Q CLEARANCE

In a stunning departure, the bestselling author of JAWS, THE DEEP and THE GIRL OF THE SEA OF CORTEZ moves out of the water and into the White House with this big, rich, deft comic novel about a presidential speechwriter who unwittingly becomes the target of Soviet spies.

Timothy Burnham is refreshingly indifferent to power in a town – Washington – where power is the trading currency; it's partly because he doesn't have the foggiest idea how to use it. Then, in an accident of bureaucracy, Burnham is given 'Q Clearance' – access to the highest atomic secrets – and he becomes the chosen, the one the President turns to when he wants not assurance, but the truth.

In his newly exalted position, Burnham was to find out that it was not only the President who sought the truth . . .

Here is Peter Benchley at his storytelling best – with all the brilliant ingredients of a first-rate drama combining with a new wonderful ingredient, comedy. If you pick it up, you'll never put it down.

About the Author

Peter Benchley was born in 1940, the grandson of the famous comic writer Robert Benchley. After graduating from Harvard, he went on to become a journalist and a speechwriter for Lyndon Johnson. His first novel, the now legendary JAWS, was published in 1974, followed by THE DEEP (1976), THE ISLAND (1979) and THE GIRL OF THE SEA OF CORTEZ (1982). In addition to novels, he has written for magazines including *Newsweek* and *National Geographic*.

'That rarity of rarities, a wickedly clever and intricately plotted spy-thriller which is at the same time very funny and very frightening'
Weekend Australian

'Wry and perceptive ... A good pacy read with echoes of CATCH 22 to give it distinction and flavour'
Sunday Telegraph

'An ingenious laid-back comedy, presumably written by someone with inside knowledge ... A smart variation on the theme of thud and blunder ...'
Literary Review

'Q CLEARANCE is Benchley's best since Jaws, equally gripping and with the added dimension of humour'

Daily Express

'Strong on authenticity'   *Daily Mail*

PETER BENCHLEY

Q CLEARANCE

CORONET BOOKS
Hodder and Stoughton

For Wendy
for a thousand reasons, of
which she knows only
one

Copyright © 1986 by Peter
Benchley

First published in the USA in
1986 by Random House Inc.,
New York

First published in Great Britain
in 1986 by André Deutsch

Coronet edition 1987

Third impression 1988

Printed and bound in Great Britain
for Hodder and Stoughton
Paperbacks, a division of Hodder
and Stoughton Ltd., Mill Road,
Dunton Green, Sevenoaks, Kent
TN13 2YA. (Editorial Office: 47
Bedford Square, London WC1B
3DP) by Richard Clay Ltd.,
Bungay, Suffolk.

British Library C.I.P.

Benchley, Peter
    Q clearance.
    I. Title
    813'.54[F]   PS3552.E537

ISBN 0-340-40223-7

One

'On your knees, America!'

No. Too mandatory. Too . . . military. A presidential proclamation should be forceful yet amiable, co-operative rather than coercive. Not dictatorial. Rule Number One in a democracy: don't piss off the people.

Timothy Burnham yanked the piece of paper out of his typewriter, crumpled it and aimed it at the wastebasket, then began again.

'"In God We Trust" has been a watchword for Americans since our forefathers . . .'

No. Too wordy, too mealymouthed, too avuncular. Not . . . presidential. If the President wants the citizens to pray, he should tell them to pray.

But what about that piece of parchment called the Constitution? It's none of the President's business who prays when, how or to whom. The law says he has to keep his sticky fingers off religion.

So why are we bothering with a National Day of Prayer? Burnham was damned if he knew. Why bother with proclamations, period? Nobody ever reads them, let alone heeds them. The newspapers print them between the obituaries and the neuter-your-pet notices.

Burnham wadded his second attempt into a tight paper ball and lofted a blind hook shot that missed the wastebasket by four feet. Clearly, Presidential proclamations existed for the sole purpose of giving Presidential speech writers colitis. He leaned back in his chair and put his feet on his desk and gazed out the window. Two limousine drivers were pitching pennies against the curb by the West Basement entrance to the White House.

The intercom on his telephone buzzed.

'Yup?'

'Mr Burnham, there's a Mr Renfro to see you. From DOE.'

Burnham sat up, confused. 'He's *here*?'

Nobody ever came to see the President's writers. People phoned them or sent them information, but when face-to-face meetings were called for, it was the writers who were summoned to the policy-makers. Writers were, after all, tools, to be paid no more homage than an artist accords his brush or a carpenter his screwdriver.

'What's he want?'

'He won't say. He assures me it's important enough for me to interrupt you.'

Burnham imagined Dyanna defiantly tilting her pert little nose and her sharp little chin up at the peremptory Mr Renfro, hoping for license to tell him to bugger off back to his warren in the Department of Energy.

However, Burnham was eager for any diversion from his task of refereeing the struggle between Church and State, and he was curious, so he said, 'Send him in.' He swung his feet to the floor and rolled a sheet of paper into his typewriter and faced the keys with what he hoped was an air of creativity. As the door to his office opened, he typed a garble of letters, then looked up as if resenting the interruption. He said, 'What can I do for you?'

'My name is Renfro. Preston T. Renfro. I'm with DOE.' Renfro launched what should have been a simple statement with the gravity of a formal announcement.

How does he want me to react? Burnham wondered. Tachycardia? A *frisson* of delight? For the appearance of the man denied the authority of the voice.

Preston T. Renfro was a grey-looking person. He conveyed neither rank nor ruthlessness nor intellect nor any of the several other manifestations of power. He seemed to lack even vanity, for he was bald in a pattern that would have nicely accepted a hairpiece. He wore no jewellery except an inexpensive digital watch. His suit, shirt, tie and shoes were boringly compatible. He probably did some kind of solitary exercise two or three times a week, for his skin fitted him well and he carried no obvious blubber. His face had no angles, no corners. It was roundish, a face that was unravaged by booze or tragedy or emotional tumult. He might have been a salesman, an insurance executive, a banker, a Bulgarian bureaucrat – one of those nondescript types who carries a poison-tipped umbrella with which to assassinate exiled dissidents on the Quai des Grands Augustins. Or he might be what he said he was, a something-or-other with the Federal Department of Energy.

'You can leave it open,' Burnham said as Renfro shut the door behind him. 'I have no secrets.'

Renfro hesitated, assessing Burnham before he said, 'Yes you do, Mr Burnham. As of today, you do.'

A voice in Burnham's head said, Uh-oh: this guy is beginning to sound like a refugee from a rubber room.

He wondered if Dyanna had thought to ask to see Renfro's ID. He said, 'What do you do for DOE?'

'Work for them.' Renfro took a wallet from his hip pocket and flashed a DOE pass at Burnham. It looked genuine. 'Like you do.'

'I see.' Burnham recognized the gambit of a routine power game. He decided to trump. 'The thing is, I don't work for DOE. I work for the President.'

'Let's not split hairs.' Unbidden, Renfro sat in one of the two chairs before Burnham's desk, laid his briefcase across his knees and folded his hands on top of it. 'You may work in the White House complex, but you're employed by DOE. You're paid by DOE, you're insured by DOE, and after the FBI finished with you, you had to be cleared by DOE.'

'Could DOE fire me?'

Renfro paused. 'A good question. I don't know.'

Turkey, Burnham thought. You know as well as I do that

7

DOE can't touch me. The President had me hired, and he could have me fired, but without a direct order from the President DOE has no choice but to pay me, insure me and carry me on its rolls as a high-level staff member detailed to the White House.

None of the President's writers worked for the White House, not technically. They weren't on the White House staff. In fact, almost everybody Burnham knew who worked in the White House didn't work *for* the White House: They all worked for some other agency or department or bureau.

They had to. Congress authorized a budget for the White House that accommodated 314 employees. The truth was that the great lumbering beast known as the Executive Office of the President employed 1,520 human beings, all of whom had to be paid and insured by somebody. Every President threatened to cut the White House budget. Most Presidents did make cosmetic cuts. But all Presidents quietly restored those cuts by fishing in the Federal bureaucracy for slots to fill with their own people who, thenceforth, never set foot inside the department that paid them, never met their nominal bosses, never performed a single function related to their 'job descriptions'.

Burnham's friend McGregor, for example, was officially one of two Special Assistants to the Secretary of the Treasury. When the Secretary resigned so as to be able to devote every waking hour to preparing testimony rebutting a Federal Grand Jury's indictment of him on 114 counts of inside trading, a new Secretary was nominated and confirmed. McGregor wrote the President's remarks for the new Secretary's swearing-in ceremony and was, according to custom, invited to attend the ceremony. He went through the receiving line, and when he came to the new Secretary, he shook hands and said, 'How do you do, sir? I wrote the President's remarks swearing you in. I hope you liked them. I'm your Special Assistant. You will never see me again. Goodbye.'

The Secretary, who had been prepared to say 'Thank

8

you' to some banal *politesse*, stopped at 'Th . . .' and looked as if he had been slapped in the face with a wet haddock. Another well-wisher stood before him, hand extended, but the Secretary ignored him and bent toward the President and whispered as he pointed at McGregor's back, 'Who was that?'

The President looked, squinted, glared and then said, 'A flake. I'm plagued by flakes.'

When Burnham was hired, the job lottery placed him in the Department of Energy. Like McGregor, he was a Special Assistant to the Secretary. Like McGregor, he had passed not one day, not one hour, doing anything for his employer. He had never laid eyes on his boss. He had been in contact with only one person at his parent agency, a secretary in the personnel office who fielded questions about W-2 forms and insurance claims.

There was one difference between Burnham's situation and McGregor's: the issue of national security. For years, the Department of Energy had been custodian of the keys to nuclear weaponry. As successor to the Atomic Energy Commission, DOE oversaw the research, development and construction of the flatware for the Last Supper. Let the Pentagon decide where to hide the missiles; DOE determined the content of the message each one would deliver. Only DOE knew how much to take from Column A to mix with so much from Column B to make an explosion that could turn an entire continent into a memory.

All of which had affected Burnham not a whit.

Until today.

'Why are we talking about firing?' Renfro asked. 'Nobody's firing anybody. Quite the opposite.' With a dyspeptic smile, he opened his briefcase and pulled out a white envelope which he passed to Burnham.

It was Burnham's bi-weekly pay envelope: In the upper left corner, 'Department of Energy, Washington, D.C. 20585.' In the central window, 'Burnham, Timothy Y , E.O.B 102.'

9

Burnham said, 'So?'

'Open it.'

It was just a cheque, two slips of paper, one with his name and the amount payable from the US Treasury, one with all the withholding information.

'A cheque!' Burnham said. 'Is this a voucher that I see before me, its FICA toward my breast?'

'What?' Renfro was bewildered, and bewilderment made him feel a loss of control, and loss of control made him fearful and fear made his eyelids flutter.

Burnham tossed the cheque onto his desk and said, 'Thanks for coming by, but next time why not just drop it in the mail?'

'You mean . . .' Renfro fought to keep his voice from slipping into the high tenor range. '. . . you don't see anything extraordinary about the cheque?'

'Nope.'

'Like, for example, the amount?'

Burnham glanced idly at the amount of the cheque, but it looked reasonable. 'What do I know? I put it in the bank, and I spend it, and when I spend too much the bank sends me a naughty-boy slip and I give them ten dollars.'

Renfro sensed that he was being teased, and he hated to be teased because he didn't know how to respond to teasing – 'Shove it!' being unacceptable in the corridors of DOE. But then it occurred to him that Burnham was simply being candid. He leaned forward and pointed at the cheque and said, 'May I?'

'Sure.'

Renfro plucked the cheque from Burnham's fingers and, pointing at the maze of boxes on the stub, began to speak in a low, calm voice, the voice one would use to instruct a wayward but not malevolent child.

'As of close-of-business today, you will have been with DOE for three years and six months, as a GS-15 step 8. Your base salary has been fifty-seven thousand, five hundred dollars per annum, paid bi-weekly at the gross salary rate of one thousand, one hundred and five dollars and seventy-seven cents per week, or two thousand, two hundred and eleven dollars and fifty-four cents per cheque, minus, first, Federal withholding tax of . . .'

Burnham's mind bid adieu to the torrent of statistics, and his voice hummed an agreeable. 'Mmmmmm' in tones modulated to convey concentration, fascination and comprehension.

'Now!' Renfro stabbed a particular figure, and Burnham's mind raced to refocus. 'At close-of-business today, time-in-grade moves you from GS-15 step 8 to GS-15 step 9! Congratulations!'

At a loss for an appropriate response, Burnham said, 'Right.'

'Don't you *see*?' Renfro waved the cheque before Burnham's face. 'Fifty-nine thousand, eight hundred dollars per annum, paid bi-weekly at the gross salary rate of . . .'

Burnham snatched the cheque back from Renfro, and his eyes travelled down to the last box on the stub, the one that showed the net amount. The true, after tax, in-the-pocket, spending-money increase for two week's work was $48.17. He looked up at Renfro and said, 'You do this for a living?'

'Do what?'

'Scurry from department to department, conducting . . . circumcision ceremonies to celebrate a lousy forty-dollar raise? You could've called, for a quarter.'

Renfro stiffened. 'Mr Burnham, the money is just a symbol. Elevation to GS-15 step 9 carries with it a great deal more than a raise in pay. As of close-of-business today, you will be in the – how should I put it? – in the stratosphere of DOE. You will have . . .' and here he lowered his voice in what could have been reverence or secrecy or both, '. . . you will have . . . Q Clearance.'

Burnham didn't know what to say. Was this good news or bad news? Did it mean anything, or was it but one more of the totemic badges that gave bureaucrats the incentive to go on?

He gazed at Renfro, suddenly seeing the man as more

11

than a man, as an incarnation of many things grand and grave: of the ant colony that was the Federal Government, of the paranoia and insecurity that hung over Washington like sour gas, of the entire Federal budget deficit.

'Lucky me!' he cried. 'Does this mean that I get to tear a piece off the President's niece?'

Renfro gripped the edge of Burnham's desk so hard that his fingernails left dents in the varnish. 'How *could* you?' he gasped. 'How could you joke about Q Clearance? It's no . . . no . . . joke!'

'If you say so,' Burnham said pleasantly. 'But dare I ask what the hell it is?'

'Of course.' Renfro made a busy motion with his tie. 'Of course. Code Q is the security classification used for atomic energy documents. A government employee may be cleared Top Secret – I imagine everyone in the White House complex is – but without a Q Clearance he can't see any paperwork or receive any information about atomic energy. Q Clearance gives you access to all materials pertaining to atomic energy.'

'What do *I* want with a Q Clearance?'

'So you can have access to materials pertaining to atomic energy. On a need-to-know basis, of course.'

'That's that, then. I don't need to know any of it, and I don't have any of it.'

'You will. It will be sent to you.'

'Why? I don't understand half the crap DOE sends me now. Why do I want more?'

'What you want has nothing to do with it. It's what you must have, now that you're a GS-15 step 9.'

'But I don't need it.'

'Of course you do.'

'Why?'

'Because you're a GS-15 step 9, working for DOE.'

'I *don't* work for DOE. I've never set foot in DOE. I work for the White House.'

Renfro sighed. 'I thought we'd settled all that.'

'I don't even write speeches on energy. I don't know

fission from fusion. All I know about nuclear is Hiroshima.'

'You will.'

'You mean they'll send me everything? Like where all our missiles are and what they're targeted on and the launch codes and the . . . the boom factor?'

'The boom factor?'

'Beats the shit out of me,' Burnham said. 'Sounds good, though, doesn't it?'

'I see. Another joke.' Renfro squared his shoulders and set his jaw, reminding Burnham of John Houseman on the Smith, Barney commercials. 'There are certain things you would have to request specifically and prove your need to know. But basic, Top Secret, Q-classified atomic-energy materials will cross your desk.'

'Really?' Burnham was mildly interested. 'How many?'

Renfro's smiled vanished. 'You know better than that. I'm not at liberty to –'

'Okay. Forget how many. What are they called? If I'm Q cleared for Category 7, what's higher? Category 8?'

Renfro blushed. 'Really . . .'

'You mean there's stuff so secret that no one can even know how secret? Even the names are secret? I know: They're not called secrets; they're called . . . fizmins! So you say to some guy, "Can you keep a fizmin?" and right away he knows you're okay.'

'I don't find this at all –'

'Now,' Burnham stared contemplatively at the ceiling, 'the stuff only the President can see, those are super-fizmins. The problem is, if only the President can see them, then nobody's cleared to tell them to him or type them out for him, so he has no way to get them.'

Annoyed and impatient, Renfro drummed his knuckles on the desk top.

'Tell me who can know I've got Q Clearance,' Burnham said.

'Only someone else who's Q Cleared.'

'Like you.'

Renfro nodded.

13

'How high are you cleared?'

'You're out of line.'

'Sorry. I don't mean to be nosy. The thing is, how can anybody know how high he's cleared? All he knows is what's below him. He doesn't know anything about what's above him. Right?'

Renfro hesitated, then said uncertainly, 'I suppose.'

'I mean, say I'm having lunch in the Mess with some of the guys, and the talk turns lightly to nuclear energy, and one of the guys says, "I wonder what goes into that there neutron bomb." And since I know all about those things – being Q Cleared and all – I say –'

Renfro blanched. 'You don't say a thing!'

'Take it easy. This is just for instance. I say, "I happen to know it's made up of two brindles, a gristen and a pint of phwork."'

'You wouldn't –'

'Just an *example*. I told you, I don't understand any of this crap anyway. Now, if he says, "Yeah? No shit?" then I know he isn't Q Cleared. Easy. But suppose some other guy at the table says, "Not only that, but they launch it with a twelve-volt pismo, which are manufactured at Pismo Products in White Plains." Well, no question; here's a guy with more than your garden-variety Q Clearance.'

'This is all very –'

'The point, Mr Renfro,' Burnham said sharply, 'is this: how do I know who I can talk to? How do I know who's got Q Clearance? Is there a secret handshake? Will he be wearing a code ring?'

'Don't be ridiculous.'

'Well? Is my wife cleared?'

'Of course not.'

'So what happens if we're talking about this and that, and all of a sudden I spill something to her.'

'Be reasonable. What classified material would be likely to come up in a . . . nuptial . . . conversation?'

'Piece of cake. My wife's involved with saving the whales. I say to her, "Great, let's save the whales, but did

14

you know that the only effective lubricant for the trigger devices for hydrogen bombs is sperm-whale oil? We can't save *all* the whales."'

Renfro burst out, 'How did you know that?'

'I read it somewhere. But supposed it was classified. What then?'

'*Suppose it was classified!?* That's Category 7!'

'I rest my case.' Burnham grinned.

'You weren't cleared for Category 7 till today.'

'It was in the paper. Or *Newsweek*. Or *Omni*. Anyway, suppose I said that to her?'

'She'd have to say it to someone else, and we'd have to hear about it. But technically, if you did that, you could go to jail.'

'Great. Picture this: "Hi, Hon, I'm home." – "Hi, Hon, how was your day?" – "Shut your mouth, Sweetie, if you don't want me to spend Christmas in Leavenworth."'

'This is absurd,' Renfro said, snapping his briefcase shut and starting to rise.

'Oh no you don't!' Burnham lunged across the desk and slapped Renfro's briefcase onto the floor. Renfro sat back, shocked.

'Look here, mister,' Burnham said. 'You're laying a big load on me. You're telling me that I have to learn how to blow up the world, which I don't want to know, that I have to learn to shut off a whole part of my life from my wife, which I don't want to do, and that if I make a single mistake I'm Benedict Arnold and you're gonna fry me like Caryl Chessman. Fuck it. I don't need it. I'm not flattered at being let in on The Big Secret. I don't like knowing secrets. They're obligations. So take your Q Clearance and your step 9 and your Category 7 and your forty-eight dollars every other week and go back to DOE and tell them to leave me alone.'

Blinking like a mechanical toy gone awry, Renfro said, 'I can't.'

'Why not?'

'You can't turn down a time-in-grade promotion.'

'What if I do? Forty-eight dollars is not exactly Xanadu.

'You *can't*. It's already been programmed into the computers. It's stored on magnetic discs.' Renfro paused, pondering. 'You could resign. Resign altogether. You could commit some minor infraction.'

'Like?'

Renfro shook his head.

'It's never been done. Something that would get you demoted a grade. You could appeal to the President to have you transferred to the White House payroll.'

'It's full.'

'Don't I know. You think I *like* having to deal with you people? You people who think you're above it all just because you work in the White House? Give me a career man any time, someone who knows the rules and plays by them.' Renfro bent down and retrieved his briefcase. 'I'm afraid, Mr Burnham, that you have no choice but to . . . grow up.' He stood immediately, as if expecting Burnham to take violent umbrage.

But Burnham merely smiled and said, 'I've known for years that becoming a grown-up is a consummation devoutly to be avoided. You've said nothing to change my mind.'

Renfro wheeled and marched across the office, then stopped at the door, his hand on the knob, and said, 'It's only fair to tell you: you worry me.'

'Hell, Renfro, I worry myself. But I don't lose sleep over it.'

'How did you ever get this job? You seem . . . unlikely.'

Burnham hesitated. He had no intention of telling Renfro the truth: luck, timing, a chance remark overheard at an editorial meeting about a rumour that the White House was looking for speech-writers at precisely the time when Burnham's hopes and ambitions were congealing into despair that he would never break free from the chains of weekly journalism. The truth would only confirm Renfro's appraisal of him.

So he said, 'Brilliance, Renfro. My star shone so brightly that I was chosen for the White House firmament.'

'Well . . .' Renfro said, willing to appear sceptical but not to overstep the line into blatant rudeness, '. . . I do wish you hadn't gotten this promotion.'

'So do I. But merit will out.'

'I hope you learn to take it seriously.'

'Damn straight.' Burnham winked at Renfro. 'Loose lips sink ships.'

Two

A flamethrower, that was the answer. Quick, surgical, final. Carbonize the whole business.

But where could he put his hands on a flamethrower? An Army/Navy store? Even here in DC, where a pistol was as easy to come by as an Almond Joy, he doubted that a bartender or a junkie or a swart Levantine cab driver could produce a flamethrower for less than five figures.

Of course, he could command one from the Pentagon – the utterance of the words 'White House' had necromantic powers over the entire Federal bureaucracy – but eventually he would have to explain why a typewriter jockey in the Presidential stable had a need for an instrument of incineration.

Maybe he could manufacture one himself. Fill a fire extinguisher with napalm and –

Make one? Forget it. He couldn't tie a bow tie. He required a hatchet to gain access to a child-proof medicine bottle. As animals are said to smell fear in people, so machines seemed to sense panicked ineptitude in Burnham. Clogged toilets overflowed; television sets fell into spasms of vertical rolling; light bulbs torqued themselves deep into their sockets so that at Burnham's touch they snapped off at their necks and left him to choose between laceration and electrocution.

Punt the flamethrower.

Something had to be done, though. Threats hadn't worked, nor promises, pleas, blackmail, extortion.

As he stood at the door to this garage sale that passed as a

18

bedroom, a puff of breeze entered the far window and swept his way, gathering and blending odours and finally slapping him in the face with a fetid stench that would have felled the Goth. It was a pot-pourri aroma of socks, sneakers, mould, wet wool, dirty cotton, damp rubber, sweat-soaked leather, milk, cheese, ketchup, potatoes, bread, chocolate, cardboard, cat and girl-smells that Burnham refused to try to identify.

But it was not the smell that bothered him; he was used to it, had been conditioned to accept as normal the fact that a twelve-year-old girl chose to live in a toxic waste dump.

'Let them make her own space,' his wife, Sarah, would say. 'Biorhythms go in troughs and crests, like the sea. You can't tame the sea.'

'Who wants to be a neat freak anyway?' his son, Christopher, would say. 'It sucks.'

'ShooWAH,' would say Derry, the bog creature herself, casting his way a gesture reminiscent of a Haitian voodoo adept floating a curse.

What bothered Burnham grinned at him from its place of honour stapled to the door itself – an enormous black-and-white poster of Che Guevara, complete with scruffy beard, jaunty beret and feline smirk.

What bothered him also stared at him from the far wall of the foul room – the bulbous dome of Mao Tse Tung bobbing in the Yellow River, a hoary and patently phony photograph.

And what bothered him sat in a crystal wine glass alone on a shelf, cradled in a bed of wilted ivy leaves, like a relic of the True Cross – a cigar butt sold to Derry as once having been chewed by the very teeth, caressed by the very lips, licked by the very tongue of Fidel Castro.

And what bothered him filled the room like swarming gnats, pinned, pasted, nailed and hung on wall and ceiling – pictures of Arthur Scargill and Karl Marx and Lenin, newspaper clippings about the Red Brigades and the Shining Path and the Symbionese Liberation Army and Islamic Jihad, a homemade doll representing Ho Chi Minh as an angel, a shell casing from a Sandinistra artillery round (authenticated by Cyrillic stencilling), and – most conspicuous of all, for it seemed to shout '*J'accuse!*' at Burnham – a blank square on the robin's-egg-blue wall from which Burnham had one day (finally drawing the God-damn line) ripped down an idolatrous portrait of Josef Stalin.

'He was a maniac!' Burnham had said as he tore Stalin into tiny pieces. 'He massacred twenty million of his own people.'

'So?' Derry had said.

'*So?* What kind of argument is "so"?'

'Propaganda.' Smiling serenely in her perceived triumph, Derry had retired to the den, there to take counsel from the avatars of MTV.

Burnham tried every morning to avoid noticing Derry's room, but because it was the last room before the turn at the top of the stairs, he dared not accept the challenge and close his eyes as he passed the door, for fear of missing the first step and plunging headlong down the steep, narrow staircase. So every one of Burnham's days was launched with sour thoughts about his prodigal progeny.

My daughter the Maoist. Didn't she know that even Maoists weren't Maoists any more?

Castro worship, for Christ's sake! What did a twelve-year-old girl know about Fidel Castro? *He* knew about Fidel Castro. He had been at college in 1960 when MacGeorge Bundy had sucker-punched an entire generation by parading Fidel around the campus as the saviour of the downtrodden. Burnham would never forget the speech: '*Queremos libertad! Queremos paz! Queremos pan!*' He had hollered and cheered along with everyone else. Why not? No threat there. Less than two years later, a lot of those same college boys were having their head shaved and learning how to fire M-14s because Fidel's list of *queremoses* had grown to include nuclear-tipped missiles.

Why didn't the child fall in love with a rock star, one of those harmless hermaphrodites who look like fruit salad and write profound statements about the human condition, on which they are recognized experts, having lived for the better part of two decades?

Why wasn't her room papered with posters of disaffected boys and material girls, all of them oozing with grim determination to slake their animal appetites?

Burnham heard his Puritan forebears whispering from the beyond, but he defied them. His generation had been denied the joys of premarital sex, a deprivation for which he would never forgive America. He would not so torture his children. Let her have her sex fantasies. Let her have *sex*, even! At least it was natural. Unlike Communism.

But no. Her love was not boys but Bolshevism.

What had gone wrong? Why was she not following the path cleared by the 'me' generation? Sure, a social conscience was a healthy thing: send money to Save the Children, join the march against hunger, picket apartheid. But to advocate the violent overthrow of everything?

What had he done wrong? (This was the black thought he sought desperately to escape.) The fault had to lie with him, or at least with his job at the right hand of the Supreme Imperialist. How else could he explain pubescent radicalism?

His wife called it commitment, and was proud of it. 'She just has a healthy superego,' Sarah said. 'She sees right and wrong in everything.'

Indeed, Burnham thought: she sees wrong in everything right, and right in everything wrong.

He pulled the door to Derry's room closed, took a pen from the inside pocket of his seersucker jacket and wrote on the door in large black letters; 'Danger – this room is hazardous to living things.'

Then he walked downstairs, feeling like an utter ass.

As in many old, unmodernized, skinny Georgetown houses, the kitchen in the Burnhams' house was small, dark, brick-paved and in the rear of the ground floor. It protruded, like a wen, from the back of the house, which led Burnham to conclude that it had once been a separate edifice, the slaves' quarters or the cookhouse or something

21

else historically colourful. Sarah's only conclusion about the kitchen was that it was as cold as a penguin's buns in the winter, since the central heating struggled in vain to reach from the rest of the house into the kitchen, and hot as cheese fondu in the summer, since the room's jury-rigged wiring couldn't cope with the load demanded by a window air-conditioner.

The entrance to the kitchen was topped by a six-by-six beam that capped the doorway at exactly six feet. The beam was decorated with red bicycle reflectors and tufts of hair from several mammals, meticulously applied by Burnham in celebration of the last times he had attempted to propel his six-foot-one-inch self erect through the doorway, pulping a section of his skull and blood-staining the lemon carpet. He would have removed the beam and raised the doorway if he had owned the house, but as a renter he had neither inclination nor permission to make structural alterations.

He reached the bottom of the stairs and folded his head down to pass beneath the beam and into the kitchen. He must have unconsciously closed his eyes, or he would have seen the rope of black fur under his Bass Weejun. He stepped on it, hard, and the cat it was attached to, the cat that had been sleeping mostly inside the little bathroom off the kitchen, that cat screeched like a traffic accident and shot off the floor. Burnham's head snapped back and slammed into the overhead beam, and he crumpled to his knees, grunting like a gorilla.

In the kitchen, nobody moved. Derry yelled, 'You stepped on Lehrer!' and then, as if content at having announced the day's lead story, returned to the *Post*'s funnies.

Christopher glanced up briefly from a *National Lampoon* photographic essay on nipples and said, 'Swift, Dad.'

At the sink, Sarah stopped scrubbing scrambled eggs from a pan long enough to ascertain that Burnham was only stunned, not bleeding. 'The bathroom floor's cool,' she said.

'Huh?' Burnham shook his head and lurched to his feet.
'That's why Lehrer sleeps there.'

'Oh.' Burnham poured himself a cup of coffee from the Toshiba brewer and sat at the small round table between his two children. He dropped a slice of bread into the Bauer toaster and reached for the front section of the *Post*. 'Anything happen?'

'The deficit jumped another ten billion last quarter, thanks to –'

'Thanks to us, that's who.'

'What do you mean, us?'

'Look at this.' Burnham held up his coffee cup. 'You hire the Japanese to make our coffee, the Germans to make our toast, the French to squeeze our juice and the Hondurans' – Burnham grabbed a banana from a bowl on the table, ripped off its skin and dipped the banana in his coffee – 'to feed us fruit.'

'That's not what the deficit's all about and you know it.'

'Balance of payments, then,' Burnham said, pleased at having deflected, if only momentarily, an assault on his employer and himself. 'The point is, you're subsidizing every country in the world except your own. What's wrong with General Electric? They make coffee, too.'

Derry said, 'They're racists.'

'How do you –'

'Hey, Dad!' Christopher shouted. 'Get a load of your horoscope. Man, this is heavy!' He read aloud the wisdom of the oracle of the *Lampoon*. '"Taurus: Your life isn't worth a plugged nickel. Your house, your job and your family are all forfeit, and unless you send a million dollars in unmarked twenties to the editor of this magazine, you will be cornholed to death by a tribe of Aleuts."'

Christopher rocked back in his chair, laughing in the peculiar way that made him sound like a novice with the Vienna Boys' Choir.

Sarah snapped, 'Christopher!'

'I didn't make it up,' Christopher insisted. 'It's right here. What's an Aleut?'

'Protected by the First Amendment.' Burnham smiled at Sarah, who didn't smile back.

'O ye guardian of our sacred rights,' she said 'Look who's suing the *Post* to get at some poor reporter's notes.'

'That's not me. That's the Justice Department.'

'No, it's That Man.' The words distorted her face as if she had sucked on a lime. 'You're an extension of That Man.'

'No I'm not. I'm a flunkey. A flunkey is not an extension of anything.' Burnham yawned. 'Did you put wine in the piccata?'

'Sherry. Why?'

'I didn't sleep worth a damn.'

'That's conscience, not sherry. A teaspoon of sherry won't wreck your sleep.'

Burnham sighed. 'What do I have to do, hire a taster? I am allergic to ethyl alcohol!'

'That is a load of BS.'

'Bullshit,' Christopher advised Derry, who nodded sagely.

'You think I quit drinking because I *wanted* to?' Burnham said. 'I *loved* drinking – not wisely, maybe, but too well. The doctor –'

'You believe everything that Albanian lulu you –'

'He's Armenian. And just because you haven't heard of the specialty is no reason to dump on it. He's an orthomolecular –'

'Lulu. I don't care what he calls himself. He's a blue-ribbon, prime-cut lulu. He has you convinced you're allergic to everything on the planet and he's the only one who can cure you.'

'You, madam,' Burnham said, smiling, 'are a medical Luddite.'

'What's a Luddite?' Derry asked without looking up from *Bloom County*.

'Same as an asshole,' Christopher said confidently.

Sarah poured herself a final cup of coffee and pressed the 'off' panel on the Toshiba machine, which acknowledged her touch with an obedient beep. 'I owe that yahoo one thing,' she conceded. 'Allergic or not, before you went to him you sure had a hollow leg. I've never *seen* –'

Burnham held up a finger, and Sarah knew right away what was coming – not exactly, but generally. The raised finger gave it away every time.

'That is the worse,' he said. 'A fortress which soon surrenders has its walls less shattered, than when a long and obstinate resistance is made.'

Sarah paused. 'Is there *any*thing that man didn't say something quotable about?'

'No. Thank God. Like a dirty mind, Samuel Johnson is a perpetual solace. He argues all sides of every issue. He's ammunition for any battle. And the great thing is, he's always right. Always.'

'It's not fair,' Sarah said. 'I want someone on *my* side.'

'Let us go to the next best: there is nobody; no man can be said to put you in mind of Johnson.'

'Not bad. Who said that? Maybe I'll recruit him.'

'Guy named Hamilton. Not worth it. Shaw might work for you. Or Oscar Wilde. But he's too mean. I'll think.'

Burnham emptied the dregs of his coffee into the sink, rinsed the cup and filled it with cold water. He shot his cuffs and washed his hands and dried them, then held them up as if prepping for surgery, and strode to a corner cabinet. With two fingertips he opened the cabinet door. There, arrayed above him like a phalanx, labels facing front, where his bottles of vitamin pills.

On the shelf below the bottles were seven clean Pyrex bowls, custard size, enough for a week. He took down the first bottle, the largest – vitamin C, ascorbic acid, 500 mg – and counted out the pills.

Sarah stood across the room and watched, wishing she wouldn't, incapable of not, mesmerized as thoroughly as when she saw the frog on the dissecting table in biology class.

He used to have to look at the prescription, to be sure of numbers and dosages, but now he sorted the pills as rapidly as a pharmacist: three thousand milligrams of vitamin C;

500 micrograms of B-12, 100 milligrams of B-1; 400 international units of vitamin E; 25,000 units of vitamin A; 500 milligrams of dolomite; 30 milligrams of zinc; 10 milligrams of manganese; 500 milligrams of magnesium gluconate; two 200-milligram capsules of B-6; one large yellow capsule of Zimag C, and one large mustard-coloured capsule of B-complex.

Each day's pills went into one Pyrex dish. Burnham closed the cabinet door, dumped the dish of pills into his palm and swallowed them, all at once, with water.

'Does the President know he's got a vitamin bomb working for him? Sarah asked. 'He could light your fuse and blow nutrition all over Russia.'

'Chemically,' Burnham said, chasing the pills with a last gulp of water, 'I'm the most finely tuned member of the White House staff. My body is a temple of chemical balance.'

'Have you told the President?'

'Why bother?' Burnham chuckled. 'You know what he'd say: '"Son, that's about as much use to me as tits on a canary."'

Burnham tightened his tie and brushed some Froot Loop crumbs off his loafers. 'Do you need the car?'

'Yes.' Sarah started to say why, but she intercepted the words before they could escape her mouth. She blushed.

'Let me guess,' Burnham said, grinning. 'A fund raiser at Hickory Hill. James Taylor'll be there. And Warren Beatty. And . . . let's see . . . Dick Cavett.'

Sarah's silence confirmed Burnham's guess. 'D'you know what the President said the other day? He said, "How can anybody take Ted Kennedy seriously, when he has people working for him who are all named Didi and Muffie?"' – Burnham waited a beat – 'and Sarah?'

'The hell he said that. Not to you. He doesn't say anything to you.'

'He said it.'

'To whom?'

'Evelyn Witt.'

'Doesn't that woman have better things to do than call you with gossip? Why doesn't she erase tapes, or –'

'She was doing me a favour. Warning me.'

'Tough. He's not running again.'

'He thinks, fuddy-duddy that he is, that just because he pays me fifty-seven thousand dollars a year – No! Fifty-*nine* thousand, as of last Friday – he has a right to expect some loyalty.'

Christopher said, 'You got a raise?'

'Sort of. A formality. Not really a –'

'Can I get a new box? Mine sounds like puke.'

Burnham glanced at Sarah and saw her staring at him. He tried quickly to answer Christopher, but she spoke first.

'Why were you promoted?'

'I wasn't! I mean, it was a –' He cursed himself for a fool. He envisioned suspicions rearing their heads like garden eels in the sands of Sarah's mind. A promotion at the White House had to mean the approval of the President for a job well done, and, to her, a job well done for this President was, by definition, a blow against peace, fairness, decency and the School Lunch Program. 'It was a time-in-grade thing. Routine.'

'What else does it mean besides money?'

'Nothing! Forty-eight dollars every two weeks. That's it.' Why was he lying? He was a terrible, transparent liar. His skin changed colour, his eyes refused to look at the person he was lying to, he always protested too vehemently. Why hadn't he concocted a credible evasion? 'Increased access', maybe. Something like that.

It was too late. The lie was in place and would soon fester.

He felt that he was beginning to rot.

Evidently, Sarah decided not to challenge him, for she looked away and said, 'Who does he want you to be loyal to?'

'Whoever he picks. He still has over a year to go.'

'You're supposed to hang around, wait for him to pick some . . . orang-utan . . . like the Vice-President?'

27

'I am.'

'Well, I'm not. If he thinks I'm about to support that cretin . . . The man who said ERA is a bunch of dykes with penis envy.'

'One of Ben Klammerer's lines. I think he's gone on to greater heights, like chief writer for the Teamsters Union.'

'I don't care who wrote it. The Vice-President said it.'

'It got a laugh.'

'From a pack of hyenas.'

Burnham could see that Sarah's irritation was ripening into true anger. The hand that held her coffee cup was trembling, and the sinews in her long neck pulsed against her pale skin as, subconsciously she worked the muscles in her jaw. She wanted to maintain control, but the effort was as futile as trying to stop a shaken soda bottle once the cap has been started. The pressure had momentum, and it would be released.

'You'd quit,' she said tightly, 'if you had the guts.' She set her cup down so hard that the handle snapped off.

'Noble. And what would we eat?'

'There're other jobs. You're not a complete incompetent, you know, no matter what you think of yourself.'

'Look . . .' Burnham said, stalling, praying for the doorbell to ring, or the telephone, or for the living room couch to combust spontaneously – anything to move the conversation away from this sore and tired subject. 'The job is a matter of simple economics, not principle. Fifty-nine grand is not bad pay for –'

'Crap!' Sarah said. 'That's crap, and you know it!'

Derry's head popped up from the funnies. 'Hey, gimme a break!' she said, employing one of the multipurpose adolescent tools that could be interpreted as intended to convey amazement, annoyance or admiration.

Sarah interpreted it as reproach, and she lowered her voice to the octave of reasoned discourse. 'It's power. You just love the power.'

'*Me?*' Burnham tried to laugh, but what emerged from his mouth and nose was more of a hollow bark. 'How can I love power? I don't have any.' He reached again for the paper and opened it and pretended to read.

Sarah was right, of course. Even at his level, employment in the White House was strong drink. Power seeped down from the summit and intoxicated everyone from the janitorial staff to the telephone operators. It was power-by-association, the implicit (and usually untrue) suggestion of access to the throne, of the possession of secrets. In the amorphous, indecipherable middle-level ranks where Burnham resided, where everyone was a staff assistant, a deputy special assistant or (most mysterious of all) a plain assistant to the President, it meant restaurant reservations when all tables were full, the instantaneous return of phone calls from the most power-crazed snobs in the capital, and entrée (at least once) to redoubtable Georgian manors where the glassware tinkled with clarion clarity and no wine was served before its time.

'You know what?' Christopher said, closing the *Lampoon* and sliding it into his L. L. Bean canvas tote bag.

'What?' Burnham looked at Christopher eagerly, gratefully.

'I think you guys are heading for a divorce.' Christopher's tone was flat, unjudgmental, but he did not look at either parent. He made a show of arranging his books in his tote bag.

His sister looked at him as if he had just shouted 'Fuck!' In church.

'Wha . . . gck . . .' was all Burnham could manage. He had prayed for detente, not escalation. He glanced at Sarah, whose face was purpling as if prior to a major stroke.

'You fight all the time these days,' Christopher said, standing up and slinging his bag over his shoulder. 'About everything.'

Derry stood up, too, still eyeing her brother as something from 'The Twilight Zone'.

'We do not,' Burnham said, adding with a weak smile, 'WASPs don't fight. We discuss.'

'Yeah, well . . .' Christopher brushed past him and

29

headed for the living room. He stopped at the front door, turned and waited for Derry.

'I mean, it may *seem* like fighting,' Burnham admitted amiably, 'but really it's just . . . ah . . . intense conversation.'

Derry shouldered her bag and stepped around her father, avoiding him by an unnecessary four feet, as if he had suddenly been exposed by Christopher's words as contaminated and contagious.

'Did you feed MacNeil?' Sarah asked Derry.

MacNeil was Derry's fish. Burnham had to admire Sarah: Christopher had unleashed a monster, and Sarah was concerned about a fish.

''Course,' Derry said as she left the kitchen. 'We're out of fish food, so I gave him Grape Nuts.'

'Wait!' Burnham shouted, panicked, realizing that he was about to be left alone with Sarah to deal with the monster. The monster could not be confronted, not now. It must be avoided. Burnham didn't know how real it was, from his perspective or Sarah's, but he sensed that if confronted, the monster would become undeniably real, and he wasn't ready for that. Maybe later. Maybe never. Certainly not now. 'I'll walk out.'

He sprang to his feet, tightened his tie, feigned searching for something so that he wouldn't have to look at Sarah, who, cherry pink, stood as still as Lot's wife. Burnham scurried into the living room.

His children had gone, leaving the front door open, but he spoke to them anyway, to keep Sarah from calling him back and forcing him to face down the monster.

'Right. Here we go. I'll walk you up to the bus stop. Bye, hon!' He stepped outside, pulled the door closed behind him and leaned against it, eyes closed, breathing deeply.

After ten seconds, or so, his pulse slowed so that he could no longer hear it. He opened his eyes and looked to the right, saw that his children were out of sight and stepped off his doorstep onto Prospect Street.

Back in the Kennedy days, and even into the first Johnson years, Georgetown had been clean, elegant, quiet, safe, tolerably uncrowded and discreetly expensive. It was even spared the carnage of the Martin Luther King riots in 1968 that burned down a large part of the District of Columbia. The Government simply stationed troops on all the bridges going in and out of Georgetown, and if you couldn't prove you lived there you stayed outside.

Georgetown's decline had begun in the Nixon years, but not only because the President knew it to be a fortress for his enemies, a redoubt of bleeding-heart assholes, knee-jerk liberals and media preppies who could not abide the thought that Nixon had been savvy enough and tough enough to hang in there until finally he found a way to tweak the public's reflex into giving him the White Horse.

No, Georgetown had been beset by discovery, celebrity and prosperity.

Tourists had always liked Georgetown, but the Kennedy myth – especially as it flowered in comparison to the hard, mean, greyness of the Nixon crowd – made Georgetown a shrine. There's the house he lived in. There's where the press waited (see the plaque?) all through election night and were served hot coffee and cocoa. There's where Jackie lived after the assassination. Harriman. Kay Graham, Joe Krat. They all lived here. This was it. Camelot of a thousand days.

The tiny house Burnham lived in had sold for $30,000 in 1967. Ten years later, it went (to the current landlord) for $220,000. Included in Burnham's lease was an option to buy the house. For $350,000.

Neighbourhood stores couldn't afford to keep up with the rents, so the groceries and shoe-repair places and cheap restaurants and drugstores and haberdasheries on Wisconsin Avenue gave way to boutiques and Haagen-Dazs parlours and leather-craft shops and saloons with brick walls and sawdust on the floor and movie posters and a cucumber rind in your Bloody Mary for only $4.95, plus tax. Wisconsin Avenue became *the* place to hang out, and that, of course, attracted peddlers – of belts, Indian necklaces, hot wristwatches and scarves and umbrellas and several controlled substances.

Since the controlled substances cannot exist without people to buy them and people to prey on those who have the money to buy them and on those who get money from selling them, soon society's predators came to call Georgetown home.

Not all of them lived here, just enough to make it exciting.

Early one morning, Burnham had gone around the corner to 33rd Street to get the car and had found a couple asleep in it, male in front, female in back, though he would have had hell to ascertain the gender of the creature in the back seat if one of her jugs hadn't flopped out of her shirt when she stirred. He had waited and watched for a few long moments before determining that it was probably safe for him to wake and chase them rather than trudging all the way back to the police station and getting a cop and coming back, by which time something else would have spooked them anyway.

They hadn't broken into the car. They had used a 'popper' (he saw it on the floor), a thin strip of metal that fitted between the closed window and the door and was slipped down and manoeuvered to pop up the lock. A good sign. They were professionals – in that they did it every night in order to have a place to sleep – they weren't car thieves, and they weren't looking for a fight. Burnham had no doubt that if he had come by at 8.30, his normal time, instead of 6.15, he would have seen no trace of their occupancy and wouldn't have noticed anything at all until he got in the car and was led by his nose to wonder if something had died under the front seat.

He hadn't yanked open the door and bellowed. He knew enough about junkies to know that if you surprise one in its sleep, depending on what it's been taking and what dreams it's in the grip of, you run the risk of setting off an hysterical, explosive awakening. So he tapped softly with his knuckles on the closed window. Nothing. The young man on the front seat slept with his hands between his knees, curled up in a fetal ball, which was as close as he had been to primal innocence in a couple of decades. Burnham rapped again, harder, and, with the speed of a striking viper, the man uncoiled, thrashed around in a grimy blur and ended up crouched, facing Burnham, weaving from side to side and tossing from one hand to the other a *kukhri* – one of those nasty curved knives that the Gurkhas carry to decapitate the enemy.

Burnham took an involuntary step backward on the sidewalk, raised his hands to show he was unarmed, smiled vulnerably, opened his palms as if to say, 'Golly, I'm sorry to disturb you, but can I have my car?' tapped his watch for some absurd emphasis, then spread his palms again, begging.

The man in the car scowled at him and pulled an antique gold pocket watch from his vest. He opened it, snapped it closed and rolled down the window.

'Hey, man,' he said, 'it's only six-fuckin'-twenty.'

'I know. I'm sorry . . . I . . .'

'We didn't go to bed till four o'-fuckin'-clock.'

Don't say it, Burnham told himself. He could hear his pulse thrumming behind his ears. Don't say anything about whose car it is, or what right do you have, or any of those nice middle-class things. You are dealing here with an alien. So what he said was, 'I gotta go to work.'

'Yeah, well I work all fuckin' night, is what.'

Again Burnham spread his hands: that's the way it goes. He wondered what he would do if the man rolled up the window and lay back down on the front seat. Find a cab, that's what he would do. And be late. And explain to the President of the United States, the Leader of the Free World, the most powerful and preoccupied individual since the dawn of time, why he had been unable to prepare last-minute jokes for this morning's Leadership Breakfast. 'Y'see, there was this couple crashed in my car . . .'

But the man did not go back to sleep. He reached over the back of the seat and shook the woman awake. She sat

33

up, tucked her breast back inside her shirt, scrubbed the hair out of her eyes and yawned.

Burnham felt he should look away, that he was intruding upon the matutinal ablutions of this couple. But he was fascinated, and they paid him no heed at all.

The man opened the glove compartment and withdrew four hamburger-sized glassene bags of white powder. One he dropped down inside his shirt. Three he held out to the woman, who, to Burnham's horror, hiked her ragged, stained batik skirt over her hips. She wore no underwear, and for a three-beat Burnham was sure she was going to pee in the back seat of the car. But no. There were pockets with zippers sewn into a lining of the skirt where it would fall down the front between her legs, and she stashed the three bags in them.

Detachedly. Burnham admired the hiding place. No police officer would dare shake the woman down in public. Not only would he be aware that the cache was in such proximity to the woman's naughty bits that he would run a real risk of being slapped with a charge of sexual fiddle-de-dee, but once he approached within whiffing distance of the harpy, horrid visions would come alive in his mind, of wasting diseases and running sores, and he would touch her with nothing shorter than his nightstick. By the time they reached the station house, zippers would be zipped and the skirt would be empty.

The couple got out of the car on the street side, left the front and back doors open, and shuffled off up 33rd Street.

He never saw them again.

The Burnhams had been able to move to Georgetown only because Sarah had met Muffie Cogan at a Kennedy thing, and Muffie dabbled in real estate and knew that her office was about to list an off-beat rental, a tiny Georgetown house that was available for a piddling $1,750 a month because (here was the catch) it was for twenty-one months, no renewal, which happened to be the precise number of months left in the President's term. No matter who was elected next, Burnham would be out of a job, and he had no

34

intention of remaining in Washington. Three and a half years was quite enough, thank you very much, particularly for a person who had no business being in government – let alone in the White House – in the first place.

He walked to the end of Prospect Street, turned right onto Wisconsin and headed for M Street and the bus stop. An empty cab was idling at the corner of Wisconsin and M, and he veered toward it. But the light changed, and the cab began to roll away. Burnham made no effort to pursue it. He told himself that his reluctance was economic: to spend five dollars just to avoid a fifteen-minute bus ride was profligate. In fact, his reluctance was purely neurotic: he could not make a spectacle of himself, running down a public thoroughfare, waving and shouting to attract the attention of a surly Kenyan (or so he envisioned the driver) who would, he was convinced, wait until he was two steps from the cab and then ram the pedal to the metal and squeal away, leaving this Anglo-Saxon relic in his rumpled seersucker to be the butt of sneers and snickers from the world at large.

He would surely have taken the cab if the light hadn't changed, because he disliked the bus with a visceral loathing. It was not only that buses were hot and crowded and dirty, but being on a bus constituted a kind of invasion of his privacy. When he boarded the metal container, he was thrusting himself into contact, and sometimes confrontation, with people he was not equipped to deal with, who did not play by his rules. They babbled and squabbled, their children squawled, they sweated, they smelled, they pressed against each other and stared out of the tinted glass as if everything was perfectly normal. Now and then, one of them would address him, which – even if the address was as innocuous as 'Is this seat taken?' – could unnerve him and trigger a stammer that could evolve quickly into an anxiety rush that could, if unallayed, mushroom into a full-blown panic attack.

This morning, the bus arrived promptly and took Burnham down M Street, across the bridge and down Pennsylvania Avenue without incident. A naïf from, say, the Cotswolds might have felt threatened by the two black teenagers who played a cassette deck at peak volume and said to any passenger who glanced their way, 'Loud enough for you, muhfuh?; or by the slender man in black suit, black shoes, black tie and starched white shirt who was running a column of figures on a calculator but kept making errors every time the bus joggled, and as he started the column anew sang atonally, 'Jesus loves me, this I know, for the Bible tells me so'; or by the elderly man in hat and raincoat who clutched between his knees a sign with which he was going to picket the White House:

HUSBANDS UNITE
You have nothing to lose
but your
BALLS
Throw off those apron strings!
BE A G.I.
(Gynophobes International)

But to the urban sensibility, even one as finely tuned as Burnham's, those were phenomena to be noticed and avoided but not feared.

Burnham and the man with the sign got off at the same stop, 17th Street and Pennsylvania Avenue, the corner just to the north of the White House complex. Burnham held the door until the man could angle his big placard free of the bus.

By way of thanks, the man looked into Burnham's eyes and whispered fervently, 'Beware! They're following you.'

Startled, Burnham took a step backward and said, 'Who?' And then, seeing the psychotic glow in the man's eyes, Burnham was embarrassed that he had been suckered into even momentary discomfort.

'You've got the wrong man.' He laughed uneasily. 'I'm not worth following.'

The man's eyes widened – in surprise or umbrage, Burnham didn't know which – and he hoisted his sign and spun around and marched off.

Three

Ivy Peniston felt like kicking the old rummy, she was so angry. He slumbered on the sidewalk beneath a blanket of yesterday's *Post's* sports section and beside a brace of Thunderbird empties. But kicking a rummy wouldn't do any good, wouldn't help Jerome, wouldn't even make her feel better for more than about ten seconds.

Jesus *wept*, Jerome! Typing! How could you do this to me? How could you do this to *you*? How could you flunk *typing*?

Typing can't be any big thing, just one letter after another till they make a word, then one word after another till they make a sentence, and so on till you do the right number in the right amount of time. I even bought you lessons!

She stepped around the rummy, and the lateral movement shot a twinge of pain through her bad knee and reminded her to remind Jerome to borrow an Ace bandage, one of those basketball kneepads, for her from the gym.

She turned the corner onto NE 12th Street. There was no bus in sight, so she reached inside her shopping bag and felt around for her watch. You never wore a watch in this neighbourhood, that was the law. A watch, displayed, was fair game. And you never carried a purse. Same law. But a shopping bag was all right – a shopping bag was out of bounds. It said you were a poor person, and nobody but the real bottom of the barrel of junkies would knock over a truly poor person. Especially a truly poor black person.

Especially a truly poor black female person with a limp. If one of those scum *did* go after you, usually someone would pop out of a doorway or from a store or a parked car and pummel the junkie away, which no one would think of doing if you wore a watch or carried a purse.

Ten o'clock, the secretary had said. It was twenty of. She could wait for a bus that would drop her in front of the school, or she could walk. A bus was quicker once you got on it, but at this time of day you could wait half an hour for one to come by, and for this appointment she could not afford to be late. Four years of Jerome's life were tied up in this appointment. Maybe more. Maybe his whole life. And a big piece of hers. So she walked.

George Washington Carver High School had been built of red brick which, with age and dirt, had darkened to the colour of dried blood. It had turrets and gables and grime-grey windows, and it had always seemed to Ivy to be less suited as a temple of learning than as what folks back home called a 'funny house' – an asylum for the criminally insane.

There was a mirror in the principal's office, and Ivy stopped to run a check on herself. She licked a couple of hairs down and tucked away a bra strap and was pleased: the edifice showed age and hard use – the shoulders were weary, and maybe there was a bit too much padding on the trunk – but none of that could conceal the woman of good breeding and proud bearing who lived within.

The principal impressed Ivy right away by not keeping her waiting. She was on time; so was he. The signs were good.

He was a round, jocund, black M.Ed. from the University of Pennsylvania named Luther Joslin, and he wore bifocals that kept trying to escape his ears and slide off the plateau of the end of his nose. He offered her a seat, closed the door, sat at his desk and opened a file folder.

'You come from Bermuda?'

'Way back when,' she replied, politely but briefly enough (she hoped) to discourage small talk.

'Why did you come up here?' Mr Joslin would not be denied.

'My husband worked here,' she lied. The truth was, she had been impregnated by a lieutenant (JG) stationed at the US Naval base in Bermuda, whom she had bullied into marrying her so their child could have the option of choosing American citizenship – an option she exercised on behalf of the fruit of their loins, *né* Jerome, as soon as it became apparent that he was destined to outgrow the capacity of the Bermuda school system to instruct him in the subjects in which he was gifted.

My mind, Ivy had decided, may not be a terrible thing to waste, but Jerome's is.

'What does your husband do?' asked Mr Joslin.

'Did.' She lowered her eyes. 'He's gone now.'

'I'm sorry. Why don't you go back?'

What *is* this man? Ivy wondered. A schoolmaster or an immigration officer? 'I'm an American citizen. So's Jerome. There's no going back.'

'But don't you miss the climate? The flowers? Bougain-villea. Oleander.' Mr Joslin sniffed the stale air.

She didn't miss them, so she said, 'No.'

'I've always wanted to go there, to live there, where we – black people, that is – are the majority, can make our own laws and respect our own culture and live lives of natural . . .'

The man's slipped a gear, Ivy concluded. He thinks Bermuda's some kind of nigger heaven.

'. . . and every man can pluck papaya from his neigh-bour's tree.'

And get his fingers chopped into itsy bitsy pieces . . .

'Ah well, perhaps when I retire.' Mr Joslin smiled dreamily, but his smile faded as he saw Ivy looking at him as if he was a fungus growing between her toes. 'Yes. Well, Enough about me. What seems to be the problem?' He consulted the file folder on his desk.

'The problem is that someone told Jerome he isn't going to graduate.'

39

Mr Joslin hesitated, following his finger down a sheet of paper in the folder. 'Yes. Apparently so.'

'Because he didn't pass typing.'

'Correct.'

'Typing.'

'Yes. Typing.'

'Jerome has three A's, a B-plus and a B-minus. He took an extra-credit half year of mechanical drawing and got an A-minus.'

'True. A good student all around. But he failed typing.'

'Mr Joslin, look at Jerome's grades in his computer courses. All A's. How do you program a computer? By typing in information. Jerome can type. He just can't type on a dead machine, a machine that won't answer back and take the game the next step. A typewriter's a baby toy for Jerome. It doesn't interest him; he can't concentrate on it.'

'I see. What you're saying is, he lacks discipline.'

Ivy took a deep breath, to swallow the 'Bullshit!' that wanted to escape. 'No, sir, he doesn't. He does all his school work, he works after school and on weekends programming computers – typing on computers. He doesn't lack any discipline.'

'Then let's just say,' Mr Joslin smiled a smarmy smile, 'that he lacks the discipline for typing.'

'So you won't give him a diploma.'

'I can't. The rules say every student must pass a term of typing. The board considers it a necessary skill, like reading.'

'But suppose you have a higher skill, like programming computers. Jerome'll never have to be a typist.'

Mr Joslin folded his hands and leaned forward on his desk and began, with patronizing serenity, 'Mrs Peniston . . .'

That's right, Ivy thought, look down on me. Motherfucker.

'. . . educational theory is based on the concept of building blocks. You must build a foundation on which the rest of the structure can stand. One or two weak blocks, and the entire building falls. The board considers typing one of those essential blocks.' He paused, waiting for the great weight of his wisdom to penetrate. 'But don't worry.'

'Don't *worry*? That Jerome's not gonna graduate? That after four years he's not gonna have a diploma? Don't *worry*?'

'Please, Mrs Peniston.' Mr Joslin held up a hand, as if to calm her with his aura. 'There's a solution to everything. All Jerome has to do is repeat his typing course this summer and pass the test in September. He'll get his diploma then.'

Ivy squeezed the fingers of her left hand with the fingers of her right so hard that she made the joints crack. She felt a strange battle going on in her head between the forces of reason and the gremlins of recklessness. She had to fight to keep from calling Joslin a stupid twit.

'Mr Joslin,' she said with strained calm, 'have you heard of a company called DTCo?'

'Of course. Used to be DataTech.'

'DTCo has a few jobs open in what they call their affirmative action program. They'll take a computer whiz like Jerome and pay him ten dollars an hour for the summer. That's four hundred dollars a week, Mr Joslin. About twice what I make.'

'That's great.'

'Then, in the fall, they'll send Jerome to college and train him for four years and pay for everything, and all he has to do is agree to work for DTCo for the first three years out of college. It's like ROTC. Maybe he can become a systems analyst, then maybe a senior systems analyst, and maybe make forty thousand dollars every year.'

'That's what it's all about,' Mr Joslin said.

'But you see . . .' Soon, Ivy knew, she would either weep or scream '. . . they won't take Jerome, they won't even let Jerome *compete* for the job, without a high-school diploma.'

'Oh.'

'And by the fall, the jobs'll be full.'

'I see.'

'So what I'm asking you is, you have this boy's life in your hands, you have his ticket, I'm just asking you if you'll bend the rules.'

Joslin looked uncomfortable, sweaty. He said, 'I can't.'

'I beg you. Pass him in typing.'

'No.' He shook his head. 'It's unfair.'

'*Unfair?* Unfair to who? What about unfair to Jerome? You want to let one stupid-ass rule destroy a boy's life?'

'Really, Mrs Peniston . . .'

'Really what? It isn't like he can't read. It isn't like he can't count. I don't care what the board says. Suppose they said you had to pass knitting. Would that be fair?'

Mr Joslin spread his hands. 'I don't make the rules.'

Ivy fought to compose herself one final time.

'Mr Joslin, I am a poor person. I am a . . .' she paused, commanding herself not to abase herself by playing the black fugue '. . . an immigrant. I work for a living. I have a son who has a chance to make his way – more, to make a contribution. Aren't we the kind of people this country says it wants to help?'

'Indeed. And it does. It gives you . . .'

'Except when it really counts.' Ivy stood, and the movement freed her, let slip the dogs of war. 'You could do it, Joslin. You could, but you won't. And you know why? 'Cause you're scared shitless.' She walked to the door.

Joslin was wary. He would have been frightened if she had stayed seated. A shopping bag could contain anything. A gun. Mace. A Molotov cocktail. But she had gone to the door, so he felt safe saying, 'I'm sorry you refuse to understand.'

'I understand okay.' She opened the door. 'I understand that you stink.'

Outside, Ivy sat on the dirty red brick steps and closed her eyes, squeezing back tears of rage. For a few seconds, she let herself wallow in a mire of venom and self-pity, hating Joslin and her Navy man and Washington and the United States and poverty and being black.

42

Then a hand touched her shoulder and a voice said, 'You okay, lady?'

She opened her eyes and looked into the face of a tall boy with a bookbag slung over his shoulder, who said, 'Need a Pepsi?'

'No.' Ivy shook her head. 'Thank you.'

'There's a machine inside.'

Ivy nodded. The boy bounced up the steps. 'Hey!' she called after him, and he stopped. 'Did you pass typing?'

'Don't take it till next year. But I will, no problem.' The boy grinned.

'How d'you know?'

'There's ways.'

'How you cheat a typing test? Can't cheat a machine.'

The boy grinned again, and touched a finger to his temple and turned into the school building.

Ivy wanted to chase him, to shake his secret from him. But she didn't, because it wouldn't do any good. To convince Jerome to cheat – even assuming she could arrange with his typing teacher for a special re-examination – would be a no-win crusade. If she succeeded, she would destroy his respect for her and for the ethical code she had bludgeoned into his head for seventeen years.

It wasn't worth it. If there was cheating to be done, she'd have to do it for him. Without his knowing.

She found her watch. She was on the early shift this week, but there was still plenty of time.

She headed westward, not bothering to keep track of street numbers. She knew that if she moved west for a while she'd be near work and could orient herself then. Direction never had to be confirmed. Even in a city, her interior compass performed flawlessly, an integer in her genetic code, passed down through three centuries of island people for whom a sense of direction and a sensitivity to coming weather were life-and-death instincts. She knew innately where the sun was and which way it was going, so as she walked she could keep her mind focused on its business, leaving only one channel open to be alert for traffic lights and weirdos.

Problem. There was no way Jerome was going to get a high school diploma from George Washington Carver High School this spring. Could she appeal to the school board? Out of the question. If Joslin wasn't about to bend the board's rules, the board wouldn't be about to go over his head to do something it wasn't inclined to do anyway.

Problem. Without a diploma, Jerome had no chance of landing a job with DTCo. Was there anyone to appeal to at DTCo? No.

Problem. If Jerome didn't get the job with DTCo, he would become a statistic this summer – one of the fifty percent of black youth unemployed – because except in the broad area of numbers and machines, Jerome had the ambition and intellectual curiosity of an armchair. Ivy had had to coach him, cajole him, threaten him, into a B-minus in his English course, reading the books aloud to him, making up quizzes for him to take at home, drilling him in names by making each name a number and playing programming games with the numbers.

Final problem. If Jerome became a statistic, Ivy might as well lead him to the jailhouse steps and wait for them to come out and arrest him, for it was as inevitable as high tide that someone would get hold of Jerome's itching fingers and idling mind and turn them to no good. He was naïve as a puppy and playful as a kitten, which would have been fine if they lived in some place like MacLean, Virginia, or Chevy Chase, Maryland, where there were things to do like tennis and golf, and where simple mischief didn't have a bad name, instead of in the Northeast ghetto, where many of the most popular games were played with toys from the Charter Arms Company and almost all frolic ended either in blood or in custody.

Conclusion. Jerome must get a high school or high-school equivalency diploma within the next two weeks. He must have physical possession of the piece of paper, be-

44

cause it said, clear as day, on the DTCo application, 'Proof of eligibility will be required.'

Question. How to acquire a diploma?

Option. Wait till graduation day and have Jerome put a stocking over his head and mug a graduating senior and steal his diploma. Rejected. Joslin would hear about it, and because he couldn't possibly be as stupid as he was bull-headed, would dope it out.

She called up every name of every friend and acquaintance from every corner of her life – her childhood, her Navy sojourn, the people at work, her neighbours – hoping to find a clue to access any of them might have to a high-school diploma.

Nothing.

She told herself to keep trying, reminded herself what her friend, Mr Pym, always said: free enterprise means you're free to help yourself, 'cause it's for sure no one else is gonna help you.

Mr Pym. Maybe he'd know.

Don't be foolish, girl. He's a caterer. What's a caterer know about getting hold of a high-school diploma? More'n you know, that's a bleeding fact. Besides, if he doesn't know how to do it, maybe he knows somebody who knows.

Mr Pym knew a lot about a lot of things you'd think he'd be bone-ignorant about. Like Bermuda customs. Last year, Christmastime, Jerome had made some video games for his Bermuda cousins – *made* them, out of scraps of videotape and discarded cassettes he found at work – and they seemed like perfect presents until Ivy learned that Bermuda customs wouldn't understand homemade video games and would slap a duty of about $300 on the two dozen games.

Mr Pym learned about the dilemma during idle chit-chat at his apartment one afternoon, and he said simply. 'Give them to me.' Said he had a client who travelled to Bermuda all the time and the customs people trusted him.

Lo and behold, the tapes arrived in Bermuda duty-free, delivered to Ivy's sister, Doris, by a shy white man in a dark suit and a gaudy sportshirt. They were the hit of the season.

45

She owed Mr Pym one. No, she owned him a bundle, if she counted all the little favours he'd done for her – like giving her free pain pills for her bad knee – since that day a year ago when he'd seen her coming out of work and her shopping bag had haemorrhaged and spilled her watch and her lunch box and her support hose and her Odour Eaters all over the avenue. Most people passed her by, but Mr Pym collected her stuff and found her a new shopping bag and accompanied her all the way home.

She wanted to pay him back for all his favours, but there wasn't any way. She couldn't offer him money. She couldn't cook a pie for him: he had professionals cooking pies for him all day long.

He said he didn't want anything, and he seemed to mean it. He seemed genuinely interested in her, in who she was and what her life was like, now and before, and where she worked and whom she worked for and what she liked and didn't like about everything. He said he was a collector of 'people trivia', and he encouraged her to notice funny offbeat things that happened at work.

The trouble was, the people she worked with were a bunch of downtrodden whiners with whom Ivy had nothing in common, and their problems were neither funny nor offbeat – children in jail, children on drugs, hard-hearted landlords and afflictions of every orifice and organ of the human body.

If she was going to call Mr Pym and ask for help with the high-school diploma problem, she wanted to be able to bring him a present, and if she had any hope of rooting out a tidbit that might brighten his day, it would have to concern the people she worked *for*.

Coincidentally, today might be a good day for such a discovery. Normally, all the offices had been dusted, swept, scoured and waxed, had had all loose papers removed, bagged and burned by the time she set to work on the hallway floors. But when she worked the early shift, it was she who cleaned some of the offices and removed the papers during the last couple of hours of her work day, and

46

because of the high-level goings-on that always crackled around the building it was common for several people to work late. If she kept her eyes and ears open, she might be able to pick up something that would help balance her relationship with Mr Pym.

Ivy looked up and found herself in Lafayette Park. She checked her watch. Still early. She had plenty of time to make herself a cup of tea in the employees' locker room and look up Mr Pym's *Plat du Jour* Caterers in the Yellow Pages. She crossed Pennsylvania Avenue and turned right.

As she passed through the tall wrought-iron gates, she reached down the front of her dress and fished out the plastic card with her name and picture on it that hung around her neck on a chain of little steel beads, and she let it fall outside her dress so the guard couldn't possibly miss it.

Then she walked up the long ornate staircase into the Old Executive Office Building that housed the bulk of the White House staff.

Four

'Are you gonna answer the phone or what?' Mrs Miller
shrilled around the corner from her cubicle outside Foster
Pym's office.

Pym sat at his desk and stared at the yellow light blinking
on his telephone.

Peniston, Peniston, Peniston, Peniston . . .

He urged his mind to summon name after name of client
after client. There was no Mrs Peniston. He turned his
mental Rolodex to creditors, wholesalers and former employees. No Mrs Peniston. No point in searching his file of
friends, for neither of them was a Peniston. And there *was*
no file of lovers, for there hadn't been any, unless one
counted long-gone Louise, and that marriage had not been
exactly a passion play.

'She's waiting!'

'I can't!' Pym said. 'I don't know who she is.'

'Answer the phone. You'll know.'

'Why will I know?'

'Because she'll tell you. Trust me. I know people.'

Ha! Pym sneered silently. You don't know people, Mrs
Miller. You don't know people or typing or book-keeping
or accounting or common courtesy. You don't know anything but deceit. Had I known you were Jewish, I never
would have hired you.

Foster Pym didn't like Jews. He also didn't like Cath-
olics, pregnant women, Arabs, cocker spaniels, garlic,
Manx cats, left-handed people, people with dentures,

48

Greeks, black people, lotteries and Chinese food – all foi different reasons involving, variously, childhood experiences, reading, hearsay, personal contact and slights (real or fancied).

One problem with Jews was that they took too many holidays – more than banks, public schools and mackerel-snappers. The calendar, Pym was convinced, had been invented so Jews could take time off.

Pym punched the flashing button and said, 'Hello,' and as soon as he heard the first few syllables of 'Mr Pym, this is Ivy and I'm very sorry to be bothering you at work,' he knew exactly who Mrs Peniston was and why he hadn't recalled her name: the card file in his head did not have her listed under 'P' for Peniston or even 'I' for Ivy but under 'B' for Black Woman Who Works in the White House Complex. Now that the mnemonic had been triggered, he saw her face, her background, her address, her phone number, her taste in music and the current state of their relationship.

What he could not see, and what disquieted him, was any reason for her to be calling him at his place of business. She could not have good news to relate, for she could not know what would be good news to him, at least not news good enough to warrant a phone call to him at work. On the other hand, the prospect of her having bad news for him – truly bad news – was so farfetched as to be ludicrous.

Suddenly, Pym felt an adrenalin rush in his arms and his neck and the pool of his stomach, and he smiled to himself. A conditioned sensory system had activated somewhere within him, and it was reacting like a Geiger counter closing on a uranium pile. He had been cultivating this woman for months, and now, he felt certain, she was about to bear fruit.

'Ivy!' he said. 'How good to hear from you!'

'Yes sir. I'm sorry to be bothering you at work.'

'Never a bother to hear from you, my dear.'

'I wonder if I could stop by and see you for a minute tonight after work.'

Before he said, 'Of course, my dear,' Pym paused long

enough to convey the impression that he was consulting his crowded schedule. 'Nothing wrong, I hope.'

'Matter of fact . . .'

'Jerome's all right??'

'For now. That's what I want to talk to you about.'

'Always glad to help.'

'I know,' Ivy said, 'and I appreciate it, too. And don't think I don't know I already owe you one big favour, and I'm not a person lets her debts go unpaid.'

'Helping is reward enough. What time will you be by?'

'I get off work at six.'

'Say six-thirty. See you then.'

Pym hung up the phone and, clucking smugly, leaned back in his chair to contemplate the possibilities. Perhaps it's true, he thought: all good things do come to him who waits.

The credo had been one of his favourites for the almost forty years he had served – quietly, diligently, assiduously self-interestedly – as a Soviet spy in the United States.

Fyodor Michaelovitch Pinsky had been one of the first chosen, first recruited, first trained and first sent. He didn't know why. If he had been forced at gunpoint to guess, he would have guessed that one of his primary-school teachers had detected an ear for languages in the child. Nor did he care why he had been selected. He was, simply, pleased that while scores of millions of his compatriots were being turned into dog food by Stalin or Hitler – if one didn't get you, the other was bound to – he was learning how to be an American in a big old *dacha* in Astrakhan, on the Caspian Sea, where the closest he came to armed combat was reading propaganda posters about the vile and vicious Hun nailed to the wall of the café where he spent every one of his few unsupervised moments.

Commerce didn't boom in the Soviet Union during the war: nobody had any money, and if someone came upon some money, he found there was nothing to buy with it. The law of the marketplace was barter. Pinsky had one prized commodity, his increasingly fluent English. With it he could read English-language newspapers smuggled by a sturgeon fisherman across the Caspian from Bobol, in Iran, and this tool, according to the proprietor of the café, could be used 'to shove the light of truth up the dark asshole of Mother Russia'. The proprietor (not owner; nobody *owned* anything) had opened the café under the pretense of serving the people of Astrakhan their midday meals, but his true ambition was to use it as a conduit for acquiring foods other than potatoes and fish. So he kept a flock of ducks, which he tended with loving care and cooked with Gallic panache and shared with Pinsky in return for Pinsky reading aloud to him translations of the English-language newspapers.

From the proprietor Pinsky learned to appreciate food, which, though he couldn't know it at the time, would become his life's work. His superiors didn't discourage him, for they knew that whatever employment he engaged in would be but the cover for his *real* life's work.

When his trainers deemed him to be sufficiently American to pass as an American (which turned out to be not quite the case – some Americans accepted him as an American but one who had spent his entire life in an institution, and others accepted him as a person recently arrived from Pluto), sufficiently reliable ideologically to keep the Communist faith indefinitely anywhere in the world (which turned out to be true generally, though with modifications that would have given Lenin apoplexy) and sufficiently skilled in the arcana of spycraft (which turned out to be a matter of opinion: *he* thought he was doing a bangup job, but others in the trade were less appreciative), they revealed to Pinsky his destiny: the Kremlin assumed that as soon as the war in Europe ended, the United States and the Soviet Union would fall to squabbling. And since the squabble had all the ingredients of a conflict long-lived, bellicose and perhaps apocalyptic, it was important for the Soviet Union to have moles working underground in America, establishing themselves as Americans, perhaps

51

acquiring bits and pieces of intelligence data, perhaps running an agent here and there, perhaps just standing by until such time as they would be called upon to serve the homeland. Pinsky would go to America as one of the hundreds of thousands of young men returning from the European Theatre of Operations, would assume an identity, find work and settle down. He would be an American. He would never again see his family and friends, for he would never again return to the Soviet Union unless he was apprehended by the American authorities and uncovered before he could kill himself, in which case, even if the Americans did send him home, his homecoming wouldn't be joyous since he would be shot as soon as he disembarked.

He was infiltrated aboard a hospital ship as a 'John Doe', a soldier with amnesia resulting from shellshock. After an uneventful crossing, during which he stole several hundred dollars from *non compose* fellow patients, he jumped ship in what he assumed was New York but was in fact Halifax, Nova Scotia, where the ship had stopped to unload Canadian wounded.

Like a Canada goose, with the coming of Fall Pinsky moved gradually southward. Everywhere he stopped, be it for a few days or a few weeks, the doors that opened quickest for him had to do with food. In Philadelphia, he worked as a busboy at Bookbinder's. In Annapolis, he was introduced to – and initially terrified by – softshell crabs, which he had never heard of and which looked to him like giant spiders.

By the time Pinsky's migration landed him in the District of Columbia, he was far more versed in the techniques of selecting, preparing and serving food than ninety-eight percent of the American people. He determined to construct a career in the general field of victuals.

He had also settled, at last, on a credible but vague background that he would keep ready for the day when he would have to explain himself. That day might never come; so far, he had found Americans to be astonishingly credulous. In the Soviet Union, there were papers to attest to everything – birth, education, employment, armed service, address, marital status, party affiliation – and they were demanded by every petty official one encountered. In America, it seemed, no one ever challenged anything anyone said about himself.

He moulded, fired and glazed into permanence a biographical core that began with birth in a Nebraska farm town (no one outside Nebraska knew what a Nebraska accent sounded like, so he was safe). His parents had both died in the terrible winter of 1939.

The young Foster Pym had moved around the Midwest, living with this cousin and that great-aunt, spending a term or two at the public high school wherever he was. He had tried to enlist in the Army on December 8th, 1941, but was turned down because of 'bad lungs'.

Afflicted by conscience at not being able to serve his country, Foster volunteered to work in the USO in San Diego, where he learned to cook, and for the next three and a half years he travelled from Naval base to Army post, from USO to canteen, helping out wherever he could.

Now that the war was over, he hoped to be able to put his skills to work making a living. His culinary quiver contained one special arrow, a holdover from his early years in the Nebraska wilds: he was a dynamite duck chef.

He tried the story at his first (and, as fate would have it, last) job interview in Washington, and while he was pleased that his prospective employer found no flaws in his tale, Pym knew that the man wouldn't have cared if he had introduced himself as the Wadi of Hunza: the man, who called himself Herbert Dickinson (a name which Pym's fine ear discerned as being about as genuine as the name Foster Pym), was looking for a white, polite, articulate, all-American type who could take orders and keep his mouth shut, to be the outside man for his food-supply and catering business, and Pym fitted the bill perfectly.

Pym saw the catering business as the ideal conduit for his

53

primary mission – gathering intelligence. If he were to become a businessman or a civil servant, a publicist or a journalist, a salesman or a restauranteur, he would have access to a limited circle of Washingtonians. He would be on some party lists but not on others, could never aspire to Georgetown salons or receptions at the Shoreham or candlelit dinners in MacLean. By becoming a caterer serving an international array of gourmet foods, he could cross all social, political, cultural and diplomatic barriers. He might not be invited anywhere, but he would be present everywhere. Until such time as he was given a specific mission to fulfil, he could work at becoming acquainted with the rich and powerful, at gathering gossip and at familiarizing himself with the labyrinth of decision-making in the nation's capital.

He began by learning the business; he finished by owning it. The first took six months. The second, once he had assembled all his tools, took five minutes.

With research help from associates with whom he was in contact mostly through dead-letter drops, Pym discovered that Dickinson had been Heinrich Himmler's personal chef. He had cut a deal with the American OSS, whereby he ratted on several former colleagues now eager to deny ever having heard of the SS, in return for which he was guaranteed immunity from prosecution and provided with a new identity.

Pym typed out a note, addressed it to himself at work, and opened it in front of Dickinson. It said: 'Do you know who you're working for?'

By five that afternoon, Dickinson was on a train heading west. As *lagniappe* for keeping his lip buttoned, Pym was given title to *Plat du Jour*.

Financially, Pym did well. He could afford to move out of the Northeast neighbourhood, from which whites were fleeing like rats from a fire and into which blacks were streaming like roaches to a mouldy kitchen. But he felt comfortable on familiar turf, was accepted by the local merchants and policemen and enjoyed being inconspicuous. Only once had he briefly contemplated moving. That was when he was married to Louise.

He had met Louise at a time when the fighting was winding down in Korea, at a small political gathering in a row house in Alexandria. Though no one would have thought to use the term, the gathering was, in fact, a *bund* meeting – one of the first seeds that would sprout into the belladonna known as the American Nazi Party. He had sought out the right-wing fringe groups during the height of the McCarthy frenzy because no one paid attention to them (all eyes were focused on the other end of the political spectrum) and because they showed promise of someday sowing violent discord in America.

Louise was a plain girl – fine featured, by no means ugly, but rather blah – who was searching for a cause that would light up her life. Almost anything would have served: saving the snail darter or preserving the environment or stopping nuclear proliferation, had they been issues then. But as it was, suburban Virginia was a hotbed of inchoate fascism, so fascism was what Louise embraced.

Louise and Foster lurched into a relationship based on loneliness, ignorance of and curiosity about sex, and a shared (or so she thought) passion for the perpetuation of the Thousand Year Reich. They slept together at his apartment every Tuesday (*bund* night) and Saturday (movie night) for six months. Louise announced that she had missed her period. There were endless conversations about examinations, options, embarrassment for her parents (her father was a senior official with the Census Bureau), with whom she lived. There were tears, a couple of insincere declarations of love, several more nights of thrashing on the sheets. Louise announced that she had missed another period.

They got married.

The marriage lasted almost a year, which, on reflection, Pym appraised as quite a success, considering that it was a loveless union punctuated by mistakes, misapprehensions and lies. Louise was not pregnant; she had a polyp on one of her ovaries. She hated having to heed the welfare of anyone but herself; she had always had a room of her own and was unaccustomed to a lack of privacy, had always had meals cooked for her and was a fumblefingered calamity in the kitchen, had no skill at feigning interest in Foster's health, happiness or day at the office. And she continued to be fervid in her affection for fascist blather, which had always been offensive to Foster and now became oppressive.

But Foster Pym was not about to spark a scene that would cause any lasting bitterness. It would be one thing to be a middle-class caterer with an angry ex-wife pecking at him through the legal system, quite another to be a Soviet spy with a revenge-crazed ex who hung around with a band of loud-mouthed Nazis.

So one evening, after a silent, sullen supper of day-old moo goo gai pan, Foster said cheerfully, 'Don't you think you'd be happier at home?'

There was no artifice to Louise, which made it easier. She didn't say something maudlin like, 'But this *is* my home!' or burst into tears and lament their failures. She just looked up, surprised, and said, 'I sure would!'

They agreed on a one-time payment of $10,000. They agreed that Louise would change her name back to Whelan. They did not discuss what her parents' reaction might be to having their baby back in the nest. Louise didn't care what her parents felt. She believed Robert Frost: home is where, when you have to go there, they have to take you in.

They agreed about everything, so quickly and with such good humour that they felt a new glow of fondness for one another, a glow that they fuelled with a bottle of Canadian whisky. Finally, bibulously, they agreed that the occasion called for a goodbye screw, and they tumbled into the sack.

And Louise got pregnant.

She waited almost six months before telling Foster. She hoped to be able to entice a Nazi into her bed and pin the pregnancy on him (she had dreams of spawning a fuhrerlet who would crown her Queen Mother of the Reich), but none of the SS trolls, with their acne-pitted foreheads and dyed blond hair, would succumb to her charms.

Louise didn't suggest that she and Foster reunite. She was happily ensconced in her old room in her parents' house. She didn't suggest an abortion: by now it was too late, and, besides, her father had assured her that he would pitch her into the street, with 'whore' branded on her lips, if she so much as hinted at an abortion. She didn't suggest putting the child up for adoption. She made no demands for child-support payments.

Her proposal was simplicity itself: she would sell the child to Pym.

Her logic was unassailable. She didn't want a baby. It would be a burden on her and her parents. She wanted money, which would lighten the existing load on her and her parents. Furthermore, she pointed out, Foster's devotion to Nazism (that is, what he had encouraged her to perceive as devotion) had been waning over the past year, as his catering business had been waxing. She wasn't criticizing: she understood that there wasn't much call for fascist food. Surely it would be embarrassing for Foster to be the acknowledged (albeit divorced) father of a Nazi *wunderkind*. Wouldn't it be better for him to have the child, to raise it as he saw fit?

Foster recognized blackmail, and he appreciated it: it was his kind of plan. Besides, he rather liked the idea of rearing a successor in his own image. He even permitted himself to fantasize about creating a dynasty of homegrown spies. He agreed.

Two days after the baby was born, he traded a cashier's cheque for $25,000 (he had mortgaged his business) for a seven-pound, four-ounce girl already legally named (Louise's Parthian volley) Eva, after Eva Braun.

Foster never communicated with Louise again, though he did see her twice, both times in the newspaper, standing in the background at news conferences behind George Lincoln Rockwell. After Rockwell was shot, Louise dropped from sight for good. Whenever he thought of her, which was almost never, Foster surmised that she was working as a secretary at something like a used-car agency and that she spent her evenings plotting in damp basements. He half-expected her to turn up next on a '60 Minutes' report on the search for Josef Mengele, whose purported death in Brazil he regarded as a splendid fraud. Maybe as Mengele's nurse.

Eva became the joy of Foster's life, a bouquet of posies amid the weeds of Foster's humdrum existence. A clever, sunny child, she was blessed with impossible looks: the crossing of a plain woman with an utterly forgettable-looking man had somehow produced a stunning child – corn-blond hair, grey-blue eyes, high proud cheekbones and assertive chin. It was almost as if Louise had willed her Aryan fantasies to overcome her and Foster's drab genes.

Foster continued to live in Northeast, where there was a ready supply of inexpensive, kindly black labour, which suited Foster politically as well as personally: a sociologist might have labelled him an eccentric ethnic Calvinist (or a racist), for he believed that each ethnic group had a pre-ordained place in society and that black people's place was to provide inexpensive, kindly labour.

If parents received grades. Foster Pym would have given himself solid Bs.

Spies, on the other hand, do receive grades of a sort, and it was a source of annoyance and consternation to Pym that while he thought he deserved high Bs or low As, those who judged him consistently gave him C-minuses.

Had an inquisitor demanded that he enumerate his successes, he would have listed at least four.

He had learned about the Bay of Pigs invasion a full twenty four hours before it occurred, by overhearing a tipsy New York *Times* correspondent brag to a comely maiden that President Kennedy had asked the paper to withdraw its scheduled story.

He had properly assessed the global gravity of the Watergate fiasco, by watching and listening to Ben Bradlee as he interrupted countless dinner parties for phone conversations with Woodward and Bernstein.

He had discovered that an assistant director of the CIA was a genteel junkie, addicted to paregoric.

And he had engineered an embarrassment to the Carter Administration, adding grain alcohol to the *Chassagne Montrachet* he served to a senior official of the Carter White House, a chunky, good-humored koala of a man who had only recently learned to tie a necktie, who had been seated beside the wife of the Egyptian ambassador, a raven-haired, onyx-eyed beauty with skin that shone like honey and teeth as white as Chiclets. By the dessert course, the Carter man was so thoroughly ripped that he gazed liquidly at the ambassador's wife's breathtaking cleavage, asserted vinously that he had always wanted to see the pyramids and begged ravenously to be permitted to 'munch on the Valley of the Kings' – all well within earshot of several attentive members of the Washington press corps.

Each of Pym's coups was received with an insouciant 'So what?'

Either the information received was practically useless (in the cases of both the Bay of Pigs and Watergate, things worked out perfectly without any interference from Mother Russia), or else it was regarded as inconsequential (half the Politburo was addicted to alcohol, and booze-fired *bêtises* were as common as flatulence).

The reaction infuriated Pym, who thought he had done exemplary work – especially considering that he had been given no specific assignment – and impelled him to a rash exchange that he had long since come to regret.

During his last meeting with a contact, a twilight walk in Rock Creek Park a year ago, he had endured sarcasm and condescension for nearly an hour before finally exploding, 'What do you *want* from me? You want me to run an agent in the . . . White House . . . for God's sake?'

'That would be nice,' said the wretched weasel of a man, who, apparently, knew Pym better than Pym thought, for he added. 'Then perhaps you can end your days here, instead of coming home to read the news on Radio Moscow.'

'*Home!*' Pym choked, feeling as if an ice pick had been plunged into his liver.

'Just a thought,' the man said before he turned down a bosky path and disappeared in the shadows.

The next morning, Pym's dormant haemorrhoids burst into agonizing bloom.

He began to prowl the perimeters of the White House grounds, not looking for anything specific, but hoping – almost mystically – to absorb an aura that would give him a clue as to how to proceed.

Then the poor black lady's shopping bag had burst, and he had sensed the cracking open of a door.

Next, Eva had come home to work for him, which Pym regarded as a gift, a blessing from whatever gods oversaw his life.

He had not been close to Eva since she went away to boarding school when she was ten. Her letters from Bennington had been infrequent and remote, alluding to increased political commitment in which, she was sure, he had no interest at all. He began to think of her as an adult with whom he had some distant connection. He never imposed himself on her: first, he knew she would resent and resist it; second, he quite approved of the political drift she was taking on her own. She worked for the Southern Christian Leadership Conference, then for Common Cause, then for Greenpeace.

Then she had called, from a jail in Colorado. Evidently, she had joined a radical environmental group intent on blowing up the Glen Canyon Dam.

Pym bailed her out and hired a lawyer who, for $16,000, got Eva's case separated from the others and dismissed on an obscure technical ground.

Eva came home frightened, chastened, disillusioned and in debt to her father, to whom she tearfully confessed having also committed one third-class felony and two misdemeanours for which she had never been apprehended.

Pym let her regain her strength and her composure and her self-confidence. He fed her, housed her and clothed her as she worked off her debt – which, of course, indebted her further, at least in her head, which was as Pym would have wished.

He had never told her he was a Russian spy. He knew that many American leftists had no more affection for the Soviet Union than they had for America. And he wanted her to have no leverage against him: he wanted all the ammunition, in anticipation of the day he might want to use it to recruit her. Probably, he would have found the word 'blackmail' infelicitous to describe his plans for his daughter, but probably, too, he wouldn't have denied it.

That day, it appeared, was drawing near.

Things were looking up.

Five

The West Gate of the White House was kept closed, to dissuade loons from driving up to the front door of the mansion, and it was reinforced with concrete bulwarks, to discourage maniacs from launching frontal attacks with explosive-packed laundry vans. But there was a pedestrian-access path beside the guardhouse in which sat, most mornings, Sergeant Roland Thibaudeaux of the White House detail of the Metropolitan Police Force. Each morning, Burnham would wave and say, 'Morning, Sergeant T,' and Sergeant Thibaudeaux would wave and say, 'Morning, Mr B.'

It was their private ritual joke, their acknowledgment of eccentricities of language and quirks of human nature. The first time they had met, Burnham had pronounced the Sergeant's name in its original French form: 'Tee-boe-doe.'

The Sergeant had corrected him: 'It's Tibby-doo.'

'It is?'

'Yup. Come from up Norritch [Norwich], Connecticut. My father used to say, "T'aint my fault some frog got into Granny's jammies. We're Americans and that's that."'

As he passed by the guardhouse, Burnham waved and said, 'Morning, Sergeant T.'

'Halt!' The Sergeant slid open the bulletproof window, smiled apologetically and tapped his left breast.

'Again?' Burnham chuckled. 'What was it this time?' He reached into his pocket for his White House pass.

Among the scores, the hundred, the countless symbols of

power and privilege in official Washington, one of the most prized, especially to those young ambitious and unknown to the public, was the White House pass. It was a laminated plastic card, printed with a colour photograph and the name of the bearer, and it looked like a driver's license. But it was awarded only after the bearer had been blessed with an offer of a job in what were called 'the highest councils of government', a job that, it was determined, required him to have access to the President of the United States, and had been sanctified by a Full Field Investigation by the FBI, which included, among other things, interviews with the candidate's grammar-school classmates about their recollections and impressions of him as a fifth-grader.

Technically, the pass meant that the bearer could go to work in the morning. Actually, in the eyes of the rest of Washington it was affirmation of his worth as a human being. With that pass he could cash cheques at strange banks, open charge accounts at restaurants, do favours for Congressmen (taking constituents through the West Wing of the White House and the private family quarters while the President was away), impress the drawers off girls by arranging to have the White House telephone operators page him during a date, and, perhaps most delightful of all, comport himself with an air of polite restraint which suggested that so full was his brain of classified, super-sensitive material that his every word must be weighed before it could safely be uttered.

Even the lowliest member of a typing pool bore his or her White House pass as a badge that set him a substantial half-step above his peers, for the mere existence of the pass suggested proximity to the President, and proximity was the capital's highest currency.

Every member of the White House staff, whether he worked in the White House or in the Executive Office Building next door, was supposed to wear his pass every second he was on the premises. This was a club, and as long as everyone displayed his membership card, the Secret Service was cool, the police mellow.

The fact that a White House pass would have been easy to steal and easier to forge was never mentioned. It was a symbol.

For the first few months that he worked as a speechwriter for the President, Burnham wore his pass dutifully, clipping it to his jacket when his overcoat came off, then to this shirt when his jacket came off, remembering to take it with him even when he went down the hall to the john. Then he began to notice that the more senior staff were neglecting to wear their passes.

He said nothing, asked no questions, but observed that while there was distinct status in possessing a White House pass, there was even greater status in possessing one and not wearing it: it implied that the bearer was *so* in at the White House, *such* a veteran, *so* well known to the police and the Secret Service, that it would have been absurd to require him to wear his pass. After all, did the President have to wear a pass?

One morning, he left his pass at home. On purpose. He went to work early, prepared to be sent home to fetch it. As he passed through the West Gate, feeling like a priest sneaking into a Marilyn Chambers movie, he saluted and said, 'Morning, Sergeant T,' and the sergeant glanced up and saw his face and smiled and said, 'Morning, Mr B.'

That whole day, Burnham had felt very close to the seat of power.

Nowadays, he always carried his pass with him – he'd damn well need it if he were summoned to the Oval Office (the chances of which were about as great as his election to the Papacy), for the phalanx of Secret Servicemen that guarded the Presidential corpus were strangers to him, and he to them – but he seldom wore it.

And truly, once one's face was known around Fortress White House, there wasn't any need for a pass. No wino would ever get close enough to the President to sit on the end of his bed and chat him up, like that guy had done to the Queen. Without a pass, he'd never get upstairs in the mansion. He'd never get on the grounds.

But once in a while, something happened that shook everybody's confidence and made a *frappé* of the White House routine, and then one of the staff pygmies, a Special Assistant to the President for Ukases and Edicts, would snap off a memo to the entire staff, a memo that always began with the magic words 'The President wants . . .' and bingo! Everyone from the Executive Dog Walker just about up to the First Lady of the Land would walk around with their passes riveted to their foreheads.

Once, it had been a woman who had scaled the fence down by the Ellipse and had triggered the electronic alarms in the ground. They nabbed her as she was sprinting across the South Lawn carrying a bird in a paper bag. She wanted the President to bless her parakeet. Its name was Onan, she said, because 'he spilleth his seed upon the ground'.

A pass emergency was declared whenever there was a riot in the ghetto, which usually happened somewhere at least once a summer. The implication was, of course, that without a pass it was impossible for the police to distinguish between rioters and the President's staff two miles away inside the White House.

Burnham found his pass. 'What is it this time?' he asked Sergeant Thibaudeaux.

'Some fella come to the East Gate, looking' for a ticket to the tour, just like a reg'lar visitor, only missin' a few dots on his dice 'cause he said he had an appointment to see the President.'

'He have a gun?'

'Nope. Just said he had to see the President. Said he had orders.'

'Who from?'

Thibaudeaux smiled. 'His toaster.'

'His toaster?'

'Every day. Said he took his marching orders from his toaster.' Thibaudeaux shrugged. 'Anyhow, a memo come through 'bout an hour ago.'

Burnham aimed the clip on the pass at his jacket pocket, but he missed, and the card fell to the ground. He bent

65

over, and here was the unmistakable, awful sound of tearing thread, and he felt a cool breeze blow through his boxer shorts. He stood up, and as he reached gingerly behind him, his hand touched not the rough texture of seersucker but the smoothness of Egyptian cotton, from just below his belt right down to his crotch.

'I've been holed,' he said, 'just like a clipper ship on a reef.'

'Flapjacks,' Sergeant Thibaudeaux sympathized. 'Flapjacks do it to me every time. 'Swhy I steer clear of flapjacks.'

Burnham attached his pass and smoothed his jacket and turned his stern to the Sergeant. 'Does it cover?'

'Sorta. Long as you walk like you've got the piles and nobody's chasin' you.'

'You're a comfort, Sergeant T,' Burnham said. 'You know what the trouble is with modern society?'

'There's only one?'

'Well, one of the main ones. It's that we don't listen to warnings. Since light first peeked through the cracks in my eyelids, this day has been rife with warnings. If I were primitive man, I would've cast my spear into the earth and turned back into my cave and said "fuck it". Or whatever was the fashionable phrase of the day. But I don't have that luxury. I must press on,' Burnham pinched the rear of his trousers together, 'and strive to build a better tomorrow.'

Thibaudeaux smiled and said, 'Have a good day.'

'I have other plans.' Burnham turned away and made his way toward the White House, as guilty and crazed-looking a figure as had ever pranced up the path – glancing furtively from side to side, clutching the seat of his pants, trying to walk without moving anything above his knees.

At the end of the path, Burnham turned not into the West Wing of the White House but to the right, across West Executive Avenue and into the Executive Office Building, the heap of grey granite blocks that housed the Office of Management and Budget, the staff of the National Security Council, the White House switchboard (in the cellar, staffed by dogged operators who boasted that they could find anybody, at any time, anywhere in the world, and who liked to tell reporters about the time they rousted an errant advance man from the bed of some broad in Canberra, Australia), a cafeteria that specialized in ciguatera, scores of members of the White House staff (including the speech-writers), and the offices and staff of the Vice President of the United States, a man picked to run with the President for three reasons: he was so rich (oil) as to be incorruptible, so stupid as to be incapable of devious backroom ma-noeuvrings on behalf of his friends, and from a state and region (Houma, Louisiana) that the President could never have carried on his own. (The only liability that the Presi-dent's men saw in the Vice President was that he was so popular at home that some of his chums talked openly of shooting the President just so good ol' Leroy LeDoux could have a crack at the top job.) When the President had announced his selection of LeDoux for the ticket, the Majority Leader of the United States Senate had pro-tested, albeit privately, 'But he's a bigoted, bullheaded ignoramus!'

'Maybe,' the President had replied, 'but don't they deserve to be represented, too?'

To many members of the White House staff, assignment to the EOB was exile. It did not correspond to their vision of their own importance. They were not working *in* the White House; they were not working at the President's side. Through the corridors of the West Wing of the White House there coursed a constant current of excitement, of drama, of historical moment. Through the corridors of the EOB there coursed an occasional messenger with a super-market cart full of routine mail and, now and then on slow summer days, a rubber ball thrown back and forth between two of the President's writers who had nothing to do but didn't dare go home.

Burnham loved the EOB. He had an enormous office, twenty by thirty feet, on a ground-floor corner of the building with a pleasant view of the South Lawn and the

Ellipse. The windows were tall and the ceilings were high, and there were easy chairs and a great conference table (for gin rummy) and a massive oak desk and a typing table and a word-processor that he hated and an electric typewriter that he loved and a phone console with sixteen buttons and three television sets (one of his early assignments had been to monitor the evening news on all three networks and to analyse each for anti-Administration bias) and a huge leather couch which came in very handy when the quest for *le mot juste* became exhausting.

Burnham's boss did work in the White House. His name was Warner Cobb, and he was a conduit and co-ordinator of the President's spoken and written words: speeches, letters, proclamations, messages to Congress, personal mail, congratulatory blather, political nonsense – it all passed over Cobb's desk. The President's Appointments Secretary gave Cobb a list of the upcoming week's speeches; legislative assistants outlined the needs for messages and statements; the correspondence office sent batches of mail. Cobb then assigned the work to the six White House writers, read the results of their efforts before forwarding them to the President for signature or delivery, and passed back to the writers the President's response to their work (when and if the President chose to respond), which was the writers' only measure of their worth as craftsmen.

Cobb's office was in the basement of the West Wing. The President had personally insisted (the highest of all flatteries) that Cobb work in the business end of the White House itself, so that he would be available instantly on summons. There had been no office space availabe.

Then make him an office, the President had said.

And because he was the President, it was done.

And though Cobb himself had nothing to do with the construction of his office, he became the object of loathing of the women who worked in the White House, for his office was built by removing two stalls from the four-stall ladies room on the basement story of the building.

The office was furnished with one small metal desk, one

small metal swivel chair and, facing the desk, one small straight-back chair where a secretary could sit to take dictation. Dictating took longer in that office than in most, for it was usually punctuated by the sound of rushing water. There was no window, so Cobb never knew what the weather was doing outside, and because he chain-smoked Gauloise cigarettes in his airless cubicle, when he emerged into the world he was surrounded by a miasmic reek that led cosmopolites to wonder if he was an attendant on leave from a Parisian WC.

Burnham's resistance to working in the White House itself was not only hedonistic; it was also practical. There was no need for speechwriters to reside close to the President, and with a White House staff of 314 in a building that could accommodate fifty or, at most, seventy five workers, office space had to be assigned on a need basis.

Burnham further disagreed with those of his colleagues who believed that each writer should have a POTUS phone in his office. Another status symbol. Those who had the special phones had been deemed vital enough to the welfare of the Republic to be kept on the shortest leash possible: When the President of the United States (POTUS) wanted to reach you, he wanted to reach you *now*, without having to diddle around with busy signals and secretaries and switching delays, so he picked up the phone and punched your number, and in your office your POTUS phone buzzed with a nasty, urgent noise like when something goes wrong with your convection oven or when you wanted to push your English muffin down for a bit more browning but the toaster's too hot and rebels. Whatever you were doing you stopped, and you snatched up the POTUS phone and said, 'Yes, Sir!'

The second most important man in the Federal Government was Mario Epstein. He had *two* POTUS phones in his suite of offices. He also had a phone in the government car assigned to him, a phone in his own car, and, in his home in Cleveland park, sky-blue phones with locks on them in his bedroom, his study and the kitchen.

Epstein's title was, simply, Special Assistant to the President. His real job slot was, not so simply, Deputy President of the United States for the Economy, for Keeping Malcontents From Burning Down the Cities, for Convincing All Minorities That The Administration Cherished Them, for Mollifying Women, for Convincing Old Folks that Social Security Cheques Could Be Stretched Beyond Cat Food, for Delivering the Jewish and Italian Votes, and for Counselling the President as to Which of His Foreign Policy Advisors Were Trying to Blow Smoke Up His Ass.

The President didn't like Epstein very much, but he needed him. 'He's so mean he wouldn't give you the clap,' he told a Cabinet meeting one day, with Epstein sitting in the background against the wall, 'but I'll tell you this: that man can spit miracles.'

Epstein did not want to be liked. He wanted to be feared, for he believed, quite rightly, that fear was the only engine that could galvanize a bureaucracy as huge and obdurate as the Federal Government. He knew every man, every position, every salary, over which the President had control, and he used that knowledge as a whip. He also knew how to deal with those over whom the President did not have control, those with Civil Service tenure. There were all manner of intricate weapons that could be used to make a man's life miserable if he would not co-operate – shrinking his office, reducing his staff and finding fault with everything he did being among the more innocuous options.

The President had barely known Epstein prior to hiring him. The President had embarked upon his first term with a coterie of cronies that the press had immediately dubbed 'The B Men,' because every one of them was a banker, a broker, a businessman or a booster. They had a lot of splendid ideas, and no idea whatsoever about how to implement them.

What these guys know about government, went a favourite line of the time, you could stick up a gnat's ass and still have room for the Vice President.

The B Men had nothing but contempt for Washington,

and Washington returned the sentiment. So, naturally, they accomplished nothing but the alienation of everyone with whom they came in contact.

The President stood by his friends with admirable loyalty, until one day when the assistant in charge of the President's reading matter made a slip and let him see an editorial in *The Washington Post* which said, in part, 'In terms of leadership, decisiveness and accomplishment, this President makes Jimmy Carter look like FDR.'

Even then, the President did not march through his staff with a scythe. He hired one young man, whose name he had forgotten but whom Evelyn Witt, his personal secretary and one of his oldest friends (she had been with him for thirty years), helped him recall: Mario Epstein.

Epstein had applied for a staff job when the President was still in the Senate, and he had impressed the Senator mightily, but on hearing that a run for the Presidency was not only possible but imminent, he withdrew his application. A run for the Presidency meant a long campaign, extensive public exposure and constant contact with people of various opinions, abilities and personalities.

'I'm a perfect staff man,' Epstein had told the Senator, 'but I'm a perfectly terrible politician. I'll do you more harm then good. For you, success is being loved and admired; for me, it's being hated and feared. After you win, think of me again.'

Evelyn Witt discovered that Epstein had since worked for two Senators, one liberal and one conservative, and had been fired by both because of his inability to deal with the constant demands for compromise. He had gotten a job as the untitled deputy to the chief executive officer and sole owner of a company that supplied tungsten elements to Defence Department contractors, weapons manufacturers and a handful of unnamed foreign governments.

The President admired many things about Mario Epstein. He had graduated from Harvard College, Harvard Law School and Harvard Business School, which was good because it gave him first-strike credibility on the Hill and with the press. (You have to prove a Harvard man wrong; somebody from, say, Bucknell, has to prove himself right.) He was married (good, because he wouldn't be a flagrant tail-chaser) to a woman who taught endocrinology at John Hopkins (good, because she had a life of her own and wouldn't lie around the house watching 'General Hospital' and bitching about the hours he worked). She looked like the love-child of a bulldog and a ten-speed bike – all wrinkles and bones and teeth and nails (good, because nobody in his right mind would try to get at the President through Epstein through her). He coveted power for its own sake, for what it could accomplish. He loved to watch the ripple effect of a Presidential command, and sometimes he issued Presidential commands solely for the pleasure of watching them work. He had no personal ambitions. At forty one years old, he was in day-to-day control of the largest, most complex, most powerful machine the world had ever known.

There were valid knocks about Epstein, and the President was aware of them. The man was completely, unashamedly amoral. He could not be consulted about what was right, or just, or compassionate, but only about whether a certain programme could be made to work. He had respect for decisions, but not for the process, the give-and-take, that led to decisions. He had no patience with discussions, only with conclusions. It had taken him longer than most to assemble a functioning staff because of what he and the President referred to as 'the Epstein paradox': he had to employ, to implement his orders, people who could deal with other people, but such people were often constitutionally incapable of working for a person who could not deal with other people – namely, Epstein.

Eventually, though, he did build a staff, and his operation, which consisted of about two dozen men and women, some in the White House, some in the EOB, became known informally and with no affection whatever as Atilla & Co.

Epstein removed – quietly, one by one – all of The B Men. First, he cut their access to the President. Second, he replaced their assistants with his own people and made sure that every decision they made was cleared with his office. Third, those who were not impelled by boredom and frustration to quit were assigned as ambassadors to backwater countries. Ronald Reagan had raised to new heights the art of dumping incompetent political hacks into the ambassadorial ranks, and his administration had taken so much criticism that Epstein could pump at least two dozen yahoos into foreign embassies without risking unfavourable comparison in the media. He de-fused objections by the appointees by having the President announce the appointments – with fulsome praise and outrageous promise – before informing the appointees. Any man who declined an appointment would seen churlish, ungrateful, unAmerican.

The one person to whom Epstein deferred without hesitation was the President – in part because the President was his employer and provider and could deprive him of his cherished power with a single word, but also because Epstein did respect the office of the Presidency, and when the weight of that office was broadcast through the anger of a man who stood six-foot-four and weighed two hunded and thirty pounds, the man suddenly became twenty feet tall and weighed a ton and was awesome and truly frightening.

When Epstein's POTUS phone rang, he always grabbed it immediately, because he knew that, to the President, the speed with which you responded to his summons was an absolute indicator of your loyalty to him.

And so it was with bewilderment that Epstein's senior secretary, a condor named Esther Tagliaferro who had been at the White House since Eisenhower's second term, one day heard the POTUS line in Epstein's office buzzing unanswered. She knew he was in the office: he had just returned from lunch downstairs in the White House Mess and had told her to remind him to call Commander Larsen, the Navy officer in charge of the Mess, which meant that he had a complaint about the preparation of a certain dish, the quality of the salad dressing, the limited choice of entrées on the day's menu, the freshness of the bread, the presence in the Mess of a person or persons he considered inappropriate to eat in company as august as the Second Sitting, or the conduct of one of the Filipino messboys, as obsequious a covey of Orientals as had ever confirmed the tacit racism in the American military.

Esther knew Epstein wasn't on the phone to someone else: she had placed no call for him, and neither of his private, direct lines was lit. Besides, he would have abruptly cut off anyone to answer the POTUS phone.

That left only one possibility, and it put Esther in an awkward position. If she went in and picked up the POTUS phone, she risked a dressing-down from the President. No one but the principal was supposed to answer a POTUS phone. If she let the buzz continue (she could envision the muscles in the President's jaw beginning to twitch), the rest of the day was as good as shot. The President would set sail upon a sea of rage. Then, as apologies and explanations filtered through to him, he would slide into a sulk. Then, as understanding nudged petulance aside, he would feel guilty, and the last few hours of the day would be taken up with his attempts to soothe all the feelings he had bruised.

Screw it, she thought. She had been tongue-lashed by past masters. LBJ had once said to her, 'Esther, I 'spect you don't have sense enough to pour piss out of a boot with the instructions written on the heel.' She could weather any salvos *this* President could fire.

So she entered Epstein's office, eyeing the closed door at the far end of the room, knowing he could hear the buzz, imagining him frantically torn between personal need and professional duty, and picked up the POTUS phone.

'I'm sorry, sir, he's . . .'

'Epstein!'

'No, sir, he's . . .'

'Who's this!'

'Esther Tagliaferro.'

'God dammit, Esther, where is he?'

Her first impulse was to say, 'I don't know,' but three decades of experience with seven Presidents told her that that response was not only unacceptable, it was impossible. An Epstein was *never* out of touch.

So she said, 'He's . . . indisposed, Mr President,' and she thought: I bet that's a new one for you.

'He's *what*?'

'Indisposed, sir.'

She heard a quick, incredulous suck of breath. 'Do you know who this is?' The voice was calm, as if it thought it was dealing with a child or a deranged person.

The possibilities that rattled through Esther's head included: 'What number were you calling? 'Could you spell that?' 'May I ask what this is in reference to?' May I refer you to Mr Epstein's assistant?' 'President of what?' and 'Sure you are, and I'm Princess Diana.'

'Why yes, sir.'

'Tell me. Tell me who this is.'

To her surprise, Esther found herself growing angry, angry at being patronized by the President of the United States, angry at being sneered at by a man who had worked here for six years when she'd been here for more than thirty, and to her amazement she heard herself say, 'Mr President, do you want me to spell it out for you?'

'What?'

'I said; Mr Epstein is in-dis-*posed*.'

There was a pause, and the President said quickly, 'Oh. Oh.' But his retreat was momentary. 'Esther,' he said, coming back strong, 'I don't want you to go home, I don't want Epstein to go home, I don't want *any*body going home tonight, until there's a phone in that crapper!' The line went dead.

The door at the far end of the room flew open, and Epstein emerged looking like a fundamentalist Baptist caught in a raid on a cathouse – belt unbuckled, zipper at half-mast, one trouser leg hitched in a sock, face flushed, tie askew – from the only private lavatory in the West Wing of the White House except for the President's own.

That was how Epstein got his second POTUS telephone.

And that episode, the details of which leaked from office to office, was why Burnham wanted no part of a POTUS phone. He held the heretical belief that peristalsis was a private affair.

Furthermore, a POTUS line violated Burnham's instinct for self-preservation. It permitted no time for a calculated response, for the creation of excuses and evasions. It forced spontaneity and candour – bad news for a person interested in survival.

Burnham wanted as many baffles as possible between himself and the Oval Office. When he first arrived at the White House, he had longed for proximity, had striven always to be accessible to the President. Though a day's work was done, he would linger in his office into the evening, until he could ascertain that the President had left the Oval Office for the mansion. And even then he would call the White House switchboard and tell the operators exactly where he was going and when he would arrive.

Just in case.

By now he knew that the only good news from the President was no news. If the President wanted to deliver a compliment, he sent it through Warner Cobb. If he wanted to see someone not on the POTUS network, he would have the individual summoned by Evelyn Witt or the secretary to the Appointments Secretary. Only if he was incensed or flustered or unable at that precise moment to reach a particular high-level aide would he directly contact a middle-echelon esne like Burnham.

It had happened to Burnham once, by accident. He had stayed late at the office because he had a date to meet Sarah at 7.45 at a theatre a few blocks farther downtown. His secretary, Dyanna Butler (who came from Richmond, where, apparently, exotic spelling of first names was mandatory), had long since left for her apartment across the river in Arlington, so he was alone with Walter Jackson

76

Bate's biography of Samuel Johnson when the phone rang.

He picked it up and, because he detested the military habit of answering with his last name, said simply, 'Hello.'

A voice thundered, 'You a writer?'

In the next few seconds, Burnham recognized the voice, assumed that he was wrong, wondered whether it was a joke or an impersonation, decided that it wasn't, and concluded that, in fact, he was being telephoned by the President of the United States. Who was waiting for a reply. From him.

'Sir?'

'I said, are you a goddam writer?'

'Ah . . . well . . .'

'Judas Priest! Goddam Cobb has taken a powder and now I can't find anybody speaks English.' (Warner Cobb had left the building to attend a retirement dinner for a State Department official, one of the many details relevant to this phone call which Burnham would learn over the next twenty-four hours and a fact that the President could have discovered by calling the switchboard instead of impulsively using the POTUS system, giving up and shouting at an operator, 'Get me a writer!' The operators knew that Burnham was the only writer still in the building.)

'Yessir. A writer.'

The President seemed to take a deep breath, for when he spoke again, his voice was calm, controlled. 'I thought we had a deal, son.'

'Sir?' He doesn't even know who I am, Burnham thought.

'I thought we agreed that you fellas were going to help out your President . . .'

'Yes, sir . . .'

'. . . by phoneticizing names that no goddam human being in the civilized world can be expected to pronounce right.'

A clue. Something had gone wrong with a speech, a name had been mispronounced. But which name?

Burnham didn't know all the speeches the President gave Only Cobb knew the entire list.

'Yes sir. We phoneticize them all.'

'You do, eh?' The voice was rising again, rearing back like the fat lady gearing up for the last aria of the opera. 'How about . . . Kat-Man-Fucking-Du?'

Oh shit. *It was his speech.* Last night. A short, inconsequential toast to the Prime Minister of Nepal. He had spoken to Cobb about Katmandu. It was a rule that all foreign names were to be phoneticized for the President, no matter how simple or familiar. Sha-MEER;. Gor-ba-CHOV. The problem with Katmandu was that it was phonetic as is. For the sake of the gesture, in the text he had spelled it Kat-man-DOO.

'Yes, sir. Katmandu.'

'You know where Katmandu is, son?'

'Yes, sir, I do.'

'Do you suppose it would be fair of the President to ask you to share that knowledge with him?'

'Sir?'

'I'm gonna tell you something that I would tell Cobb if he wasn't out tomcatting when he should be at his desk working like the taxpayers pay him to do. I want all you goddam writers to stop jerking off . . .'

'*What?*' What's he talking about? Burnham waited, and the President continued.

'. . . with chicken-shit names like Katmandu and Nepple and the rest.'

Now the silence was of a broken connection. Burnham stared at the telephone receiver, as if willing it to surrender more information, not realizing that he had been given the final clue.

The next day, Burnham and Cobb together reconstructed the few minutes that preceded the phone call. The President had been walking from his office back to the mansion when he had spotted a copy of the 'Style' section of the *Post* lying open on a table. He stopped and turned the pages till he found the gossip column – the Disposal of

Washington Tripe – that always gave him a lash to use against some member of his staff. There was nothing of interest until the last item, under the headline

WHITE HOUSE COUP

The President tried to score points with another Third-World nation last night, but as usual, to use one of his own favourite phrases, he just 'slobbered a bibful'.

At a small dinner for the Prime Minister of the Himalayan nation of Nepal, the President praised the Prime Minister, the King and the country, citing contributions made to the world community – and then proceeded to pronounce the name of the country 'Nepple'.

Some pacifier.

The Secret Service man with the President told Cobb that the President had dropped the paper 'like it was covered with maggots' and had lurched so spastically toward the nearest phone that he feared the President might have had a stroke.

Burnham's secretary, Dyanna Butler, was thirty years old and single, which meant that at the core of all her moods were confusion and a sense of betrayal, anger and feelings of resentment. Everything in her upbringing had conditioned her to believe that it was impossible to be thirty years old and single; the two states could not exist together; they were contradictory. She was from a 'good' Virginia family, in which care in breeding and documentable height of family tree were acceptable substitutes for wealth and talent. She had gone to Foxcroft and Sweetbriar, had been presented to society (a second mortgage on the family home, Fox Knoll, had seen to all three), had impeccable taste in clothes, was a creditable cook (people praised her gazpacho and salmon mousse), held a relatively prestigious (for a young woman) Government job and was good-looking in a clean, Olivia-Newton-John way.

She couldn't, for the life of her, figure out what had gone wrong. Granted, she worked in a town where single women outnumbered single men by two or more to one. But she had beaten worse odds than those in college; she had been a standout. 'Always remember, honey,' her father had told her, 'wherever you sit, that's the head of the table.'

Burnham could have given her a couple of pointers, from the perspective of a disinterested older observer, had she sought his counsel, but she wasn't about to confess that any cog in her transmission had slipped, and he wasn't about to involve himself in anything that would complicate his existence.

One simile that had crossed Burnham's mind about Dyanna was that she made Narcissus look like Mother Theresa. Her nails were honed and tempered like Toledo blades; the several elements of her eyes were plucked, highlighted and outlined as if they were to be presented to a sheik on a plate; her hair was washed, set, combed and, finally, sprayed into carrara permanence. She was a Barbie-Doll pietà.

As a conversationalist, she was an enraptured listener and a fascinating raconteuse, as long as the subject was herself. When the subject of the conversation wasn't herself, she attacked and wrestled with it until it *became* herself.

Too cruel, Burnham admitted. Dyanna was amiable and often thoughtful, and she did protect him, however much to protect him was also in her interest. She knew a lot about the Federal Government and the people in it. She was a superb typist, a mistress of the IBM Correcting Selectric III as Casals was a master of the cello. She was polite on the telephone, didn't spend all her time yakking with friends and didn't (so far as he knew) gossip about him, not that there was much to gossip about.

Because Dyanna was incapable of assigning blame for any part of her dilemma to any flaw in herself, she decided that the reason she hadn't met Mr Right was that she didn't move in the right circles – meaning, the circles travelled by men who were bright, sophisticated, wise and wealthy enough to appreciate her manifold assets. And the reason she didn't move in the right circles was that fate had cursed her with a succession of second-rank bosses.

The acquisition of Top Secret Clearance had not, as she has assumed it would, been her passport to glamour and romance. Her first job had been in the typing pool, where she worked nights tapping out routine messages to Congress. Then she was promoted to the office whence emanated routine Presidential correspondence, where she typed letters that were sent out over a Presidential signature inscribed by a mechanical pen, form letters that responded to comments from citizens, special blessings to couples celebrating their fiftieth wedding anniversaries, and, in one instance that cost her boss an official reprimand, a message congratulating a rabbi on his fifty years of Christian endeavour.

Her next job had been as one of two secretaries to a special assistant to the Vice President, which meant that at least she was in daily contact with other living human beings, although most of the contact consisted of placing phone calls to people in Louisiana who treated her like a hooker.

And now she worked for Timothy Burnham – definitely better than the Vice President's office, but still not in the White House itself, which was where she longed to be. She knew she couldn't reasonably aspire to work for the President directly – each of his secretaries had been hand-picked from a retinue of long-time retainers – and she was smart enough not to want to work for the President: the men who went in to see the President were so intense, so distracted, so nervous or so exalted (kings, for example) that they wouldn't conceivably notice a pretty young thing, no matter how striking she might be.

Her ideal was to work for someone like Mario Epstein – surrounded by a large staff of eligible men on the way up; visited by figures of renown and power in and out of government, people who would appreciate a secretary

81

putting them through before someone else; with instant access to, and constant contact with, the President.

At this rate, though, Dyanna would be fifty before she reached the level of secretary to an Epstein. So she had reluctantly hitched her star to Burnham's and was forever urging him to reach higher, to volunteer to write the most difficult messages to Congress, which would mean weeks of late-night involvement with Epstein's staff, to write memos to the President suggesting ingenious ways to attract public support for favourite programmes, to have confidential lunches with media biggies and submit perceptive reports to the Oval Office.

These suggestions she made in the name of the common weal, and Burnham would nod solemnly and take notes which he would tear off the pad and stuff in his pocket, since he didn't want her to discover that his notes were line-drawing speculations about how she would look in a series of sexual contortions with a variety of land mammals.

This morning, as usual, Dyanna sat at her desk with a mug of coffee, a manicure set and the society pages of the *Post* spread before her. She looked up, startled, as Burnham flung the office door open, popped quickly inside and shut the door behind him and stood, panting, against the wall.

'Good morning?' she said.

'No, no it isn't,' Burnham replied. 'Have you got a needle and thread?'

'Why?'

'Because I have had a small misfortune.' He turned his back and pointed at his trousers. 'I would show you the extent of the damage, but I fear that the sight of an expanse of boxer shorts would throw you into a fever. Do you . . .'

'I remember once, it was prom night, senior year, and I had this brand new dress on, a copy of a Galanos I think it was, Mama said I looked so pretty she couldn't remember when, and I was reaching up to do something to my hair, it had just been styled and all, and . . .'

Burnham walked through the door into his office, letting

her yammer on. There would be no stopping her; her monologues had the momentum of a locomotive. He checked his desk for phone messages (there were none), for mail (none) and for work. His IN box was a teak rectangle to which was affixed a pewter plaque inscribed with Burnham's favourite quote from Dr Johnson: 'No man but a blockhead ever wrote except for money.' A gift from Sarah in the days before she had been infected by principle.

The shallowness of the stack of papers in the IN box told Burnham that his work load was light – a couple of personal letters for the President, a proclamation for something like National Self Abuse Prevention Week, and one or two 200-word addresses that might be delivered, or might be released as if they had been delivered, to groups from the districts of some Congressmen to whom the President owed a favour. ('Representative Whipple has told me a great deal about the fine work you ladies are doing in the Leesburg Macramé and Dialysis Society. As you know, Dick Whipple is one of my closest friends and most trusted advisors, an American who . . .')

He could knock off the whole day's work by noon, which meant that he could safely leave the building for lunch. Maybe if, as seemed likely, the work loads of McGregor and Butterworth, Burnham's two good friends among the other writers, were as light as his, they might conspire to discover the President's schedule for the rest of the afternoon, and if the coast was clear they might abandon ship for a Lucullan two- or three-hour curative lunch, which itself would call for the cure of a two-hour nap.

Perhaps the day could be rescued, after all.

'. . . no time at all for a proper sewing job,' Dyanna droned on, 'so Mamma jig-timed it upstairs and found some safety pins, can you believe it, and pinned me from the inside out, and not a soul ever knew. Not even Trevor, he was my date, and we were not exactly strangers if you get my meaning, even though nothing ever really *hap*pened.'

Burnham waited a beat or two, to make sure Dyanna

hadn't stopped only to get a fresh breath, then said, 'Do you have a needle and thread?'

'What for?' Dyanna arose from her desk and stood in the doorway.

'I told you.' Burnham gestured at his trousers.

'That's not my job.'

'What's not your job? To get me a needle?'

'I don't have to sew anything.'

'I'm not asking you to . . .'

'I don't even *have* to get you coffee. It's only the goodness of my heart.'

'Don't sew.'

'I could file a grievance.'

'I don't *want* you to sew.'

'You don't?'

'I'll do it. Can you just get me a needle?'

'Do *you* know how to sew?'

'Spare me your sexist drivel and get me a needle.'

Caught, Dyanna blushed, turned to her desk and rooted through the drawers.

Burnham pulled off his trousers and sat behind his desk and spread the split seat of the seersucker pants across the blotter. It was agape from the base of the fly to the belt loops. The seam had a little flap inside it. Where did that go, inside or outside? Did you sew from the inside out or the outside in? How close together should the stiches be?'

Dyanna returned with a needle and a spool of dark blue thread, and not until she placed the needle and thread in Burnham's hand did she realize the implication of the pants on the desk. If the pants were on the desk, what was on him? Another fuchsia flush started at her neck and crept quickly up to her cheeks.

'I know what you're thinking,' Burnham said.

'You do not.' Now the blush was making her temples tingle.

'What colour are the shorts? Are there garters or knee socks? Knobby knees? Milky white thighs?'

'You're sick!'

Burnham tried twice to thread the needle and missed both times.

'Here.' Dyanna took the needle and thread from him, threaded the needle, turned the thread, bit off the end and tied it, and handed it back.

'Thanks.' Burnham pinched the two sides of the seam together and, from beneath, plunged the needle up through the fabric.

'That's not the way to do it.'

'That's the way *I* do it.'

'It's not the right way.'

'Hey.' Burnham looked up at her. 'I don't think this is a team sport. Either I'll do it or you ca do it.'

'It's not my job,' Dyanna said weakly, torn between the opposing forces of her femininity.

Burnham took another stitch. The phone rang. Dyanna didn't budge. It rang again.

Burnham looked at the phone. 'Is that your job, or do I have to hire a specialist?'

'Oh,' Dyanna said, as if coming to. 'Oh.' She reached across the desk and punched the blinking light button and picked up the receiver. 'Mr Burnham's office.'

Like a dog sensing something preternatural, Burnham felt a galvanic crackle coming from Dyanna, and he knew there was trouble. He looked at her and saw her mouth hanging half open and her fist clenching the phone. His mind galloped among the possibilities. One of his children had been injured. Sarah had been in a car accident. His mother had been assaulted in the Ritz Carlton in Boston War.

'Yessir,' Dyanna said. 'Yessir.' She hung up.

Burnham stared at her, holding his breath.

'The President wants to see you.'

Burnham sighed. And chuckled. No war. No kidnapping. No maiming. 'Sure.' He held up his pants. 'Thoughtless bitch always calls at the worst times.'

'He does!' Dyanna was stunned.

No, Burnham thought. No. She's serious. 'What about?'

'He . . . Mr Cobb . . . didn't say.'

'When?'

'Now. Right *now!*'

'I can't! I don't have any pants!'

'What do you *mean*? You *have* to!'

'Like this?' Burnham jumped up, knocking his swivel chair spinning behind him, and waved a hand at his plaid boxer shorts, at his pasty white thighs marred by tiny bruises from the allergy shots he poked into himself four times every week, at his hairless, wrinkled knees and at the navy blue cotton socks that came up just beneath them. 'You're not allowed to see the President of the United States without pants on. It's . . . it's illegal!'

'Put 'em on, then. Just don't turn around.'

'And walk like a duck with a broom up its ass? No thanks. Tell him I'm in a meeting.'

'Are you *crazy*?' Dyanna shouted. 'Here. Gimme here. For pity sakes.' She snatched the trousers from his hands, looked at the ragged stitches he had made and tried to bite the thread to draw them out. But he had double-stitched and pulled them so tight that she couldn't get her teeth around them. 'Give me some scissors!'

Burnham opened the top drawer of his desk. 'I don't have any scissors!' He looked at his watch, as if suddenly aware that he was keeping The Most Powerful Man In The World waiting because he had a rip in his pants. 'Hurry!'

'I can't! I can't get the stitches out!'

Burnham yanked open drawer after drawer. Pads and paperclips and rulers and rubber bands spewed out onto the rug. No scissors. But he spied a solution. He grabbed the trousers back from Dyanna and laid them carefully across the blotter. He placed her hands at the top and bottom of the huge rip and told her to pull hard, keeping the rip closed.

He picked up his big desk stapler, fitted it over the top of the trousers and, working from the top downward, slammed the staples into the fabric – bam! bam! bam! He flung the stapler aside and examined the pants: they would hold, unless the President intended to grapple with him.

'Remember now,' Dyanna said as she watched Burnham hop delicately into the trousers, 'whatever he wants, say yes. I 'spect he wants you to do a special job of work for him, something real important like where my contacts could come in real handy, and you can tell him that. If it's travel, and they say he's thinking of going to Europe and maybe Asia at least one more time, don't worry about Sarah and the kids 'cause I'll make sure someone looks after 'em while we're away. It could be that he wants us to move into the White House so's he can call on us more often, and that's okay too, it won't be as big as this but lots more exciting and if we have to we can share an office 'cause there's not that much phone-calling to be bothersome, you know that.'

Burnham listened to her with one ear. Most of his brain was engrossed in defence preparedness – trying to isolate the possible areas of vulnerability. He had never before been summoned to see the President, and he didn't know what such a summons meant. If a phone call was usually bad news, what was a meeting? Potential catastrophe.

Burnham had met with the President several times, but only as one of the group of writers. Usually, after the President had expressed displeasure with a number of speeches ('My cat shits better stuff than that!'), Cobb would counsel gently that it was difficult for the writers to write a given speech unless they knew what the President wanted to say, and since the President's normal response to an inquiry about what he wanted to say to a group was 'Oh, something nice,' the writers were left to guess what the President thought would be nice.

'They're my writers,' the President would say. 'They're supposed to know what I want to say.'

'But sir,' Cobb would reply, 'it's hard for them to anticipate you if they don't know you.'

'If they don't know me, how come they're working for me?'

'They're professionals, sir, the best money can buy. That's what you ordered, after the . . . Brandon business . . .' (The six professional writers had been brought in as firemen, to douse the conflagration ignited by Brandon Mundy, the President's second cousin, whom the President had brought with him to the White House as his 'personal wordifier'. Mundy was a mean, vindictive poetaster whose work had been published in *The American Rifleman*, *Grit* and *Velvet* and who worshipped Ezra Pound for his war-years poems. The first speech Mundy had written for the President, to an Italian-American group, had begun, '*Io sono uno WOP*. And I'm proud of it, 'cause I know that WOP means you came to this country With Out Papers, and that means you really wanted to get in.' Mundy's second effort had been an address to a right-to-life group, and it had contained the sentiment, 'To paraphrase Marie Antoinette: Let 'em use coathangers.' There had been no third Mundy speech.)

'You're right. I did.' The President would ponder for a moment and then say, 'Warner, I want every one of the writers to spend a full day right at my side, twenty-four hours stickin' as close to me as my shorts. One by one, I want 'em to see me, hear me, smell me, feel me, get to know my every mood, so when they get an assignment they can say by instinct, "*This* is what my President would want to say."'

Cobb would agree, and a day later he would write a memo to the President with a proposed schedule for the writer-in-residence programme. The memo would not be answered. Cobb would send another one. It, too, would go unanswered. In three or four weeks' time, Cobb would get a call from the Appointments Secretary, informing him that the President thought that a more economical way to get to know the writers would be to gather with them for an informal session in the Cabinet Room. 'No other staff,' the President would be quoted as having said. 'Just some real give-and-take with my boys.'

The meeting would last exactly one hour. The President

would point to each writer in turn and ask for complaints, comments, suggestions. The words of each response might vary from individual to individual, but the substance was identical: it was difficult – nay, impossible – to do the job the President wanted without more contact with the President.

To each the President would reply, 'Damn right. That's why we're here today.'

Whatever time was left over the President would devote to reminiscences about his childhood or his time in the Senate or Great Men He Had Known – 'So you'll have grist for your mill and know what's behind this fella you call the President.'

It was a completely predictable ritual.

Within a week after the meeting, each writer would receive a photograph of the assemblage taken by the President's personal photographer, a Pakistani named Naj who had worked the USIA for two decades. The President would have inscribed each picture with the most coveted of phrases: 'To: With gratitude from his friend and President, Benjamin T. Winslow.'

To Burnham's knowledge, none of the writers had ever met alone with the President. Why now? Why him? He wasn't even the senior writer, or the most important. He rarely got big foreign-policy speeches to sculpt. That was Butterworth's ken. And McGregor got to enunciate all the economic thunderclaps.

'What have I done?' he suddenly cried aloud.

'What? Nothing.' Dyanna was smoothing his lapels and checking his tie. 'You'll be fine, Mr Burnham honey. Okay. Now *go!*'

Something didn't feel right. His hands. His hands were empty. 'Get me some papers!'

'Papers? Newspapers?'

'No! Papers papers! Documents! You can't walk around the West Wing without papers. Everybody's always got papers. Otherwise you look like a butler.'

Burnham didn't remotely resemble a butler, but Dyanna

wasn't about to argue. She dipped her hand into the IN box and plucked out a proclamation and a State Department proposed first draft of a Presidential greeting to some visiting poobah. Then, for icing, she tore two message slips off a pad, ticked the box marked 'urgent' and scribbled on one 'Margaret Thatcher – please call soonest' and on the other 'Andrei Gromyko returned your call.' These she stapled prominently to the top sheet of a yellow legal pad which she placed atop the other papers, all of which she thrust into Burnham's hand as she propelled him toward the door.

'*Go* for it, Mr Burnham honey,' she said as she held the door for him. 'It's first down and goal to go!'

What is going *on*? Burnham shouted at himself as his shoes clattered down the marble corridor and he unconsciously checked his collar buttons, his tie, his shoes and the shoot of his cuffs. Why am I here? I'm just a nice boy from the northeast who does what he's told as best he can. I should have stayed in New York. Journalism's an honourable profession.

He pushed through the swinging door and walked down the ramp to West Executive Avenue, the thin ribbon of concrete that separated the White House from the Executive Office Building and provided parking spaces for the small armada of White House staff cars and for the private vehicles of about three people in the solar system, including Evelyn Witt and, should he for some reason choose to drive himself to work rather than wait to be picked up at home, Mario Epstein. It was here on West Executive Avenue during times of Deep Crisis that the Secretaries of State and Defence were seen on television disembarking from their limousines and marching sombrely into the West Basement, because that was the quickest route to the Situation Room, the nerve centre from which the first salvos of Armageddon would be fired – before everybody who was worth saving boarded the aircraft that would take them into the bowels of a Maryland mountain.

As always, a phalanx of GM sedans sat, nose-in to the

curb, engines idling so the government chauffeurs could enjoy air conditioning while they dozed or read or composed screenplays that would free them from the drudgery of driving bureaucrats who treated them like old furniture through the scelerotic Washington traffic.

Striding purposefully across the avenue, pretending to read a draft proclamation for White Cane Safety Day, Burnham looked up just long enough to glance at the sedans and wonder if it was possible that this meeting with the President would result in his being initiated into some new knighthood so exalted as to entitle him to what was called 'portal-to-portal' – meaning that a black sedan picked him up at the house every morning and returned him there at night. Not bloody likely. True, things were a lot better than in the days of the Carter Proletarian Presidency, when the higher you were ranked the more ardently you had to pretend to embrace the plebeian ethic, and Cabinet Secretaries, for Christ's sake, were driving to work in Volkswagen Beetles. But better or not, one still had to be several rungs closer to Olympus than Burnham was to get portal-to-portal.

Besides, this cozy little fantasy was founded on the assumption that he was being summoned to receive *good* news.

Burnham opened the door into the West Basement. It was dark in there, and cool, and the air conditioning made a soothing noise that reminded him of staterooms on ships at sea.

A few feet ahead, on the left, one door this side of the one marked 'Ladies', was the door to Warner Cobb's office. To the right, down a short staircase, was the White House Mess, which was – but only in the Second Sitting – the most exclusive luncheon club in Washington, where delicious, inexpensive (subsidized) meals were served in opulent surroundings to the princes of the White House royal family: Special Assistants, Special Counsels, the President's private secretaries, the Vice President (who had had to fight off an attempt to stick him in the First

Sitting), and, when a whim led him to break bread with those who served him, the President himself. The Second Sitting sat from 1.00 to 2.00.

The First Sitting, of which Burnham and the other writers were members, sat from 12.00 to 1.00. Burnham, pleased though he was to have been awarded the perk, rarely attended. The membership of the First Sitting was, in general, about as much fun as mononucleosis. Second- and third-level myrmidons on the White House staff were exactly what they should be: second- and third-level functionaries who did one job with mechanical precision, be it advancing Presidential voyages, sifting political requests, flying the Presidential planes or operating the White House social office.

Burnham didn't consider himself above the others, he existed apart from them.

The other writers could be jolly companions, but they didn't have to go to the Mess to see one another. Much more lively was to go out into the world, where one didn't have to speak in a murmur while scanning with one's ears the other conversations in the room in search of White House gossip.

Warner Cobb's battery of secretaries sat somewhere in the White House, but Burnham had no idea where. They could not have been in or near Cobb's office, of course, since the two-stall office was barely big enough for Cobb alone, and near his office was nothing but the remains of the ladies' room and a narrow corridor. This arrangement was not ideal for Cobb, but it suited the writers just fine: if they needed to see Cobb, no secretary barred the door; with no anteroom before his office, he could not command them to wait in the anteroom. If he was in, he had to do business with them without resorting to status games.

Not that Cobb was the kind who enjoyed such petty juvenilia, but you never knew. Big offices with anterooms and lots of secretaries had a way of turning any head. It was like giving a loaded pistol to a child and telling him not to shoot it. He'd *have* to try it once or twice, and once he saw how much fun it was, there might be no stopping him.

Cobb was an unpretentious man trying to do an impossible job for which he had had no training, for which there was no such thing as training – that is, to maintain a productive, even creative, dynamic between a President who thought all writers were either left-wing rabble-rousers, right-wing messiahs, snobs, natives of New York or Boston or San Francisco ('Hot beds of assholes, and I can prove it!'), or out to get them, or any combination of the above, and six professional writers who were skilled at articulating matters of policy and politics, who knew the tricks of rousing and holding an audience, who agreed generally with the stated aims of President and party, who had been respected – even lionized – in their prior occupations and who were therefore unaccustomed to, and unhappy at, being considered by their employer as (the President had offered both appraisals several times) 'as useless as a spare prick at a wedding' and 'a necessary evil – like farting'.

Burnham listened at Cobb's door before he knocked, a courtesy to avoid interrupting phone calls. He heard Cobb's old Royal typewriter clacking away, so he knocked and opened the door and went inside. Cobb was bent over his typewriter, the bald spot on the crown of his head gleaming like a new dollar, and he held up a finger that said 'Be with you in a minute' and continued to compose one of the myriad memos he sowed about the Federal Government each day – suggesting ideas for Presidential remarks, for groups who should be addressed, for organizations that would serve well (if unwittingly) as conduits for new proposals, for things that needed saying and things that should be left unsaid.

And for new acronyms.

The President was in love with acronyms. If a programme was marginal in substance, it was made worthy, in the President's eyes, by slugging it with an acronym. He liked NORAD and the DEW line, was nostalgic for the

WACs and a strong supporter of NATO, SEATO and CENTO. He signed a bill changing the name of the Naval facility on Andros Island by the Tongue of the Ocean to TOTO. He wanted young people to train for government service in YONGOV, wanted businessmen to hire the handicapped through BUSCAP, and lobbied for a Gerald-Ford-like economic slogan that, unlike Ford's Whip Inflation Now (WIN), would attack *all* the gremlins in the economy. But he abandoned the effort when he found that no one could pronounce the acronym he had proudly fashioned for Whip Inflation Now and High Interest Rates Too For Rising Employment (WINAHIRTFRE).

Cobb finished typing and spun in his chair to face Burnham. 'Hi,' he said.

'This is a joke, right?'

'Nope.'

'What, then?'

'I don't know. The boss called me bright and early and said, and I quote, "Get me the fella wrote the O'Leary thing." And I looked on my list, and lo and behold, it was you. Lucky you.'

'What O'Leary thing? What . . . oh. *That?*' Days ago, last week sometime, Burnham had written a couple of hundred words for the President to deliver at a surprise appearance at a dinner for Mary O'Leary, a former Oregon State Attorney General whom the President had nominated for a Federal judgeship. Burnham had been instructed to keep the remarks short and free of controversy, and to begin them with one or two soft jokes – not thigh-slappers but mildly amusing one-liners to establish fellowship with the audience. All this Burnham had done. Or thought he had.

'What went wrong?' he asked Cobb. 'What could've gone wrong?'

'Nothing, far as I know. I told the Signal Corps to send me the tape, but it isn't here yet.'

'Then what's this *about*?' Burnham felt frantic. There

was an unsavoury smell to the summons, the bitter smell of surprise.

'Beats me. For what it's worth, he didn't sound pissed. Just sort of matter-of-fact.'

'Icy, you mean. Wonderful. Let's wait for the tape.'

Cobb shrugged. His phone rang. It was answered by a secretary somewhere, and then a buzzer sounded once, meaning that the call was from inside the White House and Cobb was to answer it personally. (Two buzzes signalled him to speak on the intercom line to the secretary.) Cobb punched the flashing button and said, 'Cobb . . . Oh, hi, Evelyn. Yep, he's right here . . .'

Burnham felt sweat on his palms and under his arms.

'Okay,' Cobb continued. 'It's his candy store. Right away.' He hung up and said to Burnham, 'He wants to see you now, so you better haul ass.'

Burnham took a deep breath and stood up, clutching his papers. 'Okay. Let's go.'

Cobb shook his head. 'He said alone.'

'Oh, shit.'

'Yes.' Cobb nodded. 'I would say that is a fair appraisal of the situation.'

Burnham smiled weakly as he reached for the door and said, 'Say later that my demise eclipsed the gaiety of nations.'

Burnham's breath was coming too fast, and, climbing the stairs to the first floor of the White House, he gripped the bannister and fought to breathe rhythmically. He turned the corner and walked down the corridor past Epstein's office, where Esther Tagliaferro orchestrated the medley of bells and lights that began every morning just before 8.00 and tailed off every evening just after 8.00 and kept eight healthy American women so busy that no two dared visit the ladies room at one time; past the perpetually closed door of the office of the President's Appointments Secretary, a quiet, retiring man who wielded immense power by virtue of controlling access to the President, power about which he cared little since he served the President only in

95

payment of an enormous unspoken debt owed by his father to the President's father, power in return for which he had to function supercurricularly as Special Assistant to Receive Unfocused Presidential Abuse and to Keep From Public Scrutiny Awkwardnesses and/or Embarrassments Committed By the President or Members of His Immediate Family; toward the two Secret Service praetorians who flanked the door to the Oval Office.

That door opened, emitting Mario Epstein and the Secretary of the Treasury, a middle-aged polymath named Jerome Goodman who had been educated at Harvard and Stanford and had since educated others at Harvard and Stanford when he wasn't rescuing some conglomerate from the chapters or writing, under a pseudonym, a series in intricately plotted crime novels that elicited from critics phrases like 'wickedly clever'.

Epstein and Goodman did not look up. They looked at each other's shoes, the way important people always do when they exchange profundities on the hoof. Burnham was pretending to read his Important Papers, and if some kindly muse had not told him to look up at the last second, he would have barged into both men. But he did look up, and, with the quickness of a startled tarantula, flung himself flat against the wall. Epstein and Goodman flowed by, unaware.

Burnham saw one of the Secret Service men notice him plastered against the wall, and frown, and say something to the other Secret Service man, who looked, and frowned, and then recognized Burnham and grinned.

Burnham shook himself together, the way an actor does before an entrance, and walked with measured pace down the hall, pretending once again to peruse his documents. He nodded gravely as he passed the Secret Service men, and walked beyond into Evelyn Witt's office, the anteroom to the Oval Office.

Evelyn Witt was in her mid-fifties, and she had been with the President since her early twenties. He had brought her with him from Sandusky, Ohio, when he had come to

Washington as a freshman Congressman. When he resigned his seat to join the Navy to fight in Korea (a meticulously planned fit of patriotism that freed him, on his return, to allow himself to be drafted for nomination to the Senate), she joined the Navy, too, as an ensign. At his urging, she stayed on in the Navy and did not take part in the Senate campaign, which was the smartest thing she could have done since it kept her off the political battlefield and out of the public eye and made it seem eminently sensible for him later, as a Senator and member of the Armed Forces Committee, to request her transfer to him as a Naval aide.

He thus acquired, at no cost to his staff budget, a cherished, trusted assistant who owed him her entire professional life. She thus acquired a job in which her promotions were mandated by her boss and his colleagues, her benefits comprehensive, her pension generous and guaranteed, and her status secured by rank and respected by law.

At the moment, though she did not wear a uniform except when there was some benefit to be garnered from a display of feathers, she was a captain in the United States Navy, and she and the President had already discussed the timing of her final promotion so that a few weeks before he left the office of the Presidency, the Congress would confirm her as Vice Admiral Evelyn Chester Witt, USN. She lived with her mother.

Because of her relationship with the President – they had a favourite bit of banter, in which she would say, 'I'd better get this right or you're sure to fire me,' and he would say, 'I could never fire you, Evie, you know that. I'd have to have you killed,' and then they would both laugh – Evelyn was above White House politics, so she could afford to be, and (save at times of extreme stress) as, kindly, solicitous and considerate of those she called 'those poor mites' who had to deal with, bow to and be terrified of Benjamin T. Winslow.

She was particularly nice to the writers – or so it seemed

to them, anyway – perhaps because she perceived them as they perceived themselves, as a pack of lost souls staggering around in the dark, serving the unservable, with no authority and a lot of accountability.

She looked up as Burnham entered her office, and she said, 'Good morning, Timothy. Thank you for coming. You look awful. Are you all right?'

'Of course I'm not all right. I'm a basket case.'

There were many people in the White House you could finagle, with a smile or a bit of slick patter. Evelyn Witt was one of the few you couldn't. She knew too well the power of the aura – some thought of it as a miasma – of the Oval Office and the man who occupied it. She had dealt with the Congressman who had taken that one extra belt of vodka in pathetic hope of brewing enough courage to go toe-to-toe with Ben Winslow, only to slide into a spasm of uncontrollable hiccoughs and, finally, a fitful slumber right there in her office; with the dashiki-clad cannibal, Colonel Roe his name was, who swept into the Oval Office full of macho Third-World bullshit and demanded this and that, and that for his trouble found himself referred to in public by the President as Chairman Moe; with the newly crowned sheik of some date-picker's paradise who spent his time with the President discussing Great Ladies I Would Like To Fling My Bones Upon and who tried to entice two of Evelyn's younger assistants into coming back to the desert 'for a little holiday'.

'With anybody else,' Evelyn said, 'I'd ask if it was a hangover.'

'I wish it was a hangover. Then I'd know it would get better. No. Life. Fate doth conspire against me. First thing I did today was smash my head on a beam. Next thing was tear the a . . . the seat out of my pants. And now this. D'you know what it's about?'

'No more than you do.'

'Can you find out for me? Please?'

Evelyn smiled. 'No time. He's only got a few minutes before he has to speak to' – she consulted the President's schedule on her desk – 'the American Association of Junior Labor Leaders, in the Rose Garden.'

'I guess that's a comfort.' Burnham tried to sound convinced. 'How much damage can he do in a few minutes?'

She started to smile again, at Burnham's innocence, but then she snorted instead as she recognized the desperation in his voice.

'Go on in,' she said, pointing to the closed door to the Oval Office. 'He's waiting for you.'

Burnham turned and faced the door. A knot of pain dug at his colon, and he had a fleeting terror that he would defecate on Evelyn's rug. The sweat under his arms was not trickling, it was coursing. He hoped he didn't stink. He wiped his handshaking hand on the seat of his trousers and reached for the doorknob.

He had never been in the Oval Office, but he had seen so many pictures of it that he found nothing unfamiliar. He even knew about the tiny pock marks he saw on the cork floor by the door leading to the Rose Garden – the marks left by Dwight David Eisenhower's golf shoes, covered over by other floors laid by other Presidents but revealed anew at the command of this one.

The President was in the far right corner of the office, his back to the door, bent over his 'signing table', an early American pine refectory table on which the secretaries placed all the letters, messages, memos, speeches, executive orders, proclamations and other papers that needed Presidential approval, disapproval, initials or signature.

Burnham took a step into the office and shut the door quietly behind him, and suddenly there was something brand new to his senses. It was the smell. Automatically, he decided it was the smell of power, but no; that was too easy. It had in it a faint aroma of cologne (Old Spice, he thought), and furniture polish, and clean, dust-free upholstery, and a tang of a substance with chlorine in it, and altogether it smelled of care, of concern, of gravity. This was not an office frequented by laughter.

'Ah . . . Sir?' Burnham wasn't sure the President had heard the door.

'Right with you.' The President signed a final paper, closed and put away his fountain pen, straightened up, turned around and smiled.

He walked toward Burnham, so Burnham walked toward him, hoping that motion by him would not be misconstrued as an assumption of equality, and they met in the centre of the Oval Office.

The President held out his hand, so Burnham held out his hand, and when the two hands met, the President's hand ate Burnham's hand, swallowed it and then returned it intact.

The President looked directly down into Burnham's eyes and said, 'How you doin', Tim?'

Timothy, Burnham said to himself. Timothy. 'Fine, sir,' he said, looking up into the eyes of the biggest person in the world.

The human being himself was large – three inches taller than Burnham and forty pounds heavier, with feet so mammoth that (he liked to joke about himself) his shoes 'came from a partnership 'tween a blacksmith and a saddler' and his hands were used, when he was young, 'one for a maul, th'other for an anvil.' He insisted that physically he was the perfect paradigm of the American farm boy, as imagined on postcards and recruiting posters; his official biography had him growing up on a small mom-and-pop dairy farm in central Ohio. And he had tricks that made him seem even bigger; he always stood as close as he could, often smotheringly close, to people shorter than himself, which increased the angle at which they had to look up at him and emphasized the different in their stature, and that, in turn, became a symbolic representation of the difference in their importance and position and achievement, all of which was supposed to make them understand that one of nature's immutable laws was that Benjamin T. Winslow was smarter, wiser, better, than they and that to disagree with him was not only stupid but absolutely, ineffably *wrong*. And because only people who are unsure of themselves, or are lying, or are wrong, look away during a one-on-one palaver, Benjamin T. Winslow never unlocked his eyes from the eyes of the person he was challenging or fighting or seducing.

Taller people posed a special problem, and they were kept at the greatest possible distance from the President. None was permitted to work near him.

This large human being also knew how to use the majesty of his office to magnify him into superhumanity. 'Jimmy Carter was quite the genius,' Benjamin Winslow would say with a sorry sigh. 'He turned the Presidency into a toilet and then dove in and pulled the chain.'

No one ever called the President anything but 'Mr President.' Ever. It was supposed that his wife called him 'Benjamin' or 'Ben' or even something private and endearing, like 'Bunny' (the mind reeled), in private, but in public she never referred to 'Benjamin' or 'Mr Winslow' or 'my husband,' but always to 'the President'.

'Hail To The Chief' was played at every opportune occasion. At state dinners, the President danced twice, once with his wife and once with the wife of the guest of honour. No other beauty – be she Christie Brinkley or Meryl Streep – was permitted to partake of the imperial two-step. He never joined a singer on a stage for a chorus of 'Blue Skies', never made light remarks about the United States, never made a public slip stronger than 'hell', and never in public called anyone by his or her first name. No entertainer was Willie or Frank, no politician Tip or Teddy or Bob or Strom. Everyone was Mr and Mrs (that trick he had learned from a man whose verbal skills he admired, William F. Buckley, Jr. It always made Buckley seem at once respectful and superior).

'The American people don't want their buddy for a President,' he explained to a *New York Times* reporter in a rare moment of candour. 'They can't look up to their buddy. Their buddy can't give them hope or make them proud. They want a goddam leader! That "goddam" is off the record.'

And yet he had to balance distance and majesty with humanity. He had to be a man if not *of* the people, then *from* the people. Up from the people. Now and then he had to let his roots show through. And where those roots didn't exactly fit the need of the moment, why, he'd prune them, cutting this one short and grafting a little colour onto that one.

He put his arm around Burnham's shoulder and led him toward the sofa. 'Fine,' he said. 'That's a good thing to be. I'd say I'm fine, too.'

Where are we going? Burnham wondered. Why are we going to the couch? There are plenty of perfectly good chairs all over the place. What does he want to do with me? Make out? Oh shit. Don't laugh. Not now.

But the image of the President of the United States, suddenly overwhelmed by a steamy passion, flinging some benighted, unknown wretch onto the floral-print sofa and pouncing on top of him to smother him with kisses, started Burnham smiling and then gurgling to suppress a laugh.

'What say, son?'

'Nice, Sir. I was saying that it's nice that you're fine, too.'

'Damn right.'

Burnham didn't have a chance to sit on the sofa; the President sat him on it. He guided him by one elbow, like a tugboat turning a tanker, and smoothly shoved him backward until his legs hit the front of the sofa and he fell.

The President did not sit. He stood over Burnham and looked down on him, and Burnham saw so far up the man's immense nostrils that he felt like a tourist at the base of Mount Rushmore.

'Comfortable?'

'Fine, sir. Thanks.' Burnham leaned forward and placed his Important Papers on the coffee table in front of the sofa – just in case the President should want to know what he was working on these days.

'How's Sarah?'

Sarah! Jesus! Burnham thought. This man doesn't miss a trick.

'Oh, fine. Fine.'

'Still working for Te . . . Senator Kennedy?'

Oh-oh. So *that*'s it.

'Ah . . . now and then . . .'

'Fine with me,' the President said quickly. 'Don't misunderstand. It's every American's birthright. If she can make the voters forget there was a time when he didn't know right from wrong, or right from left –' he chuckled maliciously '– why then more power to her. Of course, if I was running again,' the President grinned at Burnham, 'you and I might have a word or two about it.'

'Of course, sir. But . . .'

'But I'm not. So it's no problem. No problem!'

He's trying to make me feel at ease, Burnham decided. Why? What's coming next? The sweat that had dried coolly on his hands began to run warm again.

The President turned away and took a few casual steps across the office. 'Tim,' he said, 'I am the President.'

'Yes, sir,' Burnham said to his back.

The President stopped, spun, glared and said, 'Is that funny?'

'Sir?' Burnham's heart whacked against his rib cage.

'I said, is that funny? Is the Presidency funny?'

'N-n-n-n-n . . .' Burnham clamped his lips closed.

'Is it funny to be President?'

Burnham wanted to say something like 'I wouldn't know, I've never tried it,' but he couldn't. He couldn't say anything. A jerky sequence of 'S' sounds bubbled from his mouth.

'Is it funny to be responsible for the lives of two hundred and forty million Americans?'

What is going *on*? Burnham howled to himself. 'N-no no sir.'

'Is it funny to be custodian of the untold millions of the unborn?'

Burnham didn't bother to attempt a reply.

103

'Is it funny to bear the burden of knowing that if you make one mistake, one wrong decision, those unborn and their offspring and *their* offspring – maybe they'll all be mutants – will look back and say, "It's your fault, Mr President"?'

This time the President waited, and Burnham forced his mouth to fashion the two simple words. 'No . . . sir.'

'Then why the jokes?'

'Wha . . .?'

'I am not a funny President.'

'I . . .'

'A President who wants to look funny is an asshole. To coin a phrase.'

Burnham's brain clawed through the drawers of memory, searching for any candidates, any jokes he had written that could have gone wrong.

'The press is drooling for a chance to make the President look like an asshole. You know that, don't you?'

'I . . . I . . .'

'You mean you *want* to make your President look like an asshole?'

'N-n-n-n-n . . . NO!'

'Well, then . . .' By now the President was towering over Burnham, his arms outstretched in a gesture of majestic outrage, the American eagle betrayed by one of its own chicks. He dropped his arms and, his head hung with the expression of a wounded parent stung by the serpent's tooth of a thankless child, retreated to a chair opposite Burnham and put his feet on top of Burnham's Important Papers on the coffee table. 'It seems you've got some hard explaining to do, Tom.'

Tom? Now what? First it was 'Tim.' He got Sarah's name down cold. Now 'Tom.'

Then Burnham knew: he was about to be fired. For, there was, in the Winslow White House, a rule: Him Whom The President Wishes To Dismiss He First Makes Lowly. And what better way to abase a staff member, to make him seem a bagatelle and his dismissal a trifle, than not even to know his name?

Still, Burnham didn't know what his offence had been, and he was damned if he would go ignorant into ignominy. Curiously, he felt relieved, as if the certainty of his doom freed him from the conventions of cowering before the throne, and he was able to say, without once stammering, 'I'd be happy to explain, Mr President, if you'd tell me what the hell you're upset about.'

The President's eyes narrowed, and his ears flattened noticeably against the side of his head. Like a pit bull. 'I'm sick and tired of writers going around with their thumb up their ass and their mind in neutral.'

'What?' Burnham knew now that he was as good as gone; he had nothing more to lose. 'What in the name of Jesus does that mean?'

It was another of the down-home, good-ole-boy back-woods sayings that the President collected like other people collect stamps. He didn't care what part of the nation a saying came from, if he liked it he adopted it and attributed it to one or another member of his family – a family whose cast of imaginary (or at least untraceable) characters grew and spread metastatically across America and its past.

'It means that a President who puts his trust in writers who think the Presidency's a joke' – a buzzer sounded urgently on the President's desk – 'has about as much chance of making it into the history books as a fart in a cyclone!'

As the President rose to answer the buzzer, his shoe dragged Burnham's Important Papers off the coffee table onto the rug. Absently, forgetting for a second who he was, the President leaned down and scooped up the papers and put them back on the table, glancing at them – with a brief snap of double-take, first at the papers, then at Burnham – as they left his hand.

Burnham saw the President frown as he turned toward his desk, noticed that he seemed distracted as he listened on the telephone, was surprised at his vehemence when he said into the phone, 'Then let 'em wait, God-dammit! All they're gonna do is grow up to be burrs under the saddle of America anyway!'

As the President returned to Burnham, his face seemed different, softer somehow, and when he held out his hand, he said simply, 'I'm sure glad we understand each other, Tim.'

'Sir?' Burnham hopped to his feet, thinking: I don't understand a thing.

'We're both doing the best we can, and that's all any of the bastards can ask.' The President handed Burnham his papers and led him toward a door. 'You do your job, I'll do my job, and we'll try to co-ordinate 'em better. Right, Tim?'

'Right. Sir.'

'You bet, Tim. That's great. Thanks for coming by.'

Before Burnham could reply, he found himself in the corridor between the two Secret Service men, the door closed behind him, the President gone. He felt that the Secret Service men were eyeing him quizzically, as if he had been spewed out of the office like a chaw of tobacco from an angry pitcher, so he cleared his throat gravely, checked his watch blindly, tucked his Important Papers under his arm and walked down the corridor.

He hadn't gone twenty feet when he felt the meltdown begin. It was like the sequential failure of the elements of a computer: first the sweats, pouring down his neck, under his arms, off his fingers; then tachycardia, the heart hammering faster and faster, from eighty to a hundred to a hundred and twenty to a hundred and forty beats a minute, bringing with it the short, panting breath of hyperventilation; then, as the brain began to hunker down in defence against malnourishment, tunnel vision, everything blurred but the tiny object at the absolute centre of vision, and that so clear that he could read the address on an envelope being typed by a secretary in an office thirty feet away; now the next-to-last stage – he had had this before, but never in the White House; my God! what would happen if he passed out right on the floor of the West Wing of the White House? –

the accumulating panic and the onset of unconsciousness, all vision pulsing in and out, a tingling in the hands and arms.

He stopped walking and leaned head-first against the wall and took long, deep breaths.

A passing secretary stopped and said, 'Are you okay?' and he nodded and said thickly, 'Thinking. Gotta work something out.'

His head cleared. He knew where he had to go, but he didn't know if he could make it. He turned and aimed for the railing at the top of the staircase that led to the basement.

He made it in four steps, gripped the railing and took three deep breaths.

He went down the first few steps, stopped at the landing and targeted the short staircase leading into the Mess.

He made that crossing without stopping, and now he knew he would make it, and as soon as he knew that, the panic began to subside.

It was still early in the morning, but the waiters would be in the Mess, setting up for lunch, and he didn't care if they were there or not because what he wanted – what he *had to have* – would be on every table in a bowl decorated with the Great Seal of the President of the United States.

Burnham focused on the table nearest the door, took two steps and flopped into a chair. His fingers felt for the sugar bowl, flipped the top off it, and raised the bowl to his lips. He stuck his tongue into the bowl and curled it like a dog taking water and lapped sugar into his mouth. The granules dissolved and slid down his throat, and he lapped again and again.

In a few seconds he felt the tingling leave his arms, and his hands were steady enough so he could put the bowl on the table and spoon the sugar into his mouth. He swore to himself – as he had sworn the time before and the time before that – that he would carry a Milky Way or a Snickers bar in his pocket every minute of his life from now on. If he had pumped some sugar into himself *before* he saw the

President, this never would have happened. He could prevent the hypoglycæmic-shock reaction by overdosing sugar before the onset of stress. Or so Dr Arunian had assured him.

Free-floating anxiety, Arunian had called it, caused by hypoglycæmic-shock caused by the body's natural reaction to acute stress, which is to gobble up all the sugar in the system.

Carry a Snickers bar, and you'll be fine.

But how was he supposed to know the President was going to do a number on him?

Besides, have you ever carried a Snickers bar in your jacket pocket in Washington, DC, in the summer?

All these thoughts ran through his mind, and ne was feeling much better, almost functional, when he sensed someone standing next to him and looked up into the limpid black eyes that resided in the round brown face of L. Reyes, Chief Steward of the White House Mess, who had been observing Burnham with fascination and some alarm.

'May I help you, sir?'

Burnham swallowed another spoonful of sugar and shook his head. 'I'm fine, thanks,' he said, and by now he was.

'We're not open yet, L. Reyes said.

'I know.' Burnham nodded. 'I'm just having a coffee break.'

'But you're not having any coffee.'

'Of course not.' Burnham popped one last dose of sugar into his mouth and daubed at his lips with a napkin. 'That's because you're not open.' He stood, and smiled at L Reyes, and left the Mess.

By the time he arrived at Cobb's door, Burnham was feeling, if not euphoric, at least like (whose simile was it?) the very button on Fortune's cap. He rapped lightly on the door and, hearing no voice within, opened the door and entered.

Cobb was waiting for him, hands folded on his desk, head

cocked like a puppy who senses something exciting in the wind but doesn't know what it is.

'Come in, my boy,' he said, gesturing grandly at the chair opposite his desk, 'and give me a word of wisdom.'

'Jesus Christ!' Burnham said, the fires within stoked high by glucose. 'I was done, fired, out on my can, and then . . .'

Cobb held up a hand. 'I know all about it.'

'You do?'

'Well, not *all*,' Cobb said. 'But two minutes ago, I hung up with Himself.' He pointed to the POTUS phone. 'He chewed me out for not telling him what a great job you were doing, then he said – and I do *not* know what the hell this is all about – "No no, I guess you didn't know either." Then before he slammed down the phone he said I was to be sure to involve you more – involve you in what? – because you're too valuable to waste on petty shit. Period.' Cobb smiled. 'Whatever you did, share it with your old buddy. You slip something in his coffee?'

'Nothing! I don't know. I know he called me in there to fire me – why, I don't know, but . . .'

'I do.'

'Why?'

Cobb reached for the 'play' button on his cassette recorder. 'It wasn't your fault, but you were as good as gone. Listen.'

It was the Signal Corps tape of the President's address to the dinner for Mary O'Leary. It began with an unfamiliar voice saying, 'I have a special message here for Mary, from a very special person, and . . . no, by golly, I'll be ding-donged but that special person has decided to deliver his message in person. Ladies and gentlemen, it is my honour to present to you the President of the United States!'

Loud applause, whistles, cheers, and then the President's voice saying, 'Thank you, thank you,' in a way that urged the audience to stop clapping and sit down.

When the crowd sounds had died, there was the soft crinkle of two sheets of 20-lb, Kokle Finish, Berkshire Parchment Bond being unfolded and smoothed on the podium by the Presidential hand, then the last-minute heavy hush that always precedes a Presidential speech. And, at last, the voice that had been described a myriad times by a myriad scribes as having true Presidential timbre beginning to read the words typed on the Presidential speech typewriter that produced quarter-inch-high letters.

JUDGE THOMPSON, LADIES AND GENTLEMEN AND ESPECIALLY MARY.

I WANTED TO COME TONIGHT, BECAUSE THIS *IS* A SPECIAL NIGHT AND YOU ARE A SPECIAL PERSON AND . . . I ASSURE YOU . . . THAT IS *NOT*.

(Polite laughter from the audience. Burnham said to Cobb, 'Nothing there to get pissed about,' and Cobb shook his head and said, 'Wait.')

AFTER SUPPER TONIGHT I PUT ON MY JACKET AGAIN, AND HELEN SAID TO ME, 'WHERE ARE YOU GOING?' AND I SAID, 'THERES A DINNER FOR MY FRIEND MARY O'LEARY. I THINK I'LL GO HAVE A CUP OF COFFEE WITH HER.'

WELL, HELEN LOOKED KIND OF SAD, AND I SAID, 'WHAT'S THE MATTER?' SHE SNIFFLED AND SAID, 'I *KNEW* YOU DIDN'T LIKE MY COFFEE!'

(More polite laughter. Burnham said to Cobb, 'I'm not proud of that, but it's not an indictable offence.' The President continued.)

EVERY PRESIDENT DOES THE BEST HE CAN IN HIS JOB. HE CAN DO NO BETTER. AND WHEN HIS TIME IS DONE, THERE ARE CERTAIN THINGS HE CAN LOOK BACK ON WITH PARTICULAR PRIDE

WHEN MY TIME IS DONE ONE THING OF WHICH I WILL BE PROUDEST IS OUR RECORD IN HELPING WOMEN ACHIEVE THE FULL AND COMPLETE EQUALITY IN AMERICAN SOCIETY THAT IS THEIR BIRTHRIGHT.

110

(Long, sustained applause. Burnham said to Cobb, '*That* must've given him a high,' and Cobb replied, 'Oh yeah, by now he was on a roll.')

WE HAVE APPOINTED MORE THAN TWO HUNDRED WOMEN TO IMPORTANT POSITIONS OF GREAT RESPONSIBILITY IN THE FEDERAL GOVERNMENT AND THE JUDICIARY. I HAVE NAMED AND SEEN CONFIRMED BY THE CONGRESS TWO WOMEN ADMIRALS AND THREE GENERALS. AND THERE WILL BE MORE, I PROMISE YOU.

(More applause. Burnham said, 'Damn right there will. Evelyn Witt, for one.')

THE APPOINTMENT OF MARY TO THE FEDERAL-BENCH GIVES ME PARTICULAR PLEASURE . . . IT IS RARE FOR A PRESIDENT TO FIND AN OLD AND DEAR FRIEND SO HIGHLY QUALIFIED FOR SUCH A VITAL JOB.

AND SO, LADIES AND GENTLEMEN . . .

('Listen now,' said Cobb.)

I ASK YOU TO JOIN ME IN A TOAST TO A GREAT FRIEND, A GREAT WOMAN, A GREAT AMERICAN . . . WHO WILL SOON BECOME A GREAT JURIST . . .

LEARY O'MARY!

(The silence was so total that Burnham thought the tape had ripped. But then he heard a few isolated laughs, a few coughs, the tinkle of glassware, the scrape of chairs shifted nervously on the floor, the thud of a hand covering the microphone.)

The President's voice, frantic:

MARY O'LEARY! MARY O'LEARY!

There was laughter, and applause, and the tape stopped. Burnham said, 'He blamed *me*?'

Cobb nodded. 'It got worse. The Signal Corps guy who brought me the tape said Mary O'Leary got up to reply, and everybody was feeling fine – except the President, and he was covering himself pretty well – and O'Leary, the dizzy dame, thanked the President and asked everybody to join *her* in a toast to – you won't believe this – to her great friend, President Winslow T. Benjamin.'

'Oh my.'

'And that's not all. She got a huge laugh, a real ball-buster, the place went nuts, and the President had to sit there and smile like he thought the whole thing was hilarious and play the good sport while all the time he felt like a complete asshole.'

'So how's that my fault?'

'You know as well as I do, around here fault is in the eye of the fault-finder. He couldn't do what he would've liked to do, fire everybody involved – the driver who drove him there, the dude who introduced him, the secretary who typed the speech, O'Leary herself. So he had to blame the poor schmuck who wrote it. He told the Signal Corps guy that that's what had been on the page he read from.'

'That's bullshit!'

'Who cares? The point is, your tits were the ones in the wringer. And the question is, why didn't he squeeze?'

'Warner, on the grave of my sainted mother . . .'

'Your mother lives in Scarsdale.'

'Yeah, but she can't live forever. On the blood of my children, then, I do not know. I was in there, he was yelling at me, I almost had a convulsion in the Oval Office, and the next thing I know, Pow! I'm his bosom buddy.'

'Congratulations,' said Cobb. 'I guess.'

'No. No congratulations. I don't like it.'

'Please. Spare me the 'umble-man act. Ninety-nine percent of the human race would sell their souls to have the President say "howdy" to them, let alone say how valuable they are.'

Burnham raised a finger in what Cobb, like Sarah, recognized as his Johnsonian posture, and asked ponderously, 'Why should he flatter me? I can do nothing for him. Let him carry his praise to a better market.'

Cobb did not smile. He nicked at a pencil eraser with a thumbnail, then said, 'What is it with you and Doctor J? You keep him on your bench, like a ready reserve. He's your favourite pinch-hitter.'

'Yep.' Burnham felt himself reddening. He begged Johnson to help him now, but the good doctor declined; he had scorned self-puffery. How could Burnham explain his implausible adoration of a man who had been dead for two hundred years, a man with cosmic perceptions and timeless intuitions, a man who had answers for questions that would not be asked for centuries?

He said to Cobb, 'Do you like yourself?'

'What? What's that got to do with anything?'

'I don't like myself a lot. I'm okay, I guess, but I don't see a hell of a lot that's special. I'm average, a reactor, not an actor. I go along. Johnson was everything I'm not, so when I'm cornered, I turn to him and he always helps me out. He's . . . my friend.'

Now Cobb was embarrassed: He had anticipated an off-hand explanation and had received a confession. 'Well, I know one person who disagrees with you,' he said, 'at least about yourself.'

'Who's that?'

'The President of the United States.'

Dyanna would love it. She wouldn't understand it any better than he did, but she would love it because it meant there would be more contact with the White House and with the Oval Office directly. She might even get to speak to the President himself on the phone, and for certain she'd have to carry stuff at least as far as Evelyn Witt's office, which meant walking through those charged corridors peopled with the men who ran the world, an occasional one of whom would likely cast an appreciative eye on the Dixie dream.

The fact that *some*one stood to benefit from that bizarre

conversation with the President pleased Burnham, so he decided to recount it to her with enthusiasm rather than with the amorphous shadow of foreboding that he sensed was truer.

He pushed open the door to his office and said, 'Wait'll you hear –'

'Sssshhh!' Dyanna sat at her desk, fingers to her lips, eyes wide, and pointed theatrically to his inner office. 'He's come back!' she whispered.

'Who?'

'That Mr Renfro. And he brought a box.'

Burnham peeked into his office and saw Preston T. Renfro looking out the window at the Ellipse. A cardboard crate, large enough to contain an electric typewriter, rested on the floor beside Burnham's desk.

'Sorry to keep you waiting,' Burnham said as he strode into the office. 'I've been with the President.' Carefully carelessly, he tossed his Important Papers on the couch.

'So I understand,' Renfro said. 'My visit is timely indeed.'

'What'd you bring me? A box of secrets?'

'Droll, Mr Burnham,' said Renfro's mouth, contradicting his eyes. 'Very droll. Do you have a knife?'

Burnham didn't have a knife, so he turned to call to Dyanna, but she was already passing through the doorway, a letter opener held like a dagger in her hand.

Renfro slit the tape that sealed the crate, then popped the staples and lifted out a beige rectangular metal box, approximately twenty-four inches by eighteen inches by eight inches, with wide slots in the top and the bottom and a power cord gathered in a bow by a wire bag-tie.

'Where's an outlet?' he asked, and he directed Dyanna to pick up a large square wastebasket and follow him.

Dyanna set the wastebasket by the electrical outlet, and Renfro placed the rectangular box atop the wastebasket and plugged in its cord.

'What is it?' asked Dyanna.

'A document shredder.'

'Wow! Neat.' Dyanna smiled at Burnham and said, 'See? I told you.'

Told me what? Burnham wondered, and then he realized that Dyanna was connecting the arrival of the shredder to his summons to the Oval Office. Well, let her; it'd brighten her day.

'What do we shred?' Dyanna asked Renfro.

'You, madam,' Renfro replied frostily, 'do not shred anything.'

'Well exc-ee*yooze* me!'

'You have to be cleared to shred,' said Burnham. 'Can't let just anybody shred. It's a privilege you have to earn. You start by tearing. Then you learn how to rip. Then you rend. Finally you master shredding.'

Renfro shot Burnham an acid glance and said to Dyanna, 'That will be all.'

But before Dyanna could depart, Burnham said to Renfro, 'Don't you think she ought to at least know what it is I'm shredding? So she can make sure I get it to shred.'

'You tell her nothing. She has no need to know.'

Burnham shrugged, and Dyanna turned and left the office, pulling the door closed with just enough unnecessary force to punctuate her displeasure.

Renfro activated the shredder, took a blank piece of typing paper from Burnham's desk and fed it into the slot in the top of the shredder. The machine gobbled it with a contented humming noise. When the paper was gone, Renfro lifted the shredder off the wastebasket and showed Burnham a small pile of white strips.

'Fettuccine.' Burnham said.

Renfro sighed. 'If you must.'

'A really top-top-top-secret document would be fettuccine atomico.'

'Everything in Category 7 is top-top-top-secret. Remember that.'

'An Iranian student could reassemble those secrets, y'know.'

'Nothing's perfect. We don't have to make it easy for them.'

'Who's "them"?'

'Whoever.'

'I don't see what good this does,' said Burnham. 'Everything in the joint is burned every night anyway.'

'But first it's collected by the janitorial staff, and the janitorial staff is not Q cleared. Imagine –' Renfro lowered his voice '– what would happen if a member of the janitorial staff got hold of a Category 7 document.'

The man's serious, Burnham thought. All he could think to say was, 'Staggering!'

'DOE is not the United States Navy. A Walker scandal will never happen to us.' Renfro put a hand on Burnham's arm. 'Right, Mr Burnham?'

'Right, coach.' Burnham recoiled. 'Is that all I'm supposed to shred? Category 7 stuff?'

'Not at all. Let's see.' Renfro scanned Burnham's desk and saw, as a bookmark in his Bartlett's *Quotations*, an information stub from a recent paycheque. 'Great Scot!' he said, and he yanked the stub from the book. 'Never leave these around. Always shred them. Nobody needs to know you work for DOE, let alone as a GS-15 step 9. It's a giveaway that you have Q Clearance.'

'Mum's the word.' Burnham plucked the stub from Renfro's fingers and fed it to the shredder. 'It's fun,' he said. 'Kind of like feeding flies to a spider.'

Renfro flipped through the papers in Burnham's IN box but found nothing that needed treatment more special than the normal day's-end conflagration in the basement of the building. There wasn't a single Top Secret paper in the box.

'I had no idea White House work was this . . . routine,' Renfro said.

'You mean boring. I told you. Sometimes we classify things for the sheer hell of it.'

'You *do*?'

'Sure. "Eyes Only" is a favourite. Like, "Eyes Only to

McGregor: I have a squash court for seven o'clock." Stuff like that.'

'Don't you realize that all gets archived?'

'Not if we throw it away it doesn't.'

'But you *can't* throw away "Eyes Only" material.'

Burnham looked at Renfro and smiled and said, 'Renfro, you're a great American.'

Renfro was beginning to blink again. 'Let's see what you have in your pockets.'

'Got a warrant?'

'I'm not getting personal!' Renfro barked. 'I only want to show you what should and shouldn't be shredded. Sometimes people carry things on their persons that they shouldn't, and they throw them away in any old receptacle.'

Burnham shrugged and slipped his hands in and out of his several pockets. He found two pieces of paper. One was blank: he carried it to make notes on, in case a felicitous idea should come to him on a bus or at lunch. He glanced at the other and handed it to Renfro. 'Just this.'

'What is it?'

'A prescription . . . sort of.'

'For what?' Renfro studies the sheet of paper. 'What's Z imag?'

'Vitamins. Things like that.'

'You don't need a prescription for vitamins.'

'For some kinds you do. It's . . .' Burnham paused, searching for a simple explanation that wouldn't involve all the arcana of orthomolecular medicine and force him to defend its apparently eccentric tenets to a man who, Burnham had no doubt, would condemn them as sorcery. Like most people, Renfro would know vitamins only as food supplements. He would never have seen the reaction in an allergic person to a dose of, say, niacinimide – the instantaneous blotching on the face, the hive-like welts that would wax and wane like boiling tomato sauce. He would never have seen a child with a zinc imbalance – the pustulant sores, the pestilential itching, the swelling that could shut the eyes and close off the œsophagus. He would not know of the torment a human being goes through by overdosing a simple thing like B-6 – the ghastly, *guignol* nightmares that jerk you awake every fifteen minutes and eventually, after many sleepless nights of horror, begin to come during the day as hallucinations similar to, and occasionally mistaken for, delerium tremens.

He would not know any of these things, and so wouldn't understand that the purveyors of certain vitamins insisted on seeing a doctor's authorization before they peddled potential poisons to people on some freaky chemical crusade.

Burnham settled for: 'Those are special ones. I'm allergic.' That usually worked.

'Oh.' Renfro handed the prescription back. 'That you don't have to shred.'

Burnham noticed that there was an expiration date on the prescription and that it had passed weeks ago, so he dropped it into the wastebasket.

'As a general rule,' Renfro said, 'aside from Category 7 documents, use your common sense. Anything that would tell anybody more than you would want anybody to know – shred it.'

'Done and done.'

'Good. If you have any questions, don't hesitate to call me. Do not use the DOE switchboard. Our association is nobody's business. Here is my direct number. Commit it to memory. Do not write it down.' Renfro recited the seven digits, sounding like the robot voice on the phone that gives you the new number to which the number you dialled has been changed.

Burnham repeated the numbers once, at Renfro's insistence, but he had already concluded that it would be more fun to tweak Renfro by calling him through the DOE switchboard, so he determined to forget the numbers as soon as Renfro left.

On this way to the door, Renfro's omnivorous eyes lit upon the Important Papers Burnham had tossed on the couch. He bent over and studied the telephone-message slips Dyanna had stapled to the top page of the papers. He touched each one with a fingertip, as if to confirm that they were real.

'Have you returned these calls?' he said.

'Not yet.' Burnham had never looked at them, had no idea what they said.

'As soon as you do, shred them. Shred them immediately.'

'Right.'

When the door had closed behind Renfro, Burnham went to the couch and picked up the Important Papers. As he read the message slips, he grinned: Dyanna's ambition for him knew no bounds.

Dyanna pushed the door open and said, 'What a rude man!'

Burnham pulled the message slips off the legal pad and held them up to her. 'You,' he said, smiling, 'are a piece of work. Did that saucy Thatcher ever call back?'

Dyanna blushed. 'I just thought –'

'Look at this.' Burnham was feeding the messages into the shredder. 'Sucker's got some appetite. You s'pose we could turn it into a planter? Begonias'd look nice.' He reached to turn off the shredder and the fabric in the seat of his trousers pulled right and two staples sprung free. 'Whoops!' he said. 'Where'd I put that needle and thread?'

'Sit at your desk and give 'em to me,' Dyanna said. 'I'll do it, while you tell me about the President.'

'But that's not your job.'

Dyanna smiled and held out her hand. 'Things are changing. I can tell.'

Six

By five o'clock, Ivy was desperate. She had been working for seven hours, and she had seen, found or heard nothing – not a scrap of juicy gossip, not a heated exchange between overworked secretaries, not a rumour of high-level hugger-mugger – with which to amuse, delight or intrigue Mr Pym. In an hour and a half, she would be visiting the man's home to ask a big favour of him, a dangerous favour, and she had promised to deliver something in return.

He didn't seem to care, but she did: she couldn't bear to be a beggar.

Sweet baby Jesus, come through for me now, she whispered as she wheeled her utility cart – loaded with mop, broom, dust rags, toilet paper, paper towels, furniture polish, trash bags and light bulbs – down the marble halls of the Executive Office Building.

She had spent the first few hours of her shift in the cafeteria, cleaning up after the breakfast crowd, then after the coffee-break crowd, and setting up for lunch. During her own lunch break, she sat in the kitchen and ate the food she had brought from home, two chicken legs and a cucumber sandwich.

From 3.00 to 4.00, she stocked the ladies rooms with paper products. At 4.00, she took a break and had a cup of tea, with which she washed down two more yellow pills, for her knee was swollen and sending arrows of pain up and down her leg. At 4.30, she launched her cart slowly down the second floor corridors of the EOB, hoping to find an empty office to clean, an office whose occupant had called in sick or had left for the day or was out of town on business.

But a sliver of light shone beneath every door, and from within she heard telephones ringing and typewriters clacking.

By 5.15, she had circled the entire second floor and half the first floor, and still she had found no unoccupied office. She was tired, and her leg hurt, and she was beginning to despair and to conjure imaginative apologies for Mr Pym, when she saw a door open at the end of the corridor and a couple emerge, laughing.

The man was tall and slender, good-looking if you liked white-bread looks, and he wore one of those light, blue-and-white-striped summer suits that make the slim look slimmer and the fat look foolish. He carried a small athletic bag like Jerome's – well, sort of like Jerome's, for where Jerome's was made of plastic-rubber stuff, this one was of old, well-worn leather – and a midget racquet for a sport that wasn't tennis.

The woman looked as if she had been made in a toy store: small and delicate and perfect. Everything about her was just so – her little feet in their high-heeled pumps, her helmet of hair that defied a saucy breeze to muss it, her fingernails that probably had more coats of lacquer than a German car.

The man said something, and the woman laughed again and reached inside the closing door and snapped off the light. Together they walked out of sight toward the door that led to West Executive Avenue.

Ivy waited for a moment, to be sure they had gone, then pushed her cart down to the empty office. The name-plate beside the door said 'Timothy Burnham' and 'EOB 102'. Nothing about who he was or what he did or whom he worked for. Well, hard darts. It was 5.20, and in seventy minutes she had to be across town at Mr Pym's place. She didn't care if this Burnham fellow was a masseur or a mail clerk. She'd find *some*thing in his office for Mr Pym.

She cracked the door and put her back to it, pushing it open as she pulled her cart after her and flicking on the light as she passed.

121

This first, small room was the secretary's. Nothing worthwhile here. The typewriter was covered, the desk bare and the file cabinets closed and locked.

She turned to her right and pushed the cart before her into the main office. Even before she had put a foot inside the office, she felt a shiver that was part excitement, part shock and part uneasy fear.

This was the biggest office she had ever seen – bigger than her apartment, bigger than the whole ground floor of her house in Bermuda. There were conference tables and sofas and easy chairs, huge windows through which she could see the White House and the Washington Monument, and, behind the desk, signed photographs of the President together with this Burnham person.

Oh my, girl, she thought. Looks like you struck the mother lode. No question: *big* doings go on in this place. But you best be careful. It's one thing to pinch a little something to tickle Mr Pym's fancy, quite another to get nicked for sticking your hand in the big-time cookie jar.

She had no illusions about Mr Pym; she was confident she had him pegged good and proper. All his talk about being interested in people's 'quirks and foibles' was just that: talk. What he really wanted was dirt. Who had the skeletons in the closet, who had the power to do what and to whom. He was in a competitive business, catering to the movers and shakers, and spicy scuttlebutt was cash money to him. If word got around that he could provide more than canapés and veal birds, that he was party to the inside skinny on some big hitters, his business would grow like Topsy.

She had no illusions about herself, either. She was tired of playing the game strictly by the rules. If she didn't take the initiative now and then, she'd end her days sitting in a wicker chair with no one to care for her but a cat. Jerome was her only hope and computers were Jerome's only hope.

Fair enough. Time to become a free-style, free-enterprise entrepreneur.

But don't be rash. The place could be bugged. There could be a camera in the chandelier. Ever since that money-mad ex-Navy man had whipped up a whole litter of spies, people were seeing spies behind every blade of grass. They might not be so quick to understand her point that there was a difference between spying and muckraking.

There was a wastebasket by the desk, and she went to empty it, but there was something sitting on top of it, a machine that looked like a telephone-answering machine, only thicker, or a copier, only it wasn't a copier. She lifted it up (anyone watching from the chandelier would think it natural for her to remove the machine to get at the wastebasket) and set it on the floor. The wastebasket was full of paper spaghetti, some of which seemed to have writing on it. Maybe this would intrigue Mr Pym. She emptied the basket into an unused plastic trash bag and replaced the machine.

She began to dust the glass top of the desk and noticed on the far corner an appointment calendar. Maybe it would tell her more about who this Mr Burnham was. But she didn't dare flip through it in view of the chandelier (which, by now, she *knew* to contain a camera; guilt was already creating phantasms in her head), so as she rounded the desk, she hit the calendar with her hip and knocked it onto the floor behind the desk. She grumbled aloud (for the benefit of the microphones that might be behind the paintings or in the electrical outlets or even in the dingle-dangles on the chandelier) and knelt – slowly and carefully, supporting herself on the edge of the desk so as not to insult the ligaments in her knee – behind the desk, out of sight from the chandelier, and said, 'Where'd you get to? Come back here. Way over there? Damn!', talking a torrent of nonsense to cover the sound as she flipped through the pages of the calendar in search of tidbits about its owner.

'Ivy, my dear!' Foster Pym forced a smile as he held the door open. 'How good to see you! Come in, come in!'

Clutching her bulging shopping bag, feeling dowdy and frumpy, Ivy tried to square her shoulders and stand tall, so she wouldn't look like a bag lady. 'Evening, Mr Pym. I'm really . . .'

'Come in, my dear!' Pym took the shopping bag and helped her into the apartment. He felt her limp. 'That pesky leg is bothering you again, isn't it?' In the past hour, he had read over his notes on Ivy, had refreshed himself about her likes and dislikes, about her son, her ailments and the pills he had given her. He hoped she had become dependent on the pills.

'It's nothing I can't live with,' Ivy said as she allowed herself to be led into the apartment. She wasn't here to complain about herself. She heard 'Clair de Lune' playing on the phonograph in the living room, smelled cinnamon toast and strong tea.

'Do you have enough pills?' Mr Pym was the most thoughtful man she had ever met.

'I have a few left. It's funny about those pills. Most of the time, one does the trick, but now sometimes it takes two. I wonder if they make up different batches.'

'It's possible.'

'Or maybe I'm building up a resistance to them.'

'No. Different batches, I'm sure. Don't worry, I have plenty. I'll give you some more before you leave. Why don't we have some sherry?'

'Fine, fine.'

Pym went into the kitchen, and Ivy leaned back in the sofa and stretched out her leg and closed her eyes. The lilting music was cleansing. It seemed to suck the pain from her knee and the worry from her head. She could feel her face and forehead soften.

Pym carried the sherry on a silver tray and poured it from a cut-glass decanter into tiny crystal glasses. This man, Ivy thought, this man knows how to *live*. No pint bottles and Dixie cups for him.

She told him her problem. Jerome's problem. Their problem.

Halfway through the tale, Pym knew what the request would be, but he let her finish. He wanted to make her ask, didn't want to make it too easy for her. He wanted her to be fully aware of the magnitude of the favour she was asking.

She would not be permitted to blind herself, as she had in the Bermuda videogames caper, to devious procedures. She was asking him to commit an illegal act on her behalf, and he wanted her obligation to be complete.

She finished. Pym furrowed his brow and sighed and picked at a loose thread on the arm of his chair.

'You do have a problem,' he said.

Ivy looked at him. He was frowning. Had she gone too far? Had she insulted him? Stupid! she said to herself. 'I understand . . . I shouldn't have . . .'

'Even if the diploma was possible,' Pym said, 'DTCo might want a transcript, SAT scores, all kinds of things from the school.'

Her fear evaporated. At least he wasn't angry. He was trying to help her. Maybe he could, maybe he couldn't, but so far she hadn't poisoned their relationship. 'I know,' she said. 'It's probably impossible. I shouldn't have asked.'

Pym held up a hand. 'No, no. I just have to think.'

Change the subject, Ivy told herself. Now. Don't let him think so hard that he blows a fuse and decides he can't help. 'I brought you something.'

'Oh?' Pym looked up and smiled.

Ivy reached into her shopping bag and pulled out a plastic trash bag tied with a twist-tie. 'I was on the early shift today, and one of the girls was sick so they sent me to do some of the offices I don't usually do, and I was in the biggest office I have ever seen – it was as big as a cricket pitch – and this fellow has a machine on top of his wastebasket.'

'A machine? What kind of machine?'

'I don't know. But look at this.' Ivy reached into the trash bag and pulled out a handful of strands of paper spaghetti.

The easy smile froze on Pym's face. Mother of God! A shredder. Take care, now. 'Whose office was it?' Pym felt that his voice sounded urgent, and he tried to smile again.

'Someone named Burnham. Timothy Burnham. What's all this for, d'you think? Everything in those offices gets burned anyway, every day. Why would they do this?'

'I can't imagine,' Pym said. He held out his hand, and Ivy

passed him a bunch of the strands. Some of the strands were blank, some had pieces of letters on them, some pieces of numbers. He pretended to try to decipher a message in the strands, while through his mind ran the various possible possessors of the shredder. Who in the EOB would be exalted enough to warrant a shredder? The Vice President, of course, if he demanded one, but from what Pym had heard about the relationship between the President and the Vice President, he doubted that the Vice President would ever be trusted with a document classified higher than 'Confidential'. Members of the National Security Council staff, he supposed. And that was about it.

Pym felt his adrenalin beginning to flow, but he willed himself to stay cool. 'Fun!' he said. 'I wonder if we could put it all back together?' He knew full well that the re-assembly of shredded documents would be accomplished only with a microscope, surgical tools and an infinity of time and patience.

'Whoo!' Ivy said, pleased that Pym was pleased. 'Maybe, if you've got a year or two.' She reached into the trash bag and came out with more masses of paper. 'This stuff doesn't quit.'

'What else do you know about Mr Burnham?' Pym asked.

'Not much. But there was *some* stuff in the basket that wasn't wrecked.'

Ivy handed him a couple of pieces of paper.

One was a pay envelope from the Department of Energy.

Why did the Department of Energy have a man in the White House? Pym was familiar with the curiosities about the White House staff, with the fact that more than three-quarters of the President's men were detailed from other agencies for purposes of clerical obfuscation. It was not inconceivable that an Energy man would be sent to the White House, but if the Department were forced to sac-rifice a job, surely it would choose one in fossil fuels or rural electric power, not atomic energy. Yet this man, whoever he was, was of a rank high enough to be given a shredder.

Fossil-fuel experts did not need shredders. Obviously, this Burnham had access to atomic-energy secrets.

The second piece of intact paper seemed to be a prescription of some kind. Twenty or thirty chemical combinations were printed on the paper, of which a dozen had been checked by the doctor whose signature was on the bottom. Some were routine: B-12, B-1, B-6, ascorbic acid. Some were exotic: lecithin, pantothenic acid, dolomite. Some sounded as if they were used in the manufacture of automobiles: chromium, zinc sulphate, manganese 10. And a few Pym recalled seeing in articles about mental illness: lithium, Elavil, Tofranil.

'You think he takes all these?' Pym asked aloud.

'He must be one sick fellow,' said Ivy.

'Or the healthiest man in the world.' Pym smiled. 'I doubt that any disease could get through all that.'

'Well, he exercises, I know that.'

'What d'you mean?'

'I saw him leaving the office today, and he had one of those little racquets they play . . . ah . . . squash with.'

'I wonder where he plays.'

'There's a Y on 17th. I pass it every day. But I don't know if they have squash.' Ivy remembered the appointment calendar. 'He's playing tomorrow, too. It's the only appointment he has for tomorrow. His calendar says "Twelve noon, squash with . . ." and then a question mark.'

'He plans to pick up a game, then. Wherever he plays has a pro who matches players up.'

Ivy laughed. 'Dick Tracy!'

Pym laughed, too. 'I love puzzles like this.' He got up to refill the sherry glasses and change the record.

If 'Clair de Lune' had been soothing, 'La Mer' was almost anaesthetic. Ivy felt that if Pym were to leave the room for five minutes, she would drift off into a lovely sleep.

Pym returned to his chair. 'Let's see if we can take all the evidence we've got and discover this Mr Burnham's story.'

127

He began to sort through the strands of paper, tossing aside the blank ones and laying out those on which there was some writing in neat lines on the table beside him. Mostly, Pym was radiating enthusiasm for Ivy's benefit. But there was an off chance that two or three strands would fit together and disclose a bit of valuable information about Burnham's job.

Ivy was delighted. Mr Pym seemed genuinely pleased by what she had brought him. She had delivered. Even if he couldn't help her with Jerome's problem, things were back in balance, and she needn't feel embarrassed about calling him again.

A key turned the lock in the front door of the apartment, and a woman walked in. She was young, in her late twenties, and beautiful in a careless, confident way, as if she knew that nature had created in her a splendid creature of perfect proportions, and she saw no reason to gussy herself up with hairdos or makeup, jewellery or chi-chi clothes. Her hair reminded Ivy of goldenrod, for its yellow was dusty rather than shiny, and it fell ungoverned to her shoulders. Her nose was straight and sharp and must have been made for her face, unlike those noses that seemed to have been placed at random on inappropriate faces. Her eyes were a light grey-blue: any darker, they would have been nondescript and boring; any lighter, they would have been scary. Her skin was faintly, smoothly tan, as if she had once spent so much time in the sun that the melanin in her skin had moved permanently to the surface. She wore a blue cotton shirtwaist dress and brown leather sandals.

'Hello,' she said pleasantly and with an ease that told Ivy she was at home here.

My, my, Ivy thought. Mr Pym is full of surprises. He has himself one top-shelf girlfriend. 'Hello,' she said.

Reluctantly, Pym abandoned the strands of paper. 'Eva, this is Ivy Peniston. Ivy, this is my daughter, Eva.'

Daughter! Ivy stared. My God! They must've crossed Mr Pym with that Cheryl Tiegs woman.

Eva smiled and said, 'Hello again.'

'Eva is a . . .' Pym glanced at her. '. . . nutritionist.'

'At the moment,' Eva said.

'Look, Eva.' Pym pointed to the strands of paper on the table. 'Ivy brought us a nifty puzzle.'

Pym sketched for Eva what little he and Ivy knew about Burnham. Then he gave her the prescription sheet and said, 'Does this make any sense to you?'

Eva read the paper carefully, noting each of the vitamins and chemicals that had been checked. 'He's hyper-hystemic,' she said. 'He's allergic to a lot of things, probably including foods. He may or may not be a kind of alcoholic. Sometimes he has broad mood swings. He had trouble remembering his dreams.'

Ivy was amazed. 'You got all that from that piece of paper?'

Eva smiled. 'One of the Greenpeacers I worked with was an orthomolecular shrink. We never ate right, and he used to pump us full of nutritional supplements. You spend six months with someone on a boat, you learn whatever he has to teach.' She said to her father, 'The man is like a Ferrari: he works like a dream when he's finely tuned, but one little thing goes out of whack, he'll fall apart. What is he to you?'

Reflexively, Pym lowered his eyes and turned his head. 'Nothing. It's just for fun.'

Eva looked at her father. A smile started on her lips, but she suppressed it.

Pym tried not to look at Eva. He was a child caught in a clumsy lie, and he knew he was blushing. He busied himself with the decanter of sherry, finding a glass for Eva, filling it, spilling some, wiping up the spill, handing her the glass.

Ivy sensed that her presence had suddenly become an intrusion. The last thing she wanted to do was annoy Pym, leave him with an unpleasant aftertaste. Time to go. 'Well,' she said, leaning forward and fitting her feet back into her shoes, 'I should be going.'

Pym helped her up and fetched her shopping bag. 'Why not leave all this with me?' he said, gesturing at the strands of paper scattered on the floor. 'I'll play with it and see if I can make something of it.'

'Fine.'

'And keep your eye open for any other piece that might fit the puzzle.' He winked and smiled and hoped he looked mischievously conspiratorial.

Ivy nodded. 'I'm on the early shift all week.' She took a step, put her weight on the bad leg, and the unexpected pain stopped her short and made her gasp.

'Ivy!' Pym felt her totter, and he grabbed her.

'It's all right,' Ivy said. 'She stiffened up on me. I have to work 'er some.'

'Have some more sherry.'

'No thanks. 'F she complains about walkin', she sure don't want to crawl me all the way home.'

'I'll get you some more pills.' Pym looked at Eva, who came and held Ivy's arm while he fetched the pills.

In the bathroom, Pym knelt and reached under the sink. He used a nail file to pry loose a square tile behind the sink's drain pipe. He had been hiding his pharmacopoeia behind the sink for years. Granted, the chances were greater that he would be struck by lightning or bitten by a puff adder than that he would be raided by the police for having a stash of deviously acquired prescription drugs, but just as he had been trained to arrange elaborate blind drops for passing information, to speak in absurdly circumlocutory language when dealing with his contacts, to burn all his typewriter ribbons, so too he concealed anything that might raise an eyebrow if it were discovered in a random accident, like a fire or a flood from a broken pipe in the apartment upstairs.

There were a dozen bottles of pills in the hole in the wall – Valium, Dexedrine, Demerol, Seconol, Antabuse (capital for causing spectacular, mysterious illness at a cocktail party, should such an occasion ever arise) and four bottles of Percodan, the morphine-based pain-killer on which, Pym was certain, he now had Ivy hooked like a striped bass.

He poured twenty Percodan pills into an empty plastic vial, replaced the bottle in the hole and the tile in the wall, and returned to the living room. Ivy was sitting down again, holding another glass of sherry and a five-dollar bill. Eva stood before her, looking like a concerned and caring nurse, the sherry bottle in her hand.

'I thought we should have a taxi take Ivy home,' Eva said to Pym.

'Of course. Good for you. Is he on his way?'

Eva nodded. 'Be here in a minute.'

Pym handed the pills to Ivy, and she smiled at him. Her eyes were glassy, and it took her a moment to say, 'Thank you.'

'Let's help her downstairs,' Pym said. 'I don't want her waiting alone on the sidewalk.'

'About Jerome . . .' Ivy as she struggled to stand.

'Ah yes . . .' Pym's mind charged ahead, searching all avenues for access to a high-school diploma. 'Can you borrow a diploma from someone who graduated last year? From the same school.'

'I 'spect Jerome can get one.'

'Good. As soon as you get it, you can consider it done.'

'I don't know how . . .' Ivy felt herself beginning to weep. Tears were backing up behind her eyes and wanting to squeeze out. For God's sake! she thought. What's going on? I'm grateful, but it's not worth falling apart over. She swallowed, cleared her throat.

'Now, now . . .' Pym patted her on the shoulder and led her toward the door.

The taxi was waiting. Pym and Eva helped Ivy into the back seat. Pym took the five-dollar bill from Ivy's fist and gave it to the Sikh driver, told him Ivy's address and told him to keep the change – a two-dollar tip at least, Pym guessed.

'I don't know what the chemistry is,' Pym said as the taxi rolled away, 'but blacks have a terrible weakness for alcohol. Goes right to their heads.'

Eva didn't reply. She was recording the taxi's licence number.

'Sikhs don't rob people,' Pym said.

'How do you know he's a Sikh? Maybe he's a Mexican with a turban.'

'What kind of talk is that from a socialist?' He hoped his voice sounded light and jocular.

'I don't turn my back on anybody.' Eva said. 'Not any more.'

In the taxi, Ivy leaned her head against the back of the seat. Her stomach was rolling, and her brain felt like dough. What *happened*? One minute she was fine, the next she was pissed as a goat. That last glass of sherry must've done it. Foul brew, served like wine but with a kick like booze. No wonder the British Empire rotted away.

And probably the pills didn't help.

She rolled down the window.

Remember, girl, if you're going to spew, spew to leeward.

'Who was she?' Eva asked as she and Pym re-entered the apartment.

'Nobody.' He couldn't look at her. He sensed that he was at a crossroads. He could take the safe path, say nothing, or . . . He busied himself collecting the sherry glasses and putting them on the tray.

Eva grinned. 'Don't bullshit me, Pop. You can tell me. You having a little fling?'

'A *what*?' A series of muscle groups tightened in shock, snapping him upright and clenching a hand that held a sherry glass so hard that the stem of the glass snapped.

Surprise had twisted the grin on her face into a grimace. She said, 'Sorry. I didn't –'

'No,' he said. 'I'm sure you didn't.'

Pym looked at Eva and saw that her face was radiating uncertainty, bewilderment and (maybe he was seeing too much, but he didn't think so) the first few wrinkles of fear.

He stepped through the crossroads.

The time had come.

'Get a jacket,' he told her. 'We'll go for a walk.'

Seven

Burnham left the YMCA at 7.30. He had played well, had split games with a quick and hairy ferret who worked for the Treasury Department. The man was younger than Burnham, had sharper reflexes and was more aggressive, bumping Burnham off the 'T' and wielding his racquet more like an axe than an epée. Burnham had won his points with wrist finesse and ball control, and by the end of the fourth game he had perfected a maddening tactic of dinking the ball low into the far corner, just above the tin, which had brought his opponent to his knees, cursing and flustered. Burnham won the fourth game 15–6, and he left the court feeling deft, clever and – intellectually if not statistically – the clear winner. The match mirrored his day, which had begun rough and uncertain and had ended on an unexpected high.

The match had been arranged by Hal, the unofficial pro at the 17th Street Y, which was known informally and unpleasantly as the Walter Jenkins Memorial Y, after the unfortunate aide to Lyndon Johnson, whose career had screeched to a seamy halt when he was apprehended in an unspeakable act with an unidentified stranger in one of the men's room stalls.

Hal (whose last name was known only to himself and to God) could never have been formally employed by the YMCA or any other organization that pretended to conform to conventional morality, for he was, by his own admission, an accident of nature. It was, he told Burnham one evening after drinking half a quart of Scope mouth

133

wash, as if his manufacturer had gathered components for disparate devices and forcibly assembled them into a bastard machine that could perform no socially acceptable function. Once, Hal had probably been pretty – back in the days when he lived in California and made a living, he said, as 'catamite to the stars'. He would have been slight and delicate and fair. But now his skin was the colour of old bone, his gums had receded so far that his teeth looked as if a fair breeze would cause them to fall like apples from a tree, and his remaining hair – meticulously moulded around an insane yellow toupée that would have passed for a decent blond merkin – had been peroxided so often that it was the colour of water.

Lacking the courage, the intelligence and the resources of Quentin Crisp, Hal had not dared flaunt himself in police society and so had gone underground. If he could not secure a proper job by normal means, he would fashion one for himself. Passing through Washington a few years earlier, he had spent a few nights at the Y and had noticed that the athletic facilities were tacky and unsupervised. Men and women (for, financial exigencies had long since forced the YM and YMCAs to share the same building) had to provide their own locks, their own towels, their own soap and had to wear shoes everywhere for fear of contracting some exotic parasite. They could not play squash on short notice, for court time was allocated on a first-come, first-served basis, so an individual had to call an opponent whose schedule matched his own, then show up and wait and hope that his entire lunch hour wouldn't be spent waiting for a court.

Quietly, Hal began to spend his days in the cellar of the Y, dressed in white-duck trousers, white tennis shoes and a polo shirt from the Malibu Beach Club. He bought two dozen cheap towels and rented them for fifty cents apiece to people who had forgotten their own. Then he provided padlocks for rent, and sold soap. Finally, as he saw the frustration of players whose opponents failed to appear or who couldn't get court time, he began to book games.

Knowing that people tended to obey any sign that looked official, he brought a snappy placard that said 'RE-SERVED' and pasted it on one of the four squash courts. Regular pairs could call Hal and book the court and know that they would get to play. His tips for providing this convenience ranged from a couple of dollars to as much as $20. Before long, all four courts were under Hal's control, and as he came to know the skill levels of the various players, he was able to match partners. Nowadays, all one had to do was call Hal and say he would like to play at such-and-such a time, and he would be sure of having a court and an opponent who would give him what Hal liked to call 'a rum go'.

Burnham sometimes wondered idly about Hal's private life, but he never asked, and Hal was too smart and too circumspect ever to let slip anything personal. (Even his one indiscretion, in the grip of Scope, was not so much a complaint as a matter-of-fact observation). Hal would tell anyone who would listen about the sordid tragedy of Walter Jenkins, but Burnham had the sense that telling the tale was a kind of therapy for Hal – as if cautioning himself that a stupid slip could destroy the life he had so carefully built for himself.

Burnham's opponent today was a conversational fewmet, which was too bad because half the enjoyment of a vigorous workout came from pleasant, vacuous, locker-room banter. He shed his clothes quickly, scurried into the shower and, by the time Burnham arrived, had soaped himself so thoroughly that he resembled an overtaxed Brillo pad. He left the locker room before Burnham.

As Burnham emerged, he saw Hal gazing contemptu-ously at the man's departing back and holding between his fingertips, as if it was a wet and dirty sock, a single dollar bill. By now, it was an accepted routine that each player in an arranged match would give Hal $5, and Burnham had dutifully folded a five-dollar bill in his palm. As unobtrus-ively as possible, he exchanged it for a ten-spot from his wallet. He smiled as he gave it to Hal, and Hal's return smile said that he appreciated the gesture.

'He was a referral,' Hal said.

Burnham shrugged. 'It happens.'

'Not twice.' He pocketed the bill. 'Tomorrow?'

'How about noon?'

'I'll find you somebody jollier.'

Outside, the evening was fine. The infernal sun that had baked the city all day had finally moved behind the Virginia hills, and the air had cooled to a point where Burnham's pores soon closed and did not pour forth defensive sweat. He decided to walk home.

He climbed Pennsylvania Avenue and crossed the M Street bridge, and not till then was the peace of his promenade smashed by the painful shriek of Pratt & Whitney jet engines. A south wind was the curse of Georgetown, for it mandated that the glide path of all aircraft destined for National Airport was directly over the gilded ghetto.

Burnham had long felt that no one should be allowed to fly over Georgetown, not because of the noise (he rather liked the idea of Katharine Graham being forced to observe a moment of silence in deference to People Express), but because flying over Georgetown was destructive of fantasies. It was like watching a sci-fi movie being shot (the actors acting to a blank wall which the special-effects wizards would later transform into an invading armada) or learning how the magician makes you believe he's cutting the woman in two.

From ground level, Georgetown was like the back lot at the Burbank Studios. It could be any number of things: quaint, colourful, historical, chic, dangerous. What it could not be, and what nobody ever tried to pass it off as, was grungy.

From the air, Georgetown was grungy. The houses, with their filthy roofs and tiny gardens, were packed together like cattle in pens. The alleys between the backs of the houses were littered with trash bags and garbage cans. The carriage lamps and the washed bricks, the leaded windows and the brass door knockers all were invisible.

From the air, Georgetown was revealed as the slum it used to be.

Burnham pushed open the door to his house and knew instantly that something was amiss. From the second floor came none of the accustomed cacophony of two tape decks playing two different songs by two different groups, as each child did his and her homework to his and her muse. No food odours came from the kitchen. The kitchen had not been used since breakfast.

His first conclusion was that Sarah had been asked to stay late at work, addressing envelopes or laying out the draw for a celebrity tennis tournament, and had farmed the kids out to friends' houses. But that made no sense: the children were old enough to be alone in the house until he came home, and he was capable of subduing a couple of lamb chops and a box of frozen spinach for them. His second conclusion, a fleeting fantasy that his family had been kidnapped, was dispelled by a pungent aroma of wine. Red wine. Good, expensive red wine. A drinker might not have noticed it; the wine had not been spilled or liberally poured, merely opened and reduced by a single glassful. Burnham had not had a drink in a year, and his nose for alcohol was as keen as a shark's for blood. It could detect vodka in orange juice, bitters in ginger ale and ethanol in any combination through even a screen of Binaca.

He shut the door and turned left and saw Sarah. She was dressed in a white silk blouse, with a demure little bow at the neck, and a tweed suit. He didn't know she owned a tweed suit. What was she doing, applying for a job? Before her on the coffee table was a single tulip goblet and an open bottle of Margaux. A $22 wine. Judas Priest! Was *Town & Country* coming by? She sat on the sofa with her knees together and her hands in her lap. She hadn't been reading or watching television or doing a crossword puzzle.

He said, 'Hi . . . Hon?' as he shut the door.

She smiled at him, a vague, perfunctory smile appropriate to direct at a doorman or a train conductor.

Burnham felt a change in the atmosphere, as if the barometer was falling, but he sensed that his behaviour now wouldn't affect anything, that whatever was going on had already happened. So he strode across the room and said, 'Where are the troops?' and flopped in a chair beside the sofa.

Sarah didn't answer. She just smiled again, more faintly.

Burnham felt like an unwitting participant in a Cheyenne religious ritual. He leaned forward and filled Sarah's glass and sniffed the bottle. 'Times like this I miss the stuff. Wait'll you hear what the leader of the free world . . .'

'Timothy.'

That's all she said. Timothy.

Well? 'That's my name.'

'I want to talk to you.'

Oh God. It was the monster. The children had rolled back the rock from the mouth of its cave that morning, and sometime during the day it had emerged. Try to stuff it back.

He forced a feeble laugh. 'Their antennae are something, aren't they? They see things about you, feel things, even before you do.'

'I want to talk to *you*.'

'What does that mean? *You*.'

'Just you. No Dr Johnson. All right?'

Now he had to force himself *not* to smile, for now he knew who the third person was whose presence, whose guidance, he had almost tasted since he walked through the door, the force that had staged this scene. 'How's Sonja?' he said.

Sarah blushed, instantly and lividly. She said, 'Sonja has nothing . . .' But then she stopped, for the lie was absurd.

Sonja was Sarah's guru, a term that Sarah despised and denied. Nor would she accept 'counsellor', 'therapist', 'leader', or even 'moderator'. She insisted that Sonja was nothing more nor less than a friend, although, pressed, she would concede that Sonja was the wisest, kindest, most perceptive friend she and the other members of the Thursday afternoon reading group had. Sonja was a freelance copy editor, and she had edited a huge tome that discussed, analysed and evaluated every one of the mental, psychic, pseudo-religious and psychosomatic disciplines that had surfaced since the sixties. She knew everything about EST and Esalen, biorhythms and biofeedback, multimodal therapy and the Moonies. She knew techniques for everything, from fifty ways to leave your lover to regulating blood pressure through breathing to talking yourself into or out of an orgasm.

'She conned you into this Dress for Success number, right?' Burnham gestured at the tweed suit and said, attempting to imitate Sonja: 'If you have an impression to convey, a strong appearance can be a strong ally.'

Sarah stiffened. 'I don't intend to argue with you.'

'Who's arguing?'

She took a deep breath. 'When I married you . . .'

Oh-oh, he thought. The big guns are firing already.

'I . . . I knew that you were not a man of high principle, that you functioned in response to what could be called a situational ethic.'

She was beginning to piss him off. 'Don't say "what could be called." Say "what Sonja calls."'

'Damn you!'

He looked at her eyes, and he saw the telltale signs that tears were trying to escape and that she was trying to contain them. He felt sorry for her. What she was doing was important enough to her, and frightening enough, to have led her to seek help and to follow Sonja's loopy instructions. The least he could do was let her play herself out.

'Okay,' he said, but couldn't stop himself from adding, 'We were at the part where I'm not Patrick Henry.'

She seemed not to hear. She pressed on. 'I could deal with that because you were smart and clever and fun. And you are basically a good person. You care for me and the kids, and you don't go out of your way to hurt people. I allowed myself to hope that as we grew together, we would develop strong beliefs and that at least some of them would be in the same things.'

Politics again, he thought. Warmed-over horseshit. Mentally, he sighed a martyr's sigh and steeled himself for a tedious replay of one of their standard arguments. 'I never once said that working for the President was . . .'

'Let me finish. Please.' She waited until he nodded assent. 'To have you work for a man for whom I have no respect, for whom none of my friends have respect, for whom no civilized human being *can* have respect . . .'

'– except fifty-six per cent of the American people –'

'. . . has not been easy. The children were right. We have been fighting more. But I could live with that, because I loved you, part of you at least, and I kept hoping that someday there might be a miracle and you'd suddenly grow up.'

Inside Burnham's head, Dr Johnson was outraged. He begged to be released into the fray, he waved weapons of destruction tantalizingly behind Burnham's eyes. Burnham had to swallow him back into his guts.

'Then this morning I discovered that it was hopeless.' She stopped.

'This morning? You mean that pretty little argument in the kitchen? Come on . . .'

'When I went around the corner for the car, there was this couple, these two people, the most disgusting, filthy, revolting creatures I have ever seen . . .'

'Living in it!' Burnham laughed aloud.

Sarah looked puzzled. 'Yes.'

'Usually they're gone by then. They must've had a bad night.'

Now Sarah was amazed. 'You admit it? You know them?'

'I don't *know* them, for crissakes. I ran into them just the way you did. But at six-thirty, not nine o'clock. They're harmless.'

'I see.'

140

Burnham stopped laughing. '*They're* what all this is about?'

'No.' Sarah put a hand into one of her suit pockets and left it there. 'They left, but not before showering me with every four-letter word in the book, and I aired out the car for a few minutes and came home and got some Glade for the back seat. I got in the car and started it, and I must have had an anxiety backlash . . .'

Anxiety backlash! *Dear* Sonja.

'. . . because when I was backing up, I put my foot on the accelerator instead of the brake, and I hit the curb and something was knocked loose and fell on the floor.'

'What was knocked loose?'

Sarah brought her hand from her pocket and opened it. 'This.'

'What's that?' It looked like a blazer button – round, silvery, with fine crosshatched striations.

'Please, Timothy. Don't insult me.'

'"Please" what? What is it?' He plucked it from her palm.

'It's a microphone! A bug, they call it. And you know it.'

Burnham turned the button thing over in his hand. On the back was a small magnet that would hold it to the metal beneath a car's dashboard. 'I don't understand,' he said, and he didn't. 'What are you accusing me of?'

'You put it there! You, or your . . . your *people*.' She spat the word, as if his people were a loathesome assembly of vile creatures.

'Why? Why would I bug my own car?' He shouted, 'You're nuts!'

'It's not just *your* car. You know it; they know it. They know that it's also driven by someone who works for one of the few men with the courage to stand up to that . . . that grotesque who calls himself the President.'

'For God's sake, Sarah. Be serious.' But as he protested, Burnham searched his mind for alternatives. No question, this thing was a bug. But who would be trying to bug whom?

141

He wasn't worth bugging. A monitor of his conversations with himself as he drove to or from work would have heard an occasional curse at an inconsiderate motorist or a vituperative reply to an inane news item on the radio. And surely, Sarah didn't spend much time in profound policy discussions with senior members of the Kennedy staff as she drove back and forth across the Key Bridge.

Maybe they hoped – who could *they* be, anyway? – simply to gather dirt, gossip about something sensational, like a Chappaquiddick for the eighties. Maybe . . .

Maybe they knew something he didn't. Was Sarah having an affair with the Senator?

He looked at her and saw that she was staring directly and righteously into his eyes. The moment didn't seem propitious for a descent to lubricity.

'I have never been more serious,' she said.

'Sarah . . .' Burnham fingered the bug, as if to rub it would force it to divulge its secrets. 'Whatever you think, I don't know anything about this. Instead of accusing me, let's try to work it out together.'

'Timothy.' She wasn't listening. She wasn't going to listen. 'I have always known you were unprincipled. I did not know you were unscrupulous, that no depth was too low for you.'

'Hey! You haven't –'

'I don't want to hear a lot of lame lies!' Sarah's fists were clenched, and she was trying not to shout. 'I told you, I don't intend to argue with you. I believe you were responsible, directly or indirectly, for that microphone. But I am a fair person. I want to give you a chance to prove that you had nothing to do with it.'

'How noble. How about taking my word?'

'Here are your options: tomorrow morning, you resign from the White House and issue a public statement accusing the administration of having a Watergate morality and deploring its behaviour.'

'You're crazy! How about proof?'

142

'The proof is in your hand,' Sarah said, pointing at the microphone.

'There's no proof of who did it. For all you know –' Burnham was hoping his mind would keep pace with his tongue '– those street people left it there by mistake.'

'I believe they put it there, but not by mistake. Those street people work for the President.'

'Sure.' Burnham snorted. 'And their job is to skulk around Georgetown bugging cars.' Jesus, Burnham thought as he spoke, can that be true? The creeps had been around for nearly a year. He decided to try sweet reason. 'I know that what you do is important to you, Hon, and it may turn out to be important to the country, too. But don't you think – won't you at least consider – that to imagine that the President of the United States has dispatched a bunch of hippies to bug your car so he can overhear your every word, don't you think that smacks just a little bit of paranoia?'

Sarah said, 'Will you do it?' She had no intention of listening to him. Sonja had programmed her just like a floppy disc.

'What'll we live on?'

Sarah seemed to sense that she was winning. She leaned forward, and her eyes shone. 'Something. Anything. At least the dollars will be clean. We can live with ourselves.'

Who does she think I am? he thought. Jesse James? 'I don't have any trouble living with myself.'

She stiffened again. 'I do.'

'You said options. Plural.'

'You leave.'

'Leave what?'

'Leave here. Leave the house. Leave us.'

Doctor Johnson was not in the game, so, in his anger, Burnham called on David Mamet. 'Fuck you, Joan of Arc! You're not happy, *you* leave.'

'All right.' Sarah stood and smoothed her skirt and walked to the closet beside the front door. 'If you believe you can feed the children and do their laundry and take them to their lessons and remember when their dentist

143

appointments are and be home every night by seven, I'll leave.' Sarah opened the closet door. Inside were two suitcases, packed and standing side by side. One was Sarah's heirloom Vuitton, plastered with Cunard and French Line stickers. The other was his own heirloom Mark Cross that his father had passed on to him when he went away to college, its oiled leather and brass hinges gleaming even in the dim closet light.

'Your choice,' she said. She held the door open and stood aside, reminding Burnham of Betty Furness doing a 1950s Westinghouse commercial.

She had thought of everything. Rather, Sonja had thought of everything. He had no room to manoeuvre. Either, or. Two absolutes. One would spell poverty, the other loneliness.

He knew that, really, he had no choice. He could not be the one to stay and care for the children, and he would not quit his job. He did not commit the crime of which he had been accused, and (the determination blossomed within him) he was damned if he would let himself be pussy-whipped – especially not by that dingbat surrogate, Sonja – into pleading guilty.

He walked toward the closet. He wanted to ask a thousand questions: what would she tell the children? When would they speak with one another again? Was this a separation, or was she planning to file for divorce? What had she packed in his suitcase? Where was he supposed to go?

But all he did was pick up his suitcase and open the front door and walk outside.

'I booked a room for you,' Sarah said.

'Where?'

'The Y.'

Burnham took a step away, and then he stopped, for at last Dr Johnson had joined him. 'Nobody has a right to put another under such a difficulty,' he said. 'You and Sonja should remember that it's always much easier to find reasons for rejecting than embracing.'

Sarah slammed the door.

Once, in prep school, Burnham had been hit in the testicles by a lacrosse ball, a pound of hard rubber travelling at forty or fifty miles an hour. He had collapsed, and just before he vomited he imagined that his insides were being torn from him by a clawed hand.

He felt the same way now. He retched in the gutter, but because he had not eaten in many hours, all that came up was bile.

He was dreaming he was on a school bus. All the other kids were fully dressed, but he was naked. They didn't seem to notice, certainly not to care; they chattered merrily away. But *he* cared. What would happen when he got to school?

He couldn't remember why he was naked. Had his mother sent him out of the house without clothes, or had he taken them off at the school-bus stop? If he knew why, maybe it would be all right.

The dream was familiar; he knew what would happen next. But he was scared nonetheless. The bus turned into the school driveway. A pretty girl with a ponytail, a girl for whom he had been showing off for weeks, got up and took her bookbag from the overhead rack and walked down the aisle towards him. When she reached his seat, she looked down and smiled and said, 'Don't hide your dick,' and then walked on to the front of the bus.

Obediently, he removed his hands from his lap, and the kids around him all laughed and pointed at the shrivelled little worm hiding between his legs.

A door banged shut, and someone screamed, 'Asshole!'

This wasn't in the script. He looked around, but he couldn't see a door, couldn't locate the screamer.

'Asshole!'

It wasn't part of his dream. He opened his eyes.

Everything was grey. He could tell by the feel of the sheets that he wasn't in his own bed. The room held a faint astringent odour, like Mr Clean. Was he in a hospital? Jail? Dear God, had he done it again, gotten wasted and blacked

145

out and been lost downtown and gone to some skid-row dive of a flophouse? Had his buddies put him on a plane again, like the time in college, with no money, no driver's licence, just a one-way ticket to Pittsburgh? Fearfully, he put out a hand and felt the sheets beside him, praying he would touch no other body, no glutinous thigh of a sodden slut who would giggle and recall for him the noisome misdemeanours of the night before.

No. He was alone.

He sat up, and there was no pain, no foul taste, no sensation that his brain had slipped its moorings and was floating free in the cabinet of his skull.

All at once, the pieces came together, like backward-run videotape of a shattering glass. He knew where he was and how he had gotten there, and he felt grateful and strong, grateful at being strong enough to have weathered the storm with Sarah without being compelled, as once he would have, to repair to a dark saloon where a sympathetic anaesthetist would help him remove himself from himself.

Out in the hallway, the door that had slammed now opened on creaky hinges, and an oriental voice said something oriental that was undoubtedly so poisonous that, in the orient, it would have resulted in bloodshed.

Burnham looked at his watch. It was 6.30. The rising sun might have shown in his window, if his window hadn't been opaque with grit and facing an air shaft. He flicked the wall switch behind the bed, and the cold light from the bare ceiling bulb brought out all the character in the room's decor: that is, it revealed the room as suitable as a holding cell for a psychotic killer. There was the steel-framed bed on which Burnham sat, whose hard-used springs had given up and now formed a pocket as deep as a first-baseman's glove. There was a straight-backed chair and a square wooden table, on which every hooligan who had ever lived had carved his initials.

There came a knock on Burnham's door, three quick raps of a knuckle.

'Just a sec!' Burnham hopped up and scrambled for his

146

trousers. He wasn't about to answer a door in his boxer shorts. Not here. Who knew what were accepted practices in the corridors of the Y? He was no fool; he had seen *The Ritz*.

There was no one at the door, but at his feet Burnham saw a copy of the *Post* and a brown paper bag. He picked them up. Inside the bag was a container of coffee, a stirrer, a cup of dairy substance and a packct of Sweet'n Low, On the bag, scribbled in pencil, was a note:

Why you're here is your business.
My business is to welcome you.
See you at noon.

H.

Hal. Burnham smiled. He must have checked the register.

Burnham arrived at his office at eight. He had finished the coffee and the paper, shaved, showered and dressed, had breakfast at a cafeteria, and still it was only 7.45. He had nothing to do, nowhere to go and nothing to read, so he went to work.

He dialled Cobb's number – Cobb might be able to help him begin his inquiry into the likelihood (however remote) that the bug in his car had been planted by someone in the Administration – but there was no answer.

He decided to go have a cup of coffee at the Mess. For company, he took along a volume of Boswell's *Life of Johnson*. Another great thing about Johnson: you could re-read him forever and always find something new. Open Boswell to any page, and you were sure to find something Johnson said that hadn't etched itself on your mind the first time you read it, or the second or the third. It was Burnham's Bible.

He had never before been in the Mess in the morning, and he was surprised to find it crowded. There were no seatings in the morning; serfs sat cheek-by-jowl with knights.

147

Evelyn Witt waved pleasantly to him as he came in, but she didn't beckon him to join her. She was sitting with two of her deputies, and from the chastened looks on their faces, Burnham guessed that Evelyn had been giving them hell.

Three Air Force officers sat together. Burnham recognized one of them: Brigadier General Woody Ravenel, who was the pilot of Air Force One. One of the others was a bird colonel, the last a light colonel who was obviously older than the other two. Burnham assumed that the light colonel was the infamous Clip Dixon. Eighteen months ago, Dixon had been the President's pet pilot. He was sure to become a general officer before the end of the President's term. But one day, Dixon had been escorting the President off Air Force One at Andrews, and the President had started toward the wrong helicopter.

'That's your helicopter over there, sir,' Dixon had said.

'Son,' the President had smiled, 'they're *all* my helicopters.'

They had both chuckled at that one. The trouble was, Dixon had repeated the story at the Mess, and one of the people he had told had told someone else, and the next morning the anecdote appeared in the *Post*.

There was no penance he could do. He had sinned and been caught, and this lord was a lord not of mercy but of vengeance. Dixon would end his career as a light colonel, and because the spread between the retirement pay of a light colonel and a brigadier general is the difference between ease and penury, the sins of the father would be visited upon the wife and the children and the parents-in-law.

Two members of the National Security Council staff played pocket chess over their cups of tea.

Four women from the 'east side' – the social office in the East Wing – huddled in grave conference over the seating plan for tonight's State Dinner in honour of the dictator of some Asian ministate. From what Burnham could overhear, an Asia scholar from Columbia had had the tacky brass not only to decline the invitation but to accept and then renegue at the last minute, after his card had been printed and his seat assigned – at the right of one of the poobah's wives. Evidently, the scholar had objected to an esoteric point in the Administration's Asia policy and had decided to shaft the President publicly, not realizing that the President had no idea who the man was and that the only people he was shafting were four overworked young women who had nothing to do with policy and, in fact, couldn't have pointed to Asia on a map.

A Filipino steward showed Burnham to a small table for two nestled against the far wall. Burnham ordered coffee and opened his Boswell. He heard a familiar voice nearby. It was not loud – barely above a whisper – but it was angry, emphatic and contemptuous. He looked up.

Beside him, at another table for two, were the Secretary of State and Mario Epstein. Epstein was excoriating the Secretary. The Secretary's face was heliotrope with rage and humiliation; so much blood had rushed to his face that his neck had swollen and threatened to pop his Tiffany collar pin. His eyes were fixed on his coffee cup, and his hands gripped the sides of the table so hard that he barely moved each time Epstein jabbed him in the shoulder with a finger.

The Secretary's appointment had been a token tossed by the President to the eastern establishment. He was the only male heir to a huge chemicals fortune which had permitted him, his father, his grandfather and his great-grandfather to dedicate their lives to public service. He had graduated from Princeton and the Yale Law School and had served, briefly but creditably, in the Foreign Service until he received the first of a succession of increasingly important appointments to various international commissions, committees, delegations, negotiations, parleys and palavers. He taught seminars, wrote articles and books, moderated television shows and won formidable awards from obscure groups for his devotion to international understanding. He was debonair, and impeccably tailored, diplomatic, handsome . . . and safe.

Though well educated and widely experienced, he had no ideas of his own. He was a talented synthesizer incapable of creation. He fitted perfectly into the President's Cabinet.

The last thing Benjamin Winslow wanted in Foggy Bottom was a free thinker. One Henry Kissinger was enough for a generation. If the supervision of the nuclear arsenal was too important to leave to the generals, then foreign policy was too important to leave to the striped-pants brigade. In the Winslow Administration, foreign policy was born and bred in the White House and merely enunciated by the State Department.

Epstein jabbed the Secretary again, and Burnham wondered what transgression the man had committed. Hubris, probably. The Secretary must have had the gall to issue a policy statement without clearing it with Epstein or the President's National Security advisor – one and the same thing, really, since the National Security advisor, Dennis Duggan, had been recruited from the Brookings Institute by Epstein and (it was rumoured) didn't dare belch without first clearing it with Epstein.

But why would Epstein have chosen the White House Mess as the forum in which to dress down the Administration's own Cary Grant, when he could have ranted at any decibel pitch he chose behind the closed door of his own office? Looking at the Secretary of State, Burnham suddenly knew, and he felt the pride of perception. Epstein would have recognized three choices: the privacy of his office, the open public – that is, in front of his subordinates or the Secretary's or (the unthinkable last resort) the press – and the semi-privacy of a place like the Mess.

The second option he would have abandoned immediately. The Secretary would have felt compelled to resign (rich WASPs could afford to take offence at anything, so you had to be careful how you abused them), would have become the darling of the nation's op-ed pages, talk shows and think tanks and would suddenly have found himself wielding a great deal more clout as an adversary of the President than he had as an ally.

The first option was no good, either. In private, the Secretary would have defended himself vigorously, would have scored several telling blows, and Epstein would have had to argue with him, deal with him, negotiate. Epstein loathed the very thought of dealing and negotiating.

A semi-private room was the answer, for here Epstein had a hands-down advantage. He had no hesitation about offending anybody anywhere at any time. He would castigate waiters, upbraid chefs, insult hosts and belittle dinner partners with gay abandon. But the Secretary was too well bred. He would never make a scene in front of strangers. He would eat bad food, drink bad wine and suffer appalling boors with polite forebearance rather than raise his voice or (God forbid) tell them to buzz off. In this circumstance, the Secretary was forced, by genetics and environmental training, to endure Epstein's attack in silence. At most, he would say something like, 'Respectfully, Mario, I must disagree with you.'

Burnham realized he was staring. He should look away. But it was too late. Epstein must have sensed an intruder, for his head snapped around and he glared at Burnham and said, 'You got a problem?'

'Me?' Burnham squeaked. 'No!' He flapped his hand over his book. 'Confusing translation.'

Epstein kept staring at him until Burnham hunched over and surrounded Boswell with his arms and appeared to be about to eat the book.

He hummed, to block out the conversation at the next table, as he tried to focus on Johnson, so he didn't hear Warner Cobb walk up to his table and say, 'Hi.'

Cobb gazed quizzically down at the humming machine consuming the book, then pulled out a chair and sat down.

Burnham felt the table shake, and he looked up. 'Oh. Hi,' he said. 'I tried to call you.'

He told Cobb about Sarah finding the microphone in the

car. He did not tell him how their discussion had ended. It was none of Cobb's business. Besides, Burnham had no idea how long his problems with Sarah would last, and he had not had time to absorb them, to adjust to them. He was not ready to become a White House staffer with Personal Problems. Personal Problems were a liability. At best, they were a source of gossip and sympathy. At worst, they could affect security clearance, assignments and access to the President. They could be used as a synonym for instability and unreliability. To the President, an aide with Personal Problems was a flake.

'She must be pissed.' Cobb said.

'You could say.'

Cobb smiled. 'Is that why you're in early?'

'Sort of. She thinks . . . no, she knows that she's being bugged because she works for Kennedy.'

'That's paranoid nonsense.'

'That's what I told her. Can you find out?'

'What would we do it for? He isn't running again. Even if he was . . . Man! If there's one lesson from Watergate, when it comes to that kind of shenanigans, *watch your ass.*'

Burnham nodded. 'Can you find out?'

Annoyance flicked across Cobb's face, and then he realized that Burnham was not so much disbelieving him as begging to be rescued. 'For real? I doubt it. If anybody was doing it – and I can all but guarantee you they're not – they'd hardly admit it to me. But I can get you an answer. What makes you think she'd believe us?'

'I don't know. She won't believe *me.* Maybe if I look as if I'm making an effort, raising hell in high places, she'll see reason.'

'It's none of my business, but . . .' Cobb paused. 'Maybe she doesn't want to see reason.'

'That, Warner, I can't deal with. I can't do anything about it, so there's no point thinking about it. I'd rather bear the ills I have, then fly to others that I know not of.'

'Very healthy. Okay. I'll check around. I'll make sure you get a categorical denial from usually reliable sources very close to senior officials high up in the Administration. Unofficially.'

'And off the record.'

'Right. Now, if I may . . .' Cobb took some folded papers from the inside pocket of his jacket. 'This morning I got a call from the boss. I was at home. In bed. Asleep. He seemed annoyed that I wasn't on station in my splendid office. It was six o'clock.'

'Power knows no time of day.' Burnham smiled. 'And absolute power never sleeps.'

'Johnson? I like it.'

'I just made it up.'

'Oh. Too bad. Let's find somebody to attribute it to. Anyway, Himself has a job for you.'

'You mean he asked for me?'

'Specifically. And even by your right name.'

'Why?'

'Who knows? It must be more of the magic you worked on him yesterday. I wouldn't worry about it. He gets these infatuations. It'll pass. They always do. Sometimes, the people even survive. There's a State Dinner tonight.'

'I know. For the Gizmo of Grunt.'

'Please. Show some respect. It's for the Pasha of Banda.'

'Banda.' Burnham tried to read Cobb's eyes, to see if he was being thrown a curve. He wasn't. 'Warner, I went to fine schools. I have travelled. I read the gazette. I monitor the electronic marvels of the age. I think of myself as respectably informed. But never in my life have I heard of the nation of Banda.'

'You are so . . . parochial.' Cobb grinned. 'In the Timor Sea, of course. Critical. Very critical. A citadel of democracy.'

'No doubt with a population of six anthropoids, a derelict copra industry . . . and fifteen trillion barrels of oil.'

'Approximately.'

'So what's the problem: we phoneticize "Banda". The President calls him a great American and gives him a set of cuff-links and a gift certificate to Orvis.'

'The President received a draft of a toast for the dinner from the NSC. I don't think he liked it.'

'You don't think.'

'His words were . . .' Cobb consulted some scribbles on the folded papers, '. . . Warner, I got the toast for the whosiwhatsis tonight. That dog won't hunt.'

'"That dog won't hunt?" Where'd he get that one?'

'T. Boone Pickens paid a visit the other day. T. Boone Pickens likes to say things like "That dog won't hunt."'

'Did he say exactly what was wrong with that dog?'

'No. His next words were . . .' Cobb turned the paper on its side to decipher more scribbles. '. . . "Get Tim Burnham to do me a proper toast. Tim probably knows this fella. He's well wired."'

'"Well wired." What does *that* mean?'

'I was going to ask you.'

'*Me?*'

'You're the one he was talking about.' Cobb slid the folded papers across the table to Burnham. 'Have a look at it. Run it through your typewriter. Give it some of that old black magic.'

'And all I have to go on is: "That dog won't hunt."'

'That may say more than it seems. The President is not without instincts. He didn't get to be President by being thick. I think he smells something wrong – maybe not with the speech but with the visit, or with the Pasha himself. *Some*thing has set off an alarm in his head, even if he doesn't know what it is.' Cobb smiled. 'He has great faith that you'll find it for him. After all, you're well wired.'

'You want to give me a hint about how I find it?'

Cobb shrugged. 'If I were you, I'd call the CIA.'

'What d'you mean, call the CIA? You can't just call the CIA.'

'Of course you can. They're in the book.'

'Why are they going to talk to me?'

'You're one of the President's men, Timothy. They *have* to. Never forget it.'

Burnham picked up the folded papers. 'What about the

154

NSC guy who wrote this? Maybe he's already called the CIA.'

'The NSC hates the CIA, and vice versa. They don't speak.'

'Wonderful. I . . .'

A shadow fell across the table. Burnham looked up into the pointing fingertip of Mario Epstein, who loomed above him.

'You!' Epstein growled. 'What's your name?'

'Huh?' Burnham was startled, and had he tried to say anything more, he would have stammered.

'Do you work here?'

'Yes. I –'

Cobb to the rescue. 'Mario, this is –'

Epstein ignored him. 'What do you do?'

A steward came up behind Epstein and said softly, 'Phone for you, sir.'

Epstein shot a final venomous glance at Burnham and turned on his heel.

Burnham saw, beyond Epstein, the blue-pinstripe back of the Secretary of State hurrying out of the Mess – a proud man, a kind and good man, probably, a man who wished ill to no one and who strove to make the world a better place, now humiliated, pummelled into submissive jelly by a bullying schmuck. Burnham felt sorry for the Secretary, wanted to shout encouragement to him – 'Don't take that shit!' – and at the same time hated him as a reminder of his own cowardice in melting before Sarah's swami-inspired fusillade. Nice guys finish last. Rudeness is its own reward.

Enough.

Burnham snapped, 'Hey!' The sound of his own voice surprised him, for he had made no conscious decision to speak.

Jolted, Epstein stopped.

'What about you?' Burnham said. 'Do you work here?'

Epstein's eyebrows popped upward until they formed perfect crescent moons above his tiny eyes. His mouth opened, but no sound emerged.

All the colour drained from Cobb, as if someone had pulled a plug in his toes.

Burnham continued to look expectantly at Epstein, as if awaiting a civil reply to his civil question.

Epstein pointed at Cobb. His pointing finger trembled. 'I'll see *you* later,' he said, and he departed.

'That was not smart,' Cobb whispered to Burnham. 'Not smart at all.'

'Why are you whispering, Warner? You told me: I'm one of the President's men. I'll never forget it.'

Burnham signed his cheque and pushed his chair back from the table.

His wife had kicked him out of the house. His home was a cubicle in a den of outcasts, misfits and deviates. He had just committed an unforgivable act of lèse-majesté against the second most powerful man in the country, and the odds were that by noon he would be out of work.

He should have been frightened, depressed and confused.

But he had done something, actually become – if for only a moment – an actor instead of a reactor.

He felt terrific.

Dyanna had just arrived by the time Burnham returned to his office. She wore a dress of yellow cotton decorated with blue butterflies. She was humming the theme music from *Gone With The Wind* and arranging a huge flower display on her desk.

'What's the occasion?' Burnham asked her.

'You are.'

'I am?'

'These flowers symbolize power and success. Roses are for lovers. Lilies are for dead people. These are for people on the move.'

'They are?'

'Uh-huh. I read it in "Ask Beth".'

Burnham did not inquire as to what 'Ask Beth' was. The explanation would be bound to include a numbing *recitatif*

156

of an entire chapter from her childhood, and he was on a detail for the Leader of the Free World.

'Forgive me if I shut the door,' he said. 'This Q Clearance business is a bore.'

'Of course. I'll hold your calls.'

Not bad, Burnham thought as he crossed to his desk. The real reason he had shut the door was that he had to call the CIA, and he had never called the CIA before, and he didn't want Dyanna to hear him make an idiot of himself on the phone, and it never occurred to him that he could ask her to get the CIA for him. But he hadn't had to explain anything. Q Clearance said it all. Convenient. It could be used for playing solitaire or reading a book or taking a nap.

He dialled the White House switchboard and said, 'This is Timothy Burnham.'

'I know,' said the operator.

'You do?'

'Sure. Your light just went on.'

'Oh. Can you tell me how I get hold of the CIA?'

'Who in the CIA?'

'Ah . . .' He had no idea whom he should speak to. He didn't think of the CIA as people. It was a creature that lived in as enchanted forest in Langley, Virginia, and emerged on misty nights to commit dark deeds that no one ever heard about until, eventually, a wizard named Seymour Hersh unearthed and exposed them in the pages of *The New York Times*. No one seemed to exist in the CIA: they existed only after they left, when they assumed the identity of 'former CIA employee' and went on to play a role in real life as convict, corpse, author, turncoat, informer or unimpeachable source for '60 Minutes'.

'The Director?'

'Ah . . . okay, sure.' The Director! Wait a minute! He didn't even remember the Director's name. The Director was a professional non-person, a computer genius who was said to be as smart as Einstein, as ruthless as Goebbels and as reclusive as Howard Hughes. The President had learned a lesson from the bad publicity that had accrued to Ronald

Reagan from the appointment of bulldog Bill Casey. Winslow wanted a man who was squeaky clean, hard as nails and totally unconcerned about his image or his personal welfare.

The Director's name almost never appeared in print. He refused to give interviews. He refused to testify before Congress – or, if he did testify, did so under such elaborate secrecy and with such intimidating mien that none of the solons dared violate his confidences. He had made it clear from the outset that he didn't give a damn for subpoenas or contempt citations. They could cite him for anything they chose, but he put them on warning that he would ignore any and all summonses and was prepared to precipitate a Constitutional crisis by forcing them to send Federal marshals to Langley.

Accused once of lying in a deposition to the Senate Select Committee on Intelligence, the Director issued a public statement that said, 'Of course I lied. That's part of my job. I'm paid to keep the secrets. You can't keep the secrets if you don't lie.'

In public, the President's attitude toward the Director was that of an indulgent parent toward a naughty but prodigious offspring. In private, he considered the Director one of his greatest assets, a lightning rod who deflected unwanted static from the Presidency, a vital bulwark of the independent Executive Branch.

Burnham didn't want to speak to the Director, had no desire to get into a pissing match with a junkyard dog. The operator could give him the Director's number, but he didn't have to dial it. He'd locate a basement-level functionary who could give him the information he needed.

But the operator didn't give him the number. She put him through.

'Four-four-nine-one,' said a voice.

'Ah . . . ah . . . is this the . . . ah . . . Director's office?'

'Four-four-nine-one.'

'This is the White House.'

'Who in the White House?'

'Timothy Burnham.'

'Spell it.'

Burnham spelled it.

'Hang up.'

'What?'

'Hang up!'

Before Burnham could hang up, the line went dead.

Thirty seconds later, one of the lights on his phone console flashed, then his buzzer buzzed. He picked up the phone and punched the intercom button.

'It's the CIA!' Dyanna said breathlessly.

'Who in the CIA?'

'He didn't say.'

Burnham punched the flashing button. 'Burnham.'

'What can I do for you, Mr Burnham?'

'Who is this?'

'You called us.'

'Is this the Director?'

The voice stifled a laugh. 'Hardly.'

'How come you made me hang up?' Burnham wasn't peeved, merely curious.

'An elementary precaution. I could call back through the White House switchboard and verify who you were.'

'Oh.' Burnham's impulse was to tell this man that he had been assigned to write the President's toast to the Pasha of Banda and that he needed background material on the Pasha. But before the first word could escape his lips, he sensed that that gambit would sound too routine. The upper echelon of the Central Intelligence Agency would take umbrage at being treated like a Stop'n Shop for White House writers. Instead, he said, 'The President is meeting today with the Pasha of Banda. The NSC briefed him on Banda. He found the briefing inadequate.'

'What did he expect?' The voice chuckled, and Burnham knew he had chosen the right tack.

'He feels there are things he hasn't been told.'

'He's right.'

'He told me to call and . . . get your input.' Whoever you are, Burnham thought.

'He told you to?'

There was only the slightest emphasis on the word 'he', just enough to make Burnham swallow and wonder whether this disembodied voice would insist on verifying that, too. 'Absolutely. He's not without instincts, you know. He didn't get to be President by being . . . gullible.'

'No, no,' the voice said quickly. 'Of course not.'

Good, Burnham thought. He's on the defensive. Now flatter him. 'He said to me, "Check with them. If anybody knows this fella, they do. They're well wired."'

'He's right. Okay. You got it.'

'Thanks. It's EOB 102.' He was about to hang up, when a question occurred to him. 'By the way, how come you didn't have any input into the original briefing?'

The voice paused. 'The President knows where we are. He has our number. If he wants help from us, all he has to do is ask. If he wants to rely on . . . amateurs . . . that's his business.'

Offended vanity. Burnham couldn't believe it. The CIA was like a teenager who hadn't been asked to the prom till the last minute. Suppose this Pasha was a Libyan thug bent on putting a bullet in the President between the coq au vin and the Cherries Jubilee.

The voice must have read signals in Burnham's silence, for it said, 'If this guy was dangerous, we'd ring a bell. But he isn't. He's a punk.'

'Right. If I have any questions, who do I ask for?'

'Four-four-nine-one.'

'Okay, four-four-nine-one. Over and out.' Burnham hung up, unfolded and smoothed the papers Cobb had given him, and began to read the NSC draft of the toast.

It was a predictable four hundred words of vapid bushwa: a welcoming paragraph that included a light reference to the similarities in the climates of summertime Washington and year-round Banda; a paragraph detailing the history of the fruitful relationship of mutual respect and co-operation between the Republic of Banda and the United States (the word 'history' being almost hyperbole in itself, since the Republic had been carved out of the jungle barely thirty months ago); a paragraph predicting an even more fruitful relationship in the future (but never mentioning oil); a paragraph praising the Pasha's contributions to the community of nations, and, finally, a paragraph praising the Pasha personally and ending with the obligatory toast.

Nothing here to get excited about, Burnham decided. He wondered what the President had objected to.

The door opened. Dyanna spoke softly, as if she were entering a temple and didn't want to disturb the priests.

'Mr Burnham, your mail is here. Your . . . special mail.' She crossed the office and handed him a large manila envelope on which the Department of Energy's return address was prominent in the top left corner.

'How did it come? An armoured car? A state trooper?'

'No, sir. Regular interoffice mail, with the other junk.'

'They send James Bond over here to threaten my life if I ever open my yap about what's in it, and then they put it in the mail?'

'Yes, sir.'

'Look at this!' Burnham pointed to a printed notice on the bottom of the envelope: 'If found, return immediately to the Department of Energy. Do not open or read.' 'Why don't they for chrissakes slug it "Please forward to the Russian Embassy"?'

'Yes, sir.' Dyanna backed out of the room and closed the door, to leave Burnham to read his Q Clearance mail.

Though the envelope had been slugged with no classification, each document within was marked TOP SECRET – Q CLEARANCE ONLY in bold black letters.

Burnham didn't understand any of the documents. One was an interminable paper – in technical language pocked with the misuse of the word 'parameters' – that seemed to have something to do with the properties of fission. One was a succession of mathematical formulaes, none of which was remotely familiar to Burnham, whose math education had stopped with basic trigonometry. Two were speeches by DOE officials that had been delivered to scientific gatherings and were therefore (or so it seemed to Burnham) matters of public record and should not have been classified at all. And one spelled out the specific benefits offered by his medical plan for reimbursement for purchases of prescription drugs.

Burnham turned on his shredder. It hummed hungrily. He fed it first the technical paper, page by page, enjoying his alchemical power to turn secrets into strands of trash, then the two public speeches and the medical-plan advisory. He paused, as if to let the machine digest its main course before he fed it its dessert of mathematical formulae.

There was a shy knock on the door, and Dyanna poked her head into the room and said, 'Would you like some coffee?'

Burnham smiled. It was against Dyanna's nature to offer to perform domestic services for him. He imagined her sitting at her desk refereeing a battle between her self-respect and her curiosity. Clearly, curiosity had won in the early rounds. Well, what the hell . . . Secrets were only fun if they could be shared. 'Sure,' he said. 'Thanks.'

The coffee was already in her hand, already sweetened. She crossed to his desk and handed it to him, trying dramatically not to let her eyes stray to the shredder, or to the paper still in his hand.

'What do you make of this?' Burnham handed her the sheet of formulae.

'I shouldn't . . .' Dyanna made a show of demurring.

'If you can understand it, you deserve to see it. Anyone who can read this garbage should be Q Cleared automatically.'

Dyanna plucked the paper from his hand and ran her eyes down the page. Burnham could see a mist of bewilderment cloud her eyes like cataracts.

'Golly,' was all she said.

'My sentiments exactly.' He took the paper from her and

held it above the shredder, to which he spoke as if it was a performing seal. 'Ready, Smiley?'

'It has a name?'

'I think "Smiley" fits, don't you? He eats the secrets so the bad guys can't get them. And we give him the secrets, so we're Smiley's people.'

Burnham enjoyed his little joke. Dyanna, who thought he was speaking Dutch, nodded politely and said, 'Why, yes.'

'Don't forget to buy Smiley his begonias. We'll put topsoil in his mouth there, and plant the begonias, and all the doo-doo will go right down into the basket.'

The outer door to the office swung open, and Dyanna looked grateful for the distraction.

A short young man with a crew cut and a set of pectoral muscles that threatened to pop the buttons on his drip-dry shirt was holding an envelope. Dyanna reached for the envelope, but the man shook his head – no – and gestured at Burnham. Dyanna ushered him into the office.

'Mr Burnham?'

'Yes.'

'I'm from Langley. May I see your identification?'

Burnham showed him his White House pass.

The man proffered a slip of paper for Burnham to sign, acknowledging receipt, then surrendered the envelope.

Burnham said, 'Since when do you characters pack heat on your home turf?'

'Beg pardon?'

Burnham pointed to a prominent lump beneath the trouser leg on the man's right calf. 'Either you've got a compound fracture of the tibia, or else you're wearing an ankle holster.'

The man stopped breathing.

'Don't worry,' Burnham said. 'My lips are sealed.'

The man left quickly. Dyanna looked at Burnham and said, ' "Pack heat"?'

'This Q Clearance is great.' Burnham grinned, 'Whole new perceptions flood my brain. I feel . . . cosmic.'

Dyanna's eyes were as big as golf balls.

Burnham opened the CIA envelope and turned toward his desk. He expected to hear Dyanna leave, and when he didn't, he stopped and looked at her.

The siren song of secrecy had captivated her. Her hands fluttered, trying to appear busy, and her mouth worked, trying to form words.

Burnham went to her and took her by the elbow and gently led her to the door, saying, 'Sorry.'

Dyanna mumbled something apologetic.

Burnham sat behind his desk. The CIA document was three pages long, single-spaced. It was described as 'A Psychiatric Profile of Babar Sumba Emir, Pasha of Banda'.

Amazing, Burnham thought. Everybody thinks that the CIA has been emasculated – look at Iran, look at Nicaragua, look at Jamaica – but they keep on truckin'. They've got shrinks in the bedrooms of the palace in Banda. How do you con a pasha into lying on a couch and telling you about his mother and his dreams and his terror of spiders?

The answer was, Burnham discovered, you don't: what the paper didn't admit, but what was quickly clear, was that the paper was a *long-distance* psychiatric analysis of the pasha, conducted by two Freudians in a room in Langley, Virginia. They had never spoken to the pasha, never met him, never even seen him. The grist for their analytical mill came from field reports, newspaper accounts, rumours and top-secret cables from American Embassy personnel desperate for guidance about dealing with a head of state of an emerging nation that promised to provide America with a significant percentage of its oil needs well into the Twenty-First Century, whose behaviour could be described by the most charitable of Pollyannas as 'disturbingly eccentric'.

Burnham knew nothing about psychiatry, but he supposed that long-distance shrinkage, when applied to a person of intelligence and subtle character, would be useless.

In this case, however, it was probably quite effective, for very little actual analysis was necessary. The mass of intelligence about the Pasha pointed to a conclusion for which a PhD was wholly unnecessary: the Pasha was a certifiable madman.

The man claimed to be a direct descendant of Buddha. His documented youth as a banana-picker had, he said, been lived by someone else. He had been jailed for stealing a box of ballpoint pens, had escaped by setting fire to the jail and hiding in a cistern while the building (and twenty four other prisoners) burned to charcoal around him. Emerging from the ashes, he was dubbed a phoenix by a rum-soaked English missionary who saw the hand of God in everything from kwashiorkor to pink gin, and Babar Sumba took the opportunity to discard his mortal past and to declare himself a creature born of the fire. People flocked to him, first out of boredom and curiosity, then for amusement, then for excitement, for his answer to all problems was to set them afire. ('Pyromania has been a compelling force in the Pasha since early childhood,' the report read.)

When Banda became independent, Babar Sumba was one of three candidates for the presidency of the new Republic. He disposed of one of his opponents by dousing him with gasoline and setting him afire. The other withdrew.

Then an Amoco team discovered oil, which Babar Sumba interpreted as divine affirmation of his leadership. Being President was no longer enough. Nor did he want to be a king or a sheik or a sultan; the world was full of them. So he decided that he was Pasha – not *a* pasha, but *the* Pasha.

He hired a chic American architect to begin work on a palace of Carrara marble and gold leaf. He decreed a 'Miss Banda' contest and took all twelve finalists as his wives. (One rebelled, so he had her smeared with jellied gas and touched off in front of the other eleven.)

He had no opponents. Somehow, though, the goon squads he dispatched into the highlands always unearthed a dissident or two for him to burn. The fact that the goon

165

squads had been told that if they didn't locate a dissident, one of their own number would be sacrificed undoubtedly sparked their zeal.

A year ago, the Pasha's wives had begun to bear children. (As he read on, Burnham's eyes bugged and he couldn't suppress a gasp and a bubble of nausea.) As luck had it, of the first eight children born, five were female. The Pasha was displeased. Male children were prized. One male could service a dozen females. A surfeit of females was worse than a redundancy: it was a burden on the economy and on the social structure of Banda. Worst of all, a majority of female children in a litter of eight might reflect badly on the genetic divinity of the Pasha.

By blind lottery, the Pasha selected four of the five female children and ordered that they be burned alive.

Burnham put down the paper without reading the medical jargon diagnosing the Pasha's psychosis. Who cared what they called it?

The President shouldn't have him in the house.

He called four-four-nine-one at the CIA. 'A punk!' he shouted. 'You call that man a punk? He is a fucking maniac!'

'To each his own. We can't run the world.'

'We've got to advise the President not to see him.'

'What's this "we" stuff? You tell him what you want. I'm not in the principle business.'

'All right, I will.' Burnham paused. Principles. What would Sarah say? Was this a question of principles? Deciding not to entertain a psychopath? It was basic morality. Morality and principles weren't necessarily the same thing.

Were they?

Four-four-nine-one spoke up. 'It's none of my affair, but you're walking in a mine field here. Banda's a strategic bonanza for us. It's not only the oil, even though that's the big-ticket item. The Pasha's gonna let us put in a deep-water terminal, and if it should happen to have all the capabilities of a naval base, well, he let us know he's not one to criticize. It'll be a backup for Subic Bay until the

Philippines cave in and go radical red – and that is going to happen, Mr Burnham, believe me – and then, overnight, it'll replace Subic Bay. Now, what d'you think the Pasha's gonna do if the President boots him out? He may be nuts, but he's not stupid. He knows what he's got. He'll get back in his gold-plated 747 and go straight to the Ivans.'

'But . . .' Burnham sputtered. 'Suppose some reporter gets hold of this? The man cooks *children!*'

'Who cares? I mean . . .' Four-four-nine-one cleared his throat. 'That's a rhetorical question. First of all, most of the public doesn't believe the press any more, unless it re-inforces something they already know or want to believe. Oh sure, some of those knee-jerk groups like Amnesty International will raise a stink, but they're always yelling about something. Most of the public has a selective mem-ory: they remember what they want to remember. At the moment, they don't remember who Somoza was or what he was like. Where's the public uproar about our great and good friend Stroessner in Paraguay? Zip. They don't even care that we hired Klaus Barbie after the war. I tell you, everybody over here was walking on eggs when *that* broke. But it lasted two days, and then pffft! Gone.'

Burnham insisted. 'I don't think you appreciate what a good reporter could do with a monster like this.'

'And I don't think *you* appreciate the public's capacity for not giving a damn. The next time the Arabs stop fighting long enough to kick up the price of oil, or the Ayatollah gets really pissed and closes down the Persian Golf, and we're back to two-hour waits in line to buy two-dollars-a-gallon gasoline, do you really think Joe Sixpack and Betsy Buick are gonna thank the President for kicking out the little brown oil man – just because he likes to set fire to other little brown people?'

'But . . . I . . .' Burnham felt a stammer coming on. Then he said, 'I see.'

Four-four-nine-one was silent, and Burnham thought that he could feel the man smiling.

'Principles are expensive,' said four-four-nine-one.

'Why didn't the NSC tell the President?'

'How long have you been at the White House?'

'Why?' Burnham saw no reason to confide in a stranger the fact that while he had been at the White House for years, he had been alone with the President exactly once, yesterday, and had never been in a position of advising him to do or not do, say or not say, anything.

'The NSC doesn't want to clutter his head. The decision has been made, by them and State – which means by Mario Epstein – and facts will just confuse him. Look: put principles aside for a second and consider two practical issues. One, will the President listen to you?'

Burnham spoke before he had time to consider his words. 'I doubt it.'

'Me too. So all you'll do is start a fight that you're bound to lose. Two, it's too late to stop it now. The Pasha's already in the air, and unless you've got the clout to deny him landing rights at Andrews, the visit's gonna happen. It strikes me that all you can do is cut your losses. Give the President a draft that will keep him from looking like a complete ass.'

Burnham smiled to himself. 'Yes. I think he'd appreciate that.'

'Send me a copy if you want.'

'If there's time.'

'No. On second thought, forget it. I don't want to know.' Four-four-nine-one paused. 'I think you're a dangerous person to be involved with.'

Burnham laughed and hung up. He felt good, almost elated, and he had no idea why. His mind was a conflicted mess. For the first time in his months at the White House, he was faced with an issue of right and wrong – and not just with the absolutes, but with their many subtle shadings. Right would be to turn the Pasha away at the gate, but it would probably also be wrong for the country. Besides, he had no power to enforce a right decision. Epstein would slice him up like liverwurst and feed his pieces to the Pasha

168

on a plate. So he would have to seek a compromise between his own feelings and the NSC draft and Epstein's militancy and the President's . . . the President's what? He had no way of knowing what the President wanted to say. All he knew was that the President had detected an unsavory odour about the Pasha's visit.

It was troublesome. Difficult. Fascinating. Scary. Heady.

He re-read the NSC draft of the toast. Diplomatic platitudes galloping on a field of boundless praise. He underlined a couple of useful statistics, then set the draft aside. He turned on his IBM Correcting Selectric III, rolled a sheet of paper around the platen and straightened it, flexed his fingers and held them poised above the humming keyboard. He felt like Robert Stack at the controls of a B-29, about to embark on a mission in *12 O'Clock High*; like Matthew Broderick tapping into the Pentagon's nuclear codes in *War Games*.

He began to type.

An hour later, he was finished. The speech was still four hundred words long. It had to be. ('I will have four-hundred-word toasts,' the President insisted, 'four paragraphs long, with four sentences to a paragraph, four words to a sentence and four letters to a word. I won't have the goddam duchess passing out in her Jello.') But otherwise, it bore no resemblance to the NSC draft.

The light-hearted comparison of Banda's weather to Washington's was gone. Burnham had decided that there should be no comparison of Banda with anything in the United States. In its stead was a reference to the length of the Pasha's journey and recognition of the fact that issues of great moment were always more fruitfully discussed face-to-face.

Instead of a recitation of Banda's relationship with the US, the President would (respectfully, not condescendingly) refer to Banda's youth as a nation and express his hope that the Pasha would look to older nations for examples of wise leadership – touchy, but phrased so delicately

(Burnham applauded himself) that only a master of fancied slights could take offence.

The body of the speech detailed the agreement that the President and the Pasha would be working to achieve. It contained phrases like 'mutual interest' and 'bulwark of freedom' and gave the President the chance to (as Burnham knew he would) ad-lib about the great strides in education, health and social welfare that Banda would undoubtedly make with the bonanza from its new-found wealth. (This would be the President's hedge against the day when and if the Pasha was unmasked as a vicious tyrant. 'He swore up and down to me that he was going to pump that money into social programmes', the President would say. 'What was I gonna do, call the man a liar? Look how long it took John Kennedy to get wise to Fidel Castro.')

There was no praise for Banda, not for the Pasha himself. Burnham opted to praise Banda's people, some 30,000 rice farmers, banana growers and sugarcane workers. Many of them had but to look over their shoulders to see the Bronze Age, and the vast majority were illiterate. Their deities were the very practical gods of sun, rain, moon and fire. They were afflicted by leprosy, rickets, beriberi, yaws, dengue and most of the other wasting and rotting disease. But Burnham referred to none of that: he called them good, simple, God-fearing people whose lives would probably be changed by affluence but who, the President would pray, would retain their basic virtues.

Finally, there was the toast – to Banda, to the people of Banda, to the opportunities for the people of Banda, to co-operation with Banda, and – almost, but not quite, as an afterthought – to the Pasha of Banda.

Burnham was proud. The toast was good. It said what he wanted to say, albeit mostly by omission. A perceptive diplomat or an astute reporter would be able to read between the lines and realize that the Pasha was a man the President intended to feed with a long spoon.

He gave the toast to Dyanna to type clean and in delivery form – triple-spaced, wide margins, each new statement beginning a new line, every place name and proper name phoneticized ('BAHN-da', 'BAH-bar SOOM-bah ay-MEER'). Later, after the President had approved the text, it would be typed on heavy bond on the speech typewriter. Then he returned to his desk to ponder the cover memo he would send to the President.

The memo was more of a challenge to Burnham than the speech itself. He had to appear informed but not presumptuous – after all, the National Security council was a team of professional experts, and he but a petty scribe – helpful but not pushy – a writer's franchise was to enunciate, not formulate, policy – confident but not critical – the NSC draft was first-class, of course, but perhaps a few altered phrases would better convey the President's message.

The memo could contain no slips, no errors, no double-entendres. Communicating with the President was an unforgiving art. There was no such thing as a confidential – let alone secret – communication. It was seen, first, by a secretary, then (more often than not) by anyone who happened to be in the room with the President chose to check the missive's accuracy, then (inevitably) by Epstein, then, finally, by the archivists who had to find a slot for it in the vast mountain of Presidential papers that would eventually repose in a multi-million dollar Winslow library in Ohio. A simple memo could become a footnote to history, and the careless writer who let slip an offhand remark or a lame witticism or a sly barb at a staff rival ran the risk of becoming a carbuncle on the ass of posterity.

Burnham wrote and rewrote, crushing discarded attempts into paper balls that he aimed at his wastebasket and that invariably missed since most of the mouth of the wastebasket was covered by the shredder.

When at last he had a document he liked, he pulled a clean sheet of White House stationery from his desk. 'The White House, Washington', was all it said. Nice understatement. He intended to type the final draft of the memo himself, partly because he often rewrote when he retyped, but also because he felt proprietary toward the memo: it was *his*, his statement, his position, his first foray into the no-man's-land of policy.

He hesitated briefly before applying the ultimate classification slug. It was not to be used lightly. Staffers had been chastised, even demoted, for scattering it indiscriminately about the Executive, treating it like a tool to enhance their own stature. Burnham had never used it at all, except in jest to the other writers, knowing that it would humbug no one but the archivists. It wasn't that the classification was particularly effective, but rather that it was regarded as a privilege reserved for the exalted.

What the hell . . . this was a memo based on a Top Secret CIA paper that accused a head of state of being a homicidal pyromaniac. If this wasn't an appropriate occasion for the ultimate slug, what was?

So he typed the portentous words: EYES ONLY.

THE WHITE HOUSE
Washington

EYES ONLY

Memo to the President
From: Timothy Y. Burnham
Re: Banda toast tonight
Here is a new draft of tonight's toast to the Pasha of Banda.

The President's instincts were acute: the Pasha is not a man with whom the President should appear to be on friendly personal terms. He is a man of unstable violent personality, and there is evidence that he has slaughtered many of his own people.

I believe that this draft acknowledges the need for co-operation between the US and Banda without, in any way, endorsing the Pasha himself or his lunatic views.

The President should be aware that the Pasha has several wives, of whom three will be at the dinner. It is

172

important that the President avoid dancing with *any* of the Pasha's wives, since the Pasha might, on mercurial whim, offer a wife as a gift to the President. Declining such a gift from a man who believes he is God incarnate could be extremely awkward.

Burnham was pleased. The memo flattered the President without criticizing the NSC. It documented the case against the Pasha without going into such lurid detail that the President would worry that he had been suckered by staff flakes into breaking bread with a dime-store Hitler. And it demonstrated that Burnham was, as advertised, well-wired and savvy enough to propose a way for the President to avoid unnecessary embarrassment.

He buzzed for Dyanna. When he gave her the memo, he saw her face light up as she saw the EYES ONLY slug. Then, discreetly, she looked away.

'Make two copies,' he said, 'then put the original with the original of the toast, and –'

'Take them to Mr Cobb.'

'No.' Burnham had decided to route the memo direct to the President, as he felt he had Cobb's tacit leave to do. Time was short; the President had requested Burnham by name, so Cobb would not presume to edit the draft before the President saw it. And the normal routing procedure would place a draft with the NSC, from which aggrieved protests were bound to erupt. 'Walk them over to Evelyn Witt and tell her we're on a tight deadline.'

'Yes, sir!' Dyanna smiled a smile that Burnham thought she would have reserved for a marriage proposal from the Secretary of State.

Burnham looked at his watch. It was 11.40. 'I'm going to play squash. I should be back by one or a little after.'

'Right!' Dyanna wheeled as enthusiastically as a Parris Island recruit and marched out of the office.

Watching her go, Burnham thought: there's something pathetic about this. Today we are rich in the coin of the realm. The President likes us, and so we exist. We are

173

affirmed. Tomorrow he may not like us, and we will be denied, we will not exist.

And that kind of thinking, he said to himself as he stood and pushed his chair back, is a waste of time. You want to play the game, you play by the rules.

He kept his squash bag and racquet in a cabinet beneath a bookcase. He opened the cabinet. It was empty. It took him a second to remember: of course it was empty. He had left his racquet and clothes in his room, four stories above the squash courts.

His room. It didn't sound right, didn't feel right. Wasn't right.

He hadn't thought about Sarah all morning, and now that he did, his stomach began to hurt. He felt guilty about not having thought about her, and stupid for feeling guilty because he hadn't done anything – *she* had done it all – and cowardly for feeling helpless because there had to be *some*thing he could do – he wasn't going to let fifteen years of marriage go down the chute because of a misunderstanding – and tormented because he knew that it wasn't just a misunderstanding – that was only the trigger, Sarah was falling (had fallen?) out of love with him because she couldn't separate her emotional life from her political life – and angry because that wasn't fair, and confused because maybe it *was* fair to use a person's attitude toward the Big Issues as a basis for an emotional attachment, and frustrated because why should stuff like Apartheid be allowed to wreck his marriage, where is it written that we all have to be our brother's keeper all the goddam time? – and determined that he was going to fight.

He picked up the phone and dialled his home number.

No answer.

He felt like a whoopee cushion sat on by a fat person.

174

Eight

He refused to change in his room and ride the elevator down to the basement. He was not ready to acknowledge that he was a resident of the YMCA, did not want to have to answer questions from anyone he might encounter in the elevator or in the hallways by the squash courts. Besides, he enjoyed the camaraderie of the locker room.

So he threw his squash clothes into the bag, grabbed his racquet and descended to the locker room.

Four men were already in the locker room: a pair from State, who played together often, and a pair whom Burnham didn't recognize but who knew each other and were obviously matched against each other. Burnham changed slowly, expecting a lone man to rush into the locker room at the last minute, tearing at his tie and kicking off his shoes, complaining about the traffic or the lack of parking spaces or thoughtless superiors who had burdened him with urgent trivia.

But no one appeared, which meant that Hal had been unable to find an opponent for him. Either he would have to play alone, which would give him little exercise and no pleasure, or he would have to endure forty minutes of being cut to ribbons by Hal himself. Hal was self-taught, but he played squash every day and was quick as a cougar and mean as a shrew. His racquet was a scalpel with which, methodically, he dissected an opponent.

At the first stroke of noon, Burnham left the locker room and walked to the row of squash courts. Hal was standing by the door to court number 1. He was a symphony in white, from platinum skull to ivory skin to milky polo shirt to Cloroxed ducks to vanilla shoes. Someone stood behind him, in the shadows, an opponent.

Burnham smiled, relieved.

'Timothy Burnham,' Hal said formally, 'meet Eva Pym.'

A woman.

She stepped around Hal and extended her hand. She looked nervous.

She looked nervous? Burnham was suddenly frantic. He wanted to call for help. He had never played squash with a woman. How do you play squash with a woman? The rules must be different. No bumping or checking? He'd have to go easy on her. How do you go easy on somebody in a squash game? Suppose she was good, better than he. Suppose he lost. This was supposed to be an hour of relaxation and exercise, not a test of his manhood and self-esteem. If he won, he won nothing, he was *supposed* to win. If he lost, he was a . . . a wimp. He'd rather play against Hal. At least he expected to lose to Hal.

The kaleidoscope of anxieties jangled in his mind for perhaps a second, just long enough for him to realize he was staring at the woman's hand. He took the hand and grasped it and said, weakly, 'Hi.'

'Timothy works for the White House,' Hal said brightly, providing (as he always did for new opponents) conversational fodder. He was as considerate as a hostess at a diplomatic soirée. 'He lives in –' he hesitated for a split second '– Georgetown. Eva is a caterer and a nutritionist. She insists that I start taking a high-potency B-complex vitamin.'

The woman took a step forward, into the light, and Burnham saw her for the first time. Her blond hair was tied back in a ponytail. She wore no makeup. Her nose was straight, her cheekbones high, her jaw strong, her lips thin and perfect, her skin like polished walnut. She wore a baggy Bennington College sweat suit, but the muscles in her arm suggested that her entire body was fit and finely tuned.

She was beautiful.

Burnham felt faint. Suppose he hit her with his racquet. It was one thing to hit a man; men were supposed to be scarred. But if he opened a nasty gash on this face . . . he'd probably go to jail.

Please. Let the President call. Anything.

'I left this number,' he said to Hal.

'Don't worry.' Hal grinned. 'I'll tell the President you're in a meeting.' He put one hand on Burnham's arm, the other on Eva's. 'Enjoy yourselves, children.'

Burnham pushed open the door to the court. He started to duck down to go through the small opening, then caught himself and backed off and gestured for Eva to go first.

She refused, waving him ahead. 'No sexism in combat,' she said.

When they were both inside the court, Burnham shut the door, isolating the two of them in a brilliantly lighted white box. 'Have you played a lot?'

'In college. Not much since. I hope I can give you a game.'

'Me too,' No! Asshole! 'I mean . . . I hope *I* can give *you* a game.'

'Never mind.' She smiled. 'We'll have fun.'

Burnham dropped a squash ball from his hand onto the wood floor. It didn't bounce, but rolled languidly against the wall. The hard rubber ball was cold, and the rubber had no elasticity. He should have held it under a hot-water faucet for thirty seconds.

'I'll warm it up,' he said, and he began to rub it between his palms.

'Here.' Eva reached under her sweatshirt, hunched her shoulders, and brought out a squash ball. She flung it to the floor, and it bounced to her waist. 'Let's use mine.'

Burnham gazed at her dumbly.

'A bra,' she said with a little laugh, 'is a coat of many colours.'

177

Burnham wanted to grab the ball from her, to feel it, examine it, smell it. She had kept it warm in her bra, in the fold of her breast.

I can't play squash, Burnham concluded. This woman is going to drive me mad.

Stop it! Do what Milan Kundera says: separate your sexuality from your self. Compartmentalize the elements of your humanity. It may be possible to regard a sexual partner as an athletic opponent, but it is impossible to regard an athletic opponent as a sex object. See yourself in segments.

What?!

He wasn't going to go mad. He had *gone* mad.

Eva hit the ball at the front wall.

Surprised, unready, Burnham flailed at the ball and missed it. It dribbled into the back corner. He picked it up and squeezed it, not knowing what to expect. It felt like a warm rubber ball. Nothing breasty about it.

He hit the ball at the front wall. She returned it. He returned it. She returned it. He returned it. She returned it. He hit it harder. She walloped it. He retrieved it off the back wall and belted it cross-court. She took a step, dropped her racquet head and whipped off a backhand that fired the ball on a sharp angle to the front wall, whence it caromed to the side wall, dropped to the floor . . . and died.

Burnham was in trouble. She was strong, quick, sure-handed and experienced. She had good ball sense.

By the end of the brief warm-up, Burnham knew that his only chance for victory lay in surprise, in constantly changing the game on her, breaking her rhythm, keeping her from setting up for the smooth strokes that she hit better than he. He resolved to imagine that she was the hirsute Treasury drone he had played the day before. He would let her get into a point, and then he would dink her to death.

They played for the right to serve. Eva won. Burnham stood in the receiver's box, his eyes focused on the front wall, waiting to see the black missile streak toward him. But nothing happened. He glanced to his left.

She was removing her sweat suit.

'Not fair,' he said before he could stop himself.

'What do you mean?'

She wore a white Bennington T-shirt through which her bra was plainly visible, and white runner's shorts with high swoops over each hip that did not cover all the firm flesh at the bottom of her bottom and that revealed the sharp outline of her miniature underpants. Her calves were turned as perfectly as if on a lathe, her thighs taut and lined with muscle fibres. Her tan continued well up under her shorts. Her chest was ample, her arms highlighted by hillocks of tricep.

Everything about her seemed to have been made to strict specifications.

'Be still my beating heart.' He blushed.

'Don't worry, Mr Burnham,' she said nicely. 'I'll get your heart working.'

Ah, but she's slick, Burnham thought. First she exposes an expanse of shiny-thigh. Then she feigns innocence of its seismic effect on me and maintains a facade of formality by calling me 'Mr Burnham'. Then she assumes the posture of an authority figure, a trainer.

'Your serve, Miss Pym.'

She lofted the ball high, aiming to have it caress the side wall and drop softly, without a bounce, at Burnham's feet. But he jumped the ball on the fly and swatted it smartly to the front wall, low, just above the tin. She lurched forward but could not reach it before it bounced twice.

'Good shot,' she said.

They changed sides. She served again, and stepped into the centre of the court, onto the 'T'.

The serve was a good one. It dropped like a dying duck an inch from the side wall. If Burnham swung at it, he would smash his racquet head against the wall. He took a step back, hoping to catch the ball on its bounce off the floor, but the ball was spinning crazily, and it jumped off the floor directly at his face, so he took another step back – and crashed into Eva.

179

They hit back to back. Her weight was forward, on the balls of her feet. His was backward, on his heels. So when they collided, she tumbled forward and he fell on top of her. He spun as he fell, instinctively (like a cat) trying to position himself to break his fall with his hands. One of his hands hit the floor to the left of her left shoulder, one to the right of her right hip. His right knee came to rest between her thighs. His head, the heaviest of all his corporal equipment, plunged deep into her left armpit.

His face was buried in the soft flesh of her underarm, in the swell of her pressed breast. His nose felt snug warmth and smelled soap and salt and a faint blend of spices.

He didn't want to move. He wanted to lie there and pull the covers up and take a nap and . . .

He felt a swelling in his shorts, taut pressure against the pocket of his jockstrap. Dear God! He was getting a hard on. (Milan Kundera wept.) He felt it spring free of its pouch. It was probably poking out the leg of his shorts. He didn't dare stand up.

'Are you okay?' Her voice came from inside her shirt.

'Yes. You?'

'Well . . . I have this head in my armpit.' She laughed.

He snapped his head back. 'Sorry. Sorry.' He pulled his head free and, bit by bit, disengaged his body from hers, backing away on his hands and knees. Before she could turn around, he bent down and checked his shorts. There it was. Judas Priest! He swivelled on his knees, turning his back to her, and shot his hand down the front of his shorts. He grabbed the offending member and, disregarding its painful protests, wrenched it back to a respectable stance. He pulled the tail of his shirt out of his shorts and let it hang out.

'You play for keeps, Mr Burnham,' Eva said, smiling.

He wanted to ask her to call him Timothy, but he thought not: he had forced quite enough intimacy on her for the time being. 'I *am* sorry, Miss Pym.'

'No harm done.' She found the ball in a corner. 'That was a let, so it's still love-one.'

'No, no, I insist. Your point. I never got near the ball.'

'Let's play it over.'

Keep arguing, Burnham told himself. Stall for time, till the creature in your pants dies a natural death. 'No, really. Your point. One all.'

Did she know? Her eyes left his face and travelled quickly down his front. She smiled and shrugged and said, 'Okay. Whatever you say.'

Burnham won the first game, 15–12. He was sure she had let him win, because she had stayed a point or two ahead all the way to 11-all and then, inexplicably, had made three unforced errors in succession. He double-faulted at 14–11, then she missed an absurdly easy shot to lose the game.

He was positive she had let him win when she thrashed him in the second game, 1–7, never ahead by less than four points, drawing him back and forth across the court like a fly on a spinning rod.

He didn't know why she had let him win the first game – a kindly gesture to his male ego, perhaps – but he was determined to take, not be given, the third game.

As the loser of the previous game, he served first. He knew she expected a high, slow dribbler, so he boomed a line-drive serve that zipped behind her and took her by surprise.

He swung at his second serve as if he were going to pattycake the ball, but at the last instant snapped his wrist and fired a low bullet that struck her in the hip.

Two-love.

As she prepared to receive his third serve, she looked at him with a theatrical sneer and said, 'I see your rotten plan. Vietnam squash.'

'What?'

'You plan to blow me away, turn me into a parking lot.'

'Beware, arch fiend.' Burnham chuckled. 'You haven't seen the half of it.'

He hit a dribbler and moved out onto the 'T'. She returned it hard down the centre, right at him. He stepped out of the ball's way and slashed it, floating a wicked slice that would die when it struck the front wall.

But the ball flew higher than he had hoped, and she had time to dash forward and scoop it up.

He could tell by the way she held her racquet as she ran that she meant to dink the ball into the corner, so he charged after her.

She wristed the ball softly into the corner. He reached around her and caught it an inch from the floor and flicked a little lob that soared over her head.

She shot her arm up, but the ball was already behind her head. She staggered backward, swung wildly, stepped on Burnham's foot, slammed her rear end into his shoulder and collapsed on top of him.

He lay on his back. Her pony tail was in his mouth. It tasted sweet and salty. His panting breath moved the little hairs around the base of her neck. He could see far into the pink cavern of her ear. She rolled off him and drove a heavy thigh into his crotch.

Not again, he prayed. I can't hide it this time.

She rolled onto her knees and elbows. He could see, down the front of her skirt, her breasts heaving as she breathed, and he yearned for one to escape its silky prison and flop free.

'We have to stop meeting like this,' she said. 'You're a married man.'

'How do you know?'

'Everybody's married.' She smiled. 'Aren't they?'

'Are you?'

'No. Who'd want a wife who can't get out of her own way?'

They both laughed, and they helped each other up. Her arm, as Burnham touched it, was slick with sweat, and once again he felt the creature stirring in his shorts. Quickly, he removed his hand, but he could not bring himself to wipe his palm on his shirt. He kneaded his fingertips together.

Now the creature struggled again to slip its bonds. He

dropped his racquet and, as he turned to fetch it, wiped his hand on his shirt tail. 'Now. Where were we?'

'What do you say we flip for the third game?' she said. 'I don't think either of us'll survive it if we play it.'

'Okay. Rough or smooth.' Burnham spun his racquet. 'Rough.'

Burnham examined the telltale string. It was smooth. 'Rough it is,' he said. 'The day is yours.'

Why did he do that? he wondered as Eva gathered up her sweatsuit. Why did he want to play the gallant? Who was he trying to impress? Himself?

In the corridor outside the court, Burnham looked at his watch. It was ten to one. He wanted to ask Eva to lunch, but he didn't dare. He should go back to the office, he told himself, in case the President called. But that wasn't it; he was lying. The fact was, he *was* married, and to ask a young woman to lunch constituted a kind of infidelity. No. Even that wasn't the whole truth. He could take *a* woman to lunch – Dyanna, say – without burdening himself with guilt, because Dyanna caused no turmoil in his loins. But to go to lunch with a young woman over whom he had already sprung not one but two impudent boners would be more than a lunch: It would be a date. Like Jimmy Carter, he would be committing adultery in his heart. He had so far been trying to maintain a conviction that the sorry state of his marriage was no one's fault. The misunderstandings would eventually sort themselves out. But if he added adultery to the mix – even mental adultery, spriritual self-abuse – the balance would tip against him; he would become the villain.

He and Eva walked toward the locker rooms. A few steps before the point where they would have separated, Hal intercepted them.

'How was it, children?' she asked cheerfully.

'A scrimmage,' Eva said. 'I thought I might have to have his nose removed surgically from my armpit.'

'Lovely.'

'I was about to make a peace offering to Mr Burnham.'

183

She glanced at Burnham with a half-smile. 'Like buying him lunch.'

Burnham stopped breathing. She had read his mind. Maybe she had read his shorts. What should he say? He should beg off. He could use work as an excuse. The White House was always a valid excuse for anything. No one understood what went on in the White House, but everyone assumed it was a cauldron of constant crises.

But he didn't want to beg off. He wanted to have lunch with her. He said, 'Oh.'

'A gentleman must accept,' Hal said, reaching out to pat Burnham's shoulder.

Burnham recoiled from Hal's touch, raising his hand and pretending to be gravely concerned with the time of day. 'I'd like to . . .' he said, leaving an implicit 'but' hanging in the air.

'The President won't miss you,' Hal said.

'All right,' Burnham said. 'Sure.' He looked at Eva, whose smile made him uncomfortable. It wasn't a flirting smile, but it was knowing, as if her sensors had plucked the conflicting signals from his mind, appraised his temptations and determined how to exploit them. He felt that she knew more about him than she had any reason to know. And that, he reassured himself, was patently absurd.

'I'll see you back here in . . . ten minutes?' Eva said.

'Ten minutes.'

In the shower, Burnham did battle with guilt, and, to his surprise, won an easy victory. His mind was finely tuned to self-interest, and it concluded that infidelity was defined by intent. If he were to be mugged in an alley and raped by the Rockettes, no infidelity would exist. Just so, he had decided not to ask her to lunch. His intentions were pure; he could not be responsible for hers. He suspected that arguments could be made against his conclusion, but he chose not to entertain them. For the time being, he was secure.

The only uncontrollable element hung in a froth of soap suds between his legs. 'You, sir,' he said sternly to his quiescent penis, 'are well advised not to betray me again.'

184

When they were outside the Y, Eva said, 'Where do you want to go?'

'Anywhere. As long as it has a menu.'

'A menu?'

'I have to order myself. I can't take the blue-plate special.'

'Why not?'

'I have a bunch of food allergies. It's no big thing, but I have to be careful.'

Eva thought for a moment. 'I know a place. We can custom-order anything you want.'

She led him up toward 19th Street. 'What are you allergic to?'

'Everything known to man, and then some. Tomatoes, egg whites, beef, corn, cane sugar, milk, wheat, yeast.'

'You can't eat any of that?'

'I can eat them, but only every other day and in low doses. If I make a mistake and have something two or three meals in a row, I get zapped. It's easy to make a mistake. Corn, for instance, is in damn near everything – diet colas, jams, jellies, ice cream and so on. So's cane sugar.'

'What happens to you?'

'Rashes, hives, bleeding gums, dandruff, stomach pains, headaches, depression. The whole ball of wax. I never know till it happens. I went to a dinner party one night, and there were beet shavings in the salad, and I didn't know it till I fainted at the table.' Burnham grimaced at the memory. 'Nice.'

'Really!'

At 19th Street they turned north. The street was crowded, and Burnham was nervous. This was his neighbourhood. He probably knew fifty people who worked in the buildings within three blocks of the White House. Suppose one of them saw him. Suppose Sarah saw him! No. She was in Virginia. But maybe she had a dentist appointment downtown. Suppose he bumped into Warner Cobb. Okay, suppose he did. If Cobb had the bad taste to bring it up, he'd tell the truth: he played squash and then went to lunch with his opponent. What was wrong with that? Nothing. Only people with salacious, suspicious minds would rush to judgment. People like himself.

He smiled at his own stupidity and, to free his head from the fearful topic, said, 'If you're a nutritionist, you probably know all about this stuff.'

'Not all,' Eva said quickly. 'Not by any means. I see kids who are allergic to peanuts and ice cream. I know the basic stuff about B-6 and Vitamin C. But that's about it.'

'What do you cater?'

'Lunches, dinners, dances. Anything. I work for my father.'

'And you went to Bennington.'

She smiled. 'And I went to Bennington. Have you always been in government?'

'No. Hell, no. I fell into it. I was a journalist.'

'What does a journalist do in the White House? Work in the press office?'

'No. He writes speeches. And proclamations. And messages to Congress. And letters to the President's aunt.'

'Must be interesting.'

'Sometimes. Rarely.'

Eva stopped. 'Here we are.'

It was an oriental food shop. In the window were teas and herbs, fruits, roots, nuts, powders, berries and what appeared to Burnham to be dried pieces of animals.

'It's not Chinese or Japanese,' Burnham said. 'I don't recognize the writing.'

'It's Vietnamese.'

'I don't speak Vietnamese. How'm I supposed to order?'

Eva put both her hands on his upper arm. Through the light fabric of his summer suit, Burnham felt her fingertips nestle in his armpit. Her touch was soft and warm and (now he was projecting) full of promise.

'Trust me,' she said.

Burnham looked down into her eyes. On this bright day, they were the faded blue of a tropical dawn. He said, 'I do.'

There were four Formica tables in the rear of the shop,

served by a slight Vietnamese who might have been thirty or fifty. He greeted Eva with a genial '*Bon jour, mademoiselle,*' and she replied, '*Ça va,* Tuan?'

'Where did you learn about Vietnamese food?' Burnham asked as he sat down.

'The war was still going on when I was a teenager. My girlfriends and I had no way to protest. We couldn't resist the draft. We couldn't go to North Vietnam. So we dressed like Vietnamese and ate like Vietnamese. Cultural empathy.' She smiled. 'It made us feel good.'

The menus were in French as well as Vietnamese. Burnham read French, but because the French words were translations of Vietnamese descriptions, he recognized nothing. The menu might as well have been in Aramaic.

'See anything?' Eva asked.

'I'll have two Saltines and a cup of tea.'

Eva studied the menu. 'Is there anything you react violently to, that makes you strange or fall into a fit?'

'Beets.'

'That's it?'

'Far as I know. But go ahead and surprise me.' Burnham laughed. 'We'll have an adventure in dining.'

Eva summoned the waiter and began to order, snapping off complex instructions in rapid-fire French.

Somewhere far back in the building – in the kitchen, perhaps, or a storeroom – a phone rang and was answered.

A reflex was triggered in Burnham. He interrupted Eva and, in French, asked the waiter where the pay phone was.

'*Dans le W.C.,*' said the waiter, pointing in the general direction of the kitchen.

Burnham found the men's room to the left of the kitchen door. It was small, clean and remarkable only in being completely free of graffiti. To distract his itchy-fingered clientele, the proprietor had hung a poster-sized photograph of Nguyen Cau Ky which had been appropriately desecrated by pens, pencils, erasers and blood.

Burnham dialled the White House number and said to the operator, 'This is Timothy Burnham.'

187

'I know.'

'You *do*?'

'Just kidding.' The operator snickered. 'Keep you on your toes.'

'Right.' Burnham told her where he was, gave her the number on the pay phone, and hung up.

By the time he returned to the table, the waiter had departed. Eva was sipping a glass of tea. 'Calling Big Brother?' she said.

'Just checking in.'

'Everywhere you go.'

'Everywhere. Twenty-four hours a day, seven days a week.'

'Suppose you forget?'

'Odds are, that'll be the one time something hits the fan and they have to reach you.'

'What can they do to you? I think I'd give them the wrong number just to see what happens.'

'Once, you might.' Burnham smiled. 'Not twice. There's a chain reaction. Whoever's trying to reach you – and God forbid it's the President – first screams at his assistant, who screams at his assistant, who screams at your immediate boss for having such an irresponsible half-ass on the staff, and he screams at the telephone operator who couldn't reach you. By the time they finally find you, half a dozen people have been yelled at – and they've all been told that the President himself is pissed purple, whether or not it's true – and they're all convinced that their jobs have been placed in jeopardy because you, you thoughtless schmuck, forgot to call in. Now you've got a handful of new enemies, and if there is one thing you do not need, it is more enemies on the White House staff. The quota you have already is quite enough to make your daily life a thrilling parade across a bed of hot coals.'

The waiter brought two bowls of steaming soup. It was khaki-coloured and contained floating bergs of something squooshy.

'What's in it?' Burnham asked.

'Don't ask. Eat.'

'You mean I don't want to know.'

'No.' Eva smiled. 'I mean I'm not sure.'

'It smells . . . good.' The steam that rose from the soup smelled exotic and pungent, spicy and ripe.

The taste was entirely alien to him – not vegetables, not fish, not meat. But it wasn't unpleasant. It tasted . . . nourishing.

Eva said, 'Can I ask you something rude?'

'Sure.'

'When we were playing squash – or mud wrestling, or whatever it was we were doing – I noticed that . . .' She stopped.

'What?'

She was blushing. 'I can't believe I'm saying this.'

'You're not. Yet.'

'I noticed that you don't . . . smell.'

Burnham laughed – not a harsh, arch laugh, but a laugh of true amusement.

'That's funny?' she was perplexed.

'What do I smell like?'

'Nothing! That's the point. You sweat just like a human being, but you don't smell. I sweat, and I smell like a goat.'

'Not exactly.' Burnham said, and he believed he could still taste her pony tail in his mouth.

'You don't smell at all, of anything.'

'Well . . . I had taken a shower, and my clothes were clean.'

'Not even soap. Or laundry detergent. You have a non-smell.'

'That's why WASPS have trouble with girls. We don't leave a spoor.'

'You had trouble with girls? I don't believe it.'

Burnham was flattered. He didn't delude himself about his looks. He was good-looking, in an antiseptic, Protestant way – tall, well proportioned, symmetrical, unblemished. But not intriguing-looking. He didn't turn heads.

The main course arrived, which was fine with Burnham,

because the conversation was travelling into undiscovered country from which, he worried, he might not find a return.

The food was as mysterious as the soup – multicoloured vegetable-like things bathed in a spicy sauce and dotted here and there with chunks of meat-textured delicacies. Like the soup, it tasted nourishing, worthy. But it also contained surprises: hidden bits of pepper that ambushed the tongue and made Burnham gasp.

'*Are* you married?' Eva asked suddenly.

'I guess.'

You turkey! Burnham assailed himself. Why did you say that? What do you want to do, spill your guts about your troubles with Sarah, about the bug in the car, about the fact that she kicked you out of your own house?

'You *guess*?'

'I said "yes",' Burnham said. 'My mouth was on fire.'

'Oh,' She nodded. 'The good men are.'

The conversation was escalating in spite of him. He knew he should try to turn it around, but, at the same time, he didn't want to.

Suddenly he noticed that his fingertips felt warm. Not tingly, as they did when he hyperventilated, just warm. His earlobes, too, and a patch down each side of his neck. He assumed that these were the first signs of an allergic re-action to something in the food. He put down his fork, and he waited.

'Something wrong?' Eva said.

'I don't know.' He paused. 'No, I don't think so.'

And then a rush of warmth, of mild euphoria, flooded his guts, as if a dam of goodness had burst inside him. He was suffused with a sensation of calm and well being and – as he looked across the table at Eva – gratitude and generosity and affection. None of which made any sense.

'What's *in* this stuff?' he said.

'Nothing. Why?'

'I feel ...'

'What?'

'I don't know. Fabulous!'

'What, you mean high?'

'No! Yes! I'm not . . . Just fabulous.'

Eva looked at him, and in her eyes Burnham saw a great deal more knowledge than she was willing to share with him. 'I told you to trust me,' she said.

'Holy smokes.' Burnham sat back and closed his eyes, letting the wonderful feeling wash over him.

'Hey!' a man's voice called out, shattering Burnham's peace. 'Somebody here named Burns?'

Burnham opened his eyes. The man stood in the door of the men's room.

'Anybody here named Burns?' the man said again.

'I'm Burnham.'

'Yeah, well, whatever. There's a call for you.'

Under his breath, Burnham whispered, 'Shit.' He took a couple of deep breaths and stood up, holding onto the table just in case.

Eva stood up, too, and took his hand. 'Are you okay?'

'Sure.' Burnham grinned. 'My pretty poisoner.'

The receiver was dangling from the phone box. Burnham picked it up and said, 'Hello.'

'Mr Burnham?' It was a White House operator.

'Yes.'

'One moment, please, for the President.'

The word 'No!' burst unsummoned from Burnham's mouth. He couldn't talk to the President, not here. You don't talk to the President of the United States from a public toilet in a Vietnamese hashhouse.

'I beg your pardon?'

'I . . .'

'One moment, please.'

There were two clicks on the phone line, and then a voice said, 'Timothy?'

Evelyn Witt. Thank God.

'Hi, Evelyn.'

'Where are you?'

'Ah . . . around the corner. Getting a sandwich.'

'How soon can you be back?'

191

'Couple minutes.'

'Good. The President wants to see you.'

'When.'

'Five minutes ago.'

'I'm on my way.'

'Good.'

Burnham had almost replaced the receiver when he heard Evelyn say, 'Timothy?'

'Huh?'

'If he asks, you were in a meeting over at State. That's why it took you a few minutes to get back.'

'Okay. Who was I meeting with?'

'Anybody. It's just that, in the mood he's in today, our rights to life, liberty and the pursuit of food do not exist.'

'Thanks, Evelyn.'

Burnham hung up, checked in the mirror to make sure his tie was straight, and returned to the table.

'Problems?' Eva said.

'Apparently. Himself has been scouring the town for me.'

'I thought you said a writer's life was boring.'

'It is, usually. But for some reason, I've suddenly become a critical cog in the machinery of the Republic.'

'The caterpillar becomes a butterfly.'

'Right.' Burnham tried to smile. 'And you know how long butterflies live. Anyway, I've got to go. I'm really sorry.' He reached for his wallet.

Eva held up her hand. 'Your money's no good here. My treat.'

'Can we play again?'

'Any time.'

Burnham hurried toward the door, shouldering his way through the crowd at the take-out counter, muttering 'Excuse me, excuse me.' Halfway down the aisle, he suddenly stopped and turned back, muttering to the annoyed people he shoved aside, 'Forgot my wallet.'

'I don't know how to get hold of you,' he said to Eva.

She handed him a slip of paper on which she had written

192

her name, address and phone number, and she smiled warmly and said, 'I thought you'd never ask.'

Outside, Burnham ran, for he was not around the corner, he was a full five blocks from the White House.

Sergeant Thibaudeaux saw him coming from a block away – a tall, thin figure running flat-out toward the West Gate of the White House, hair flying, tie askew, coat-tails trailing like a cape. He didn't recognize Burnham at first, so he stepped outside the guardhouse, put his right hand on the butt of his pistol and, with his left hand, held the bullet-proof door of the guardhouse open between himself and the approaching man.

Assume everybody's a loon, was Sergeant Thibaudeaux's motto, and you'll make it to supper without being blowed up.

Burnham tried to dash through the gate without stopping, but Sergeant Thibaudeaux stood resolutely in his way. Even though he now recognized Burnham, he wasn't about to take any chances: for all he knew, Mr B had come unwrapped that very morning and got himself fired and had his pass lifted.

Frantically, Burnham searched his pockets for his pass, spilling coins and lint balls and bits of paper onto the pavement. 'The President wants to see me!' he said.

'Who told you, your hair dryer?' Sergeant Thibaudeaux rocked back on his heels, appreciating himself.

At last, Burnham found his pass in his shirt pocket, flashed it at the sergeant, and continued up the path.

The air-conditioning in the West Wing was running on its afterburners, and Burnham felt that he had walked into a meat locker. The sweat on his forehead dried and caked his soaking hair into ringlets. His shirt stuck to his armpits.

He turned into a lavatory, straightened his tie, dried his face and ran his fingers through his hair. His hands were shaking. He checked his pulse: 140. He had just eaten, so he shouldn't be at risk for a sugar crisis. Trouble was, he had no idea what had been in the food. It had made him feel terrific, but that didn't mean sugar, necessarily.

Be smart, he told himself. You don't want to pass out in the Oval office. He found two old Hershey Chocolate Kisses in a jacket pocket, unwrapped them and picked shreds of foil from the brown goo, and swallowed them. Insurance.

By the time he turned into Evelyn Witt's office, his pulse had dropped to 80 – higher than his normal resting pulse, but, he reassured himself, that was only natural since he felt neither normal nor restful.

'What have I done?' he asked Evelyn.

'I don't know, Timothy. Your speech came over an hour ago – that sweet little girl of yours brought it – but he was in a meeting with the Majority Leader and then on the phone with his brother who wants him to write a letter of recommendation for his son to Amherst, so he didn't get to it till about twenty minutes ago. Ever since he read it, he's been bellowing for you. I think his blood pressure's probably two thousand over fifteen hundred. Did you write something naughty?'

'I don't think so.'

'Well, maybe . . .' She smiled, and Burnham knew she was hoping to seem encouraging, '. . . Maybe you didn't *do* anything.'

'It's been nice knowing you, Evelyn.' Burnham started for the door to the Oval Office.

'Timothy . . . do you remember Willa Badham?'

'No.'

'I guess she was before your time. Yes, back in our first term. She was a staff assistant in some office or other, about your level, and for some reason the President took a liking to her. He wouldn't let her out of his sight, as if he felt the Presidency depended on her. He does that. Not often but he does that.'

'Cobb told me. How long did she last?'

'Oh . . .' Evelyn turned away, fiddling with some papers. 'A long time.'

'Six weeks?'

194

'Well . . . about.' Evelyn added quickly, 'But she wasn't fired. She quit.'

'Why?'

'She had a little . . . breakdown. Well, not really a breakdown, more of a . . .'

'Collapse?'

Burnham looked at Evelyn and saw her sneaking a glance at him, and he laughed. And then she laughed.

'Go ahead in,' she said.

Burnham tapped lightly and opened the door. The President was standing beside his desk, speaking on the phone. He saw Burnham and, with a curt wave of his hand, motioned him in. Burnham stepped into the office and closed the door behind him.

'Now you listen here, Admiral,' The President said into the phone. 'I don't give a shit if that sumbitch has got solid gold handles on the pissers and a diamond-studded steering wheel. I'm not gonna pay five billion dollars for a submarine!' He slammed the phone down and snapped, 'Where you been, Tim?'

'At State, sir. The traffic was terrible.'

'Shoulda called a helicopter.'

'Me?'

'Damn right. When the President wants you, he wants you.'

'Yes, sir.' Like a quarterback surveying a defence, Burnham tried to appraise the President's mood, looked for signs that would foretell an imminent blitz. But he didn't know the man, he had no scouting reports. The President seemed calm – icy, maybe, but in control. For all Burnham knew, however, he was like a mamba, a silent killer who struck with no warning, rather than like a cobra who gave showy notice of an impending attack.

The President reached across his cluttered desk and picked up a few sheets of paper. He held them up to Burnham. Exhibit A.

'The fella who wrote this, Tim . . .' With a mean little grin, the President crushed the papers into a ball. '. . . that

195

fella, if he had a brain, why, he'd be outdoors playin' with it. That fella does not have his President's best interests at heart.'

Goodbye, Burnham thought. There went my speech, there went my job, there went my life. Now: how to get out of this office without losing something really important, like a couple of quarts of blood or a kidney or two.

The President cocked his arm and fired the ball of papers at the portrait of Abraham Lincoln that hung over the fireplace. Then he pulled from his jacket pocket more papers, which he dangled before Burnham's glazing eyes.

'Now, the fella who wrote *this*, Tim, this fella is a true source of comfort and strength to his President.'

Cobb. Cobb had rewritten his speech. Somehow, he had intercepted Burnham's draft – either in Dyanna's office or Evelyn Witt's – and, in vengeful spite at Burnham's attempt to go around him, had sent the President not only his new draft but also Burnham's draft (its rumpled corpse had bounced off Abe Lincoln's proboscis and now lay beneath a coffee table), no doubt with a note telling the President that he had read Burnham's draft and had found it 'a little flaccid' (or something equally sly and condescending) and had taken the liberty of 'punching it up'.

The President proffered the papers to Burnham. 'Tell me if you don't think this fella is a great American.'

Swell. As his final act in this life, Burnham was being forced to sing a paean to his assassin. As he extended his hand, a sour, metallic taste suffused his mouth, as if he had just had his teeth cleaned.

He meant to pretend to glance at the first page (once a girl tells you you're ugly, he reasoned, there's not much fun in having to admire the true beauties she parades by you for comparison), but as his eyes swept over the ten-pitch, Bookface Academic IBM type, he saw a familiar phrase. Then another. Then a third. Then he actually read an entire paragraph.

It was his speech. Verbatim. Cobb hadn't stabbed him.

196

(Guilt for having suspected Cobb fluttered across his mind like a hunting bat and flew away.)

He was the great American, the source of comfort and strength to the Leader of the Free World.

He said, 'Ah . . .'

'This is the finest toast I have seen since I took my first oath of office.' The President snatched the papers from Burnham's fingers. 'This is a toast that if they gave Nobel Prizes for toasts, this one would be a shoo-in.'

Come now, Mr President, Burnham thought. Great, yes; epic, perhaps; but Nobel Prize . . . ?

'I'm serious.' The President's look reproved Burnham for his modest thoughts. 'Do you know why?'

'No, sir. I was just trying –'

'Because it's savvy. It's deep. It shows long-term thinking.It has the best interests of the country at heart. And most of all, it shows that this writer is in tune with his President.'

Humbly, Burnham hung his head.

'Any hack could fawn all over of some two-bit muckety-muck, but it takes a *writer* to see through all the fog and tell it like it is. Where'd you get this stuff?'

'Sir?'

'No. Don't tell me. I don't want to know. Better you do your job and I do mine. But, Tim, I have to be frank.' The President took a step toward Burnham and put his arm around his shoulder and began to walk him around the office, like a comrade trying to sober him up for the long drive home.

'Yes, sir,' Burnham said. 'Please do.'

'This toast worries me.'

'It does?'

'Yessir. Fact is, I'm 'bout as worried as a pregnant fox in a forest fire.'

'Really? What is it that –'

The President stopped walking and clutched Burnham's shoulder and drew him even closer. Three inches shorter than the President, Burnham found himself staring into the

197

pores on the man's chin, could feel the President's moist breath warming the tip of his nose.

'Tim, I've got the State Department. I've got the National Security Council – though what those dipsticks keep secure is a mystery 'bout as great as the goddam Sphinx. I've got about a billion people working for me in the Federal Government, and at least a million of them are s'posed to know something about foreign policy. Right? Is that asking too much?'

'Yes . . . no, sir . . . right.'

'Then why is it, Tim –' the President resumed his promenade '– that of all those millions of people, people the tax-payers pay billions and trillions of dollars, only one man knows his ass from live steam?'

'Well . . .'

'Now, the fella who wrote that . . .' The President pointed to the ball of papers beneath the coffee table, which Burnham assumed was the NSC draft of the toast. '. . . he didn't have the guts to put his name on it. And he was right, too, 'cause when I find out who he is, he's gonna be lucky to get a job writing four-letter words for the Scrabble company.'

'I'm sure –'

'Where've you been keeping yourself, Tim?'

'Sir? I've been –'

'Never mind. Past is past. I should be grateful – the *country* should be grateful – that you're here now.' The President gazed at the ceiling. 'It's a comfort to know that somebody up there still looks out for us.' They had reached the couch. Gently, the President eased Burnham down into the soft upholstery.

'How's Andrei?'

Andrei? Burnham thought. André? André who? My dinner with André? Andrei? He said aloud, 'Gromyko?'

The President guffawed. 'Who do you think? André Previn?'

Burnham forced a choking laugh. Who does this man think I am? 'Well, I –'

'I may want you to –' The President whirled at the sound of a door opening behind him.

Burnham peered around the President and saw Mario Epstein, accompanied by the National Security Advisor, Dennis Duggan. They had entered through the small office that adjoined the Oval Office, the Sanctuary where the President went to relax, for it had a bar and a bathroom and a television set and a favourite sofa on which he could stretch out and nap. Burnham had heard that the President called it his 'flatter palace', for there he would entertain guests who could be cajoled into doing his bidding by being stroked and fed Jack Daniels in the President's private retreat.

Epstein was one of four people with unrestricted access to the President (the others were his Appointments Secretary, his wife and Evelyn Witt), and it was known that he did not abuse the privilege. Something was up.

Burnham knew that he should stand and make a discreet exit before being asked to leave, but the prospect of being privy to a crisis – even to the first few sentences of a crisis – was irresistibly seductive. He stayed seated.

'What is it?' the President said sharply.

'Got a problem,' Epstein said, waving a piece of paper. Duggan stayed a step behind Epstein. He was in his early fifties, contemplative and professorial, with a silver-grey crew cut and a pipe that never left his mouth except when he gestured with it. He was Epstein's man. He never communicated with the President except through Epstein, never visited with the President except in Epstein's company, never ventured an opinion unfamiliar or unacceptable to Epstein. In effect, he was Epstein's National Security Advisor.

'What else is new?' the President said. 'The world is full of problems.'

'Yes, sir,' Epstein said, apparently perplexed at the President's obduracy. 'But I'm afraid this one needs the President's attention right away.'

Burnham was surprised that the President didn't turn

and ask him to leave. Nor did he cross the room and huddle with Epstein and Duggan by the signing table. He stayed where he was and said, 'Okay. What is it?'

Epstein held up the paper again. 'I'm afraid this is for the President's ears only.'

There it is, Burnham thought. Okay. He started to stand.

But the President pushed him back down on the couch. 'Bullshit, Mario. Feel free to speak in front of Tim.' He took a step to the side, and for the first time Epstein saw Burnham.

'You!' Epstein all but shouted. His mouth hung open for a fraction of a second.

Duggan looked at Burnham, then at Epstein, then back at Burnham. He sucked on his pipe. He had no idea what was going on, but he knew better than to get mixed up in it.

Burnham raised a tentative hand and said, 'Hi again.'

'I figured you two knew each other,' said the President. 'Go ahead, Mario.'

'But who *is* he?' Epstein fought to suppress the outrage that bubbled beneath his skin.

Good question, Burnham thought. I've been wondering myself.

'A friend, Mario,' the President said, and he winked at Burnham. 'A real good friend, come to help me in my hour of need.'

Burnham was sure he was mistaken: the President of the United States could *not* have winked at him. He had a fleeting fantasy that he was a player in a remake of *The Prince and the Pauper*. Lurking somewhere in the corridors of the mansion must be the genuine dauphin.

'Who does he work for?' asked Epstein the inquisitor.

'Me, Mario.' The President paused. 'Just like you do.'

'Yessir,' Epstein said quickly.

The President cast a satisfied glance in Burnham's direction, as if he was pleased to discover that Epstein was as ignorant about Burnham as he was. 'What you need to know, you know,' he said. 'And what you don't know can't hurt you.'

I'm his secret weapon, Burnham concluded. He doesn't know anything about me, and he's glad. He must think that my cover is so perfect that *no one* knows anything about me.

'Now, Mario, what's on your mind?'

Epstein was staring at Burnham, willing his eyes to pierce the shell of mystery. He exhaled, visibly, and the air hissed as it passed through his teeth. 'Cuba,' he said to the President.

'Cuba? What's that stogie-smoking hippie up to now?'

'An American-flag vessel, a yacht, is in Havana Harbour.'

'Castro captured it?'

'No, sir. It came in there on its own. Apparently, it broke down offshore and sailed in.'

'Why didn't it go to Guantanamo? There're Americans there.'

'I don't know, sir. This came in to Dennis an hour ago, from the Marine general down there. We don't know any of the "whys".'

'Castro won't let him go?'

Epstein shook his head. 'The captain won't leave. He – so to speak – is requesting asylum. But somebody's yelling out of a porthole that he doesn't want asylum. He's yelling "Rape" and "Kidnap" and bloody murder. So Castro's just sitting back – watching, I guess, and laughing his head off.'

'What do you mean, "so to speak"?'

'Apparently, sir,' Epstein cleared his throat, 'this whole operation, the whole crew, everybody on board is . . . well . . . gay . . . but even . . .'

'*Fags?*' the President roared.

'Not exactly, sir.' Epstein looked like a child who had just wet his pants.

Sitting on the couch, Burnham delighted in watching Epstein squirm.

'It seems that there are transsexuals aboard – one, maybe two. Transsexuals are –'

'I know what they are!' The President sighed. 'Christ on a

201

flaming crutch! I got the Russians want to blow me up, the Senate wants to cut my balls off, a cannibal coming for supper, and now a ship of fairies has run aground. Well, my decision is, let 'em rot.'

'I'm afraid that's not an option, Mr President.'

'Why not?'

'They're American citizens.'

'That's beside the point.'

'No, sir. That *is* the point.'

Loath though he was to do it, Burnham awarded a point to Epstein.

Epstein continued. 'You see, sir, the captain has rafted his boat to a Russian oil tanker. He says if he doesn't get asylum, he'll blow everything up – tanker, boat, Russians, everything.'

'Can he do it?'

Epstein looked to Duggan, who eased the pipe from his mouth and said slowly, 'We doubt it, sir. He's forty-eight feet long, the tanker's over six hundred feet. Even if he was a hundred percent ballasted with C-4 explosive – extremely unlikely, in our estimation – he'd have to position himself perfectly in order to inflict substantial damage on the tanker. The chances of him actually sinking the tanker are, we judge, nil.'

'But,' said Epstein, 'we can't take the chance. Even if he puts a hole in it, the Russians will raise holy hell.'

The President sighed. 'So what are our options?'

'Two.' Epstein said, 'and neither very attractive. One, go through the Swiss and try to convince Castro to give them asylum, just temporarily, to defuse the situation.'

'Sure, why not? The prick sent us all *his* fairies – and a thousand lunatics to boot – from Mariel.'

'We don't think he'll do it. Why should he? He'd love to see some crazy Americans blow up a Russian tanker. Two, General Starkweather, the Marine general, wants to send a SEAL team in tonight and take the *Bilitis* – that's the name of the yacht – from the water. The problem there is . . .'

Burnham stopped listening. He was frozen. *Bilitis*. He should have guessed. There couldn't be two such bizarre crews, not even on a planet with four and a half billion people, and though some of the details were different, the substance was unmistakably similar. But he had been so beguiled by the intoxicating brew of international crisis, had heard it with such fascinated detachment, that he had never made the connection.

Epstein was concluding. '. . . constitute an invasion of Cuban territory.'

'So,' said the President. 'What do you recommend??'

'Dennis and I think you should tell General Starkweather to go ahead and send the SEALs. But we have to try to buy time. The . . . captain . . . says he's going to blow everything sky-high at five o'clock.'

'Call him and tell him we're working on it.'

'He won't speak to us, sir. He says he won't speak to anybody but Castro himself.'

'Maybe he'll speak to me. I hate to put the Presidency on the line for a bunch of fruits, but if –'

'No, sir. I'm afraid he specifically excluded you. He made a statement on his radio saying that you were prejudiced against . . . his kind.'

'I'm not prejudiced. I'm biased. There's a difference.'

'Yes, sir.'

Burnham stood up. Rivulets of sweat ran down his sides and soaked the elastic in his boxer shorts.

'Mr President?'

Epstein looked at him as if he were a herpes lesion.

Duggan sucked on his pipe and contemplated him as if he were a new species.

The President said, 'Yes, Tim?'

Burnham stepped forward. 'It's three o'clock.' No, no! Not that! He cursed himself. What an opener! They've got to think I'm nuts.

'Thank you, Tim,' the President said. His head was cocked at an interesting angle.

'Ah . . . sir . . . what I mean is, there are two hours till

203

the deadline expires. I wonder if . . . may I have one hour to work on it?'

'You!' snorted Epstein.

'You think you can help, Tim?' said the President.

'I th . . . I hope so, sir.'

The President looked hard at him, and Burnham had to fight to keep from looking away. But he kept his eyes locked on the President's.

'What makes you think you . . .' The President stopped. Then he smiled and said, 'You got it, Tim.' He turned to Epstein. 'Mario, give him the paper.'

'But, sir –' Epstein was aghast.

'Give him the paper, Mario!'

Tight-lipped, Epstein stepped toward Burnham and handed him the Telex sheet that had come into the Situation Room. Burnham glanced at it just long enough to see that it was slugged: TOP SECRET – URGENT.

He turned toward the door. The President walked with him, his arm around Burnham's shoulder.

'I'm counting on you, Tim.'

'Yes, sir. If I need some help with communications . . .'

'Communications!' the President said. 'Shee-it, son.' He yanked open the door to Evelyn Witt's office and barked, 'Evelyn, Tim is on a special assignment for me. Top priority. Whatever he needs, you see he gets it. Planes, choppers, the goddam Third Marine Division if he wants it.' The President patted Burnham on the back and walked back into his office.

Burnham heard the President say, 'Now, Dennis, I want to know which one of your wimps wrote that crap for the swami toast tonight.'

Evelyn Witt smiled at Burnham and said, 'Welcome to hard times.'

Burnham felt his hands shaking. He stuffed them into his pockets before Evelyn could see them. 'I think I'd like to take a nap,' he said.

Evelyn pulled a pad and pencil toward her. 'What do you need?'

'Is there such a thing as a secure open phone line?'

'Where to?'

'The middle of Havana Harbour.'

'If there isn't, I'm going to take my cat and move into a cave. I'll set it up. Anything else?'

'I can't think of anything. But if I do, can I call you?'

'Timothy . . .' She reached up and touched his cheek. 'You're sweet to ask, but don't ask any more.'

'What?' Lord, Burnham thought, I've had this job for sixty seconds, and already I've put my foot in it.

'You don't *ask* anybody. You *tell* them.'

'Oh. Sorry.'

'And you never apologize. Never.'

'Oh. Right. Thanks.'

Burnham turned left outside Evelyn's office, and walked quickly down the hall past the Secret Service men guarding the President's private office, past the closed door of the office of the Appointments Secretary, past the regiment of Epstein's harassed secretaries. He turned right and took the stairs to the basement two at a time.

No one noticed him, and it occurred to him that he was moving through these hallowed halls in a way he had never moved before – as if he belonged there. Hurrying. Preoccupied. Confident. Defying anyone to stop or question him. He was on priority business for the boss.

He felt strange: nervous but not frightened, challenged but not worried. He should be berating himself for an idiot – there was a good chance he would come out of this looking like a presumptuous, feckless fool – but instead he felt a little glow of self-satisfaction at his daring (he would never have called it courage). He had seen a chance to help the President, help the country and help an unfortunate friend (a distant friend, but a friend nonetheless), and rather than refuse the risk, he had volunteered to take it. If he succeeded, he would be doing himself a favour, too: Virtue Plus Twenty Percent.

If he failed . . .

He pushed open the door of the west Basement and strode across West Executive Avenue.

He didn't intend to fail. He was sure he was right about *Bilitis*. The parallels were too great to be coincidence.

Unless . . .

His foot struck the curb on the far side of West Executive Avenue, and he tripped.

Suppose Toddy Thatcher wasn't on board. Suppose he had sold the boat to one of his chums. Suppose . . . No. It couldn't be.

Toddy Thatcher was Sarah's cousin. He had been a source of concern to his family since the fourth grade, when he started avoiding the boys in his class and associating only with the girls. He had been asked to leave Groton, not because of any overt homosexual activity – he didn't consider himself a homosexual, he considered himself a female – but because he refused to be a boy. He wouldn't undress in the boys' locker room, wouldn't sleep in the same room with his room-mate, insisted on trying out for the girls' field hockey team (and threatened to file a lawsuit when he was denied permission), and circulated a newsletter called *The Daughters of Bilitis Gazette*. School officials tried to accommodate him for a year but then concluded that he was too disturbed – and too disturbing – to function in the Groton community.

Psychoanalysis proved to be a waste of Toddy's time and seventeen thousand of his parents' dollars. He regarded his penis as a cruel joke played on him by a male chauvinist god.

He acquired a high-school equivalency certificate from one of the academies that advertised on the inside covers of matchbooks. He let his hair grow, took female hormones and applied depilatories daily to his soft, fair face and his slight body. In the fall, without his parents' knowledge (by this time, his parents had given up on him; to them, he was an eccentric roomer who, instead of paying rent, was given an allowance), he applied and was admitted to Elon College in North Carolina.

As Teresa Thatcher.

Sarah's branch of the family, including Burnham, had lost touch with Toddy for several years. He had gone underground, someone said. He had joined a commune. He had had surgery, though to do what, no one was certain.

Burnham liked Toddy, who was bright and congenial and, as he had grown up, funny about what he called his 'perversion'. He hoped Toddy had found a way to be happy.

A year ago, Toddy had resurfaced at a Christmas gathering at his parents' home. As Teresa. He dressed like a Teresa. He looked like a Teresa. And he said that he was about two-thirds of the way through the long process of mechanically *becoming* Teresa.

His ambition was to become a businesswoman, and, as he told Burnham on the telephone, the business he intended to start was Lesbian Charter Boating.

'This is the age of specialization, Timothy. I have to find my slot.'

'But Toddy –'

'Teresa.'

'Teresa. Don't you think this . . . slot . . . is a little narrow? Is the clientele big enough?'

'*Big* enough? You have no *idea*. They're out there, millions of them, longing to escape the yoke of maleness. I offer them relaxation, sisterhood, no macho Long John Silvers calling them dumb broads.'

'Do you know how to sail?'

'I'll learn. But first I need a boat. I want you to recommend a boat broker.'

'What kind of boat?'

'You tell me. All I know is, I'm going to call her *Bilitis*.'

Burnham had made a couple of calls to brokers he had known when he was writing America's Cup pieces. He had prepared a short list of boats that sounded possible and had sent it off to Toddy. A week later, he had received a huge bouquet of spring flowers from an FTD florist, with a note enclosed that said: 'I'll name the nicest powder room on

207

board after you, so everyone will know that Timothy Burnham gives good "head". Love, T.'

That was the last he had heard of Toddy.

Burnham marched into his office. Dyanna was at her desk, shaping her nails into scimitars.

'Have a nice lunch?' she said, with a conspicuous glance at the clock on her desk.

'Grab a pad and come in here.' He continued toward his desk, shedding his jacket and tossing it toward the couch.

'Something's wrong with our phones,' she called after him. 'I think they're out.'

'No they're not.' Burnham sat down, gathered all the papers on his desk – the CIA report on the Pasha, the drafts of the toast, his DOE mail – into a pile and dropped it onto the floor. He placed a yellow legal pad and two sharp pencils before him. Then he unfolded the Telex and smoothed it on top of the legal pad.

Dyanna stood in the doorway, holding a pad, frowning.

'Sit over there,' Burnham said, pointing to the conference table, on which was a telephone console. 'How's your shorthand?'

'Rusty.'

'Oil it up. I want you to listen to this conversation and take down every word.'

'Whatever for?'

'Because I said so!' Easy, Burnham thought, easy. Even Stalin didn't start the day hollering at the help.

Dyanna reacted as if he had slapped her. Her head jerked and her mouth opened.

He wanted to say 'Sorry,' but then he remembered Evelyn Witt's admonition about apologizing, so he said, 'I'll start again. We have to try to stop someone from blowing up a Russian ship. If we succeed, you'll probably be made Vice President of the United States. If we fail, you'll end your days as a bag lady in Rock Creek Park. Okay?'

'Wow!' was all Dyanna said, but she smiled.

'If I snap my fingers at you during the conversation, you

get off the line and call the President's office and tell Evelyn I need a confirmation of authority.'

'To whom?'

'Whoever's giving me grief. You'll have written down his name. Okay?'

'Yes, sir!'

Burnham punched a button on his phone console and picked up the receiver. Dyanna did the same on her console. There was no dial tone. Dyanna shrugged, saying, 'See?'

Then a voice said, 'Yes, Mr Burnham.'

Burnham winked at Dyanna. 'Who is this?' he said.

'Pingrey, sir, Thomas L. Sergeant First Class.'

'Here's what we have to do, Sergeant. In Havana Harbour there is an American yacht called *Bilitis*.' He spelled the name. 'I want you to raise him for me. He's got single sideband, VHF and AM. I doubt he has anything newer.'

'No sweat, sir.'

'Wrong. He says he won't speak to anybody but Fidel Castro. I do a lousy Castro impession.'

'Yes, sir.'

'I think he'll speak to me. Personally. No White House, no government, no military, and especially no President. Try to raise him on my name alone. Timothy Burnham.'

'Yes, sir.'

'While you're setting that up, get me General Starkweather at Guantanamo.'

'Your name alone?'

'No. The White House, the President, the cosmos. God, if you have to.'

'Yes, sir.'

'You want to call me back?'

'No, sir. Hang on?'

As he waited, Burnham reread the NSC Telex, searching for any clue to Toddy's state of mind, to what had made him snap, for Burnham was sure that something had short-circuited inside that gentle person. But all he was able to do

209

was reinforce his fear that within three hours, one way or another Toddy Thatcher would be dead.

'Starkweather,' said a voice forged from old machine-gun parts.

'General, this is Timothy Burnham, in the White House.'

'So they said. You work for Duggan?'

'No, s –' Forget the 'sir'. 'I work for the President.'

'Sure. So do I.'

'The President wants me to get the *Bilitis* out of there.'

'He wants me to, too, and I'm here and you're there.'

'General . . .' Burnham broke the pencil in his hand. Not yet, he told himself. Save your big guns. 'I intend to get the *Bilitis* out of there. Until and unless I say so, you are not to send any SEALs, any Marines, anybody anywhere near that yacht. Is that clear?'

'Look, Mr . . . Burnham. I got a possible *war* on my hands down here. I'm not gonna take orders from some –'

Burnham snapped his fingers at Dyanna. She punched a new button on her console and tapped out a four-digit number.

When the general had finished, Burnham waited a beat, and then he said, with what he hoped was menacing calm, 'You fuck with me, General, you're fuckin' with your heartbeat. In thirty seconds, you're gonna get a call, and when I come back on the line, you'd better have lost your fuckin' *attitude*, or you're gonna wish you'd chosen a career in the Salvation Army.'

Burnham punched a button that cut Starkweather off.

He was appalled at himself. His heart was tripping along at about 150. 'Fuckin' with your heartbeat?' Where had he dredged that from? To a Marine Corps general? What had he done? He didn't know how to handle power; he'd never had any before. Giving him power was like putting a blind man behind the wheel of a tank. The President wasn't about to let Timothy Y. Burnham become Commander-In-Chief. Was he?

Dyanna was staring at him, stunned, 'Wow!' she said.

'See if you can get General Starkweather on the line again.'

Dyanna spoke to Sergeant Pingrey and, a moment later, said, 'Just a moment, General.' She nodded to Burnham.

Burnham took a deep breath and picked up the receiver. 'General.'

'You have my apologies, Mr Burnham.'

The feeling inside Burnham was orgasmic, an explosion in his pleasure centre that sent radial messages throughout his body. He had never talked back, even to a taxi driver, didn't dare send putrid food back to a restaurant's kitchen, became aphasic when confronted by aggressive strangers. Now, suddenly, armed with a cause and with authority, he had become a force to reckon with. Or, at least, a human being.

And he hadn't stammered.

'Accepted. It's hard to keep lines of authority straight. We're both just trying to do our jobs.' Oh, spare me your smarmy garbage, Burnham told himself. You sound like the President. He said, 'Are we agreed? You'll do nothing till you hear from me?'

'Agreed. You're aware of his deadline? 1700 hours.'

'Yes. I better get to it. Thanks, General.'

Burnham counted back from 2400, just to make sure that 1700 hours was five o'clock. Then he picked up the receiver and waited for Sergeant Pingrey.

'Mr Burnham?'

'Go ahead.'

'I've got his SSB wide open, and I've jammed the rest of the neighbourhood, so he can't talk to anybody but me. But he won't talk. He doesn't believe it's you.'

'Put me on, then.'

'He says the President's trying to trick him. He says he won't recognize your voice on the radio. He may be right.'

Burnham thought for a moment. He could mention Sarah's name or Toddy's parent, or Groton or Elon, but Toddy would know that by now the government could have obtained all those names.

211

The answer came to him. He blushed and laughed to himself and said, 'Sergeant, ask him if he still has the plaque on the powder-room door . . .' He looked over at Dyanna, feverishly scribbling in shorthand. '. . . the one that says that Timothy Burnham gives good head.'

Pingrey sounded as if he had swallowed his tongue.

Dyanna's pencil stuttered on the page, and her ears became a pretty crimson against her yellow hair.

'Oh, and Sergeant: address him as Miss Thatcher.'

'Yes, sir.'

The line was dead for fifteen seconds, and then: 'Timothy?'

'Toddy?'

'Timothy!'

'Sorry. Teresa.'

'How are you?'

'I'm fine. Teresa. But that's not why I'm calling.'

'No.'

'What are you doing down there?'

'Things got out of hand, Timothy.'

'What things?'

'You don't want to know. It's sordid.'

'I've *got* to know, Teresa, if I'm going to help you.'

'What are they going to do to me, Timothy?' There was fear in the voice.

Be careful, Burnham told himself. You don't want to provoke anything. But he . . . she . . . has to know how serious this is. He felt lost. He wasn't a hostage negotiator. All he knew about hostage negotiating was what he'd seen on *Hill Street Blues*.

'If you let me help you, nothing,' he said. 'If you don't, I'm afraid they may hurt you.'

'I have nothing to live for.'

Burnham paused. 'This is Timothy you're talking to, Teresa, not Phil Donahue. Don't pull that "I'll Cry Tomorrow" crap on me.' He held his breath, praying that the line wouldn't go dead.

A tiny laugh squeaked forth from Teresa, and she said, 'You're too *much*.'

'Tell me what happened.'

'We had a break between charters. I was going to do some work on the boat. One of the Jacuzzis was leaking.'

'Jacuzzis? You've got Jacuzzis on a sailboat?'

'And a sauna and a massage room. Anyway, a friend called and said she had a friend who had just broken up and was a *mess* and needed to get away, and would I take him for a little cruise? Well, you know me, I'm a sucker for a broken heart, so I said I would, and this boy came aboard.'

'A boy?'

'Oh all right, a young man. I'm not *crazy*, Timothy. He was a sweet little thing, and very sad, so I took him under my arm, and one thing led to another, and, well . . . here we are.'

'Oh no you don't, Teresa. Step by step, if you please.'

He heard Teresa sigh. 'All *right*. We left Fort Lauderdale and sailed down the coast and hopped along the Keys. We spent a couple of days in Key West and had a ball. We left Key West, and I still had a week before I had to pick up my next charter, so I thought we'd take a spin to the Bahamas. This boy and I had become soulmates. It could have been more than that. It *should* have been more than that, but there was a problem: He isn't interested in girls, and I'm a girl.'

'That is a problem.'

'I was going mad. Biology was keeping us apart. Then the truth hit me like a ton of bricks.'

'It did?'

'You remember I told you I was having all those operations?'

'Sure.'

'I ran out of money before the end. Daddy wouldn't give me the money for the last operation. He thought soy beans and pork bellies were a better investment than turning a pitiful wreck of a Toddy into a joyous sprite named Teresa.'

'You mean . . . you're not a girl?'

213

'Ninety-nine and forty-four one-hundredths per cent pure. There's just one little item remaining.'

'Called a –'

'You call it that if you want. I call it the devil's plaything. But yes. That hateful creature is still hanging around. I thought to myself: well, maybe for once in its life, it can be useful.'

'So you told him.'

'Not exactly. The night we left Key West, the other girls – the mate and her mate – went to bed early. I had the watch, and Ian – that's the boy – was with me in the cockpit. What an ironic name.'

'Ian?'

'No. Cockpit. There was a nice breeze from the south-west, so we were on an easy broad reach. I could handle the wheel with my toes.'

Burnham was impressed. 'You've learned a lot in a year.'

'I'm adaptable, Timothy. If I'm anything, I'm adaptable. Anyway, we were having a lovely time, but then he got anxious. He started to apologize: he liked me, he respected me, all that nonsense, but he just couldn't *relate* – his word – to a woman. I was in a fever. I couldn't stand it any longer. Maybe the Pinot Chardonnay made me do it, I don't know, but I stood up and tore off my shorts and *showed* him. 'It's all right!' I cried. 'I *can* be yours!' I knew this would solve our problem. He'd be enchanted.'

'And?'

'He freaked out. He screamed. He pointed as if it was going to attack him. He jumped up on the fantail and tried to hide behind the backstay. I was terrified he was going to fall overboard. Or jump.'

'What did you do?'

'Nothing! I just stood there. I was shocked. I mean, I expected him to be surprised, but I didn't think he'd go bananas. He looked like he'd seen an alien. It doesn't do much for a girl's self-esteem, I can tell you.'

'No.'

'I promised I wouldn't hurt him, but he wouldn't listen.

He ran below and locked himself in his cabin. I tried to reason with him, but every time I tapped on his door, he yelled "Rape!" and demanded to be put ashore. So I thought: well, this little affair has gone about as far as it can go. I went to start the engine. I wasn't going to waste time sailing back. If the little sissy wanted to get home, I'd take him home.'

'The engine wouldn't start.'

'Right. We'd been having a problem with some of the injectors, but nothing serious. All of a sudden, it was serious.'

'Why didn't you sail?'

'I tried. After about an hour, the southwest wind veered to the northwest, then to the north, then it settled into the northeast. You know what a northeast wind is like in the Gulf Stream.'

'Garbage.'

'It grew and grew and grew. I bet that by two in the morning it was blowing forty knots. Waves were breaking onto our midships. Down below, Ian was howling like a tortured cat, and one of the girls was throwing up all over everything. I don't mind telling you, I was scared out of my wits. I knew God was punishing me. I didn't know for what – just for being me. I guess. That got me depressed. After a while, I didn't care if we sank.'

'You wouldn't sink. Those boats are built like steel.'

'Not with a hole in the bow.'

'What?'

'I told you one of the Jacuzzis was leaking? It turns out, a gasket in a return valve had worn away. The mate went down to turn on the bilge pumps and found out we were taking sea water up through the Jacuzzi in the bow. I couldn't keep pounding into the sea, or we'd fill.'

'So you ran from it.'

'I had to. I came down to bare poles and turned south.'

'Didn't you know what was down there?'

'Of course I did! You think I wanted to come to this tacky dump? I put out a sea anchor to slow us down. If the stupid

215

wind had stopped blowing, I wouldn't be here now. But it didn't, not until we were about fifteen minutes from being *on* Cuba. I had three choices; turn around and head north again, with a foot of water belowdecks, and maybe run into another blow and this time sink for sure; try to beat my way around the Cuban coast and go south to the Caymans, which would take at least a couple of days *if* we didn't get fired on by Cuban patrol boats; or sail into Havana Harbour, which was dead ahead. I sailed into the harbour.'

'Wise choice. But why did you have to ask for asylum?'

'Asylum! I never asked for asylum! I asked for assistance.'

'*What?* Who did you speak to?'

'Some Hispanic. On Channel 16.'

'Did you ask in English or Spanish?'

'God, Timothy! Who speaks Spanish?'

Burnham paused. He sent his mind forward two or three steps, hoping it would scan all the possibilities. Had the Cubans misunderstood? Had they deliberately set out to cause mischief?

'Is it true that you're threatening to blow up that Russian ship?'

'*What* Russian?' Theresa gasped. 'Omigod! That thing is a *Russian*? I don't want to blow up anybody. I just tied a line to him because my anchor windlass shorted out, and if I put a hook down here, I won't be able to get it up.'

'Sweet Jesus,' Burnham said. 'Who have you talked to?'

'Nobody, except that . . . Oh my!'

'What?'

'I don't believe it.'

'What?'

'That little *putz*.'

'*What*, for crissakes!'

'As we were coming into the harbour, I heard Ian screaming out his porthole. Rape, pillage, carnage, the whole number. I thought that wasn't a very smart way for us to throw ourselves on the mercy of a Communist dictator, so I went below and dragged him out of his cabin. I told him

216

our situation, but he wouldn't listen. He kept calling me names. So I punched him.'

'You punched him.'

'Well? I didn't *hurt* him, not really. I just bloodied his nose. Then I went up top. Five minutes later, I heard a commotion below. The mate had caught him broadcasting on the single sideband. She said he was saying "Rape!" and "Murder!" and a lot of dirty names into the radio. I don't know what-all he said, or to whom.'

'Where is he now?'

'Lashed to the mast. Bound and gagged.'

Burnham wondered if *any* of the information in the NSC Telex had been true. 'They say you refused to talk to the President.'

'That I did do,' Teresa said. 'I don't like him.'

'You don't like him.' Burnham squeezed his eyebrows with his fingertips.

'No. I'm sorry if that upsets you, but I don't.'

'Teresa . . . let me tell you what the situation is.'

'I just *told* you.'

'Have you ever heard of *Rashomon*?'

'You think I'm illiterate?'

'You just told me your side of the story. Now I'm going to tell you the other side of the story, and, unfortunately, that other side is the current reality.' He told her about the NSC Telex, about the threat to the Russian tanker, about the SEAL teams poised to strike under cover of darkness, about the Cubans hoping for trouble, about the deadline.

'But I never said any of that!' Teresa protested.

'Never mind. The message you send doesn't matter. The message received is all that counts.'

'What can I do?'

Burnham closed his eyes. An idea that had been ricocheting around the back of his mind lurched forward. He didn't know if it was any good, but he had no alternative.

'Hold on a second.'

He cupped the phone and said to Dyanna, 'I want you to

217

call Evelyn. Tell her I want somebody from the State Department to call the Cubans. Direct, not through the Swiss. Tell them that the yacht is crewed by sick people, diseased people, contagious people. Two of them have AIDS. It is going to be leaving the harbour, and we will pick it up outside and remove it from Cuban waters. Got that?'

'Yes, sir.' Dyanna looked terrified. She started to dial.

'And, Dyanna . . .'

'Yes, sir?'

'You can be polite with Evelyn. You should be. But don't *ask* her to do this. *Tell* her it's what we need. That's what she'll expect, and it's what she'll respect.'

'Yes, sir.'

Burnham spoke into the phone. 'Teresa, can you start your engine?'

'I think I can get her going on two cylinders, but I wouldn't trust her to –'

'That's good enough. I just need you to go a couple of miles. Got a white flag?'

'A white flag? No.'

'How about a white shirt?'

'*I* don't, but . . . Yes. Ian's wearing a Ralph Lauren that's white. Sort of. It had blood on it.'

'Never mind. Run it up your mast.'

'What am I doing, surrendering?'

'In a way. Now: I want you to do exactly as I say. First, fly that shirt. Second, start your engine. Third, untie yourself from that tanker. Fourth, head straight out of the harbour, nice and easy, until you're a couple of miles offshore, then turn southwest and just putt along. An American boat will come and take you in tow.'

'But what'll they *do* to me?'

'Nothing. I promise. They'll tow you to Guantanamo. I'll take it from there.'

'We're freaks, Timothy!' Teresa was panicking. 'Don't you know what Marines do to freaks?'

'Calm down, Teresa. Don't *you* know what Marines hate worse than freaks?'

'Nothing! Except maybe Communists.'

'They hate the brig. And bread and water. And two years at hard labour. And dishonourable discharges. And if any one of them does anything to you, that's what he's gonna get.'

'You can do that?'

'You better believe it.' Burnham wasn't sure *he* believed it, but he had to offer the guarantee.

'My!' Teresa said. 'You *have* done well.'

'Think you can do it?'

'Yes, if nobody shoots at me.'

'They won't,' Burnham said hopefully. 'and Toddy . . . Teresa . . . if this all . . . *when* this all works out and you're home safe and sound, I'll make sure you get your operation.'

'Who's going to pay for it?' Teresa laughed. 'The President?'

'Sure.' Burnham laughed, too. 'That's what America's all about, right? We take care of the tired, the poor, the huddled masses –'

'And the wretched refuse of your teeming shores. That's me. Wretched refuse.'

'Stop snivelling. Go rip the clothes off that pansy.'

'Timothy!'

'I've got to make a couple of calls to your . . . welcoming committee. This line'll stay open. If anything goes wrong, if you just want to talk . . . anything . . . give a holler and they'll get me. Okay?'

'Okay.'

Burnham looked at Dyanna as she hung up the phone.

'It's done,' she said, and she exhaled visibly.

He smiled at her. 'How do you feel?'

'Like the time I broke up with my first steady. It was real hard at first, but then I got warmed up, and –'

'Good.' Burnham asked Sergeant Pingrey to connect him to General Starkweather.

'Starkweather.'

'Timothy Burnham, General. The yacht is about to leave the habour. He'll –'

'He's surrendering. The Cuban's are gonna take him. I've got to –'

'How do you know? You're to-hell-and-gone down in Guantanamo.'

'I know, that's all. My men are –'

'Your men are to stay right . . . where . . . they . . . are. Is that clear?'

'But –'

'He is *not* surrendering. The Cubans know all about it. They'll let him go. He'll go offshore and head down toward you. I want you to dispatch a boat fast enough to get to him in a hurry and big enough to give him a tow back to the base.'

'What makes you so all-fired sure?' Starkweather added, with blatant contempt, 'Sir.'

He's been sitting around fuming, Burnham decided, bitching to all his junior officers about interference from the goddam egghead civilian know-nothings, and because they all value their lives they've been kissing his ass and telling him he should take control of the operation.

Time to put the general in his place again. He was astonished to find himself grinning.

'Because, General, he is doing what I told him to do.'

Starkweather paused. 'You talked to him?'

'At length, General. And I instructed him what to do. And I spoke to the Cubans –' What the hell, Burnham thought: in for a penny, in for a pound. '– and they have agreed to let him go. And you, General, if you have any interest in keeping your star and taking a cushy job with some weapons manufacturer when you retire and playing golf with the members of the Armed Services Committee, instead of retiring as a colonel and running a trailer park in Salt Lick, Florida, you, too, General, will do what I tell you.' Burnham took a breath. 'Understood?'

Two seconds passed before the general said, 'Understood.'

220

'You will take the yacht to Guantanamo, and there the crew will be treated with – and I mean this with absolute insistence – the utmost courtesy and respect, no matter what some of those bald goons who work for you may think of them. Aboard are three women and a man. The man is disturbed. His hallucinations started all this ruckus. He has been restrained, and I think he should be kept restrained until he can be transferred to the States. The vessel is in need of repair. You will have it repaired. When it is seaworthy, you will escort it out to international waters. Until that time, the crew will be your guests, and they will be treated as if they are the daughters of the President himself. Understood?'

'Understood.'

'Believe me, General, I will hear about it if there is a fuckup.' Pleased with his exit line, Burnham started to hang up. Then he remembered something, and he said, 'General?'

'Sir?'

'I have here the Telex you sent to the NSC. Where did that information come from? About his asking for asylum and threatening to blow up the Russian tanker.'

Starkweather's reluctance to answer was palpable. 'Is this line secure?' he asked at last.

Burnham assumed it was, but he wasn't certain. He chuckled derisively. 'Is this line *secure*?'

Starkweather lowered his voice, as if to ensure secrecy. 'LPers.' he said.

'What's an lp?'

'LP-*er*. Listening Poster. Infiltrators. They monitor radio transmissions, keep their eyes open. They don't miss a trick.'

'Do they speak Spanish?'

'Of course!'

'Then I fail to understand how . . .' Burnham stopped. He understood. 'But they don't speak English.'

'Why should they? The Cubans speak Spanish. Our men here translate for them.'

221

'I see.' Burnham waited, wondering if the synapses in the general's brain would suddenly begin to connect the neurons of cause to the neurons of effect. But the man's synapses, apparently, were off-duty. So Burnham said simply, 'Thanks, General,' and he hung up.

He punched up his open line to *Bilitis*. 'Teresa?'

'Hi, Timothy.'

'It's all set. They're on their way.'

'I'm almost at the mouth of the harbour.'

'They're not chasing you.'

'No.'

'When you get home, I want you to do me a favour.'

'Anything. I owe you my life.'

'Put a new plaque on the boat for me.'

'Saying?'

'"No man will be a sailor who has contrivance enough to get himself into a jail, for being in a ship is being in a jail, with the chance of being drowned. A man in a jail has more room, better food and, commonly, better company."'

Teresa laughed again. 'Who said that?'

'A friend of mine. And when you get the plaque all screwed into place . . .'

'Yes?'

'Sell the boat and be a decorator.'

Burnham put the receiver back in its cradle. He stood up and stretched. He felt elated, better than when he had written a good speech, better even than when he had been praised by the President himself. He had actually *done* something, and what he had done was good – good not only in the sense of well done, but also good for someone else. Maybe he had saved lives, maybe he had done something for the country. The idea of leaving his mark on the world had always seemed preposterous to him. But now, suddenly, he wondered, for he knew that a measure of his satisfaction came from the certainty that he had left – if not a mark, at least a tiny scratch, upon the wall of posterity.

A sweet little irony occurred to him then, and he

savoured it: he had acted on principle, had actually done something selfless, and the beneficiary was a member of Sarah's family. She would have to appreciate him, to acknowledge that for once he had done something worthy.

He looked at his watch. It was too early to call her: she would still be out selling macaroons for Kennedy. But when he spoke to her later on, and told her that Cobb had vowed to investigate the source of the bug in her car, and regaled her with his tale of rescuing Toddy from being garrotted by a Mohican-cut anthropoid camouflaged in lamp-black, she would have to relent. Without intention or design, he had bought himself a ticket home.

He had always believed in the apothegm: no good deed ever goes unpunished. Now he was finding it insufferably cynical.

He scooped his jacket off the couch and, as he slipped it on, crossed to the table where Dyanna sat, looking drained.

'Did we do it?' he said with a smile.

'Yes, sir!'

He put his hands on the edge of the table and leaned down toward her. 'I have a present for you from the President.'

'You do?' Dyanna brightened.

'He said to tell you that you're a source of comfort and strength to him.'

'Go on!'

'He told me to give you this.' Burnham reached a hand behind Dyanna's head and drew her to him. He kissed her full on the mouth.

For the first second, Burnham felt that he was kissing a piece of cold chicken. Her lips were firm and unyielding. Then they began to tremble, uneasily seeking an appropriate response. They parted, and Burnham felt warmth on his tongue. He wanted to flick his own tongue into that hot, wet cave, but no: it would be cruel.

He disengaged.

'Mr Burnham!'

'Don't blame me,' he said, slyly licking his lips to collect the sweet and fruity taste of her lip gloss. 'I was just following orders.'

'I . . . but . . . well . . .' One hand shot to her hair, the other to a button on her dress. They were diversionary hands, like a hen pheasant scampering this way and that before her nest to distract a predator from her eggs.

'You did good, Dyanna,' Burnham said honestly. 'I'm proud of you. And,' he smiled, 'you taste great.'

He walked toward the door, leaving her at the table, as red and shiny as a Bing cherry.

He was at the outer door when she thought to ask, 'Where are you going? I mean, if someone . . .'

'Where else? To see the President.'

'Oh.'

'It's hell, I know.' Burnham frowned and shook his head. 'But somebody's got to do it.'

Why had he kissed Dyanna? Why had he done that to her? For, he had to admit that he had done it *to* her. Not with her, or for her. *To* her. There were women whom you could kiss, in a burst of rash exuberance, and they would accept the kiss for what it was, a brief spasm of joy that had less to do with you or them than with the moment. He knew Dyanna well enough to know that she was not such a woman. To her a kiss was a covenant, to seal things past and promise things to come, the ultimate of which was the Act of Darkness itself, which to her (he was guessing wildly) would be a solemn ritual signifying commitment as permanent (and about as pleasurable) as a brand.

She would be confused now, wondering what he had meant by the kiss, unable to believe that it had been meaningless. Was he in love with her? Did he lust after her? What about his family? Suppose he asked her out, how should she respond? She shouldn't lead him on, but she didn't want to anger her boss, not when he was beginning to approach the throne.

The kiss to her would be like a Beckett play to a college student: she would study it, dissect it, analyse it, appraise it and inject it with the serum of significance, until at last she transformed the simple touching of four lips into a Rosetta Stone that would give meaning to her life.

That was not a nice thing to do, Burnham told himself as he turned out onto West Executive Avenue. When I return, I will apologize.

Head down, lost in thought, Burnham did not see Butterworth striding toward him, head down, lost in thought. They collided, like the *Andrea Doria* and the *Stockholm*. Burnham's bow struck Butterworth's port beam. Papers flew and fluttered down like falling leaves.

'Now look what you've done!' Butterworth said as he stooped to gather up his papers. 'Wrecked my proclamation for Rural Electric Power Week.'

'Sorry.' Burnham stooped to help him.

Butterworth flicked a wad of gum off one of his papers, and he stood up. 'Where have you been?'

'Me? Nowhere.'

'Cobb tells me the boss has gathered you to his bosom. True?'

'Hardly.' Burnham forced a weak laugh. He looked away, hoping to encourage Butterworth to join him searching for any stray papers. But Butterworth continued to look directly at him.

Ned Butterwoth was one of Burnham's two good friends on the staff. He affected the guise of the absent-minded academic, which was a calculated act, designed to keep Epstein's minions away from him, to lead them elsewhere with their assignments of interminable, repetitive, tedious, unrewarding messages to Congress, each of which involved many late nights, bitter arguments and countless drafts and re-drafts, all to no end whatever, since the President delivered his real messages to Congress in person, face to face.

Only Burnham, Cobb and a few of the other writers knew that Butterworth had a sharp and perceptive mind, an instinctive grasp of the complexities of foreign policy and the skill (when ignited) to turn out first-rate work in a very short time.

Burnham had never felt competitive with Butterworth.

He admired him, envied his facility, and consoled himself with the knowledge that Butterworth was five years older than he and had been a professional speechwriter for twenty years. Their friendship was based, in part, on the maintenance of their relative positions: Butterworth senior and superior, Burnham junior and respectful. Burnham had no desire to become a rival of Butterworth's. He had endured too many lunches at which Butterworth's viperous tongue had flayed writers who had had the temerity to accept an assignment to write a speech in the field he regarded as his private fiefdom, foreign policy.

For, as contemptuous as he claimed to be of authority, as ostentatiously blasé about power and power politics, Ned Butterworth was very human. He cherished praise from the President and framed his signed photographs, just like everyone else, and he collected nuggets of inside information and used them as prized chips in the daily game.

'I almost got fired,' Burnham said. 'If that's being gathered to his bosom, you can have it.'

'But you escaped.'

'Yeah. How, I don't know, but I did.'

'He asked for you by name, to write tonight's toast.'

'Not to write it, exactly. Just to clean up someone else's mess.' Burnham looked at his watch. 'I've got to –'

'What do *you* know about Banda?'

'Nothing!' As if pleading to the accusation in Butterworth's eyes, Burnham began to feel guilty. 'I'd never ever heard of the place.' Again he looked at his watch. 'I really gotta go, Ned.' Burnham started across the avenue.

'Rushing off to confer with the President, I expect.'

'Yeah, sure, Ned.' Burnham tossed a laugh over his shoulder. 'And tomorrow he's moving me right next to him in the West Wing.'

Shit! Burnham said to himself. I didn't ask for any of this. I didn't want any of this. I still don't.

He pulled open the door to the West Basement, and the cool darkness and the gentle hum of the air conditioning reminded him that he was entering the womb of power.

Liar. You love every minute of it.

He climbed the stairs, walked down the hall and turned into Evelyn Witt's office. 'Hi, Evelyn,' he said.

'Timothy! How did it go?'

'Okay, I think. Thanks for all your help. Dyanna was scared to death.'

'She's a sweet girl. She'll learn.' She glanced at her phone console. 'He's talking to the Speaker, but you go ahead in. He said he wanted to see you as soon as you got here.' She smiled. 'Give the poor man a word of comfort.'

'What's the problem?'

'He's been trying to write that letter for his nephew to Amherst.'

'I thought he already had a draft. MacGregor did it.'

'He didn't like it. It wasn't warm enough, didn't bring out the boy's true qualities.'

Burnham recalled MacGregor bemoaning the difficulty in finding satisfactory circumlocutions with which to praise a boy whose true qualities were twin 400s on his SATs and substantial evidence of incipient alcoholism. MacGregor had dwelt at length on the lad's athletic prowess, calling him the finest lacrosse player since Crazy Horse.

'So he's doing it himself,' Evelyn said, 'but if he puts in any of the language I've heard bouncing off the walls in there, the wretched child won't get into Dannemora.'

'I'll see what I can do.' Burnham started for the door to the President's office.

Evelyn's phone rang. She picked it up, listened, and said, 'Timothy.'

'For me?'

'No safe haven.' Evelyn smiled.

Burnham took the phone. 'Burnham.'

'Sergeant Pingrey here, sir. He's out. The Navy should have him in about ten minutes.'

'Thanks, Sergeant. You've been a big help.'

'My pleasure, sir.'

The President was leaning back in his high-backed, spring-loaded leather chair, his feet propped up on the

227

desk, the phone cradled on his shoulder, picking at his cuticles with a letter opener. At the sound of the door opening, he snapped his head around and glowered, but when he saw Burnham he smiled and waved him in.

'The problem is,' the President said into the phone, 'he tests as if he was a damn Ubangi. I've got to say I know he's smarter than his test scores, but I'm gonna need reinforcement. I need you to promise you'll make him an intern next summer. You don't have to *do* it. Just tell me you'll do it, and back me up if anybody asks . . . No . . . The damn place doesn't take a dime of Federal money, or I'd have 'em by the balls . . . Okay . . . I appreciate it. Thanks.'

He hung up the phone, swung his feet to the floor and stood up. 'Children,' he said to Burnham. 'Children are like pancakes: you should always throw out the first one.'

Burnham smiled and thought: I'll tell Sarah. That touching thought will secure the President a place in her heart.

'Well?' said the President. 'Where are we, Tim?'

'He's out, sir. No fireworks. The Navy will pick him up in a couple of minutes.'

'Damn!' The President grinned. He came around his desk, grabbed Burnham's hand and shook it. With his other hand, he squeezed Burnham's shoulder. 'Damn! How'd you do it?'

Burnham tried to appear casual, matter-of-fact, but he couldn't suppress a smile, couldn't contain the adrenalin that flooded his arteries. This, he thought, must be how Doug Flutie felt after he threw that sixty-four-yard touchdown pass in the last four seconds of the game against Miami. Sheer, unalloyed pride. 'I . . . talked him down, sir.'

'I thought he wouldn't talk to us.'

'Yes, sir. Well . . . I . . .' Don't tell him the whole truth, don't make it seem too easy, don't dilute your triumph. 'It took some work, but I got to him.'

'Damn! That's delicate stuff. You done that before?'

228

'Here and there.' Burnham looked at his feet, shoved his hands into his pockets. 'I –'

'Never mind. I don't want to know. You did it, son. That's what counts with me. Results.'

'Yes, sir. Ah . . . you should know, Mr President, I had to promise him a couple of things. Nothing too –'

'Look here, Tim.' The President squeezed his shoulder harder. 'I don't care if you had to promise him a shiny new galvanized dick.'

'Not quite, sir.' Burnham chuckled.

'You got us out of a nasty fracas down there, so whatever commitments you had to make, I'll honour 'em.'

When that requisition comes in, Burnham thought, I believe I would like to be in Fiji.

'Now, Tim . . .' The President led Burnham toward his desk. 'I want you to help me with a little personal problem.'

'Of course, sir.'

The President explained the quandary he was in regarding his nephew. The boy was not qualified to go to Amherst, should never have applied to Amherst, should have been content to attend a state university or one of those third-rate party schools named after an obscure Civil War colonel. But the boy's mother's father had gone to Amherst, and since the boy's mother – 'a stuck-up, contrary bitch, all she likes to do is come here and suck up champagne with the Brits and the Frogs' – worshipped her father and believed that Amherst could compensate for whatever qualities had been omitted from her son's genetic makeup, she had insisted that the boy apply to Amherst.

'I don't care if they pitch him out after half an hour,' the President said. 'That's no reflection on me. They all go bad someday. But if he can't even get in! Shit, if Brooke Shields can get into Princeton, my nephew can damn well get into Amherst.'

He had pulled out all possible stops. The Speaker would write a letter and would offer the boy an internship, and while Amherst wasn't in the Speaker's district, it was at least in his state, and that had to count for something.

His problem was with the letter he had agreed to write on the boy's behalf. It had to be laudatory but not absurd, general but full of specifics, brief but comprehensive.

'Would you take a shot at it for me, Tim?'

'Of course, sir.'

The President handed him a yellow legal pad and Mac-Gregor's draft of the letter, which appeared to have been attacked by pencil-wielding termites. It was scratched, torn, covered by lines. Xs and such exclamations as 'Horse *shit!*'

Burnham turned toward the door.

'No no!' the President said, taking his arm and guiding him to the couch. 'You sit right here. I'll make a couple of calls. I've gotta call a little girl in Nebraska who saved her dog from drowning. Or maybe it was her brother. Maybe it was the dog who saved her brother. Whatever.' He returned to his desk, flung himself into his chair and, over his intercom, told Evelyn to place the call to Nebraska.

Burnham hummed to himself, to blot out the President's voice, as he studied MacGregor's draft of the letter. It was a serviceable letter, but obviously written by someone who did not know the President's nephew. It was full of phrases like 'inquiring mind', 'eager to learn' and 'significant contribution to the Amherst community'. It said nothing, in about 250 carefully chosen words.

Again Burnham was impressed by the President's acuity. He could spout empty rhetoric, sign vapid letters, ooze with unfelt treacle – as long as nothing was at stake. But when substance mattered, he could spot its absence as quickly (as he once told Cobb) 'as a fly finds shit'.

Burnham began to scribble, as in the background the President lavished praise on the Nebraska girl, who had begun the conversation as 'a brave and selfless child' but had by now evolved into 'a shining example of the kind of dedicated, fearless Amerians this country will be counting on as we forge ahead to face the challenges of the Twenty-First Century.'

Under Burnham's pen, the President's nephew was being transformed. No longer was he 'eager to learn'; instead, he had 'begun to find himself after a painful growth spurt' (the miserable test scores had to be acknowledged, however tacitly). If the lad had neglected his studies, it was so he could spend time at the President's side, earning a 'lunch-pail degree' in the business of government (as far as Burnham knew, the kid had never been in Washington). What had most impressed the President, however, was a time when his nephew had broken his ankle and, defying doctor's orders, had insisted on joining a protest march against rent-gouging by slumlords in his own town (a complete fabrication: Burnham suspected that if the kid knew what slumlords were, he applauded them for being pretty clever).

Burnham read over the new paragraphs. Too much, he concluded. An utter fiction. An insult to the President to imagine that he would endorse such a patent lie.

'Well, Tim?' The President stood over him, hand extended. 'What've we got?'

'Oh! I . . . I'm not . . . I don't think you could read it, sir.' Burnham tried to crumple the paper, but the President plucked it from his hand.

'No time for modesty, Tim,' he said.

The President began to read the letter, squinting at the hastily written words, speaking the sentences silently to himself.

Now you've torn it, Burnham thought. He was sweating again. His stomach complained at the sudden onset of anxiety and, vengefully, fired a fart that was silenced by the thick upholstery of the couch.

'This, Tim . . .' The President looked at Burnham. His face was solemn. He held the piece of paper in one hand and slapped it rhythmically with the other. 'This is what I call writing.'

'Wh . . . oh . . . thank you, sir.'

'This is . . . it! This is a portrait of my nephew.'

'It is? I mean . . .' For what reason, Burnham wasn't

sure, but he felt compelled to disclaim his own lie. 'I was worried it might be a little . . . exaggerated.'

'Not a bit. It's true, that's what's important. Facts aren't important, as long as they support the truth.' The President smiled. '"Lunch-pail degree". I'd forgotten that. Damn right!'

Forgotten it? Burnham thought. How do you forget something that never was?

The President dropped the piece of paper on his desk, turned and sat on the corner of the desk. He said, 'You've been a big help to me in the past couple of days.'

'Thank you, sir.'

'Now, about this business with Andrei . . .'

The door to the private office opened, and Epstein hurried in, followed by Duggan.

'Damn it, Mario!' the President said. 'You forgotten how to knock?'

'Sir?' Epstein stopped. 'I'm sorry. I –' He saw Burnham then, but he did not acknowledge him.

'Never mind. What is it?'

Epstein waved a Telex. 'This just came in. He's out. We've got him.'

'Who?'

'The lunatic in Havana. The Navy's got him.'

'Old news, Mario, old news.'

'Sir?'

The President gestured at Burnham. 'Tim got him out, just like he said he would.'

Epstein looked at Burnham. His eyes were as cold as a crocodile's. 'I see.'

'Jolly good,' said Duggan, and he saluted Burnham with his pipe.

Epstein scowled at Duggan as if the man had a booger on his lip.

A buzzer sounded on the President's desk. He snatched up the phone and said, 'What?' He listened for a few seconds. 'Oh. Okay. Be right there.' He hung up and said, 'What the hell's a Young President?'

'Sir?' Burnham wondered if he was being asked a riddle.

'They tell me I've got to speak to some group called the Young Presidents. Don't they know there's no such thing as a young President? Soon as you take the oath of office, you're as old as the hills and twice as mossy.'

'It's a youth group, sir,' Epstein said. 'Movers and shakers.'

'Plotters and schemers, more likely. Did you write it, Tim?'

'No, sir.'

'Damn. Well, I'll go spin 'em a yarn or two.' The President patted Burnham on the back, and, ignoring Epstein and Duggan, marched out of his office.

Nobody else moved. Burnham didn't know what was expected of him, so, with a feeble attempt at a polite smile in Epstein's direction, he turned to go.

'Who *are* you?' Epstein might as well have shouted, 'Halt!'

Burnham stopped and turned his head. 'Nobody.'

Epstein nodded. 'You know it, and I know it. How come the President doesn't know it?'

Burnham said (and immediately wished he hadn't), 'He must be an extraordinary judge of character.'

'Listen you . . .' Epstein took a step toward him. 'I'm gonna find out who the hell you are.'

'Feel free. I have no secrets.'

'I don't trust you,' Epstein said, 'and I don't like you.'

'And I don't blame you.' Burnham was wearying of Epstein's bluster. 'Now, if you've finished threatening me, I'll be on my way.' He nodded to Duggan, who raised his pipe in civil reply, and walked out into Evelyn Witt's office, closing the door behind him.

Evelyn was typing. When she saw Burnham, she picked up a sheet of yellow legal paper and held it between her fingertips as if it were a dead mouse. 'This,' she said, 'this is going to be sent to Amherst College? On White House stationery? Who is this supposed to be about?'

'It contains a cosmic truth, Evelyn,' Burnham said,

233

grinning. 'The President saw it right away. Our problem is, we can't see the forest for the trees. That's why we're not President.'

'If I didn't know you so well, Timothy,' Evelyn said with a bemused look, 'I'd say you were becoming a dangerous man.'

Dyanna was preparing to leave for the day, a ritual that took her from fifteen to thirty minutes, depending on the weather, for she regarded her daily emergence into public view with as much care and concern as if she were Laurette Taylor making an entrance in *The Glass Menagerie*: First appearances formed an audience's impression of a character. If it was windy, she sprayed her hair; rainy, she covered it with a scarf; sunny, she chose one shade of makeup; cloudy, another shade.

Her mirror was propped on her desk, and she was creating a self-portrait in lip-liner.

'I owe you an apology,' Burnham said.

'For what?'

Sly minx, he thought. Trying to make believe it didn't happen. Get angry! Tell me off! Then it won't gnaw at you.

'My impetuous assault upon your person.'

'Don't be silly, it was nothing.' She stretched her mouth. But you won't forget it, will you? 'No, really, I do apologize.'

'Mr Burnham . . .' She looked at him now. 'It wasn't like it was the greatest kiss I've ever had.'

Good, he thought, there you go. 'No. But it was stupid of me.'

'Yes,' she said, and she closed the subject with, 'We all make mistakes.'

The floor of Burnham's office was littered with papers. He gathered them into a pile and dropped them beside the shredder. Before he left, he would separate the sensitive papers from the routine and would shred them. If he tried to shred everything, page by page, he'd be there till midnight.

Before he left? Where was he going to go? Back to the Y, to watch *Dynasty* in the common room with a Fuller Brush man and a couple of out-patients?

No. He was going home. Now was the time to play his trump with Sarah.

He dialled his home number. It rang four times before Sarah picked up.

'Hi, Sarah,' he said cheerily.

'Hello.' She sounded as effusive as a slug.

'How are you?'

'All right.'

She was not going to make it easy for him. He spoke quickly. 'I talked to Cobb. He promises me he'll launch a full-scale investigation into that bug in your car. He can't believe the Administration had anything to do with it – neither can I, frankly – but if it did, he'll get you an answer.'

'Get *me* an answer? What about you? Don't you care?'

'Of course! I just meant –'

'No, you don't. You just want to come home.'

'Hey –'

'You think I'd believe anything Warner Cobb told you?'

'What would you believe, then?'

'I'd believe it if they admitted it. Fat chance. Look, Timothy, I've got to go . . .'

'Where are you going?'

'Out.'

Hurry up, Burnham told himself. 'I saved your precious cousin Toddy Thatcher today.'

'Toddy? From what?'

'From being blown up, that's all.' Burnham gave her an abbreviated version of the Toddy/Teresa saga. At the end, he said, 'I really felt proud. I did something good, for once.'

He waited for her praise.

'Timothy,' she said, 'you're pathetic.'

'*What?*'

'This fairy tale and a dollar will get you a ride on the Metro.'

'You don't believe me? Call Evelyn Witt. Call the President! I spent the whole afternoon in his office. He thinks I'm terrific.'

'He has no taste. Goodbye, Timothy.'

'God damn it!' Burnham shouted. 'I'm coming home.'

'I thought you might say that,' she said evenly, 'so I changed the locks.'

'You *what*?' Sonja. This was a Sonja trick. Sarah even sounded like Sonja.

'Goodbye.'

'No! Wait!' But she hung up.

Congratulations, he thought. Welcome home.

He looked up. Dyanna was standing at the outer door. She had to have heard the entire conversation.

'I understand,' she said. 'Now.' She pulled open the door.

Burnham rested his fist on his forehead. Wonderful. Now she thinks I kissed her because my marriage is breaking up. I couldn't help myself. I was propelled by something deep. Like mortal loneliness. Or existential sadness. Or terminal horniness.

When he looked up again, Dyanna still had not left. She was standing in the open doorway, talking to a black cleaning woman, who was pointing at him.

'It's all right,' he said to Dyanna. 'Let her in.' He stood up and walked around his desk. 'I've only got one more call to make, and I can do it from your desk.'

Dyanna stepped back, and the cleaning woman shoved her cart forward with such vehemence that as it rounded the corner into Burnham's office, it rose up onto two wheels. She was in her fifties, Burnham guessed, and she had a pronounced limp. Her hair flew out from her head, and her eyes were glazed.

Silly woman thinks she's Mario Andretti, he decided. She looks wired. But then, if I had to push a cart around the EOB all day, I think I'd stick something up my nose, too.

As Burnham left his office and headed for Dyanna's desk, he noticed that as soon as she was alone, the cleaning woman seemed to calm down. She was still breathing heavily, but she began meticulously to dust around every picture in the office, only occasionally glancing his way.

He rooted through his pockets until he found the slip of paper. He stared at it for a long moment, sighed and said to himself, What the hell . . .

Then he dialled Eva.

Nine

The dustrag was a metronome in Ivy's hand. Flip-flop-flip-flop-flip-flop, it danced over the top of the dark wood frame of the old painting of the square-rigged sailing ship. Her hand lived independent of her, powered by an internal battery that she couldn't turn off. Her feet shuffled in rhythm with her hand, sending pennants of pain up her bad leg. The pain was curious: she knew it was there but she was detached from it, didn't seem to care about it.

Her eyes wandered out into the secretary's office and landed on the Burnham fellow, sitting at the secretary's desk and cooing to some honey on the phone. She sent him a thought that said, Scram: don't you have anything better to do?

She had been waiting for hours to get into this office. At first, she had been so anxious that she prowled the halls and cleaned everything in sight. Suppose she couldn't get any more papers for Mr Pym and Mr Pym lost interest and wouldn't get Jerome his diploma. Jerome would fall in with a rough crowd and start mugging people, and he'd pick the wrong dude to mug, and the dude would blow him away. The thoughts made her more anxious, and the anxiety generated more bad thoughts, and soon she was flitting around the halls like a hummingbird trying to distract herself, with the result that she tripped on a doorstep and pulled something in her bad leg. She took one of Mr Pym's pills, and not only did the pain fade but the anxiety did, too, so she took another one.

After an hour or so, she felt bathed in confidence and control, and whereas, before, she had stayed away from this Burnham's office till she was sure he had left, now she didn't care if he was there or not, so she had pushed open the door to the office and said to the Debbie Reynolds secretary, 'I got to clean.'

'Come back later,' Debbie Reynolds had said, 'Mr Burnham's still working.'

'He's not working,' Ivy had said. 'Look, he's sitting.'

'I beg your pardon!'

'You're welcome.'

Then the Burnham fellow had done the right thing and told her to come on in.

Now, if he'd just get out of here, she could do her job and be gone.

She heard him say something like, 'See you soon,' and hang up the phone, and she flopped her dustrag at one of the windowsills. Flip-flop-flip-flop. Maybe she should hire her hand out as a windshield wiper.

'Excuse me?' He was standing in the doorway.

Not bad. Civilized, anyway. Debbie Reynolds didn't say 'excuse me'.

Be polite. Don't want to leave a bad impression. Don't want to leave any impression at all. They claim they can't tell you-all apart unless you sass 'em. 'Yessir?'

He pointed to a pile of papers over by the wastebasket. 'Those all get burned, don't they?'

'To a cinder.'

'Good. I didn't want to have to sit here and shred them.'

'I'll make sure they go up the chimney.'

'Thanks. Goodnight.'

''Night.'

She waited until she heard the outer door close, then headed straight for the pile of papers.

Remember the camera in the chandelier, the microphones in the dingle-dangles. To hell with them, keep your back to them, they'll never be able to prove a thing.

She saw the first paper on the file. It was slugged TOP SECRET.

Bingo.

She turned over another paper. TOP SECRET – urgent.

Big league. This stuff'd make Mr Pym sit up and take notice. Let him dribble it out at his swell affairs, he'll be so much in demand he'll prob'ly have to sell stock in himself and become a conglomerate.

But be careful. Suppose they run a search on you on the way out.

No big deal. She picked up the two papers and, keeping her back to the chandelier, walked to the desk. She found a pair of scissors and clipped off the classification slugs.

There. Now no one can say anything.

She scooped the rest of the papers into a trash bag, tied it off and dropped it onto her cart. She tidied up the desk and looked around to make sure everything was in place.

Then she left, pushing her cart ahead of her and turning out the lights.

She was amazed at how brilliant she was.

'I won't do it,' Eva said to her father, who was slicing smoked salmon into paper-thin leaves.

'Of course you will.' He didn't bother to look at her.

'I'll leave. I'll find some other way to pay you back.'

'No you won't. You don't want to go to jail again.'

'I don't believe you.'

'Yes you do, or you wouldn't be trying to talk me out of it. You'd've left already.' He lay the razor edge of the filleting knife against the soft flesh and slashed it with quick expertise.

'But *why*? Don't you have any –'

'No, I don't. None at all. This is a once-in-a-lifetime chance for me, and it's not asking too much of you to help me.'

'They could lock me up for life! You too.'

'Only if you get caught. And if you do what I tell you, you won't.' Pym was reassured by the certainty in his own voice.

He had to convince Eva, true, but he also had to convince himself. 'Now,' he said, 'tell me.'

She told him about the squash game and the lunch and the sudden summons to the Oval Office.

'What about the allergies?'

'What I thought. He's super-sensitive to chemicals. His body overreacts to everything. I put him up with an amino acid in about two minutes. I didn't have a chance to see what'll bring him down.'

'What's he like?'

'Naïve. Out of his depth. He doesn't know who he is or what he's got. Nice. Kind of charming'

Charming. Pym didn't like that. He looked at Eva, but now she wouldn't look at him.

'What are his politics?'

'I couldn't tell. I don't know that he believes in anything very strongly.'

'Good. The mushy ones can be prodded. Is he married?'

'Sort of. Something's wrong there, but I don't know what.'

'Find out. That sounds like a real weak spot.'

She didn't respond. Pym couldn't tell if she was sad or frightened. Her face was slack.

The doorbell rang. Pym frowned and looked at Eva, who shook her head. It rang again, urgently. Pym wiped his hands on a dishrag and left the kitchen.

Ivy was through the door before it was all the way open, dragging her tote bag into the living room.

'Ivy! What a nice surprise!' Pym hated surprises, especially from people who were providing him with documents stolen from the White House.

'I know I should've called,' Ivy said, 'but . . .' With a dismissive wave of her hand, she plopped herself down onto the sofa.

She's drunk, Pym thought. Then, suddenly, from nowhere: Mother of God, she's been caught! No. Control yourself. Don't panic.

He wondered if his passport was still valid.

He forced himself to say, 'Not at all, my dear. Always glad to see you.'

Eva came out of the kitchen. She looked at Ivy for a long moment before saying, 'Are you okay?'

'Sure.' Ivy smiled.

'How's your leg?'

'No *prob*lem.'

Eva said, 'That's what I thought.'

Pym saw Eva glare at him as she turned back into the kitchen, but he didn't know why until he looked again at Ivy and saw the stuporous grin still stretching her face.

The pills. She was carrying a load of Percodan. Had anyone at the White House noticed? Had she been fired? Was that why she was here?

'How was your day?' he asked.

'Wait'll you see,' Ivy said. 'I brought you some goodies.'

Eva returned with a cup of tea for Ivy, so strong it was almost black. Ivy sipped at it contentedly.

Pym could tell that Ivy was floating in a friendly fog in which time did not exist. She made no move to show him her goodies, so he pointed at the bag and said, 'May I?'

'Be my guest.'

He dumped the tote bag in the middle of the rug and sat beside the heap of papers. The first two papers he examined had been cut by scissors. He held them up to Ivy. 'What happened to these?'

'I cut the TOP SECRET off 'em, so if they stopped me, they couldn't prove anything.'

Pym blinked and bit his lip. 'I see.' This woman, he thought, is a live bomb. The sooner Eva can get her hooks into Burnham and retire Ivy to the sidelines, the better.

He read the two papers. Before he had finished the first, he had begun to perspire. It was a CIA memorandum about America's newest Asian oil ally, Banda. If the Mother got her hands on this, she could reap a whirlwind of publicity about the friends being wooed by the West's self-styled champion of human rights.

The other had to be a joke; a transsexual plot to blow up

a Russian tanker in Cuba? But the National Security Council was not known for its pixie sense of humour.

The rest of the papers were incomprehensible – Energy Department documents and charts that looked routine but might be critical. It wasn't his job to judge.

'Lovely,' he said to Ivy. 'These are lovely.'

Ivy was leaning back in the couch now, her feet out, her shoes off. 'Glad you like 'em.'

'Yes. We're developing a nice portrait of our Mr Burnham.'

Pym was exultant. This was the material he needed. It would give him credibility. It was unimpeachably authentic and (some of it, at least) undeniably important. It was also exquisitely secret: the Energy Department papers were slugged with a classification so high that Pym had never heard of it. They were to be read only by those with something called Q Clearance.

He was itching to get to work. Evening was prime time for initiating contacts.

First, however, he had to get Ivy out of there. She looked as if she was settling in for a long stay.

He said to Eva, 'You should go or you'll be late. Why don't you drop Ivy off on the way?'

It took Eva a beat to pick up the cue, and for those few seconds there was a look in her eyes that unsettled Pym.

'All right,' she said at last.

'Okay by me.' Ivy leaned forward and, as she searched for her shoes, said to Pym, 'Having any luck with the diploma?'

'Oh!' He had shoved it out of his mind. 'Yes. By the end of the week. For sure.'

'Top shelf.' She stood up and yawned. 'I feel like I've been on a roller coaster.'

At the door, Pym ushered Ivy into the hallway, then turned to Eva and said with a sly smile, 'Remember, my dear, what the sage said: "Freedom is a precious commodity, and no price we pay for it is too high."'

Eva looked at him as if he was a stranger who had

propositioned her in an elevator. 'I'd rather remember what Janis Joplin said: "Freedom's just another word for nothin' left to lose".'

Pym started to say, 'Who?' but Eva was already following Ivy down the stairs.

Pym locked the door. He went to the phone and stood with his eyes closed, summoning the mnemonic tricks of recalling phone numbers. He had been taught a kind of meditative visionism: he told his mind to see a slot machine, and on top of the machine in bold gold letters was the word CONTACTS. His mind pulled the handle of the machine, and one by one, numbers dropped beneath each letter.

It worked the first time. Pleased with himself, excited, he sat on the sofa and dialled the number, rolling his code name around on his tongue.

'Hello.' The voice was not familiar, but that didn't mean anything. Replacements came and went. But what if they had changed the number without telling him?

Pym held a finger over the phone cradle, prepared to sever the connection immediately, and said, 'This is Mallard.'

'Teal,' came the reply, without missing a beat. 'What do you want?'

Recognition! Affirmation! He existed! He wanted to chat, to catch up, but this was hardly the time. He said, 'I want a meeting.'

'When?'

'Soon.'

'An hour. You know The Devil's Disciple?'

'The what?'

'A bar. In Georgetown. Carry a copy of *US*. I'll have *People*.'

Things were going too fast. He couldn't keep up. 'A copy of what?'

'*US, US, US!* One hour.'

The line went dead.

A bar! Since when did spies meet in bars? They were supposed to meet in parks, under bridges, on rooftops, someplace where they could talk. And what was this *US* business?

He felt suddenly very old.

He had never been in a bar in Georgetown. What did people wear to Georgetown bars? Silk shirts and gold chains? Suppose they all looked like Michael Jackson. He didn't want to be conspicuous, like an undertaker at an orgy.

Don't worry. By yourself. If somebody stops you at the door, say you're a seltzer salesman.

He chose an old tweed sports jacket, polyester slacks, cordovan shoes and a white shirt.

He put the most impressive of the White House documents into a manila envelope and went downstairs.

He had deduced the US was a magazine, so he stopped at the news-stand on the corner and bought a copy. Brooke Shields was on the cover, which made it difficult to distinguish *US* from most of the other magazines on the rack, since she was also on the covers of *Mademoiselle, Vogue, Seventeen, Self, Glamour, Life* and *National Enquirer*.

He hailed a taxi.

'Georgetown,' he told the driver. 'You know The Devil's Disciple?'

'You know the Washington Monument?' the driver sneered.

In the darkness, Pym slid the manila envelope inside the copy of *US*.

At first, he thought there had been an accident or a homicide in The Devil's Disciple. Cars were triple-parked on the street. Men and women swarmed around the stained-glass windows and swinging doors. Then, as he saw drinks passed from hands to grasping hands through the doors, as he saw desperate young women trying to bull their way into the bar, as he heard a torrent of talk and laughter that sounded like a waterfall, he realized that this was not an atmosphere of fear or anger or violence.

This was a good time.

The men wore pinstripe suits or jogging clothes, army

jackets or polo shirts. The women wore jeans or mumus, lounging slacks or short shorts, business suits or evening dresses.

Sybaris. In one of his many stops during his pilgrimage to Washington decades ago, Pym had read about Sybaris. Soon they will teach their horses to dance, he thought, and all will come tumbling down. About time, too.

The thought made him feel righteous, justified in what he was about to do. And then it occurred to him that he was doing it so that he could stay here forever, and righteousness gave way to uncertainty.

He had a more immediate problem: how to get into The Devil's Disciple.

What a stupid place to call a meeting! What was he supposed to do, set the place on fire? For sure, two 'pardons' and an 'excuse me' wouldn't work.

He could pretend to be mad, could slobber and curse and grope his way through the crowd. Middle-class Americans were terrified of crazy people. In his neighbourhood, weirdos were as common as broken glass, but in this part of Georgetown they were not acceptable.

No. He might get arrested.

He would be forceful. Americans respected force. It was synonymous with good.

He took out his wallet and held it open, so that the photograph on his driver's licence was visible. The rest of the licence he covered with his fingers.

He took a deep breath and stepped forward.

'Police,' he said. 'Stand aside.'

Two floozies stared at him. They didn't budge.

'Move, damn it!' he snarled.

They moved. One of them muttered, 'Townie.'

He shoved his way through the crowd, saying, 'Police . . . move it!' And, to his delight and astonishment, the crowd parted. He felt like Moses.

When he was inside, he put his wallet away.

The bar was five-deep with drinkers. Tables for four were jammed with six or eight. Harassed, sweating barmaids elbowed their way from table to table, delivering white-wine spritzers and *bons mots*.

Pym tucked the copy of *US* under his arm so that the logo protruded prominently. He made his way to the far wall and edged along, peering over shoulders in search of a copy of *People*.

The din was painful because it was cumulative: people unable to hear one another speak raised their voice, which encouraged their neighbours who couldn't hear themselves speak to shout, which made their neighbours, who couldn't hear themselves shout, scream.

In the farthest corner of the room, at a table squeezed between two enormous rubber plants, beneath a poster for the movie of *And Quiet Flows The Don*, sat a single man, drinking something amber, reading *People*.

The man didn't see him, so Pym had a moment to study him. He was young (in his early thirties), blond (if the hair was his) and dressed like one of the characters in that show Pym's help liked to watch on kitchen TVs while waiting for the guests to finish their dessert and move into the drawing room: *Miami Vice*. He wore a white linen jacket, a cotton shirt open to the waist, lime-green slacks and soft-leather slip-ons. No socks.

How had this creature been recruited? He was a stereotype of the American go-getter; slick, hip, rich. What could the Soviet Union possibly offer him that he would value? Money?

Maybe he was being blackmailed. Maybe he had relatives in the USSR. Maybe he was a restless failure in search of cheap thrills. Pym had read newspaper accounts about all intelligence services being plagued these days by such volatile romantics.

Still, the man was not altogether stupid, for Pym now understood the advantages of meeting in a cattle car like this: in an open park, or on a Potomac bridge, two agents could be seen and, with modern technology, easily over-heard. In here, a dozen rowdies could hatch a plot to firebomb the Vatican and nobody would suspect a thing.

247

Pym stood over the man and dropped the copy of *US* on the table. He said, 'Teal?'

The man's eyes were sleepy, the lids drooping halfway down his eyeballs. For a second, Pym thought he was drunk. But then he saw the eyes scan him like a computer searching a data bank, absorbing information from his shoes to the crown of his head.

'Hey, man,' Teal said. 'Grab a chair.'

Pym sat.

'Long time no see.'

Long time? Pym thought. How about never? He said, 'Yes.'

'What you been up to?'

'This and that. Business has been slow.'

'Sure' Teal was trying to be genial, but his hooded eyes made Pym feel he was being appraised by an asp. 'There was talk maybe you'd gone *out* of business.'

Pym felt ice in the back of his throat. 'What? That's – No!'

A waitress stopped at the table. She held a tray of empty glasses in one hand, a pencil in the other. She was exhausted. Perspiration streaked her eye-liner. Her long fingernails were cracked, the polish chipped. Her hair dangled like weeds. She smelled rancid.

'What'll it be, man?' Teal asked.

'Bourbon,' Pym said. 'Yes, bourbon.'

'And bring me another Chivas, honey.'

As the waitress scribbled, Teal ran his eyes up and down her. He said, 'Hey, babe, what's your sign?'

'Get stuffed,' said the waitress, and she turned away.

'The Constellation of Get Stuffed.' Teal laughed. 'Don't you *love* this country?'

Pym's eyes must have betrayed his surprise, for all he was able to say was, 'But what are you –' before Teal held up a hand, cutting him off, and shook his head.

'A man's gotta do what a man's gotta do,' Teal said.

'Oh.'

'So what's goin' down, man?'

'I've got a new contact,' Pym said.

'Where at?'

'The White House.' Nicely understated, Pym complimented himself as he waited for the impact of the three magic words to penetrate Teal's carapace of cool.

Teal said nothing. His expression didn't change. After what seemed to Pym to be a month, Teal turned away and took a sip of Scotch and spat out 'The White House.' Teal's contempt suggested that Pym had just revealed an agent in place at the Bureau of Labour Statistics.

'Yes!' Pym was angry, defensive.

'I don't know where you're comin' from, old man, but the fact is that nobody in the White House knows fuck-all worth fuck-all, except right up at the tippy-top. It's too compartmentalized. The NSC's a bunch of drones. One guy knows which Venezuelan has the clap, another guy knows which Nigerian has more Swiss bank account than the Swiss, and maybe a third guy knows which Berbers like to hump camels. But they never talk to each other. The only people who *really* know anything are functionaries in the State Department, the CIA and the NSA.'

'But –'

'Of course, I may be underestimating you.' Teal leaned forward, his elbows on the table, his hands folded, his eyes bulging under their lids and making him look even more like a reptile. 'Maybe you're gonna tell me that you've turned Dennis Duggan or Mario Epstein or – sure, why not? – Benjamin T. Winslow his very self. Are you?'

'Not –'

'Because if you are, I'm gonna have you sent to the funny farm.'

Never in his life had Pym struck another human being in anger, but now he had to clutch his knees to keep his hands from flinging the table on top of this impudent twit.

'Listen here, you . . . you . . . horrid little know-it-all . . .'

Teal blinked. In his time he had probably been called every street name ever coined. But 'know-it-all'?

Pym shoved his copy of *US* into Teal's lap and snatched Teal's copy of *People* from the table. 'You look at the those papers. If they're worthless, then you can put a black mark through my name and forget I ever existed. But if any brains are growing under that toupée of yours, you'll appreciate what I've given you, and you can call me.' Pym rolled up the magazine, pushed back his chair and stood.

'Toupée?' said Teal. *'Toupée?'* He grabbed a handful of yellow hair and pulled at it.

Pym could hear his phone ringing as he turned his key in the ground-floor door. It was still ringing when he arrived at the second-floor landing, but then it stopped.

He wasn't worried. Teal would call back every ten minutes. That was the established routine in such cases. Besides, it might do the insufferable snot good to be kept waiting.

Assuming, that is, that the caller had been Teal. Perhaps it had been Eva. Or Ivy. Perhaps . . .

He poured himself a glass of sherry and sat on the couch.

It *had* to have been Teal. The documents were good. Good? They were sensational! A mental defective could see that they were dynamite.

Dynamite. Perhaps Teal had concluded that he, Pym, was dynamite, too quick-tempered and unpredictable to be reliable. He shouldn't have mouthed off. Perhaps Teal was this very minute arranging for Pym to be hit by a taxi.

Stop it.

He took a sip of sherry and looked at his watch.

The phone rang.

'Hello.'

'Teal.'

'Mallard.'

'The hostess wants you to know that your *hors d'oeuvres* tonight were very good. Very, very good.'

Control yourself, Pym commanded. Don't shout 'hooray' or say something stupid like 'I told you so'.

But it was difficult, for Pym felt proud, redeemed, alive. He said, 'That's very nice to hear.'

'She hopes you will be able to do more catering for her. Soon.'

'I'm sure I will. I don't know exactly when, but please tell her I'll be in touch.'

'I will. She'll be very pleased.'

Pym was about to sign off, when he remembered Ivy. He said, 'I have to pay one of my . . . suppliers.'

'The hostess will give you an advance. How much?'

'It's not money. It's . . .' How could he say this in catering code? He couldn't. He had to be specific. But suppose somebody was listening. Nobody was listening! But suppose . . . He decided to speak quickly, as if speed would boggle the mind of any interceptor.

'I need a high-school diploma from a genuine, accredited public or private high school in the District of Columbia, this year's graduating class, along with a grade transcript showing high marks in all subjects, especially computer courses, made out in the name of Jerome Peniston.' He spelled 'Peniston.' 'And I need it fast.'

There was a silence. He hoped Teal was writing down the details of the request.

'Look in your mailbox at eleven to tomorrow morning,' Teal said.

Ten

Hair. All Burnham could smell, all he could see, was long blonde hair. It cascaded over his face, slipped between his lips, tickled his nostrils.

He held his breath, willing himself fully awake, afraid that this was another dream.

No, this was real. Through the strands of gold he saw the drab green YMCA wall, and the shafts of dirty light that seeped through the window washed the world in grey.

He buried his face deeper into her hair, touching her shoulder with his nose and smelling the rich scent of her warm skin.

They lay like silverware in a presentation case, perfectly matched, his front molded to her back. Had either one made a sudden move to either side, he or she would have tumbled out of the narrow bed.

He touched his tongue to her shoulder and made tiny circles with its tip, savouring the taste of salt and mystery.

Between his legs, a morning glory awoke to greet the day.

'Mmmmm,' Eva said, wriggling back against the gentleman caller. 'Hello to you, too.'

'I'll go brush my teeth.'

'Why?'

'I smell like a dragon.'

'I don't think you want to walk down the hall with *that* thing waving in the wind.' She pressed backward with her hips, and, like a horse turned loose after a long day's ride Burnham's beast charged for home.

Eva whirled, straddled him, locked her mouth on his, and guided him into her.

Burnham was transported. He thought of nothing, which, when he realized he was thinking of nothing, amazed him: for years, he had assumed that elaborate fantasizing was a critical key to his capacity for making love.

She had taken him to another exotic restaurant – Pakistani, this time – and once again had ordered for him. He had been edgy, almost anxious, for there could be no deluding himself about the initiative: he had made the move, and, in his mind, that made him a brother to Faust – the irredeemable sinner. But rationalizations were pounding on his mental door, pleading for the chance to soothe him. He was the wronged innocent, cast out by an unreasonable harridan. He was a human being in need of solace, and if home was not where the heart was, then he could – should – explore other vineyards.

And so on and so forth, until at last he decided to take refuge in a facile Hemingwayesque conclusion, that good is what makes you feel good.

The first course looked as though it had been pre-chewed and sprinkled with yellow dust. It tasted delicious, but even before the plates were removed he began to feel depressed, a heavy, leaden sense of unfocused gloom that made him slump in his chair and fight to keep from weeping.

Eva noticed immediately. She must have been studying him.

'Are you all right?'

'No.'

''S the matter? Sick?'

'Dead. Just dead.'

'Huh,' was all she said. She summoned the waiter and, pointing to several items on the menu, commanded him to bring them as quickly as possible. Then she smiled and took Burnham's hand and said, 'You'll feel better.'

'Who cares?' He thought it would be polite to smile back at her, but all he could manage was a lugubrious grimace. Anyway, he didn't give a damn.

The second course looked like loam sprinkled with raisins, and eating it was like gnawing on a sponge. He didn't want to eat it, all he wanted to do was be buried at sea, but she coaxed and prodded him as if he was an infant.

No more than two mouthfuls had found their way to the pit of his stomach, when the curtain of despair began to rise and a vista of broad sunlit meadows opened before him.

'Good God!' he said, grinning. 'What have you wrought?'

'We are what we eat.' She shrugged modestly.

'I guess so! Have you ever considered being the personal dietician to the free world?'

'I'd be happy being . . .' She paused, and her eyes lowered. '. . . personal dietician to you.'

'You've got it! Never leave my side. Infuse me with goodness at every step.' He looked at his hands, as if they might give a clue to this sudden surge of well-being. 'Damn!'

He ate more, and the more he ate the better he felt, and the better he felt the more he talked. He told her about his past, about how he got the job at the White House, about how he met Sarah, about his marriage and his children, about the problems with his marriage (they seemed distant and unimportant), about the President's recent inexplicable affection for him. He restrained himself from mentioning the CIA report on the Pasha of Banda and the episode with Toddy/Teresa, but his restraint came not so much from discretion as from impatience: he was in a hurry to explain everything about himself, to bare himself in homage to her, and the minutiae of his work did not reveal anything about him.

It wasn't until he had finished his monologue that he

realized that Eva had been holding one of his hands in both of hers. 'This is very embarrassing,' he said.

'What is?'

'I think I'm falling in love with you, and I'm not exactly in a position to –'

'You're not falling in love with me.'

'I'm not?'

'No. You're in love with the way you feel, and you think I had something to do with it.' She toyed with his fingertips. 'I'm flattered, though.'

'You didn't just have something to do with it. You *did* it.'

'Well, maybe a little.' She raised one of his fingertips to her mouth, and she breathed on it.

Burnham had never realized that the neural network included a highway from the fingertip to the loins, but he did not have to close his eyes to imagine – to feel, to know – that it was not his fingertip that she was breathing on, not really.

'I do know one thing,' she said softly, 'that'll make you feel good, that'll make us both feel good.'

Guilt never reared its inhibiting head that night. Burnham had no time to entertain it. In fact, he didn't even have time to remove his socks.

Now, supine, pressed into the rickety iron bed by Eva collapsed on top of him, stroking the fine hairs at the base of her spine, feeling her heart pumping as fast as his, he wondered if he felt guilty.

Sort of, he decided.

What did 'sort of' mean?

Well, he had to feel guilty, because he had broken his troth to Sarah. On the other hand, he couldn't possibly feel regret, not at the wonderful thing that had happened or at the wonderful way he felt. But –

'Don't think,' Eva said into his neck. 'Feel.'

She was right, of course, so that's what he resolved to do. Feel.

They parted at the corner of 17th and Pennsylvania. The walk had been no more than a block, but Burnham had had to struggle not to take Eva's hand and lace his fingers into hers and stroke her palm.

When they stopped, he did take her hand. 'Can you have lunch?'

'Want to play squash?'

'I don't know if I can. Or when. I told you, things are weird over there. But they won't starve me to death. Can you come to my office?'

'Okay. When?'

'Twelve-thirty? One?' Burnham didn't know what to tell her. He had no idea when he'd be free. He had no idea what he'd be doing. He had no idea, period. 'I don't know!' he said, too loudly.

Startled, she took a step backward.

'No, no,' he said, squeezing her hand. 'It's just I don't know what to tell you, and I can't expect you to hang around all day.'

'Maybe another –'

'No! I have to see you.' It occurred to him then that he was almost raving, on the corner of 17th Street and Pennsylvania Avenue. He breathed deeply, and smiled, and said, 'You know what you've done, don't you? Turned me into a junkie.'

'Really? What are you hooked on?'

'What do you think? You!'

Eva laughed. 'You're sweet,' she said, and she patted his cheek, 'but you sound like a song from the sixties. By somebody like The Temptations. I don't think that'll go over very well in the White House.'

'No.'

'Tell you what: I'll come around twelve-thirty, and if you're busy, I'll wait, and if you're still busy at one-thirty or two, I'll leave. Fair enough?'

'You're an angel.' He bent to kiss her.

She pulled away. 'Stop.' she said.

'You're right.'

'I'm serious.'

'Okay.' He dropped her hand and held his own up in capitulation. 'No more Cyrano.'

'How do I get in there?' She nodded at the grey stone wedding cake that was the EOB.

'I'll clear you at the front door. Just give your name.'

She hesitated for a second, and a trace of a frown wrinkled her brow. Then she said, 'Okay.'

He watched her until she had crossed Pennsylvania and turned into Lafayette Park. He knew he was behaving like a fool, captive of an adolescent infatuation that could, if it got out of hand, be very, very expensive.

So what? No pain, no gain, right? What was it Browning said? 'Ah, but a man's reach must exceed his grasp, or what's a heaven for?' He probably wasn't talking about reaching for heaving bosoms and steamy loins, but what the hell . . .

He turned into the EOB and skipped up the steps, feeling like Frankenstein's monster, a hollow man suddenly jolted back to life.

He flashed his pass at the police officer at the desk, left Eva's name on a list of noon-hour guests and walked smartly down the long hall, enjoying the click-clack of his footsteps resounding off the marble. At the end of the hall he turned right and descended the staircase that ended fifteen feet from his office door.

He walked directly into the office, not pausing long enough to notice that the brass nameplate-holder beside the door was empty.

Dyanna wasn't at her desk. He looked at his watch: 9.30. Curious. Was she sick?

Then he sensed something awry. It wasn't a look or a smell but more an atmosphere, or a lack of something intangible, like the feeling in an apartment when its resident has died.

The personal paraphernalia on Dyanna's desk was gone – the bud vase, the pictures of her and her parents, her calendar and her Rolodex.

257

He stepped to the nearest file cabinet and yanked it open. Empty.

Oh shit.

It couldn't have happened. This wasn't Hollywood, where you went out for lunch and returned to find that your name had been painted over on your parking space. They had to give you notice.

Didn't they?

He stepped into his office. The furniture was there, and the paintings and the curtains and the carpet. But his television sets were gone, and his desk had been swept clean: no IN box, no blotter, no appointment book. There were marks on the wall behind his chair, where his personal pictures had hung.

No one lived here.

He felt sick.

Now what? Where did he go to collect his things? His effects. Just like a dead man.

Wait a minute. Why hadn't they lifted his pass? That was the first thing they did when they fired you. He remembered hearing about a writer who had gotten drunk at lunch and had decided that his planets were in the proper alignment for deposing Mario Epstein. He had marched into the Mess and announced to all and sundry that Epstein (who was lunching with the Prime Minister of Italy) was the bastard son of Golda Meir and Al Capone. By the time the writer had reached the door to the West Basement on his way back to the EOB, the word had reached the guard, who pulled his pass and escorted him out onto Pennsylvania Avenue.

And why had they fired Dyanna, too? They couldn't blame her for what he had done. Whatever that was. Maybe she had been transferred to the Census Bureau.

Who could he ask? Cobb? No. If Cobb didn't know why he had become the President's darling, he wouldn't know why he had been magically changed into a turd.

Evelyn Witt. Maybe she had witnessed the chain reaction that culminated in the Presidential explosion that cost him his job. What was her number? Where was his White House directory? Gone.

He picked up the phone and dialled the operator. 'This is Timothy Burnham.'

'What are you doing there?'

Christ! he thought. Everybody knows.

'Trying to figure out what's going on,' he said.

'Would you like me to connect you with your office?'

'I'm *in* my office.'

'No you're not.'

'I'm not?' He looked around. What, was he on the wrong floor? No. 'Sure I am.'

'It says here you're on twenty-three-oh-six.'

'Where's that, the Bureau of Indian Affairs?'

'Not exactly.' The operator chuckled. 'But you may wish it were.'

'Where, then?'

'Ground floor of the West Wing.'

Burnham didn't know what to say, so he said, 'Oh.'

'You want me to ring?'

'No. No. Thanks.' He hung up and sank into the chair behind the desk.

The office was between Epstein's and the President's. It was the office of the President's Appointments Secretary. Or, it had been.

Unless Burnham had been promoted to Appointments Secretary.

No. Please, God. No.

Dyanna sat at her new desk. Her bud vase held a fresh white rose. Her Rolodex and her calendar and her pictures were all in perfect symmetry, as if they had been arranged by a computer. She was flushed and excited. She clasped her hands in front of her, then touched her hair, then clasped her hands again. Her eyes kept darting to her enormous telephone console, as she awaited her first Important Call.

'Good morning, Mr Burnham!' she trilled.

259

Burnham felt ashen. He assumed he looked ashen. 'When did all this happen?'

'Isn't it *fabulous*?'

'Where's what's-his-name? The Appointments Secretary.'

'They tell me Mr Dilworth moved into the East Wing.'

'But why?' Burnham waved his arm. 'We don't need all this!'

Dyanna smiled. 'Somebody thinks we do.'

Burnham walked into his office. It was smaller than his office in the EOB – but then, the only offices bigger than that one were in the Kremlin and Versailles – though still large enough to accommodate two easy chairs, a sofa, a coffee table, two end tables, a desk, a swivel chair and a full-size American flag that stood between the two huge windows overlooking the South Lawn. And whereas his EOB office had been decorated with cast-offs from the General Services Administration, this office had had the attention of the curator of the White House. Some of the furniture was from the Smithsonian collection. All the paintings were from the National Gallery.

The top of his desk (an eighteenth century kneehole number with fine gold-leaf inlay around its borders) had been arranged exactly as he had left his desk in the EOB, only neater. The lettering on his IN Box seemed to shout at him: 'No man but a blockhead ever wrote except for money!' What had been amusing in the EOB now struck him as puerile, frivolous, and untrue. He turned the box around so that the letters faced away from the door.

His typewriter and word processor were on a mahogany table behind the desk. The shredder perched over a leather waste-basket to one side.

His telephone console looked like the control panel of the Concorde: at least a million buttons, some clear, some red, some blue, some green. He'd need a master's degree just to call home.

Home. Suddenly he ached for his children. Christopher

would love this. Dad had a 'Star Wars' office. It would be far-out. Gross. Outrageous. Awesome.

He was distracted by the sight of another phone, on the other side of the desk, a white telephone with no dial, just a single red light bulb – menacing, like a poised panther.

A POTUS phone.

He stood in the centre of the room and wailed, 'Where are my friends? What am I supposed to *do* in here?'

'To begin with,' Dynna said from the doorway, where she stood like a nurse about to lead him to therapy, 'you have a Cabinet meeting in fifteen minutes.'

'*I* have a Cabinet meeting?' Burnham looked at her as if she had turned a final corner into madness. 'What do you mean, *I* have a Cabinet meeting?'

She took a step into the room and lowered her voice, grinning like a child with a naughty secret. '*He* came in and told me.' She pointed to a door in the wall behind Burnham. 'Himself! He spoke to *me*!'

'Where does that door go?'

'Into his private office,' Dyanna whispered. 'The little one.'

'And so dies freedom,' Burnham said, and he thought: I'll have to get an executive order whenever I want to take a leak.

'What? What did you say?'

'Nothing.' He sat in his new chair. It was stiff, its springs tight and recalcitrant. It discouraged relaxation.

'Can I get you something? Coffee?'

'I'd like a double Beefeater martini.'

'Mr Burnham!'

'A bottle of Thunderbird in a brown bag?' He smiled wanly.

'Would you like some coffee?' Dyanna looked stern, matronly.

'Where did you get that face? I've never seen that face.'

'You'll have to stop being silly, Mr Burnham. Our silly

days are over.' She turned her back and returned to her office.

'Why?' he called after her. 'Where is it written that powerful people can't be silly? I think a lot of powerful people are silly. Ridiculous, even.'

There was no reply. Obviously, Dyanna had concluded that his argument did not deserve the compliment of rational opposition.

He noticed a vase of pink flowers on the coffee table. 'Where'd the flowers come from?'

'Evelyn Witt,' Dyanna said.

'Nice.'

'If you say so.'

Her disembodied voice was beginning to annoy him. It was prim, sharp as a rapier, righteous. Like Tom Sawyer's Aunt Polly. One more crack from him and she'd probably storm into the office and grab him by the ear and wash his mouth with soap.

'What do you mean?'

'They're anemones.'

'So?'

Aunt Polly appeared in the doorway again. 'Anemones are very pretty. Everybody notices them. Everybody loves them.'

'So?'

'They don't last. They have a very short life. They bloom, and they die.'

Burnham laughed and said, 'Beautiful!'

'You think that's funny?'

'Don't you?' Burnham was still laughing.

'I think you're disturbed.' She turned away.

He had a few minutes with nothing to do. He decided to call Christopher. If he could decipher the mystery of his phone console.

He could ask Dyanna to place the call for him. No. There was something distant . . . Victorian . . . about asking one's secretary to call one's children.

He could have the White House operators call for him.

262

Yes. If he wasn't at home, they would find him and page him. Chris would think being paged by the White House was cool. He hoped.

He punched a button at random, got a dial tone, punched another button, beside which were the letters 'WH', and got an operator. He asked her to locate his son.

She called back in less than a minute.

'He won't take the call, Mr Burnham.'

'What? He said that?' Burnham choked.

'No, sir. I spoke to a woman. She said – here, I wrote it down – "I won't let the White House pollute his space." I don't know what it means.'

'Thanks.' Burnham hung up. He could hear his heart beating, and his palms itched with rage. He thought he would like to break Sarah's nose with the heel of his hand. He should have placed the call himself. At least he would've yelled back at her.

Ten minutes to go. He looked at his IN box. It was empty. He had no assignments. Maybe from now on his assignments would come only through the unmarked door behind him. He wanted to call McGregor and Butterworth, tell them what had happened to him, enjoy a laugh over the absurdity of it all. But he knew they wouldn't find it funny. They'd be civil, and pretend to be amused and eager to hear about it, and they'd agree to have lunch tomorrow or the day after, but as soon as the call was finished they'd be sniping at him, obeying the universal truth for men caught on a social, economic or political ladder: whenever something marvellous happens to a colleague, a little bit of me dies. They would be bitter and resentful and, worst of all, ignorant of how he had accomplished whatever it was he had accomplished, and their ignorance would breed endless nasty speculations.

There was no way he could convince them that the change wasn't marvellous, for in the White House, proximity to the President was the holy grail. He had been moved into the West Wing. Therefore, life had to be wonderful. QED.

Dr Johnson knew better. 'All envy would be extinguished,' he told Burnham now, 'if it were universally known that there are none to be envied, and surely none can be much envied who are not pleased with themselves.'

And why, Burnham thought, am I not pleased with myself?

Because I am a fraud.

And how do I know I am a fraud? Because the only thing I know about why I am here is that I do not deserve to be here.

Who am I to make that judgment? The President must see something in me.

Sarah says the President has no taste.

And why do we listen to Sarah, she who speaks well of no one who doesn't summer in Hyannisport?

Maybe I am worth something. Maybe I can actually contribute something, just by doing whatever the President wants.

Maybe power can be fun.

He gazed out over the South Lawn, past the Ellipse, at the gleaming white needle of the Washington Monument.

'I feel patriotic,' he said, turning to the field of multi-coloured buttons on his phone. 'Let's invade somebody.'

In an instant Dyanna stood in the doorway, monitoring him like an intensive-care patient. He smiled at her.

'It's ten o'clock,' she said, flat-faced. 'You're due in the Cabinet Room.'

'What in the name of the gentle Jesus am I gonna do –'

A buzzer sounded, harsh, commanding. For a moment, Burnham thought that his impious use of the name of the Saviour had tripped some secret moral alarm. Then he saw the red light flashing on his POTUS phone. He snatched up the receiver.

'Yessir!'

'Ready, Tim?' said the President pleasantly. 'We're all here.'

'On my way. Sir.' He replaced the white instrument.

We're all here? Burnham jumped up from his chair. The

entire Cabinet of the United States of America is waiting for *me*?

'Where's the Cabinet Room?' he shouted to Dyanna.

'Across the hall.'

He dragged his fingertips through his hair and checked his suit. He looked like he'd been wrinkled by a professional.

'Here.' Dyanna handed him a yellow legal pad.

'What's that for?'

'Who knows? Looks good.'

'Right. Right. Thanks.' He started out the door.

'If you need me in there,' she said, 'Just call.'

The Cabinet Room door was ajar. He pushed it open gingerly, like a chambermaid reluctant to disturb a guest *en deshabille*, and stepped inside.

There, sitting around the giant oval table, beneath the portraits of Great Presidents, were the Secretaries of Absolutely Everything with their aides attendant in chairs against the wall behind them. Each sat in his personal chair adorned with his personal plaque, which, if he was a good boy and served his President well and didn't get indicted or piss off Epstein or some vocal minority group, would be presented to him by the President upon his departure.

The President sat halfway down the table, on the south side, flanked by the Secretaries of State and the Treasury. The President saw Burnham and said, 'Good! Come on in, Tim, and shut the door.' Then he addressed his Cabinet. 'Gentlemen . . . who wants to cast the first stone?' He smiled and, without looking at Burnham, motioned him to his side.

No one spoke. As Burnham walked along beside the table, he felt eyes appraising him with amusement and contempt, as if the assembly were the first Oglala Sioux to spot Custer on the ridge above the valley of the Little Bighorn: If he kept his distance, he might survive; if he dared venture into their territory, he was chopped meat.

He saw, but did not look at, Mario Epstein in a chair against the far wall, a statue of cold stone.

He saw Warner Cobb against a wall nearer to him, doodling on a notepad. He did look at Cobb, praying for a smile of encouragement, but Cobb would not look at him.

See? Dr Johnson reminded him. Many need no other provocation to enmity, than that they find themselves excelled.

The President had placed a chair for Burnham directly behind his own, as if he expected Burnham to be an interpreter between himself and the Secretary of State. He patted the seat of the chair, and Burnham sat in it.

The President leaned toward Burnham and said, 'You know Parker?' He tapped the Secretary of State.

'My pleasure,' said Parker Randall, with all the enthusiasm he lavished on other people's servants. The Secretary wore one of those shirts without a collar, you had to attach a different-colour collar, and his Tiffany collar pin, and a yellow paisley tie. He smelled like the men's room at '21', treacly.

'Mr President?' Burnham whispered, and the President tilted backward, offering Burnham his ear. 'What do you want me to do?'

'Listen, son,' the President said out of the corner of his mouth. 'Just listen.'

'Yes, sir.' Burnham uncapped a felt-tip pen and placed it on the yellow pad that lay across his lap.

The Secretary of Agriculture spoke first. He was a spare, weathered man in his early sixties who had been a farmer and a professor of agronomy at a wheat-belt university.

He spoke on behalf of America's two million small family farmers, who were going broke at a record rate. Eloquently, he called for a Federal bail-out of the farmers, but his eloquence failed to disguise an underlying flaw in his argument: the two million small farmers produced only thirty percent of America's food, and the farms that produced the other seventy percent were healthy and successful. According to this Administration's philosophy, in a free-market economy there was no reason to bail out the small farmers. They should be allowed to collapse or to be folded into larger entities.

It was an old, familiar argument that had been batted back and forth on op-ed pages across the land.

The Secretary was in the middle of a lachrymose tale about a particular farm family, two of whose children had entered into a suicide pact in order to leave more food for their siblings, when the President leaned back in his chair and whispered to Burnham, 'What do you think?'

'Sir?' He didn't understand the question. What did he think about what?

'What do you think about what old Bledsoe is saying?'

Oh boy, Burnham thought, what do I say? Why am I suddenly an expert on farm policy? Can I just say 'interesting'? No. Does he want me to be honest? I want to tell him what he wants to hear, but what's that?

If I tell him the truth, I've got a brand-new enemy in the Secretary.

If I lie, I may have an enemy in the President.

Who would I rather have as an enemy?'

Burnham leaned forward and said, 'Sophistry.'

'What? What's that? Don't confuse your President, son.'

'No, sir.' Burnham swallowed and said, 'Bullshit.'

The President nodded and smiled and said, 'That's what *I* thought.' He turned back to the table and let the Secretary finish. Then he waited a beat and said, 'It's mouldy, Lem.'

'Mr President?' said the Secretary.

'That critter's too old to dance. Get a new one. Next?'

Burnham saw the President reach beneath the table. He shifted in his chair and saw the President's index finger on one of six coloured buttons on a panel affixed to one of the table's legs.

He expected to see the Secretary vanish through a trapdoor in the floor, or a platoon of storm troopers burst into the room and remove him from his chair.

But nothing happened.

'Next?' said the President.

The Secretary of Defence cleared his throat. Before joining the Administration, he had been president of a major supplier of jet engines to the Air Force, and upholding the sanctity of defence contracts was his private crusade. He detested the President's new policy of permitting two contractors to manufacture the same item on a competitive basis, for while he acknowledged that the policy saved money, he insisted that it inhibited research and development. A genius can't be a genius if he's looking over his shoulder at accountants all the time, went his reasoning, and since we all agree that freedom is priceless, the maintenance of freedom should not be allowed to become a matter of dollars and cents.

In public, of course, he supported the President's policy, but he had an unfortunate habit of giving interviews – 'off the record' or for 'deep background' – in which 'usually reliable sources' or 'highly placed officials' stated *his* point of view.

The result was the opposite of his intention: instead of being regarded as a patriot, in the press he was portrayed as a loudmouthed maverick. One editorial cartoon that particularly burned him showed his entire house furnished with $700 toilet seats, $2,200 coffee makers, $900 hammers, etc, etc.

Now he was asserting that the military – not he, the military – was weary of being pilloried as a gaggle of reckless spendthrifts, and he asked for unanimous Administration support of his (and the military's) efforts to keep democracy safe from godless Communism.

The President leaned back and said, 'Well?'

Burnham didn't have to hesitate. 'He's whining.'

The President twirled a pencil between his fingers.

When the Secretary of Defence ran out of breath, the President tapped the pencil's eraser on the table and said, without looking at the Secretary, 'Andrew,' (he pronounced it 'Andyroo') 'I believe you know the old saying . . .' Now he looked at him. 'If you can't stand the heat . . .'

The President let the rest of the saying float in ether, unsaid. The Secretary reddened.

The door opened, and an elderly mocha-coloured butler in a wing-collar shirt and a tuxedo entered, carrying a tray on which was a single glass containing what looked like a cola. He bowed before the President, and the President took the glass and thanked him.

Burnham assumed that the butler would take drink requests around the room, but he didn't. He turned back toward the door.

The President leaned to Burnham. 'Want something? I should've asked.'

'No, sir,' Burnham said quickly. 'No thanks.' Much as he would have welcomed a cold drink, he did not choose to be the sole man among men to be permitted to slake his thirst.

As he sat back, Burnham noticed that Epstein was eyeing him. He expected Epstein's look to be hostile, but it wasn't. It was . . . scientific, as if Epstein was studying him like a specimen to be readied for dissection.

The Secretary of State spoke up. 'I have a rather ticklish item to place on the agenda . . .'

At the sound of the Secretary of State's voice, the President stifled a yawn.

'You've got him!' Pym said. 'Well done.'

'Yeah, right,' Eva said. 'You know what I feel? Sleazy.'

'Don't think of him as a person. He's a thing . . . like that dam you were going to blow up. You're using him, plain and simple.'

'Sure.' She did not look convinced.

'You'll get over it.'

'How long do I –'

'As long as it takes,' Pym said flatly. 'They were very pleased. He's an incredible asset, and he doesn't know it. It's perfect!'

'I'm glad you think so.'

'I do.' Pym debated telling her of the dream he had had years ago, of siring a line of agents, all born and bred in

269

place. He decided against it. She wouldn't appreciate it. Not now. In fact, she looked slightly nauseated:

The phone rang. Pym picked it up and said, 'Hello.'

'Mallard?'

'Teal.'

'My delivery man tried to deliver your . . . condiments.'

'And?'

'Your damn mailbox isn't big enough! How's he s'posed to put a . . . Party Pak . . . through a little slot?'

'Oh. Where is he now?'

'A phone booth on the corner.'

'All right. I'll go get it from him.'

'How'll he recognize you?'

'I'll tell him who I am and ask him for the package.'

'No, no, no! Jesus! Think, man! Craft.' Teal paused. 'You say, "Is this phone out of order?" He'll say, "No, but I'm waiting for a call." You say, "I'll find another one, then." Got that?'

Pym smiled. In *this* neighbourhood? The exchange would more likely be: 'Is this phone broke?' 'The fuck's it to you?' 'I gotta make a fuckin' call.' 'Touch that fuckin' phone, I'll break all your fuckin' fingers.'

He said, 'Yes, I've got it.'

'I'll call him back. Give me three minutes.'

'All right.'

'By the way, the hostess was especially pleased by your . . . main course.'

Pym didn't reply. Main course?

'Your curli*cues*.'

Curlicues? What *is* the man talking about?

'Cues, cues cues! You know the ones.'

Cues? Cues? 'I'm afraid –' Oh, yes. Cues. 'Qs.' The Q-Clearance documents. From the Department of Energy. 'I'm glad she liked them.'

'She says the others showed skill and flair, but they were light and airy, like soufflés. The real meat was in the curlicues. She hopes you'll be able to give her more.'

'I'll certainly try.'

'She knows you will . . . if you want to keep her business.' Teal rang off.

It took Pym fifteen minutes to retrieve the package from Teal's courier, for Teal had been unable to contact him by phone. An addled biddy had shoved the courier out of the phone booth so she could call and harangue her daughter in Elkton, Maryland, and when the courier had protested, the biddy had brandished a sharpened knitting needle and threatened to insert it 'where the sun don't shine'. Pym took the courier aside and recited his entire conversation with Teal, and, evidently, the courier discerned enough of Teal in the tale to be convinced to turn over the goods.

The package was a worn Purolator Courier bag. Pym unstapled it and emptied its contents on the coffee table between himself and Eva.

The high-school diploma was perfect – not just realistic, but *real*, a genuine diploma with Jerome's name written in fine Gothic calligraphy. The grade transcript showed him to be prodigious in computers and math and competent in the humanities.

Ivy would be ecstatic.

That should have been all, for that was all Pym had requested, but Teal had thrown in several dividends.

There was a box that contained a tie-clip/microphone and a cigarette-pack receiver. The antenna on the receiver was activated when one of the cigarettes was shaken up out of the pack.

There was a fountain pen that shot needles out of its nib, and a small bottle of 'ink' that was really a cousin of curare.

'Who does he think I am?' Pym said. 'Colonel Abel?'

'Who's Colonel Abel?' Eva asked.

Pym smiled. 'How quickly they forget.'

There was a stack of a hundred hundred-dollar bills.

There was a small white envelope. Pym tore it open, and six transparent capsules full of a colourless liquid fell into his palm. Pym's heart thumped. He closed his hand.

But Eva had seen them. 'What are they?'

'Nothing.' He couldn't believe they had sent these.

271

'Cut the crap. What *are* they?'

'Pills.' Hurry up, he told himself, think of something. *Now*. Ten seconds more of your fumbling, and she'll guess the truth, and once she knows that if things get dicy she's supposed to bite down on one of the capsules rather than let anybody ask her questions . . . well, good-bye Eva. She'll go to the Grand Jury and beg them to hear her story.

'I see that. For what?'

Teal was crazy! Nobody had ever talked about the worst-case scenario.

Of course they hadn't. It was assumed he knew it. It had been drummed into him forty years ago.

Inspired, he said, 'For Ivy. In case she gets out of control.'

'What'll they do to her?'

'Calm her down. She can be unstable.'

'No wonder, you feed her all that trash. Don't do that to her, Pop. Let her be.'

She believes. Give in to her. Be reasonable. He said, 'You're right,' and he spilled the pills from his hand into an ashtray.

Eva picked up the last item on the table, a pair of half-glasses. 'Reading glasses? Did you ask for these?'

'No.' Pym reached for the glasses. 'Let's have a look.'

The President was asleep. His eyes were open, and he appeared to be concentrating on what the Secretary of Commerce was saying, but Burnham could tell he was sound asleep. His breathing was deep and rhythmic, and during the last thirty seconds he had begun to snore – not an obvious window-rattler, more of a staccato skip-snore.

Burnham was certain no one else had heard the President snore. The men on both sides of him were in their own dream worlds: the Secretary of State was staring into the distance (composing his memoirs, probably), and the Secretary of the Treasury was drawing his initials and his family coat of arms into a variety of crests, insignia, plaques, banners and burgees. But there was no way to

272

predict when the President would suddenly fire off a boomer that would let everybody know, that would insult the Secretary of Commerce (who, as Burnham knew too well, had a hair trigger), and that would inevitably worm its way into the columns of *The Washington Post*.

Burnham did not dare wake the President suddenly and risk inducing snorts, whinnies and exclamations that would betray him to his Cabinet. He had to coax the President back to consciousness by making him so uncomfortable that he awoke.

The Secretary of Commerce droned on, delighting in the sound of his own voice and in the knowledge that he had a captive audience of rich, slick, well-connected, blue-blooded snobs who wouldn't think of having him over for supper and who would never admit the truth, that when it came to real street-smart savvy, they weren't qualified to kiss his proletarian ass.

Burnham tapped on the President's back with the eraser of his pencil.

Nothing.

He tapped harder, drumming an irregular beat that should have been enough to interrupt the pattern of his dream.

Nothing. The President gurgled.

Burnham turned his pencil around and pressed the point against the President's back, twirling it and pushing it until the lead pierced the fabric of the President's jacket.

The President stirred and grumbled. The pencil was annoying him but not awakening him.

'I'm glad you agree, Mr President,' said the Secretary of Commerce, and on he went.

Burnham pressed harder. A small black stain circled the pencil point. Blood.

The man's not asleep, Burnham thought, he's in a coma.

But then the President shrugged and swiped at his back with an elbow, shook his head and stretched his face and ran his tongue around inside his mouth. He tipped his head toward Burnham and said, 'What's he saying? I must've dozed off.'

'Nothing,' Burnham whispered back. 'You can just say you'll take it under consideration.'

The President nodded. He waited for the Secretary of Commerce to take a breath, then said, 'Right, Norm. I'll take it under consideration.' He slapped the table. 'Well, I guess that's that . . . unless anybody sees another threat to the republic.'

The Secretary of Commerce looked as if the President had called him a Communist, or spat on his sharkskin suit. He said, 'But . . .' but he was drowned out by the sounds of rustling papers and chairs being pushed back from the table.

Burnham had to push his chair back before the President could stand up. As he stepped out of the President's way, he purposely dropped his yellow pad on the floor and, bending to retrieve it, stole a glance at the panel of buttons beneath the table. They had to be connected to crisis centres around the nation – like NORAD, SAC, NSA – for even within the womb of the White House the President could never be more than a fingertip away from the instruments of Doomsday.

The labels beside the buttons read: Coke, Tab, Fresca, Pepsi, Coffee, Tea.

The room cleared slowly, for every cabinet secretary made sure to exchange a few private words with the President, so that he could return to his department and impress his subordinates with a presidential confidence – a flattering remark about the cut of the Secretary's suit, perhaps, or a kind word about a supportive speech the Secretary had given to the Veterans of Foreign Wars or the Council of Religious Broadcasters.

Burnham watched the ritual, fascinated. It reminded him of bees swarming around their queen, servicing her and drawing sustenance from her. He imagined that each secretary had a power hard-on, and as the President put his arm around his shoulder and whispered words of praise or encouragement, the Secretary experienced the ego orgasm that made his job worthwhile.

He noticed that the courtiers awaiting their turn with the President were glancing at him, commenting about him, obviously speculating among themselves about who and what he was. Clearly, he represented a new threat to them, a filter of their access to the President. Clearly too, they disliked him, resented him and feared him – especially those who had seen the President consult Burnham before responding to their carefully honed and well considered remarks.

Enemies, Burnham thought, are sprouting around me like tulips. He didn't like having enemies, went to any lengths to avoid conflict that might create enemies, felt particularly uneasy knowing that people hated him for reasons that had nothing to do with himself. But he also knew he was safe, at least for the moment, because under the wing of the Khan all God's creatures are invulnerable.

He stood alone, not daring to scratch himself or pick his nose, for dozens of eyes were appraising him, and any barbarism would give ammunition to their ridicule.

Suddenly he realized he was enjoying himself, enjoying the attention, the consternation, the mystery he was exciting. It occurred to him that this was a kind of power. He had enjoyed himself during the meeting, too, giving his opinions about matters of national policy and seeing them instantly implemented, albeit not through his own voice.

What's your job? Ventriloquist to the President. Interesting.

Hubris.

Be careful: he that giveth, taketh away. Alone, you are nobody. You are but a reflection of the President. If he chooses to move to another mirror, you cease to exist.

Just like everyone else in this room.

He looked around for Cobb. He'd force Cobb to talk to him if he had to. Anything, just so he didn't have to keep standing here like a goddam mannequin. But Cobb had already gathered his papers and shouldered his way to the door.

He was rescued by the booming voice of Benjamin T. Winslow.

'Tim!'

The President walked Burnham to the door of his office. 'You did good, Tim,' The President said.

'Thank you, sir, but I'm not sure what I did.'

'Tim . . .' The President put a hand on Burnham's shoulder. 'You know what they say about it's lonely at the top? Well, dammit, it is! The President's . . . the President. It's like being king, don't get me wrong.'

Burnham's eyes flicked to one of the two Secret Service men. His eyes were utterly blank. It was as if the President was talking in front of his dog.

'No one tells me to put the brakes on,' the President continued. 'No one tells me when I'm off base. No one says, "Hey, Ben, don't be an asshole." I can tell we're on the same wavelength, Tim. I want you to be that man for me. Special Assistant to the President for Perspective.'

Burnham swallowed, nodded. Sure, he thought, the first time I tell you you're an asshole, I'll end up selling pencils in the park.

''Course, we won't let that interfere with your other . . . duties. Which reminds me. Soon's I catch my breath, I want to go over that Gromyko business with you.'

'Yes, sir.' There it is again. The Gromyko business. *What* Gromyko business?

The President patted his shoulder, turned, stopped and said with a smile, 'And thanks for waking me up. Damn, but those meetings could bore the balls off a buffalo!'

Burnham opened the door to his office. Dyanna sat primly at her desk, her hands folded, looking at him as if he were a child late for supper.

'There's a . . . lady . . . to see you,' she said.

'A . . . omigod!' He looked at his watch. It was 12.30. 'Thanks.' Before he pushed open the door to his own office, he said to Dyanna. 'You've got your Aunt Polly face on again.'

'My what?'

'Never mind.'

Eva was standing at one of the windows, looking out over the South Lawn. She turned as she heard the door close.

'Hi,' Burnham said, noticing that she looked nervous and uncomfortable. Well, the first time in the West Wing usually did that to people.

He tried to kiss her, but she turned away and whispered, 'Not here!'

'Why not? There're no cameras.'

'It's like . . . church. I thought you worked across the street.'

'I did, till this morning.'

'What happened?'

'The President decided he couldn't live without me.' He smiled. 'You don't have to whisper.'

'What's through there?' She pointed to the door in the far wall.

'Another office,' he said. No point alarming her.

He walked to his desk, to check for messages, assignments, mail. 'Where would you like to eat?'

'You have time?'

'Sure.' In his IN box was a memo from the Office of the Naval Aide to the President, informing him that he had been reassigned to the second sitting in the Mess. 'You want to eat downstairs?'

'*Here?*'

'They moved me in with the grownups. It might be fun.' He cast her a reassuring smile. 'Come on.'

'Suppose somebody –'

'They won't. And if they do, we'll say you're my . . . cousin from the Milwaukee.'

Eva sighed. 'All right.'

Burnham pulled the envelope of DOE mail from his IN box and carried it to the couch. He sat down and patted the

277

cushion beside him for Eva. 'This,' he said, as he slit the envelope, 'is a sick joke on America.'

'What is?' She sat beside him.

He pulled the documents from the envelope. TOP SEC-RET – Q CLEARANCE ONLY was stamped across the top of each one.

'This stuff has to be signed for every day. It has to be shredded every night. There's only one thing they can't make me do with it, and that's understand it. Look.' He passed her one of the papers. It was a chart sprinkled with numbers.

Very carefully, almost in slow motion Eva reached into her purse and brought out a pair of half glasses. She put them on awkwardly.

'I didn't know you wore glasses.'

'For reading. I just got them.' She tried to smile, but the smile died aborning.

She's embarrassed, he thought, her vanity wounded. 'Don't worry.' He patted her knee. 'Time cannot change my love, nor age impair.'

Eva looked at the document. 'It's not even in English.'

'See? Why they insist that I get this stuff I do not know. But they do.' He stood up. 'Back in a minute.'

'Where are you going?'

'Just to the john. If you can figure out what any one of those things means, you'll win a blue ribbon, two kewpie dolls and . . .' he grinned '. . . my tongue in your ear.' He walked to the door. Glancing back, he saw Eva touch her fingers to her temple, apparently fiddling with the earpiece of her new glasses.

If he had not said, 'Those things are a nuisance, but you'll get used to them,' if he had not said anything, if he had stood still and listened, he might have heard a faint click – like a fly striking a window pane across the room – and an even fainter sound of a tiny electric motor. But he did speak, so he heard nothing but the sound of his own voice.

He opened the door, closed it behind him, and said to

278

Dyanna, 'Do me a favour and book me a table for two downstairs in about ten minutes.'

'Of course. Mr Burnham . . . I need to speak to you.'

'After lunch, okay?'

'As soon as possible.'

'Right.'

He had to ask directions to the men's room, which peeved him – it branded him a new boy – but the Secret Service agent who pointed him down a flight of stairs and around a corner did not treat him like a Shiite Muslim or a motor-pool chauffeur. He addressed Burnham as 'sir' and seemed eager to be helpful. The jungle drums have passed the word, Burnham thought, pleased.

He took a leak, washed his hands and straightened his tie. He searched the mirror for changes in himself. Could power etch its signature into his face this soon? Was there a new jauntiness to his carriage, a new confidence in this bearing?

As far as he could tell, he was the same seedy WASP he'd always been.

He returned to his office, not stopping as he passed through Dyanna's.

'Mr Bur –' She rose from her chair and raised a hand.

'Right after lunch,' he said, pushing open the second door.

His first sight was of Eva standing at attention in the centre of his office. Sweating.

His second was of the President, sitting in Burnham's chair, leaning back, his feet on the desk. For one split second, the thought crossed Burnham's mind that only a man who weighed more than two hundred pounds could make that chair recline comfortably.

'Oh,' Burnham said.

'There he is,' said the President. 'I was just telling Miss – Pym, is it? – what a pleasure it is for a President to chance upon a young man as loyal and dedicated as you. Sure does ease the burdens.'

'Oh. Well . . .' Burnham blushed and looked at the floor,

shifting his eyes to the couch: All his Q-CLEARANCE documents had been replaced in the DOE envelope, and the envelope lay face-down on the couch. The President couldn't have seen Eva reading his mail. He hoped. 'I'm not really –'

'No, it's true, Tim. Where were you?'

The President's voice was not accusing, not unfriendly, but not offhand either. He was looking straight at Burnham. He wanted an answer.

'In the john, Mr President.' When the President did not respond, Burnham felt pressed to defend his right to micturition. 'It was a long Cabinet meeting.'

'Was it ever!' The President looked around the office. 'No, you don't have one. Tell you what: use mine.' He jerked his thumb at the open door in the back wall.

'Ah . . . thank you, sir, but I'm sure there are times you –'

'Use mine, Tim.' The President's voice was flat, discouraging discussion.

'Yes, sir.'

'Miss Pym says she's a nutritionist and a caterer.'

'We met playing squash.'

'Good. Good for the heart. An aerobic affair.' The President laughed at his word play.

Burnham tried to smile, but his mouth was so dry that his lips threatened to crack.

Eva's face was the colour of wet plaster.

'Well,' the President said, swinging his feet to the floor and standing up. 'I thought you might want to come to the leadership lunch, Tim.'

Burnham said, 'Of course, sir.'

Eva said, 'I should be go –'

'No no,' the President said, holding up a benedictory hand. 'You kids go enjoy yourselves. *I* don't want to go to the damn thing either, but I have to.'

'Really, Mr President, I –'

'There'll be plenty of other leadership lunches, Tim. But the chance to share a meal with a pretty girl should never be passed up. Tell you what: *you* go to the leadership lunch, and *I'll* let Miss Pym buy *me* an organic cheeseburger.' The President laughed. He shook Eva's hand and said, 'Take care of my boy.' He said to Burnham, 'See you later, Tim.'

And he was gone, pulling the door to his private office closed behind him.

Eva sagged. Her shoulders drooped, and she wiped her palms on the back of her skirt. She hissed at Burnham, 'Just another office, you said!'

'I didn't want to worry you. How was I to know?' He took a step toward her and whispered, 'He didn't see you looking through the mail, did he?'

She shook her head. 'I'd finished. I couldn't understand any of it anyway.'

'Good. Ready to go?'

'Timothy . . . I don't –'

'Don't worry.' He took her hand. 'Once he's seen you, no one else matters.'

As they walked down the stairs to the Mess, Eva said, 'How do you live with that?'

'Having to get permission to pee? I don't know yet.' He smiled at her. 'Greatness is a bitch, isn't it?'

In the Mess, Evelyn Witt was having lunch with one of her deputies.

The President's Appointments Secretary, unperturbed by his precipitate move to the backwaters of the East Wing, dined alone, reading the latest Stephen King novel. There was a petty joke among the White House staff, to the effect that because the Appointments Secretary liked to read everything Stephen King wrote, he was condemned to read nothing but what Stephen King wrote, since the Appointments Secretary's rate of reading was synchronized precisely to Stephen King's rate of writing – approximately two books a year.

The Vice President of the United States sat at a round table with five of his aides, and he held forth about bird-shooting, oil leases and poontang.

The sallow young Director of the Office of Management

and Budget shared a table with the corpulent old Chairman of the President's Council of Economic Advisors, and – at least during the few moments that Burnham waited to be seated – neither of them said a word.

In a back corner of the room sat Mario Epstein, with one of his fungible aides – a dark-suited, white-shirted, rep-tied, black-shod, thin-haired young man older than his years whom *Prevention* magazine would undoubtedly analyse as a high-risk candidate for a duodenal ulcer, a cerebral vascular accident or coronary artery disease.

Burnham and Eva were shown to a table for two against the near wall. He felt eyes following him as they walked, and he wondered if his decision to bring Eva here had been reckless. People in the White House Mess were not likely to gossip; they were *certain* to gossip – like squirrels in the fall, gathering tidbits to store away for use in lean times.

But he saw no one here who could harm him, not even Epstein, for Epstein's sting had already been removed by the President's meeting with Eva.

'You don't need the glasses to read a menu?'

'Oh. I guess . . .' She smiled. 'They're so new.'

Burnham looked at his menu. 'What's good for us?'

'Nothing. God, look at this!' She ran her finger down the page. 'Saturated fats, processed animal refuse, grease and crap.'

Burnham laughed. 'Crap, eh? Where do you see that? *Au gratin?* Al fredo? Crap Suzette?'

'Have a salad.'

They had salads and iced tea, and for dessert Burnham ordered a sherbet against Eva's caution that a person as allergic as he risked anaphylactic shock from any of the additives, preservatives and chemical toxins with which commercial processors laced their products.

Burnham signalled for the bill and turned to say something to Eva.

'Timothy!'

He looked up into the broadly grinning face of Mario Epstein. Oh God, he thought, now what?

'Ah . . . hi!' He waited for the sky to fall.

'Good job this morning.'

'Oh. Thanks. I'm not sure –'

'The President was really pleased.'

Code, Burnham decided, he's speaking in code. What he's really saying is, the President and I talked about you; the President and I will always talk about you; never think that you are closer to the throne than I.

Epstein turned to Eva. 'Mrs Burnham?'

'No,' Burnham said quickly. 'A friend. Eva Pym . . . Mario Epstein.'

'*Very* pleased to know you,' Epstein said as he shook Eva's hand. 'Timothy's a rising star here, as I'm sure he's too modest to have told you.' Then he said to Burnham, 'We'll have lunch, Timothy,' and he waved to Eva and walked away.

Eva said, 'He seems nice enough.'

'Adolph Hitler liked dogs,' Burnham said, and he frowned at Epstein's receding back. What was *that* about?

'I forgot to tell you.'

'Forgot to tell me what?'

'When the President barged into your office this morning, he called me Sarah. It was embarrassing.'

'I bet it was.'

He paid the bill and walked with Eva out of the building and down the path to the West Gate.

'How long are you going to live in the Y?' she asked.

'I keep thinking I'll be going home.'

'Do you want to go home?'

'At the moment it's not an option.'

'That's not what I asked you.'

'I know.' He smiled.

She squeezed his hand. 'Keep the room in the Y.'

They agreed to meet for dinner – that is, if the President didn't trap him – and she walked quickly across Pennsylvania Avenue while she had the light.

'Lucky man, Mr B,' Sergeant Thibaudeaux said as Burnham returned through the West Gate.

283

'My cup runneth over, Sergeant T.'

Dyanna was waiting for him, and she followed him into his office.

'What's up?' he said as he dropped into one of the chairs that flanked the coffee table.

'I had coffee this morning with two of Mr Epstein's secretaries. They were just being nice, sort of welcoming me to the White House, give me a few helpful hints and all, so they –'

'You can sit down, you know.'

'No, that's okay. I may have to get the phone. Anyway, they bought me coffee and a Danish, I don't normally eat Danish in the morning, but –'

'Dyanna.'

'What?'

'We're not really talking about Danish pastry here, are we?' Burnham didn't mean to be reproving, for he could see that Dyanna was agitated, upset; he wanted to help her edit herself.

'No. I just . . . well, anyway . . . it was Dolores and Connie who took me to the Mess, and they were telling me how things work here in the West Wing, and they asked me what it was exactly that you did, and I said I wasn't sure, really, and they said it must be tough for you having a wife who worked for Senator Kennedy, and I said how did they –' Suddenly her eyes sprang open, and she said, 'Oh!'

Burnham followed her stare and saw that the President had opened the door from his private office.

'Excuse me,' said the President.

Burnham jumped to his feet. 'Not at all, sir. We were –'

'Got a minute, Tim?'

'Of course.' He said to Dyanna, 'Remember your place. It was just getting interesting.'

He followed the President into the little office, and the President shut the door behind them.

The room was snug and cozy. It reminded Burnham of a reading room in an opulent men's club. The outside window was covered with velvet drapes, and the only light came from two darkly shaded table lamps. The wallpaper was a rich maroon fabric interlaced with delicate gold eagles. The furniture was dark green leather.

The President sat in one of the chairs and directed Burnham to the couch.

'I don't believe in bullshitting around the bush, Tim.'

'No, sir.' Burnham thought: you should give lessons to Dyanna.

'Who was she?'

'Who wa – Oh. Eva. I met her playing squash. She's a –'

'Tim.'

'Sir?' Burnham felt that he had been hit in the chest with a maul.

'We have a good thing going, you and I, but it can only be a good thing as long as we're straight with one another. Agreed?'

'Yes, sir. I –'

'Now, I venture to say' – the President leaned back and gazed at the ceiling – 'that in my time I've had more women than you've had hot breakfasts, and one thing I *know* is that I can spot a fella hypnotized by pussy a mile away.'

Burnham blushed the colour of the wallpaper. 'Mr President,' he said at last, 'I'm having a few . . . problems . . . with my marriage.'

The President nodded. 'I know.'

Burnham was stunned. 'You do? How?'

'Never mind. I just do.'

Burnham wanted to ask the President if he knew the source of the problems. No, he decided. Never volunteer. Besides, it didn't matter. The die was cast. He was now a staffer with personal problems.

'Mr President, I know that people with personal problems are a liability. If you'd prefer, I'll –'

'Hell, Tim. Everybody's got problems. *I've* got problems now and then.' He grinned. 'Yes, believe it or not, Presidents have problems, too. The difference is, you and I can't take care of our problems like other people do. We can't go tomcatting around.'

'No, sir. I –'

'They say a standing prick has no conscience, Tim. But when you're in the White House, the old stiff-stander does have a security clearance. It's classified.'

'Yes, sir.'

'We have to be like Caesar's wife: keep our screwing around under our togas.'

'Yes, sir.'

'How much do you know about her?'

'Eva? Went to Bennington; works for her father.'

'Where'd she grow up?'

'Here.'

'Where'd her father grow up.'

'I don't know.'

'You gonna keep seeing her?'

Burnham spread his hands, a gesture of helplessness. 'I suppose I shouldn't, but I want to. I want to go home, but I can't, and I'm not even sure any more that I want to. It's a mess.'

''Cause if you are . . .'

'If you think I should stop, Mr President, I will.'

'No, not necessarily. It could do you more harm than good, have you pining around with your mind on your fly. But if you're gonna keep seeing her, I'm gonna have to have the FBI do a full-field on her.'

'I see.'

'Give it some thought, Tim. Let me know in a day or two.'

'Yes, sir.'

'Sarah gonna give you trouble?'

'Trouble? She's already giving me trouble.'

'I mean about the girl.'

'I don't think she knows.'

'Assume she knows. At *least* assume she will. You have to. The world is full of people who like nothing better than to bring their best friends bad news, and this town's home to most of them.'

'I think her vanity would keep her from making a public

spectacle out of it. Charging adultery doesn't reflect too well on the . . . adulterated.'

'Remember who she works for. Senator Righteous would love it if he could drag me down in the gutter with him.'

'What do you think I should do?' Burnham looked at the President, and had to restrain himself from smiling at the madness of the moment: here he was, appealing to the Leader of the Free World as if he were Ann Landers.

'Either get separated officially, and then you can screw your brains out and nobody'll give a hoot, or say goodbye to Miss Pym and go home.'

'Separated? It's only been a few days.'

The President paused for a moment before saying, 'It didn't take her long to change the locks.'

'No.' Sweet Jesus, Burnham thought, what else does he know?

A buzzer sounded. The President picked up the phone, listened, said, 'Okay,' and hung up. 'Think about it, Tim.'

'I will, sir.' Burnham stood and reached for the door-knob. 'And thank you.'

The President waved dismissively. 'Don't thank me. I'm being selfish. You're too valuable to lose.'

Burnham returned to his office and sat in the chair at his desk.

Dyanna must have heard the springs squeak, for immediately she appeared in the doorway.

Burnham didn't want to talk to Dyanna, not now. He wanted to replay his conversation with the President. The man amazed him: every time he talked to him, he saw another side of him.

But Dyanna would not be deterred.

'I was saying, we were down in the Mess, Dolores and Connie and I, and –'

'Dyanna.'

'What?'

'I want to hear what you have to say. I really do. But I

287

want you to do me a favour: think about what you're going to say as a hamburger patty.'

'A ham –'

'In your mind, take it in your hands and compress it into a neat little patty, and then pat off all the unnecessary little edges, until all that's left is the good part. Okay?'

'Okay.' She paused. 'You remember the bug in Sarah's car?'

'Of course I remember.'

'Mario Epstein put it there.'

'*He did?*'

'Well, not personally. But he had it put there.'

'How do you know?'

'They told me. Connie and Dolores.'

'They *told* you? Just like that?'

'Pretty much. We were in the Mess, the three of us, and we had to wait awhile for a fresh pot of coffee, they must've forgotten to make more after breakfast, and . . .'

She was unstoppable, so he didn't try. He contented himself with playing Maxwell Perkins to her Thomas Wolfe, permitting her to pile mountains of raw material into a steamer trunk, from which he could sift the nuggets that would become the masterpiece.

'. . . has this couple, real creeps Connie said, who're like street people, and they keep tabs on a whole bunch of people who live in Georgetown, he has other people working for him in Cleveland Park and Capitol Hill and all over the place, and they probably wouldn't have bothered with you if Sarah didn't work for Senator Kennedy, but because she did and you were in the White House, even though not in what they call a policy position . . . Anyhow, they didn't treat it like any big deal, sort of routine, but I'm not sure they thought I'd run right out and tell you.'

She ran out of breath.

She must have a diaphragm the size of a beach ball, Burnham thought. He said, 'Where did they plant the new one?'

'New one?'

'They know she changed the . . .' He stopped himself, 'They know a lot of new stuff.'

'I don't know.'

'Can you find out?'

'I'm not sure.'

'Do they have a bug on me?'

'They've got your file out. I saw it on the desk.'

'Christ, they've already done a full-field. And more, for all that Q-Clearance garbage. What the *hell* do they think they're gonna find out?'

'Something about your connections with the Soviets.'

'The Soviets! I don't know a single Russian. Not one.'

'The President thinks you do. That's what Connie said.'

'What – Oh! That. Yeah, well, I wish them all the best. I hope they find something. I'd like to know myself. Every time I see him, he brings it up.'

'Brings what up?'

'That I'm supposed to have some fabulous in with the Russians. It beats the hell out of me.' He smiled at Dyanna. 'You are a great American, and a source of comfort and strength to me in this dark hour. I thank you.'

'My pleasure.'

'Keep listening.'

'Yes, sir.' She returned to her office, and closed Burnham's door.

He wanted to march into the President and demand that all listening devices be removed from Sarah's home, car, purse and person. Him they were welcome to investigate, from his kindergarten records to his stool samples, but they were not to drag his wife and children into it.

But he didn't. He didn't want to jeopardize Dyanna's privileged relationship with Epstein's secretaries. She had more still to learn, more to tell him, and if he blew her cover now, that channel would close permanently.

The President might well refuse. After all, he'd say, if they hadn't been monitoring Sarah he never would have learned about Burnham's personal problems, could not have counselled him about his friendship with Eva, might have been presented with a nasty surprise too late to prevent Burnham from suffering irreversible harm. He'd insist that keeping track of one's trusted aides (and, by extension, their families) was not a question of morality but of security and common sense.

The final reason that kept Burnham from bursting in on the President and taking his stand was the simplest: he didn't have the guts.

Though he had never seen it in full cry, he knew that the President had a Vesuvian temper. When the most powerful man in the world explodes in a storm of fury, ordinary mortals scurry for a lee shore. He was not man enough to stand up to a pissed-off President. Not yet.

Besides, he was just beginning to enjoy his new job, and there was nothing to be gained by throwing it down the toilet.

The worms of rationalization began to gnaw at his soul . . .

But there was one thing he *would* do, dammit.

He dialled Sarah's number. His number. His home number.

'Hello?' She sounded cheerful.

'It's me.'

'Oh.' It was as if he had pricked a hole in her balloon. He could hear a rush of escaping good will.

'How are you?'

'Late.'

'How're the kids?'

'At school.'

'Oh.' So much for pleasantries. 'I found out who put the bug in your car.'

'Oh really? Who was it?' She added acidly, 'The Chinese?'

'No. It was Epstein's people.'

'They admitted it?'

'No. I found out.'

'How?'

'Never mind. The point is, I –'

'So you're quitting.' She paused, and he could almost feel a crooked smile. 'Right?'

'The point is, I think there's another one somewhere.'

'Where?'

'I don't know.'

'Do you intend to find out?'

'I'm trying. If I do, I'll let you know.'

'Sure, Timothy. What are you going to *do* about it?'

'I think I'm *doing* something right now. D'you have any idea the risk I'm taking by –'

'Risk!' She emitted a raspy noise that passed for a laugh. 'Your idea of a big risk is jaywalking.'

Enough, he thought. I don't have to take this. 'Put a cork in it, God damn it! I've told you. You know. Now you can do what you want.'

'No, Timothy, *you* do something,' she spat. 'Or do you want me to tell the walls and the dashboard what a joke you are in bed?'

'Wha –'

She hung up.

His hand shook as he replaced the phone receiver. But as angry as he was, as fervently as he wanted to call her back and slap her in the face with his fling with Eva, he was even more startled by the depth of her rage. Never in fifteen years of marriage, not in the most bitter, vituperative moment, had she stooped to cheap, easy, tacky – and untrue! untrue! – cracks about his virility.

Never mind how you feel, he told himself in an effort to reduce his fever to a manageable temperature, think how *she* must feel. He resolved not to be angry, not to detest her, but to understand her and feel sorry for her.

Sure. You bet.

'Bitch!' he said aloud, and the world felt exquisite in his mouth. 'Self-righteous bitch!'

Foster Pym stood at the bathroom sink, letting his eyes adjust to the dim red glow from the darkroom bulb he had screwed into the fixture over the sink. He had tacked a black rubber raincoat over the bathroom window, and the few rays of light that leaked around its edges would do no harm.

When he could see, he unscrewed the right earpiece from Eva's half-glasses and, with a pair of tweezers, withdrew the strip of 8 mm film. He coiled the strip around a pencil, then slid it off into a standard 35 mm film cannister. He found an unexposed roll of film and, following Teals' precise written instructions, loaded it into the frame of the glasses.

He was worried about Eva. The confrontation with the President had shaken her badly. She had come home and declared that she was through: he could call the police, do what he would, she would rather go to jail for what she had done – naïvely or not – than risk a life sentence for something she had been forced to do. She had not so much as hinted that she might seek immunity in return for informing on him, but they both knew that the option was open to her.

He had striven to avoid a confrontation with her. He had accentuated the positive: she had tweaked the lion in his den and had lived to tell the tale.

She saw only the negative: she had been ten seconds away from being arrested by the President of the United States as a spy.

He said that demonstrated that the President was only human, not omniscient and omnipotent.

She said it demonstrated that this stupid game he was playing had dangers far beyond any possible reward.

He tried to appeal to her politically, reminding her that she had once sent him a paper she had written at Bennington entitled 'Disarming the American Bully'.

She said that was vapid bullshit and he was only interested in being allowed to live off the fat of the land for the rest of his life.

Finally, he had been forced to play two audio tapes for her, tapes in which she had innocently identified and located three of her former compatriots who were still at large and still being sought for involvement in the Glen Canyon Dam affair.

She had thrown a bottle of sherry at him and burst into tears.

He had tried to comfort her.

She had called him a ruthless bastard and asked if he had any conscience at all, even about destroying Burnham's life.

He had replied that no, he had no conscience at all, *especially* about that simpleton Burnham, at which he was shocked mute by her expression, which told him unequivocally that she was falling in love with Burnham.

Which worried him most of all.

She had poured herself a glass of vodka large enough to stun Rasputin.

He had said that drinking was a silly – not to mention reckless – way to avoid reality.

She had told him to fuck off.

He pulled the raincoat off the bathroom window, turned off the red light, and walked into the living room.

Eva was asleep on the couch.

He picked up the telephone and dialled Teal's number, and when identification had been established, said, 'The hostess's order of B-12 is in . . . Yes . . . all right . . . I'll be there.'

He hung up.

'B-12?' Eva said foggily from the couch.

'The code name for our Mr Burnham.' Pym smiled. 'You were the inspiration.'

'I was?'

'Isn't that the vitamin you said makes him believe all is right with the world?'

'So?'

'Well, if we play him correctly, he can make all right with *our* world.'

293

Eleven

Even if, intellectually, Burnham had wanted to stop seeing Eva, he could not have. He would have lied to himself as facilely as an alcoholic lies to himself to justify the 10 a.m. tumbler of vodka: it may be early here, but in Baghdad it's almost evening; I'll just have this one shooter now, and then I'll taper down tonight; I'll quit tomorrow.

For, in ways that he sensed but could not analyse, he was addicted to her. She made him feel good, and not only sexually, though that was her most obvious achievement. Her sexual wizardry had stripped ten years off his life and imbued him with a new potency and pride. She nourished him, literally, by controlling his diet – not, like a health-food nut, feeding him only what was good for him and would help prevent cancer of the colon, things like humus and bulgar, but by restricting his intake of those foods which made him feel physically fine, mentally alert and sexually immortal.

She was entirely nonjudgmental. Whether or not she was apolitical he had no idea, but whenever, conversationally, he sought her opinion about an issue that had come up during the day – for example, how to draft a statement for the President that managed to kick the ass of the President of France for harbouring 173 goggle-eyed Italian terrorists, while, at the same time, avoided driving the silly bugger farther out onto the radical fringe – her considered response was invariably based on three priorities: what would be best for Burnham, what would be best for the President, and, last and least, what would soothe the ruffled feathers of the vocal moralists.

It was so relaxing, especially compared to life with Sarah.

He had tried, every couple of days for more than two weeks, to set up a meeting with Sarah, in hopes of talking through their differences or at least of establishing a *modus vivendi* by which could see his children, whom he missed with a pain that was physical, visceral. Even his midget Maoist daughter. Sarah had refused to see him and, by now, was refusing to take his calls. If she answered and heard his voice, she would hang up immediately. Sometimes a man answered. Burnham didn't know (and didn't particularly care) who it was. He assumed it was a bright-eyed towhead from one of the Hickory Hill litters. Sarah was out. Always.

Burnham didn't know what more to do. Several of his friends had been divorced, but as acrimonious as some of the splits had been, the combatants had always talked, if only through their lawyers. How do you force your wife to return your phone calls? He should probably hire a lawyer who would go to a judge who would issue a writ (he didn't know what a writ was, but it sounded good) to be served on Sarah who would tear it up. He could stop paying his rent but that seemed self-defeating, because if the house was foreclosed upon and Sarah and the kids were moved out onto the street, he had no doubt that Sarah would find a way to have his salary attached. Without speaking to him on the phone. What he could do, and what he intended to do one of these days, was stop paying into their joint chequing account, close that account, and let her start papering Georgetown with rubber cheques. Unless she had already found a new sugar daddy to keep her in electricity and cooking gas, that should move her to make a phone call.

Meanwhile, Eva came to his office each day around noon. If he could get away, they played squash. If not, they had a quick lunch in the Mess or, if time was very short, he sent Dyanna down to fetch sandwiches for them. If he was working – editing a speech or preparing a statement or just thinking – she read. She seemed pleased to be there, and he was ecstatic to have her there. He drew sustenance from her. If he was under pressure, on a deadline, frantic to find an answer, a smile from her could (or so he felt, and, if there was truth to the precepts of biofeedback, as she insisted there was, feeling it made it so) lop twenty points off his blood pressure.

Dyanna did not like Eva. At first, Burnham thought her problem was jealousy: it was one thing for him to have a woman outside the office, but to establish another female in Dyanna's nest smacked of professional adultery. Then he realized that the problem was fear. Dyanna was afraid of Eva: she saw Eva as a destabilizing influence on Burnham, a threat to his position and, therefore, to hers. She had no control over Eva, and she knew that Eva had complete control over Burnham, which, of course, meant control over Dyanna.

Burnham spoke to Dyanna, who denied all such selfish sentiments and avowed that her concerns were purely moral: marriage was a holy vow, and Eva was a home-wrecker. She volunteered to keep her feelings to herself and to be the soul of civility around Eva, which pleased Burnham because it freed him from having to hint that he was certain that the White House could provide him with a secretary who was not a spritual sister to Jerry Falwell.

The President was unfailingly courteous to Eva, had taken to calling her by her first name, had even once asked her what she thought about a value-added tax like those imposed all over Europe (Eva denied knowing what a value-added tax was).

After the second time the President met Eva, Burnham had gone to the President and consented to a full-field FBI investigation of Eva. He said he could not imagine that the FBI would find any skeletons in her cupboard, but he agreed with the President that it was best for all concerned that she be certified officially safe.

The President had called the Director of the FBI while Burnham was in his office, and Burnham had provided the Director with what few relevant details he possessed: her name, her address, her college, her job.

Then the President had shaken Burnham's hand and said, 'If she's good for you, Tim, I know she'll be good for the country.'

The only thing Burnham had yet to do was tell Eva.

He hadn't dared. Not that he was afraid she wouldn't understand – she understood everything, that was one of her beautiful points – but she might be annoyed that he hadn't consulted with her before launching the investigation. Perhaps she had a few youthful peccadilloes that she'd like to keep private. Perhaps the FBI might dredge up an early marriage – maybe a child or two – that she had kept from Burnham. What right did he have to employ the Federal Government to steal all her personal secrets? None. Suppose she wasn't who she said she was, suppose she had been lying to him, suppose . . .

He was supposing himself into lunacy. He had to tell her, and tell her soon, before any one of the inane fantasies that competed for space in his head gelled into a credible scenario.

And before she found out on her own, as surely she would, for soon FBI agents looking like IBM salesmen would fan out across the land, asking probing questions of her pediatrician, her eighth-grade field-hockey coach and her gynaecologist. One of them would be bound to call her and ask what was going on, was she being nominated Ambassador to Mali.

On a Monday when the President was not due back from Camp David until the afternoon, Burnham and Eva went for a walk on the Ellipse. A light breeze blew from the northwest, carrying mountain pollens that irritated Burnham's allergies but keeping the humidity down so the air was pleasantly dry.

Tour buses clustered around the Washington Monument, disgorging graduating seniors from Cranbury High

School to mount the cenotaph and there, it was hoped, to osmose the glory of America's heritage amid gum wrappers, cigarette butts and Magic-Marker messages that said things like 'Scungo 154'.

Burnham and Eva circled the Ellipse without speaking – she because she was enjoying the human extravaganza, he because he was trying to compose a graceful way of telling her about the FBI investigation.

In his mind he tried: 'The President thinks so highly of you that he wants to spend a quarter of a million of the taxpayers' dollars to find out more about you.'

And: 'Our relationship has become important to more than just us. It's important to America.'

And: 'If I didn't love you so much, I wouldn't have sicced the FBI on you.'

Finally, thinking that he was actually saying something but in fact still stalling, he said, 'I have something to tell you.'

'Oh? What?'

'That first day, when the President came into my office and saw you there, he –'

'And called me Sarah.'

'That's the day. Afterwards, he called me into his office and –'

'Dad!'

Burnham stopped. Why did he stop? There were a thousand fathers here, and a thousand children calling to them. The voice was familiar. He looked around.

'Dad! TB!'

It came from behind him. He turned. There, stopped at a light, was a yellow school bus, and hanging out of one of the windows was the torso of Christopher.

'Chris!' Burnham jogged to the curb. He was excited and nervous and happy. He hadn't seen his son in more than three weeks. He wanted to say everything at once. What came out was, 'How you doing?'

'Awesome! Going to tennis camp.'

'School's over?'

298

'A week ago.'

'Oh. Right. Hey, I've missed you.'

'Yeah, me too.'

'See you when you get back?'

'Sure. I'll call you.' The light changed, and the bus lurched forward.

'Maybe I'll be home by then.' Keep him hoping, Burnham thought.

'I doubt it. Mom's already filed for divorce.'

What?' The bus was gathering speed, and Burnham ran along-side, dodging prams and hot-dog stands. 'She couldn't have!'

'She did,' Christopher said. The bus was pulling away now, and he had to shout. 'Cruel and unusual punishment, I think it is. See ya!' He waved and vanished into the bus.

Burnham stood at the corner, staring after the bus, feeling winded, shocked, betrayed, traduced, raped.

Eva came up behind him and took his hand and laced her fingers into his.

'Did you hear what he said?'

She smiled and, with her free hand, rubbed the inside of his elbow.

'I've never been cruel *or* unusual!'

They walked, and she held his hand and let him vent his sorrow and his rage and his bitterness. He plotted vengeance, and she nodded; he voiced despair, and she rubbed his elbow.

Eventually, he was empty, and then he, too, was silent.

'Nature does a wonderful thing with pain,' she said.

'What's that?'

'Builds a shell around it, insulating you from it little by little, and then one day you realize that you haven't thought about it for a while, and, what do you know, it's gone.'

'How long does that take?'

'Depends if you have somebody helping you.' She squeezed his hand in both of hers. 'You do.'

He stopped walking and took her face in his hands and kissed her.

From somewhere nearby a young male voice called out, 'All *right!*'

'Have you ever thought of being a shrink?'

She laughed. 'I didn't do anything.'

They started walking again, hand in hand, and she said, 'What was it you were going to tell me?'

'Oh. Yes.' He spoke without hesitating, because he wasn't worried any more. He loved her, he knew she knew it, and she knew he wouldn't do anything to hurt her. Besides, the whole thing made eminent good sense if you looked at it from a logical perspective.

'The President gave me two options: stop seeing you, which I don't consider an option, or make sure that our relationship won't jeopardize anything.'

'What does that mean? Jeopardize anything?'

'From a security standpoint. He feels, and I know you'll agree, that if you're going to be in my office, in my heart and my head' – he smiled – 'someone with my security clearance, with access to the things I have access to, then you'd better be secure, too.'

'What do I have to do to be secure?'

'Nothing. Not a thing. It's all done for you.'

'How?' Her pace had been in sync with his. Now it slowed. Her grip on his hand loosened just a bit.

'The FBI sends some guys around to ask questions, that's all.' He felt her fingers slide away from his. 'I know it sounds scary, but it's no big deal, I promise. The only things they care about are if you're a Nazi or a Communist or a Martian.'

He laughed. 'I think it's safe to bet you'll pass with flying colours.'

She stopped walking. She took her hand from Burnham and appeared to fish for something in her purse. Her breathing had quickened. 'Has it started?'

He chose a judicious fib. 'I think so. I don't have anything to do with it. Personally.'

'I thought you said it was your option.'

'Well . . . in the sense that once I said I wouldn't stop

seeing you, it was a given that they'd start inv . . . asking questions.' He put his hand on her shoulder. The muscles were as hard as marble. 'Hey. I'm sorry. It was selfish of me. I should've asked you. I'm really sorry. I –'

'Don't worry.' She forced a smile. She took his hand again, and her fingers felt like chilled pickles.

'I know it sounds gruesome. But it really isn't anything.'

'I guess I was surprised, that's all.' She wiggled her fingers in his. 'Feel my hand. What a chicken I am.'

'Don't be silly. If somebody told me out of the blue that the FBI was doing a full-field investigation of me, my mind'd go ape trying to remember every time I sassed a teacher or got a parking ticket.'

'Is that what they call it?' Her voice was a little girl's voice. 'A full-field investigation?'

Burnham closed his eyes and cursed himself. 'Yes. But it's really a two-dollar name for a two-bit formality.'

Eva made a perfunctory pass at her watch and said, 'Look at the time!'

'Yeah, we'd better –'

Bmeep! Bmeep! Bmeep! Bmeep! Bmeep! An urgent, abrasive, soprano signal was triggered somewhere inside Burnham's pants, like the digital wrist alarms that always seem to go off in theatres at the peak moment of tender passion.

'What's *that*?' Eva looked horrified, as if discovering that the FBI had taken up residence in Burnham's trousers.

Abashed, Burnham fumbled under the tail of his jacket, contorting himself as if possessed by St Vitus Dance, and pushed a switch that silenced the beeping. 'See?' He tried to grin. 'I get all the perks of being a doctor without ever going to med school.'

'What *is* it?'

'I'm not allowed to be out of touch any more. At all. Ever. So if I'm not near a phone, I have to carry this.' He unclipped the small black metal monitoring device from his belt. 'If they want me, they fire it from the White House.'

301

'Then what?'

'I call in, unless it's this message, and then I hie my ass back as fast as I can.' He held the device before her face and pointed to three letters flashing in the LCD window: BTW. 'Himself has returned from Camp David.'

'That's . . . creepy.'

'Yeah, well . . . extremism in the defence of liberty and all that.'

He took her arm and led her to the curb and flagged down a taxi. 'I'm really sorry about –'

She put a finger across his lips and said, 'That's okay. I understand.'

'I know you do,' he said, and he kissed her fingertips.

As he watched the taxi pull out into traffic, Burnham tried to interpret Eva's last look. It had been a smile, but a sad smile and clouded by a shadow of . . . what?

Regret? Worry? Fear?

Forget it, he told himself, don't make more of it than there is. You feel guilty, so you're looking for trouble you think you deserve.

He crossed the avenue and started around the long oval of the South Lawn.

He detested the beeper, thought of it as a leash, resented being summoned, like a lady-in-waiting, back from his lunch hour. He had several other similarly piquant sentiments about the destruction of his privacy, and he encouraged himself to flush them now, before he got back to the White House, for no matter what outcry rose from his gut, his head reminded him that these were but the prices of proximity to the President. And the rewards – in excitement, fascination, self-esteem and the deliciously naughty enjoyment of other people's envy – were handsome compensation.

Besides, he should feel grateful that he had been allowed to steal an hour away from his wall-to-wall carpeted, temperature-controlled, electronically surveilled, Secret-Service protected cloister.

Gazing at the South Lawn as he walked, he wondered if it

was true, as legend had it, that there were machine-gun emplacements beneath the greensward which, at the push of a button, would pop up and rake an unruly mob with computer-aimed tracers.

He had almost been taken to Camp David. The President had wanted him to go along, said he needed a sounding board, needed his Special Assistant for Perspective, but had changed his mind at the last minute – on the hunch that, since the gathering at Camp David was to include only the President's wife, two of their family lawyers and one of their sons, to resolve a sticky issue involving some bank loans incurred by the son (who persisted in spending his father's name like loose change whenever it could benefit him) and now under the threat of default, Burnham might be regarded by Mrs Winslow as a ringer brought in by the President to reinforce his paternal inclination to let their delinquent offspring hang.

As it was, before the trip the President had played and replayed the situation with Burnham, casting him alternately as devil's advocate, hard-nosed patriarch, pushover pop, and mother.

Burnham was becoming accustomed to being a protean figure for the President. He was an alter-ego for the man. He would argue any side of an issue, exposing weaknesses, dangers and hidden benefits.

The President trusted him implicitly, because, as he said one day, 'You got no axe to grind, Tim. You've gone as high as you can go here, and you know it. I've shown you how worthless the Cabinet is, so you wouldn't want to go in there even if I'd put you there, which I won't. You're not a lawyer, so you can't have any ambition to be a judge. And you're not rich enough to be an ambassador. I created you, and you serve at my pleasure, which means that your main interest has to be me. You know it, and I know it, so I know when you argue with me you're doing it for my benefit – not like all the rest of them, who all got some constituency or other they suck up to, even if it's just the Harvard Club, B'nai Brith or the New York Review of goddam Books.'

The President paused, squinted and said, 'You writing your memoirs?'

'Me? No, sir.'

'Good. I can't stand a man who's writing his memoirs. It skews his whole outlook. Everything he's mixed up in, he thinks of it in terms of himself: what do *I* think about this, how'm *I* doing, what does the President say about *me*, how'll history grade *me*? Shit! Only one man allowed to think like that around here, Tim, and you're lookin' at him.'

'I know, Mr President.'

'I know you know, Tim, and that's why . . . I got a little present for you.'

'Sir?' Burnham lowered his eyes, humbly, prepared to accept a tie clip embossed with the Great Seal or a signed copy of the President's collected speeches.

'I been thinkin' about this, Tim, and I've decided: you're my man.' The President paused for dramatic effect. 'I want you to write *my* memoirs.'

'Wha – Sir?'

'I know, I know.' The President raised a hand, as if to ward off an embarrassing effusion of gratitude. 'It's a heavy burden. But you deserve it. Ever since that first day, I've known you're a man with a sense of history. You can handle it. Besides, I'll be sitting by your side, helping you with every damn comma.'

Burnham was appalled. The thought of spending the remainder of his adult life sculpting self-serving reminiscences was a hell beyond imagining. And yet to decline was to buy himself a one-way ticket to disfavour.

So he said, 'I don't know what to say.'

'I know how you feel,' the President said, patting his shoulder. 'I felt that way when the Chief Justice administered my first oath of office. Don't say anything. Just take real good notes from now on.'

He had obeyed, had begun to take copious notes which, he prayed fervently, he would never have to use, except perhaps as fuel for the novel he would write. From a hideout. In Botswana.

Now, as he approached the door to the West Basement, he saw twin black Cadillac limousines idling at the curb. He recognized the drivers, which told him that the two Cabinet officers with the President were the Secretaries of State and Defence, which meant that the meeting would also include Epstein and Duggan, which meant that the subject was, as Burnham had suspected, Honduras.

Ever since Ronald Reagan had, during his last year in office, orchestrated the invasion of Nicaragua by a ragtag band of Contras, Cuban exiles, American mercenaries and assorted outcasts and survivalists – an invasion that had been squashed in a debacle widely assessed as worse even than the Bay of Pigs – Honduras had taken over the role as plague upon the foreign policy of the United States.

Los Tegucigalpeños, as the guerrillas called themselves, had looked to the south and seen that kicking Yanqui ass could be a profitable enterprise, and, with the help of their Sandinista brethren, they were hell-bent on toppling their government and forming a Central American Revolutionary Confederation with Nicaragua. The Russians were sending AK-47s, the Cubans were sending Cubans, and Muhammar Qadaffi was offering to pay for the training and transportation of any American blacks eager to join the struggle against 'the capitalist imperialist cabal.'

President Winslow was the man in the middle, hectored by one extreme to get the hell out of Central America once and for damn-well all, and by the other to get the Communists out of Central America once and for damn-well all.

The most vocal pressure on the President was to go on prime-time television and resurrect the Monroe Doctrine with ringing rhetoric and then to launch, with the support of the Congress (presuming he could get it), a full-scale, undisguised land and sea invastion of Honduras by America's Navy, Air Force and Marines. Secure America's back yard.

Once and for damn-well all.

Burnham had listened to every argument on every side a dozen times. He had spent whole evenings playing right-wing fire-brand and left-wing appeaser, while the President abused him as a fool, a dunce, a maniac and a lily-livered pussy-whipped wimp.

Never, however, had the President asked Burnham for his own advice, and for that Burnham was grateful. He didn't know what he would say. All he knew for sure was that under no circumstances, ever, not in this life or any subsequent incarnation, would he agree to be President of the United States. The fact that no President had suddenly infarcted to death in office, or been hauled away in a wagon and left to watch cartoons for the rest of his natural life, was a miracle.

Burnham walked through the door of the West Basement, climbed the stairs, passed through Dyanna's office, his own and the President's private office, and opened the door to the Oval Office. He didn't knock; the President had told him not to.

'You're nuts!' Eva shouted at her father. 'They won't stop with me. What about when they get to you?'

Foster Pym sat in an upholstered chair and picked at the loose threads in a seam of the slipcover. He was sweating, maybe from the haste of his trip home after Eva called him, maybe from the news she had delivered.

'Nothing,' he said. 'They'll find nothing.'

'Great! And then what? There is no such thing as a person without a past in this country. That's the worst thing they could find. Nothing.'

'Not necessarily. When they get to a dead end, they'll have to come to me.'

'And what'll you say? "I can't remember?"'

'Precisely. I was a John Doe. There were hundreds of John Does. Thousands.'

'They'll take fingerprints.'

'They won't find a record.'

'And? Weren't Americans fingerprinted when they joined the Army?'

'I . . . I don't know. Perhaps my hands were mutilated during the war.'

'They'll check your teeth. They can tell if dental work was done abroad.'

'I never had dental work done, not till I came here.'

He waited for her next barrage, but none came. He wanted to be irritated at her hammering, but he couldn't summon the feeling. What she was doing was useful. Reassuring, now that he had greeted each interrogatory with a credible response.

'See?' he leaned forward and patted her hand. 'Let them dig. They'll come up with a dry hole.'

'What about my mother?'

Pym paused – not evasively, but because any thought of Louise was alien to him. He hadn't thought about her in years, in any context whatever. To him she was dead, as, for all he knew, she was in fact.

Eva anticipated him. 'You can't say she's dead.'

'No, but I can say I don't have the faintest idea where she is, or whether she's alive. I haven't seen the woman in nearly thirty years.'

'Suppose they find her. How much did she know about you?'

Now Pym was uncomfortable, because he didn't have an answer. He knew how much he had told Louise – nothing – and he knew that she had been so obsessed with the resurrection of the Reich that she seemed incapable of any other concerns. *Seemed.* That was the key. He didn't know how perceptive she had been, how much she might have noticed, consciously or unconsciously, about him. Nor did he recall how careful he had been, way back then. How meticulously had he detailed his past for her? How had he excused his occasional late-night sorties into dark parks?

He decided to dismiss Louise as a threat. She was crazy then, she was probably even crazier now, and if an FBI agent should turn over a rock and find her the den mother of a *Bund* in Hopewell, New Jersey, he would hardly be inclined to give much weight to her testimony.

He said, 'Don't worry about her.'

'We *have* to worry about her. Remember what Timothy said – a Nazi, a Communist or a Martian. Well, two out of three's pretty heavy.'

'Never worry about things you cannot do anything about,' Pym said, lecturing just a little. 'We cannot do a thing about Louise.'

'There's one thing we *can* do something about.' Eva reached into her purse, took out the half glasses and tossed them into Pym's lap. 'We can stop. Right now. Before they catch us in the act. If they're watching me, you can bet they're watching Timothy when I'm with him.'

Pym toyed with the glasses, tilting them back and forth in the lamplight to see if he could discern the plastic shield over the tiny lens in the nosepiece. 'I'm afraid not,' he said, and he folded the glasses and placed them on the arm of his chair.

'What does that mean? We can do what we damn please.'

'Eva,' Pym sighed, for suddenly he felt tired and old and trapped, 'they are very happy with what we have given them so far. I don't know what's in those papers, but they're very happy. They want more.'

'To hell with them.'

Pym continued as if she hadn't spoken. 'They want more than more. As they see it, they have the most valuable agent they could hope for – a mole in the Oval Office. They want you to start pumping Burnham for information.'

'I won't do it.'

Pym sighed again. He had to make her see that the decision had been taken from his hands. They were not agents any more; they were instruments.

He said, 'What do you think they'll do to us if we refuse?'

'Nothing. Why should they? They should get down on their knees and thank us for what we did do.' She snorted. 'What do *you* think they'll do, kill us?'

'No. I don't think they'd bother. We're not worth the trouble.'

'So?'

'If we refuse,' Pym said with forced calm, 'and they decide they can't trust us any more, they'll dump us.'

'Dump us?'

'Make sure we get caught. You and me and your Mr Burnham. Especially your Mr Burnham.'

'Why? Why would they do that?'

'It would be a great coup for them. Make the American government look stupid, ineffective and untrustworthy. Make the President look like a fool. It would wreck American intelligence and security operations. Their allies wouldn't share with them any more. You remember – no, you were too young – but when they found all those spies in the British services, MI-5 and MI-6 were the laughing stocks of the Western world. Burgess and Maclean – and, later, Blunt – may have outlived their usefulness, but they had one last service to perform for Mother Russia. They turned British intelligence into a bad joke. It took years for the Brits to recover. And still nobody trusts them, not really.' Pym paused. He could see by Eva's face that she was not yet convinced, so he said, 'We're in so deep now that they'd have to sacrifice us. They couldn't take the chance that you or Mr Burnham would be seized by a sudden fit of patriotism and decide to turn yourselves in. That way, the whole thing could be covered up and denied. There would be no coup. No. They will want to control it.'

'That's crazy! They'd be ratting on themselves, admitting they're spying.'

'Don't you understand, Eva? They're allowed to spy. Those are the rules of the game. They're *supposed* to spy! All they'd be doing is acknowledging the obvious and proving that they're better at it than anyone else. It's nothing for them to be ashamed of. They'd crow!'

When still Eva didn't say a word, Pym decided to drive the last nail. 'Mr Burnham would go to jail, probably for life. He'd deny everything, but the evidence against him would be overwhelming. I'd go to jail too, and there I would die of old age unless, someday, the Americans offer to trade me for some low-level American diplomat – or perhaps a tourist – arrested in Moscow or Leningrad. Then I'd be sent home – it's funny, I don't think of it as home any more, haven't for years and years – where I'd be interrogated and, most probably, shot.' He saw her hands jump in her lap, and he continued matter-of-factly. 'Yes, they certainly wouldn't treat me as a hero for refusing to carry out an assignment. As for you, I really don't know. It depends –'

'Stop,' Eva said.

Pym looked at her. She was pale and rigid. 'I'm sorry,' he said. 'But it's true. All of it.'

'How long?' she asked.

'I can't be sure. Until your Mr Burnham loses his access to the President, I imagine, which is bound to happen sooner or later – they say this President is fickle that way – or until you lose your access to Mr Burnham; perhaps his wife summons him back to the nest.'

'She's filed for divorce.'

'Ah. In that case –'

'I can't pump him for information.'

'Why not?'

'One of the main reasons he trusts me is that I never ask him anything, ever. As far as he knows, and the President too, I know nothing about anything important, and I care less. If I start asking him questions, he'll get suspicious, and he's hardly the suspicious type, not in his state of mind.'

'What state of mind is that?'

'He's in love with me.'

'Good.'

'Even if I wanted to, and I don't, I couldn't. He trusts me.'

Pym frowned. 'What does that have to do –'

'I can't betray him. I can't!'

'You're not betraying him now?'

'That's different. I'm just reading his mail, right? It's not *him*. He doesn't ever have to know. It's not –'

'And your state of mind?' He wanted her to say it. 'You're falling in love with him.'

She looked at him, defiant, but he saw that she was gripping one index finger so hard that the knuckle shone white. 'Yes.'

'Don't,' he said.

'"Don't,"? Oh, that's helpful. Thanks very much. I –'

'You mustn't! You have to keep doing what you're doing. Nothing more, just photographing his mail, and I'll tell them they'll have to wait for an extra tidbits. They'll buy that. They won't want to lose the pictures. By and by, if we're lucky, the President will tire of Mr Burnham and adopt someone else. Once our source dries up, we can stop.'

'Why will they let us?'

'There'll be no advantage to them to expose us. As far as they're concerned, we're still trustworthy, we pose no threat to them. You don't throw agents to the wolves without a reason.'

'And Timothy?'

'They'll certainly want to leave him alone. He's perfect! He doesn't know what he's done. Five years from now, or ten years, perhaps he'll be a Cabinet officer or an ambassador or the president of a large company that makes high-technology components or even a prestigious journalist. He'll have a fat salary and a fine family and a life he'd do anything to protect. Suppose he receives a visit from someone who hints that there might be a few things in his past that he'd rather not have revealed, perhaps shows him photostats of some of the mail he never bothered to read, with a big Q-CLEARANCE stamp on it. Do you think he'd be willing to do a favour or two for this visitor?'

'So he'll never be free.'

'I'm not saying that *will* happen, only that it will be worth their while to leave him in blissful ignorance. He may never be the wiser.'

'I feel sick.'

'You can't afford to be sick. Not now. That's why it's so important that you don't fall in love with him.'

'Too late,' she said with a crooked smile. Her eyes glistened like blue marbles in a pool of rainwater. 'You're sure they'll let us go?' Her voice was clogged.

'Positive,' he said. 'Absolutely.' He turned away, wishing he were a better liar.

Burnham closed the connecting door, walked across his office, shedding his loafers as he went, and fell onto his couch.

He needed a drink. The longing was stronger than it had ever been. He craved the cool, satiny feeling as the elixir coated his throat and numbed the little nerve endings, the delicious warmth as it pooled in his stomach, the few seconds' wait for lift-off, and finally – most of all – the release as the circuits tripped one after another and shut down the thoughts that spun like pinwheels in his brain. He needed to give his brain a holiday, to let it float free in sweet nothingness.

Did the President drink? Burnham had seen him sip a watery bourbon now and again, but that wasn't drinking. Booze wasn't a toy, it was a tool, and anyone who treated it like a toy shouldn't be allowed to play with it. 'Social drinking' was an oxymoron, a term coined to sanitize the socially unsavoury. Dr Johnson knew what booze was for: 'To get rid of myself, to send myself away.'

No, the President didn't drink. Not enough anyway.

If I were President, Burnham thought, I'd make it a point once a week to lock myself in a room with no phones, only a TV set that showed reruns of *I Love Lucy*, and knock back a fifth of vodka. Just to give my brain a break.

How could the President keep all that crap in his head? Yes, no; right, wrong; black, white; night, day. Maybe he didn't keep *any* of it in his head, maybe he just let it happen around him and waited for a few drops of distillate to fall into a cup and become a decision.

The Secretary of Defence had said that the guerrillas in Honduras were intent on establishing a totalitarian Communist regime.

The Chairman of the Joint Chiefs of Staff said that two-thirds of the country were already under a totalitarian Communist regime.

Dennis Duggan puffed on his pipe and said that Tegucigalpa reminded him of Saigon near the end, an isolated enclave.

The Secretary of State said that this put him in mind of 1954, and didn't the President agree that there was an awful lot of Red-baiting going on?

The Secretary of Defence said that if the Secretary of State was accusing him of McCarthyism, the Secretary of State should watch his mouth or he'd find his paisley tie jammed up his puckerhole.

The Secretary of State said he thought things were getting out of hand and the time had come to break for cocktails and a light lunch.

The Chairman of the Joint Chiefs recommended a preemptive strike against guerrilla positions in the north.

Mario Epstein said that the guerrilla positions were changing every fifteen minutes, and that 'pre-emptive strikes' were code words for turning Honduras into a parking lot.

The Chairman of the Joint Chiefs asked Epstein if he meant to compare him to Curtis LeMay.

The Secretary of Defence reminded his colleagues that Curtis LeMay hadn't been all wrong.

Dennis Duggan asked Epstein, in an aside, who Curtis LeMay was.

The Chairman of the Joint Chiefs brought out an enormous colour-coded chart that separated all of Honduras into thousand-hectare slices and proceeded to detail the guerrilla activity in each slice.

The President asked Burnham if he wanted a Fresca, and Burnham said, No, sir, but he did ask for a Coke.

He needed the sugar.

313

And on and on it went, for three hours, ending only when the President had to depart to brief the Congressional leadership on his current thinking about Honduras.

Burnham suggested that the President tell the Leaders that this was an immensely complex situation, with potential repercussions that could last for generations, and that he had learned from the mistakes of his predecessors and was determined not to fly off half-cocked on a course of action that all Americans would come to regret.

The President liked the suggestion: it insulted everyone from Johnson Democrats to Reagan Republicans, let them know that their man (and, by association, they themselves) was responsible, at least in part, for the mess America was in and from which he was trying to rescue it, without mentioning anyone by name.

Lying on his couch, lamenting the loss of his good friend John Barleycorn, Burnham wondered if there was a pill he could take. Not a happy pill, just a goodbye-see-you-later pill. He knew little about pills, and what he did know he didn't like.

He decided to try meditation. He hadn't meditated in a year, but he remembered how. He closed his eyes and told his mind to instruct his muscle groups to relax, one at a time, and he imagined himself in the safest place of all, his childhood bedroom. He saw his bed and his hockey stick and his Mickey Mantle and Yogi Berra posters and –

'Mr Burnham?'

The voice sounded far away, like someone calling from the kitchen, but because it didn't belong in his head it was jarring, intrusive.

He opened his eyes and looked between his stockinged feet and saw Dyanna standing in the doorway.

Her face was ashen beneath its veneer of rouge, which made her cheeks look splotchy.

'I have to talk to you right away.'

Burnham expended a mighty breath and rolled upright. He opened and closed his eyes and rubbed his temples with his fingertips. His mind had begun a retreat, and to be yanked back suddenly from the lip of oblivion was painful. 'I don't suppose it can wait.'

'No, sir. Not this. I'm afraid I found out why we're here.'

'What?' He looked at her to see if she was joking. 'You mean you've solved the seminal teleological riddle? For that you woke me up? It's been lying around for a billion years. It could have waited another half hour.'

'Here.' Dyanna pointed to the floor. 'Why we're *here*.'

'I know why I'm here. The President told me. I'm to be his Boswell.'

'That may be why you're here now, but it's not how he found you.'

'What *are* you talking about?'

Dyanna opened one of her hands and showed him a Sony microcassette. 'I'm sorry,' she said. 'I mean, I think I'm sorry. I don't know! Don't you see?'

She's about to burst into tears, Burnham decided. She's come unglued.

He stood up and went to Dyanna, took the cassette from her and put an arm around her shoulder. 'We have any coffee?'

She nodded.

'Let's have some coffee.'

'Then you'll listen to it?'

'Then I'll listen to it, whatever "it" is.'

He followed her into her office, and as she fumbled for the cups and the sugar substitute and the non-dairy creamer and the coffee, the words flooded from her like water through a ruptured dike.

'I ran out of tapes for my dictation machine, and I needed another one in case the President wanted something in a hurry and you had to dictate or whatever, I didn't want to be caught without one, so I called downstairs and they won't have any new ones in until tomorrow, and our old ones have been used so many times they're fuzzy and sound like a chicken fight.'

She handed Burnham his coffee and, carrying her micro-

315

cassette recorder, followed him back into his office and shut the door behind them.

He did not try to hurry her, did not want to interrupt her, because he sensed that whatever it was she was leading up to was something about which he would need to know every minute detail.

'Well, I knew that Mr Epstein's girls have a whole bin full of these tapes, 'cause you know every phone call he has is taped and –'

'It is? Every one?'

'Uh-huh. Not so much for a record or anything, I mean this isn't Watergate or anything, he's not crazy, but just so the girls can type an accurate transcript if they need to later, and then when they're done with it or they don't need to transcribe it they just throw it in the bin and use it again. So I asked Connie if she'd lend me a tape and she said sure and she reached into the bin and gave me a whole handful of them, so I brought them back here and I picked one and put it in my machine and pushed "play" just to make sure it wasn't all crackly and . . . well, that's it.' She pointed to the tape in Burnham's hand. 'I'm sorry.'

'What are you sorry about?'

'You'll see. I mean, maybe you'll be happy. I don't know.'

Burnham handed her the tape and sat on the couch. She loaded the recorder and placed it on the coffee table.

'Sit down,' Burnham said, and he patted the place beside him on the couch.

'No, sir, I –'

'Jesus, Dyanna, I'm not gonna kiss you!'

'No, sir, I'm afraid you might strangle me.'

He smiled at her and said. 'I promise. Now sit.'

She sat on the edge of the couch, as if poised for flight, and pushed the 'play' button.

From the little speaker in the recorder came the voice of Evelyn Witt: 'Just a sec, Mario.'

Then a second of silence, a click, and the President: 'Yeah, Mario.'

Burnham pushed the 'stop' button. 'He records all his conversations with *the President*?'

'Uh-huh.'

'If the President knew, if he even suspected, he'd have Epstein's *ass*.' Burnham smiled. 'Whatever's on the rest of this tape, Dyanna, no matter what it is, I'm gonna have a medal struck for you.'

'Wait.' Dyanna's hand fluttered over her hair. 'Please wait.'

Burnham started the recorder.

'Mr President,' Epstein said, 'I've spoken to Dennis again about this Gromyko business.'

'And?' There was an edge of aggressive irritation in the President's voice.

'Sir, we hope you'll reconsider the idea of using Burnham.'

'Why? You don't think I know people? You don't think I can pick my own man?'

'No, sir . . . I mean, no, that's not what we think. He's not qualified. It's as simple as that.'

'How do you know?'

'We've double-checked his whole file. He has no experience in foreign policy. He's never negotiated anything with anybody.'

'You checked his file.' The President chuckled. 'You ever check Dick Helms's file? How about Kermit Roosevelt's? Just bureaucrats, right? A file's like the credits on a movie: it doesn't tell you anything about the story behind the story.'

'But, sir –'

'You want me to send Parker Randall? He's "qualified", alright, but you know's well as I do that he'd spend the whole time trying to find a restaurant that made you eat with eight forks and six spoons. Gromyko's dealt with nine American Presidents. He knows more about the history of our foreign policy than we do, f'crissakes. He's got no respect for college boys with on-the-job training. What he respects is someone he knows, someone he also

317

knows has the ear of the President. And that's Tim. To a T.'

'Excuse me, Mr President, but how do you know Burnham knows Gromyko?'

(Burnham said to Dyanna, 'I can't wait.' She did not reply. She picked frantically at her nail polish. She seemed to be shrinking into the couch.)

'How do I know?' the President thundered. 'I know, that's how!'

'Did Gromyko tell you?'

No reply.

'Did Burnham tell you?'

'As good as. The first day he came in here, that day I was gonna fire him for fucking up, he had a couple of phone messages on his papers. I know, 'cause I picked 'em off the floor myself. One said he should call Margaret Thatcher. The other said Gromyko had returned his call and he was to call back right away.'

(Burnham stopped the tape. He looked at Dyanna, who was wishing she could vanish into the floral print in the upholstery. He said, 'Jesus Christ.'

She nodded.

'The whole thing?' He waved his arm around the room, gathering in the White House, the Presidency, his entire life. The way a Cheyenne would point at the sky and mean the universe. 'Everything? From two silly messages you scribbled for me because I felt insecure walking around the White House without papers?'

She nodded again.

'He must've thought I was . . . I don't know. What?'

She pointed dumbly at the tape recorder, so he pushed the 'play' button.

'Phone messages?' Epstein's voice had risen half an octave. He was trying his best to muzzle a scream. 'But, sir . . . how do you know they were genuine?'

'Goddamit, Mario, don't be an asshole! What kinda jerk-off runs around writing himself phony messages to call the Russians?'

318

Epstein made a noise that sounded as if he had a piece of stew beef caught in his œsophagus, a kind of gurgly breathless swallowing noise.

Sensing that his counter-strike had drawn blood, the President resumed the offensive.

'You know, your trouble, Mario, is you think anybody who doesn't report to you and God forbid anybody who knows something you don't know, he must be a friggin' Chinaman or a spy or something. But there are people in this government that you don't know about, and some that even I don't know about, who serve their country Goddamn well in spite of you. Like Timothy. Now, if you're still nosing around him, I want you to stop it. I'm not gonna have you bitch up some major undercover operation just 'cause your pride's got piles. Understood?'

'Yes, sir. But there's one test I'd –'

'No. No tests. No nothing. Got it?'

'Yes, sir.'

'Remember something, Mario: this country's run for more than two hundred years without your hand on the helm, I don't care if Tim climbed out from under some friggin' rock. He serves his President – and without a lot of the pissing and moaning I hear from other pains in the ass around here.'

The President hung up. A second later, the only sound from the recorder was tape hiss.

'Well,' Burnham said. He rewound the tape, removed it from the recorder and dropped it in his pocket.

Dyanna sat stiffly on the edge of the couch, head high, lower lip a-quiver. 'Would you like my resignation?'

Burnham hadn't given a thought to her part in the drama, or to her reaction to it. 'Don't be silly. How could you know?' He touched her cheek. 'Besides, look at all the answers you got for us.' He patted the pocket in which he had dropped the tape.

'You mean you're happy?' Her expression had changed from lugubrious to hopeful, and the colour was returning to her cheeks.

'To have it confirmed that my life is a fraud? Not exactly. To have the answers? Relieved. And to know that the President still thinks we're doing a pretty good job . . . well, yes. I guess you could call it happy.'

Her shoulders relaxed, and she sat back in the couch. 'What do you think the test was Mr Epstein was talking about?'

'I don't know.' Burnham gazed out the window at the sprawling expanse of the South Lawn. A man in a grey suit and mirrored sunglasses passed in front of the window, his left arm ill-concealing an UZI submachine gun under his jacket. The President must be speaking in the Rose Garden, Burnham thought idly.

Machine guns every time you step out your back door. Jesus, what a life.

'But I know one thing: he's not going to call it off. Any man with the *chutzpah* to tape his phone calls with the President likes to live on the edge.'

A step before he would disappear from sight, the Secret Service agent turned and saw Burnham looking at him. He stared back – a challenging, prognathous stare.

Burnham saw the outline of the Uzi and the reflection of his own face in the agent's sunglasses.

He knew he should feel safe.

He didn't.

Twelve

Ivy's life had calmed like a shallow sea after a sudden squall.

Jerome was working. The diploma and grade transcript had gone through the system smooth as cream. He was bringing home over three hundred a week, giving her a hundred off the top.

She had seen no more of Mr Burnham or Debbie Reynolds, and nobody had humbugged her about missing papers. Why should they? The papers weren't missing. They were throwaways; she had just made sure they were thrown her way.

She hadn't had any need to bother Mr Pym, and he hadn't contacted her, so she figured everything was mellow on that front.

The interesting thing was, her leg wasn't bothering her half so bad any more, even though she had stopped taking the pills after she heard that snippy crone at work make a crack about how Ivy was probably taking a nip now and then.

Maybe the leg was reacting to tranquility. Everybody said pain was in your head, so if her head was peaceful, maybe the pain decided to take a breather, too.

The light changed, and she crossed the street. Ahead, two kids were squabbling over a bicycle wheel, a young couple sat on a stoop and alternated licks on an ice cream cone, and a woman pushed infant twins in an A&P grocery cart.

Then, ahead, signs of trouble. Shouts. A slamming door. More shouts.

Ivy stopped. She gripped her shopping bag. Her eyes sought the nearest shelter from a running crazy or a stray bullet.

Six or eight houses down the block, a door flew open and people poured out, white people, dressed all in black, with black beards and stringy black hair. Jews. Some special kind of Jews. Ivy had heard about them, had seen one or two over the years, but she didn't know they lived around here, not a whole flock of them anyway.

They were all yelling, in that weird language that nobody but God understood and even He had to use a dictionary.

Was their house on fire? There was a firebox at the end of the block, but nobody ran for it.

Maybe one of them had gone berserk and seen the devil in the kitchen.

Now they were in the middle of the street, and they formed a circle. What were they going to do, stretch a sheet between them and catch a jumper?'

No. They were going to dance. Hollering and singing and laughing, they started the circle spinning, and they dipped and kicked and squatted and hopped.

Man, Ivy thought, those folks are having themselves a *time!* One of them hit the lottery?

People swarmed out of other buildings, kids mostly but women too and a few men who'd been watching TV. Some of the kids wanted to bust into the circle, and the Jews didn't mind, they just spread the circle wider, and when a couple of the women saw it was okay, they joined too, and pretty soon the circle took up the whole width of the street.

Ivy moved closer. By now there was a circle of watchers and clappers outside the circle of dancers, so she couldn't see much, but she could hear them singing, and from the few syllables that made any sense to her – like *Gott* and *danke* and *lieber* – she understood that it was some sort of religious song of praise.

322

And I thought blacks knew how to show God a good time, Ivy said to herself. These people are pros.

Behind her a car horn blew, and she turned to see a TV truck, one of those mobile units that they always blatted about on the 'Action News' shows as if they were the greatest things since electricity, work its way through the milling people and stop in the middle of the street.

A man carrying a video camera hopped out of the truck and climbed the nearest stoop and began to take pictures of the dancers.

Another man, younger, with a coat and tie and one of those sculpted haircuts, stood right behind Ivy and, while he waited for the cameraman to finish his shot, practiced what he wanted to say into his microphone.

Ivy waited for him to finish muttering. Then she said, 'What's this all about?'

The man didn't welcome the interruption, but he said, 'They caught Mengele this morning. In Paraguay.'

'Oh.' Ivy said. 'Good.'

'You know who Mengele is: Josef Mengele?'

'Well . . . not exactly.'

'Auschwitz. The Angel of Death. He experimented on all those Jews. Killed thousands of them.'

'Oh. Right. I remember. On the news.' Ivy peered through the crowd of the dancers. 'Nice. I'm glad they got him.'

'Just in time, apparently. He had new people with him, ready to carry on for him.'

Ivy nodded. 'Put out the fire before it spreads. What'll they do to him?'

'Put him on trial. Then hang him, I guess.'

Ivy sucked on her teeth. 'They ought to skin him.'

The young man started. Then he said, 'That's interesting. How about I interview you on camera?'

'Me? I'm nobody.'

'Sure you are. You're smart, I can tell. And you're not afraid to speak your piece.'

'I don't know . . .'

323

'Wait'll your friends say they saw you on TV.'
'I look a wreck.'
'You look fine. Dignified. Honest.'
'Well . . .'

Foster Pym was in a mortal struggle with a hollandaise sauce. First he dropped an egg white in with the yolks, which confused the brew so that it wouldn't come together. Then the maverick electric stove decided to heat the left-front burner to incineration, which burned and separated the butter and left little clots of curd clinging like dough-balls to the sides of the bowl.

His problem, he knew, was that he wasn't concentrating, and the destruction of his concentration was due to his concern about Eva, who stood beside him slicing lemons with a taut-jawed determination, as if she were decapitating mice.

They didn't speak. The only human sounds in the kitchen wafted in from the living-room, where a frenetic TV pitch-man was making a last-gasp attempt to hawk storm windows to viewers waiting for the evening news.

It wasn't that Pym and Eva weren't speaking, rather that they seemed tacitly to have agreed that there was nothing new to say. They had discussed and argued their dilemma to a state of stasis. Eva continued to photograph Burnham's DOE documents but declined to relate any details of her private conversations with him. Teal continued to press for more. Pym, caught in the middle, continued to mediate, stalling Teal and cajoling Eva.

She was frightened; he was frightened. And they had no choice but to continue.

Pym looked at the mottled yellow muck in the bowl before him, and gave up. He scraped the mess into the garbage can and started fresh. He broke an egg and held its two halves over the sink, separating white from yolk.

Someone he knew must have come into the apartment, for suddenly a familiar voice was speaking in the living room. He looked at Eva, who looked at him. They both

324

frowned. He dropped the egg and walked into the living room. No one there. Then he looked at the television screen.

'Look!' he said, pointing.

'What?' Eva wiped her hands and followed him.

The round black face filled the screen. A legend on the bottom identified it as belonging to 'Ivy Peniston, Neighbourhood Resident.'

For a split second, Pym yielded to the egocentrism that afflicts all those who dwell in the house of fear: she had to be talking about *him*. Why else would a reporter want to speak to her? Surely the only noteworthy thing she had ever done was steal documents for him.

Then he heard her say: 'He tortured all those people, why give him such an easy out? I say skin him. That'll give him a lot of reflecting time.'

Ivy vanished and the reporter was talking.

'Skin who?' Eva said.

'Sssshhh!'

'. . . search for Mengele ended at exactly twelve twenty-four, eastern time, this afternoon, on a back road outside a suburb of Asuncion . . .'

'Mengele,' was all Pym said.

'Hey, terrific!' said Eva.

'. . . advance notice from the Israelis, American television was permitted to send a pool crew to film the capture. ABC's Brock Wilcox reports from Asuncion.'

The reporter was replaced by a jerky, hand-held image of a speeding Jeep approaching through dense underbrush. The breathless ABC man described the ambush in a whisper. When the Jeep was ten or fifteen yards from the camera lens, the underbrush erupted with Israeli commandos firing machine guns at the tyres and the engine compartment of the Jeep. The Jeep swerved, rose on two wheels, then settled back and stopped.

For several seconds, all that was visible was a swarm of commandos over the Jeep. Then the swarm dispersed, and two senior Israelis carefully, solicitously, helped Josef

Mengele from the Jeep and marched him, hands manacled behind his back, toward the camera.

Eva said, 'He doesn't look seventy four.'

Pym shook his head. 'Plastic surgery.'

Mengele was lean and looked fit. He walked with his shoulders back, his jaw set and his steely, droop-lidded eyes fixed on some distant point in the future or the past. He did not glance at the camera.

The camera followed Mengele until he was loaded into a truck full of commandos, then snapped back to the Jeep, where some new commotion was going on.

Three commandos were trying to wrestle a woman out of the Jeep. She was shouting, in German and English, 'I am an American! I demand to see my consul! Long live the Fourth Reich!'

The ABC man said, 'Mengele's companion refused to give her real name, insisting that she was Eva Braun, an American citizen.'

Pym felt a wave of nausea overtake him. He closed his eyes, then forced himself to open them, saying, 'It isn't true; it *can't* be true.'

The commandoes dragged the woman toward the camera. She kicked and spat and snarled like a trussed wolverine. When she saw the camera, she lunged at it and would have struck it with her jutting chin if the cameraman hadn't stumbled backward.

The image on Pym's television set was blurred and shaky, but the face that filled the frame was unmistakable. Despite the sunken eyes rimmed with purple cups of drawn flesh, despite the silver hair gathered in a severe chignon, despite the spittle-flecked lips, the face with its high cheekbones and flat forehead and potato nose belonged to no one but Louise.

The woman screamed into the cameras, *'Ich bien eine Amerikaner!'* and was gone.

'Mother of God . . .' Pym felt as if all his viscera had suddenly been flushed from him. He was dizzy and cold, and his fingertips tingled.

'What is it?' Eva grabbed his arm, for she saw that he was beginning to totter.

Pym let Eva help him down into a soft chair. 'That,' he said, pointing feebly toward the television set, 'that woman is . . .' The words seemed reluctant to be spoken. '. . . your *mother!*'

Eva's head snapped around toward the television set, but by now a sunny young housewife was extolling the anodyne properties of haemorrhoidal suppositories.

The network news came on at seven, and of course the capture of Mengele was the lead story. Eva drew a chair close to the television and sat riveted to the screen, absorbing Louise's every move and utterance, as if hoping in a few seconds to assimilate a lifetime of knowledge of the mother she had never known.

Pym slumped in his chair, unblinking, and the images from the television screen were reflected by his glassy eyes. He wanted to think, to assess risks and device alternatives, but his brain refused to entertain the thoughts that crowded his skull: it was still protesting that the two-dimensional image on the screen could not, must not, be a horrid reality.

When the story was done, Eva turned off the television set and swung her chair around. The sight of her father diluted her excitement with apprehension, so instead of asking the daughterly questions that arose naturally within her, she said only, 'What does it mean?'

Pym sighed and opened and closed his eyes a couple of times and, with a wry smile at Eva, said, 'In a word, trouble.'

'Why? They've got him, they're not interested in her. Besides, you said she's crazy. They won't give her the time of day.'

'She *is* crazy, and if they had found her picketing a synagogue in Alexandria, they'd dismiss her as crazy and good riddance. But this –' he waved at the TV – 'changes everything. She's not crazy any more. She's evil.'

'Why?'

'Because madness on this scale isn't excusable. You

327

think if they found Adolph Hitler they'd lock him up as a cuckoo? You think they'll acquit Mengele because he's insane? No. They have captured the devil, and the devil can't be nuts. People need to believe in pure evil, just as they must believe in the existence of pure goodness. And your mother – poor, unhappy Louise, and I don't know why I say that because she liked being a Nazi, it gave her something to do – will find that she has become a devil-by-association.' Pym shook his head. 'It *would* have to be the Israelis.'

'What difference does that make?'

'If the Americans had caught them, there'd be a huge legal tangle, and all manner of unpleasant little truths might fall between the cracks. They'd be prevented from speaking to anyone until they had been advised of their rights and provided with lawyers. The Civil Liberties Union would make sure they were protected against self-incrimination. Some magazine would pay them millions of dollars for the exclusive rights to their stories. Your mother would be a celebrity. The whole thing would become a gloriously bewildering circus. But the Israelis don't observe such niceties.' Pym paused. 'I wonder if Louise has ever been tortured?'

'You think she'll lead them to you? To us?'

'Not intentionally, perhaps. But yes. For sure. The Israelis will put her under a microscope. They'll study her like a new virus, learn everything there is to know about her. When they have what they need – mostly the stuff about her and Mengele – they'll give the excess to the Americans.' He tried to smile. 'We're the excess.'

'You said they can't find out anything about us.'

'No I didn't. I said the Americans wouldn't bother to dig deep enough if they thought she was just some neo-Nazi nut. But now she's not a neo-Nazi; she's a *real* Nazi. And it's not the Americans, it's the Israelis, who don't have any liberal qualms about squeezing a stone till it bleeds. Her marriage is bound to surface. So is the fact that she had a child. A child she named after Hitler's mistress.'

328

Eva froze. 'I didn't know,' she said.

'No. I didn't want you to.'

'What do we do?' Eva looked around the room as if, afraid, she was trying to locate precious things to gather for her escape. 'Do we run?'

'I don't know. I have to have time to think. I –'

The phone rang.

Pym let it ring three times, urging his mind to scan all possible callers and to prepare responses. Then he picked up the phone.

'Teal.' The voice sounded tight. Upset.

'Mallard.' Pym hoped the two syllables sounded easy, casual.

'We've got a problem.'

My God! Pym thought. Already? How could they possibly know this soon? Did they have a mole planted in the Israeli commandos? Had they already interrogated Louise and made the connection? Impossible! But they had. Don't waste your time wondering how. *Do* something. Do what? Acknowledge? Deny? Don't be surprised. Seem to be in control.

He said, 'I know. But I wouldn't –'

'You *do*?' Teal was audibly shocked. 'How? Who contacted you?'

'Ah . . .' Don't say you saw it on television, Pym commanded himself. Not privileged enough. 'Peter Jennings.'

'Peter Jennings? Peter Je – *The TV guy?* Holymotheringjesus! How did *he* find out? Why did he call *you*?'

'It's not exactly a secret any more,' Pym said. 'I mean, they had a pool crew down there.'

Silence. Pym wondered if Teal had hung up. Then, 'What's going down here, man? You been into the bourbon?'

'What? Don't be –' Suddenly Pym realized that Teal wasn't talking about the Mengele story, he knew nothing about Louise. He had another problem, a new problem about which Pym knew nothing. Pym didn't know whether to be alarmed or relieved. 'I think our wires are crossed,' he said. 'Please start again. Tell me what the problem is.'

Teal's voice dropped several decibels as he said, 'It looks like B-12's gone bad.'

Once again, Pym's mind rebelled. It had received Teal's message, but it would not process it. Access denied. Will not compute. 'What do you mean?' he asked.

'The goods the hostess has been receiving over the past week or so have been . . . tainted.'

'Tainted how? How can they . . . how can she tell.'

'She can tell, take my word. The stuff stinks, man.'

'But . . . it can't be . . . I don't . . .' Pym didn't know what to say, what to do, what to feel, except that he felt he would like to cry – not from sorrow or regret but from overload, as if to shed tears would be somehow to ease his burdens. 'What can I do?'

Teal said, 'We have to find out a couple things. Has he really gone sour, or was he just caught in a routine sweep?'

'Sweep? What kind of sweep?'

'Once in a while, when a supplier thinks his goods are being . . . diverted, shall we say . . . by unauthorized persons, he'll send out a batch coded with little marks for each of his conduits. When the diverted goods surface, he sees which mark shows up on them, and bingo! He's got the bad guy. Maybe this is what happened to B-12, he just got unlucky. But maybe he's been sending tainted goods all along. Maybe he was working for the competition from day one.'

'No,' Pym said definitely. 'Not a chance.'

'It doesn't matter, for him. Either way, his ass is grass.'

'It is?'

'Sure, man. The hostess'll never use him again. I mean, you don't hire a man who's poisoned your well. And you can bet on it, his wholesalers will know about him in a day or two, if they don't already.'

'Why? Will the . . . hostess . . . tell?'

'No way. Those marked goods are in circulation. They'll be coming home pretty soon.' Teal paused, then continued

330

in a tone of congenial menace. 'But I tell you what, man, you better hope that that's what did happen, 'cause that's the *good* news. The bad news is if the hostess decides that B-12 has been a rotten apple all along, that he's been working for the competition. She's gonna be mighty unhappy with the caterer that sent her bad goods, and for all I know she might just decide that that caterer's been working for the competition, too, and has been out to screw her from the opening gun.'

'That's absurd!'

'Hey, man . . . I'm just the messenger.'

Pym looked at Eva and saw her looking at him, and in her expression he saw reflected his own feelings of panic and impending doom.

'What do you want me to do?'

'Find out the truth.'

'But I *know* the truth! He's completely innocent. He doesn't know he's working for anybody.'

'I'm afraid your word won't wash, man.'

'What will?'

'Make them catch him. Make sure they have to expose him publicly.'

'How do I do that? They can cover up anything they want.'

'Not if you feed somebody first, like your friend Peter Jennings, feed him enough so he can ask a lot of embarrassing questions and back them up with a few hard facts. That's the great thing about America: we can keep the pricks honest.'

'Then what happens?'

'They expose him, they look like a bunch of assholes, and the hostess knows you were telling the truth.'

'To us, I mean. We're exposed, too.'

'You don't think the hostess would abandon you, do you? Once the machinery's in place, she'll have you out and on your way home, safe and sound.'

'Home,' Pym said.

'You know.'

331

'Yes, I know.'

'Okay, man? You know what you got to do?'

'I know,' said Pym, who knew nothing of the sort but who wanted to end the conversation before the numbness that was creeping through his limbs rendered him stuporous.

'Good. And take my advice: don't dick around, get on it right away, 'cause when this sucker goes down, it'll go down fast and heavy.'

Teal hung up.

Pym replaced the receiver. He felt eviscerated.

Eva watched him for a moment, then said, 'I have to warn Timothy.'

'No!' Pym clutched at the dregs of his fleeting spirit and said, 'I forbid it.'

'You forbid it,' she sneered. 'Feel free. Forbid anything you want.' She glanced at her watch and looked around the room for her purse.

'You can't help him,' Pym said. 'He can't help himself.'

'I owe him the chance to try.'

'Be smart, Eva, don't be noble. You may think he's in love with you, but when it comes to saving his own life, believe me, he'll throw you to the wolves.'

'Maybe. If he does, I won't blame him.'

When Eva had left, Pym poured himself a glass of sherry and sat on the couch. He should sort his options, locate some avenue of escape. But instead of thinking, he gazed around the room and found himself noticing things he hadn't paid attention to in years: an Andrew Wyeth print he had bought at a suburban flea market; a chipped Boehm porcelain bird; a copy of an Eames chair he had found in a second-hand store, whose leather seat had been squashed into a perfect contour of Pym's reclining posterior – the catalogue of the life Pym had fashioned for himself in America, all taken for granted till now. He regarded them with new affection, for they represented everything he had – and everything he would soon surely lose.

Burnham said, 'Thanks, Emilio,' and hung up the phone.

Eva would appear at Cantina Romana in a few minutes, and Emilio would give her the simple, terse message (never entrust a complicated message to a man for whom English was not his mother tongue): Burnham had been delayed by a sudden case of the BTWs. No matter where they had agreed to eat, she always stopped first at the Cantina, for Emilio was a reliable romantic who delighted in playing broker for their liaisons.

She might have a salad at the Cantina and then go to a movie, or browse at the bookstores or health-food stores that stayed open till nine o'clock, or wander through Georgetown and be entertained by the frenetic rutting rituals.

At ten or so, she would let herself into the tiny furnished apartment they had rented on O Street. Their landlord, who lived upstairs, was a decorator with exquisite taste and an abundance of antiques awaiting placement in great homes. He refused to rent to students, couples with children, single men with pets and single women, period ('Slobs,' he averred, 'all slobs'), which limited his potential clientele. Burnham had been honest about his situation: he was a White House employee in the midst of a divorce proceedings, who kept a room at the Y in order to accommodate the legal niceties, and who needed a quiet place to spend quiet evenings with his lady friend. The landlord must have seen in Burnham a man desperate to avoid any and all unpleasantness such as might arise from non-payment of rent, breakage or excessive noise, and so, upon receipt of two months' security and two months' rent in advance, he gave Burnham the key and his blessing..

Eva would read or watch television until about 11.30, and then, if Burnham had not arrived, would go to bed, knowing that in any event short of planetary cataclysm, he would be there before morning.

For Burnham, the arrangement was comfortable, secure and flavoured with the spice of tryst – perfect for the time being, which was all he could ask since his entire life was being lived moment to moment. His past had been stolen from him – he still couldn't believe that a fifteen-year marriage had popped like a soap bubble, and somewhere within him was the knowledge that it hadn't popped but had rotted, and someday he might invest the time and the agony to uncover the roots of the rot. Right now, he couldn't plot his future confidently beyond the next thirty minutes. He had no idea what he wanted, much less how to pursue it. All he knew for sure was that now, this minute, he felt good about himself, and that, at least, was a limb he could clutch with some feeling of safety.

He looked at his watch. Two minutes to go. An hour ago, Evelyn Witt had phoned to say that the President wanted to see Burnham at exactly eight o'clock and that Burnham should cancel any plans he might have for the rest of the evening. Burnham had said, 'Fine,' and, as he hung up, had smiled at the recollection of how he would have responded to such a summons a month ago: arhythmia, a rash, tension headaches and/or hyperventilation.

His reaction now was simple curiosity at some of the unusual signals sent by the summons. For one thing, the President had been scheduled to speak at a National Press Club dinner – Burnham had edited the speech and added a few jokes he and the President had composed together – and Presidents, no matter how roundly they loathed some or all of the press corps at any given time, did not condemn lightly the whole Fourth Estate by backing out of a major dinner at the last minute. This discourtesy would be costly, but obviously the President had determined that it was a cost worth paying.

Then, too, there was the peremptory tone of the call. Normally, the President would call himself, and ask Burnham to come by around eight, and promise to try to be finished at a reasonable hour.

Whatever was up was of an import and urgency sufficient to lead the President to dispense with all pleasantries.

Burnham decided that the leading candidate among all the possible issues was Honduras. The Congress was paralyzed by internal bickering over Honduras, and a few Senators – like Jesse Helms on the right and Alan Cranston on the left – had capitalized on the President's indecision by launching noisy campaigns that threatened to wrest the leadership role away from the White House.

The President must have finally decided to decide what to do about Honduras.

As he buttoned his collar and fiddled with the knot in his tie, Burnham realized that not once in all his musings had he considered that he, or something he had or hadn't done, might be the problem for which the President had summoned him. A month ago, imprisoned by – what did they call it? – infantile egocentrism (pumping paranoia was more like it), he would have *known* that he was the problem.

Now he knew for sure that he hadn't done anything reprehensible, and for certain that nothing he could do would be worth the President's cancelling a speech for.

Was this maturity or was it cynicism?

He tapped lightly on the connecting door to the President's little office – a reflexive, unnecessary courtesy to which the President, had he known about it, would have said something like, 'Christ, Tim, what you think I'm doin' in there, bangin' one of the cleaning women?' – then opened it, closed it behind him and crossed to the door to the Oval Office.

The President was standing alone, his back to Burnham, looking out over the darkening South Lawn. The searchlights had been turned on the Washington Monument, and it gleamed like a golden needle in the twilight. The President's shoulders drooped in a way that made him look too small for his suit jacket, as if the unrelenting demands of the office were sapping substance from the man and somehow shrinking him.

Burnham felt like a voyeur, and he cleared his throat to let the president know he was there.

The President spoke without turning around. 'D'you ever think about the unborn, Tim?'

'The unborn, sir?' What are we talking about here? Burnham wondered. Abortion? No, impossible. This President didn't need any help formulating policy about abortion. He had long since made clear his conviction that abortion was a non-issue, something cooked up by the Catholic Church and the Protestant fundamentalists as a convenient banner around which to rally their straying flocks. 'Do you mean posterity?'

'No. "Posterity" is a generality. Like "the hungry". Somebody asks you to help "the hungry", you can kiss it off without any conscience. But if they plop a starving kid named Johnny down on your doorstep and ask if you'll give him some food, that puts it to you. No. I don't give a damn about posterity – that's a lie, of course, but what I mean is, the thought of posterity isn't what makes me do something or not do something, you can't spend your life sucking up to historians – but times like this, I really do think about the unborn.'

'What are they?'

The President turned his head and smiled at Burnham. 'That's what I like about you, Tim. No bullshit. Some of the other ass-kissers I have around here, they'd say, "Right, Mr President, the unborn. I spend every waking moment deeply concerned about the plight of the unborn. Fact is, I have a bill right here that gives them each two-fifty and a Jap car."' He turned back to the window and gestured vaguely into the distance. 'I think of them as being out there, Tim, billions of them, the kids who haven't been born yet, and they're like a jury waiting to judge me. What I do now will determine the kind of lives they'll lead, whether they'll be rich or poor, happy or hungry, whether thousands of them will have to die in some foreign country while they're still green –'

Honduras, Burnham concluded. I knew it. He's trying to decide whether or not to invade or carpet-bomb or wipe the whole place off the map.

'– and they're looking down to see what decision I'll make. When I first got this job, I used to imagine George

Washington out there, and Abraham Lincoln and F.D.R., sitting in judgment on old Ben Winslow. But then I realized they're all cold as catfish and can't make any judgments. The people who count are the people still to come. You know one of the worst things I ever heard in my life? It was on "60 Minutes", and Rosalyn Carter was talking about Reagan and she said – I mean, granted, she has a bias, but this really hit me – "My grandchildren will curse that man's name." Jesus Christ! How would you like to have that on your tombstone: "My grandchildren will curse his name".'

The President turned his back to the window and reached to his desk for a glass of watery bourbon. 'I think about that a lot. I don't want anybody's grandchildren cursing my name. Drink?' He pointed to a bar cabinet in a corner of the office.

'No, thanks.'

'You don't drink at all, do you?'

'Not any more. I did. A lot. For a long time. But then it started driving the ship, and I decided it was time to get off.'

The President nodded. 'How do you get away from yourself?'

'Funny you should ask. I've been wondering the same about you.'

Burnham regretted the impertinence instantly, but before he could apologize, the President said, 'I bet you have.'

'Mr President, I didn't –'

'I bet you're the only sumbitch around here who thinks that way, except maybe Evelyn. You think any of these other fellas give a hoot how I manage to cope? No. *Whether* I cope, yeah, that they care about, but *how* – forget it. It's like being a prizefighter: between rounds, they stick smelling salts under my nose and slap me around and pop my mouthguard back in and send me out for the next round, and long as I don't get knocked out – which means they're out of work – they could care less.'

A buzzer sounded on the President's desk. 'Just as well,' he said as he reached for a button. 'Self-pity makes me

337

sick.' He leaned toward a speaker phone and said, 'Yeah.'

'Mario Epstein,' said the hollow voice of Evelyn Witt. 'He says it's urgent.'

'Everything's always urgent with him. Tell him it'll have to wait. I've got urgent business of my own.'

'Yes, sir.'

The speaker phone clicked off. The President straightened up and started to speak, but the buzzer sounded again. Angrily, the President spun back toward his desk and mashed the phone button. '*What!?*'

'Mario says it's critical that he speak to you, sir. Now.'

'Is he the President?' the President yelled at the plastic box.

'No, sir.'

'Did sixty-some goddam percent of the American people vote that half-breed egghead into this office?'

'No, sir.'

'Then you tell him that I am the one who decides what's urgent around here, and at the moment I am trying to decide whether his children – if he ever learns how to have any – will spend their lives in a palm tree being shot at by a bunch of coke-heads, which perhaps he will agree is a fairly urgent matter and whatever two-bit business he's got will wait till the morning, and unless he has got convincing evidence that the republic is about to be vaporized, *I will not be disturbed!*'

Burnham watched, mesmerized, as the President yanked open one of the desk drawers, jammed the speaker phone inside it, and slammed the drawer closed. He wondered how the President's message would be relayed by Evelyn. Surely not verbatim, but, equally surely, not too sugar-coated either: the essence of the President's mood had to be conveyed.

The President smiled at Burnham and said, 'Evelyn earns her money.'

'I'll say.'

'She's a great filter. I get to sound off, which makes me

338

feel good because there're times that smart-ass will try the patience of Job, but I can't speak like that to his face too many times or he'll eventually get so pissed he'll push his ejection button and up and quit, which I can't afford.'

'What will she tell him?'

'Pretty much what I said, but without the Don Rickles. She has a talent for delivering bad news like it was a blessing. People have told me they didn't even realize it was bad news until they hung up, and then they still had this feeling of gratitude for Evelyn. She'll be nice and polite, but she'll shut him off just like a spigot.'

'I suspect he doesn't like it when that happens.'

'Hates it!' the President grinned. 'Can't stand it. And the best part is, he won't get angry at Evelyn and he can't get angry at me – he knows if he pushes me too far I'll cut off his legs – so he'll have to swallow it. I expect if he had a dog, he'd go home and beat on it.'

The President took a sip of his drink and made a face. The drink was old; the ice had melted, and Burnham imagined that the weak bourbon tasted like tepid rinse water. The President went to the bar cabinet, measured an ounce and a half of bourbon into a fresh glass, dropped in two ice cubes and rolled them around the sides of the glass with his finger.

'Now, Tim,' he said, and he tasted his new brew, 'tell me what you think we should do about Honduras.'

'What side do you want me to take, sir?'

'Uh-uh. No more games.' The President sat on the couch and motioned Burnham to one of the chairs opposite. 'I want to know what *you* think.'

'Me? But, sir . . . I . . .' Burnham suddenly felt the old feelings returning: the tripping heartbeat, the sweat seeping into his palms. 'Why me?'

'Why not? You know all the arguments. You've taken every side.'

'But, sir . . . You've got about a billion dollars worth of the best brains in the world giving you advice. Historians,

339

military people, foreign-policy people. I think it would be presumptuous of me to . . .'

'Oh bullshit with your presumptuous, Tim. All these brains you say I've got on the payroll, every one of them has a constituency of one kind or another. If I want the military constituency, I know where to go. If I want to know what the diplomats think, I know where to go. You have no constituency, Tim. What I'm paying you for is honesty.'

'But it wouldn't be fair, sir – fair to you, that is. I could sit here and give you opinions all day –' Oh, nice! Burnham said to himself as his mind danced frantically around in a field of options, struggling to stay a step ahead of his tongue. You don't even have one opinion, let alone all these opinions you're going to give him all day '– but what would they be worth? I've been a sounding board for you, so any opinion I have would just be a synthesis of other people's opinions.'

Not bad, Burnham, thought when the President appeared not to have a ready reply but simply gazed at the ice in his glass and twirled it with his finger.

But then the President raised his eyes to Burnham and spoke with a voice as flat as lead. 'What do you think a decision is, Tim, but a synthesis of people's opinions?'

'Yes! . . . of course . . . well . . .' Now Burnham was blushing, and he could hear the march of his pulse behind his ears. 'What I mean is – it may sound paradoxical – but because I have no constituency and have nothing to lose, my opinion wouldn't carry much conviction and wouldn't be worth anything, is what I mean.'

'What makes you think you've got nothing to lose?'

'Oh. Well. I mean –'

'Let's start with the confidence of the President of the United States. I am not putting you through this, Tim, because it amuses me. I am putting you through this because I value your judgment and I think it can be a big help to the country at a time that, I'm afraid, will turn out to be a pivotal moment in our history.'

'You do?' Burnham was amazed. He wasn't aware that he had much judgment, good or bad.

'Every time over the past several weeks that I have asked your opinion and you have given it, it has been based on honesty, common sense and – I'm sure you don't have any idea you have this – a pretty sharp political sense of which option would be best for me. And every time, it has turned out that your opinion has been sound.'

'It has?' Burnham hadn't ever stopped to think that his judgment might be being judged. He had offered his opinions off-hand, and because he had never had any feedback from them, he had never thought of them as being good or bad.

'Yes, Now –' The President locked his eyes on Burnham's, forcing him to look at him '– are you finished jerking off?'

'Sir? I . . .' Burnham wanted to look away, but he couldn't. The President's eyes were like a lizard's. After a long moment, he said, 'Yes.'

'Good. Now let's come to a decision. Do you have a strong opinion?'

'No, sir. There may be one inside me somewhere, but I'm going to have to find it.' An obvious question begged to be asked, but Burnham hesitated, sensing that with Benjamin Winslow – as with any man who had for nearly seven years been the most powerful man on the planet and who was accustomed to being treated like a pharaoh – the line that separated candour from *lèse majestè* was thin and fuzzy.

Then he thought: to hell with it. I have to know. He said, 'Do you?'

The President smiled, as if he appreciated Burnham's reticence, and said, 'No. I've got instincts, and usually I trust 'em, but I'm not gonna send boys to rot in some stinking jungle on the basis of some gut feeling, the way Lyndon Johnson did. There's no Bobby Kennedy pecking at my shell.'

'Well then, Mr President, shall we take it from the top?'

341

'After you, my boy.' The President spread his hands, inviting Burnham to proceed. 'The night is young.'

Suicide, Foster Pym decided, was not an option. For one thing, it might not be an end-all. For another, as afraid as he was at the moment, he was even more afraid of dying, and as unpleasant as the fear of dying was, he'd rather be afraid than dead.

He saw that he had arrived back at the front door, having circled the block. He set off again, to walk somewhere, anywhere, it didn't matter. It felt good to be outside. The apartment had become confining. The radio and television threatened him with more news of Louise; the telephone threatened to ring with new alarms. Out here, at least, the bad news couldn't reach him.

He had to think, had to come up with a plan. A plan to do what? He didn't know. He felt too old to run, too scared to hide.

Teal wanted him to call Peter Jennings, wanted Jennings to blow the lid off the spy scandal in the White House, to force the government openly to acknowledge Burnham's perfidy. Humiliate the President. Rattle his shaky coalition in Congress. Stir the pot.

Great idea.

Just one problem: what would really be humiliated, rattled and stirred would be Foster Pym. His cover would be blown sky-high. The FBI would descend on him like a pack of vultures.

He had no desire to become a human sacrifice.

His 'friend' Peter Jennings. That was another gruesome joke. If he barged in on Peter Jennings, he'd end up in St Elizabeth's Hospital, wearing a nice white coat with sleeves that tie around the back.

Maybe he could make an anonymous phone call to the ABC Washington bureau, but that was about all.

He turned the corner. A car was parked in the bus stop. The only reason he noticed it was that the driver was smoking a cigar, and as he dragged on it, the ember

342

glowed like an orange beacon. But Pym quickly dismissed it.

People sat in parked cars at night all the time around here – junkies, pushers, hookers, cops.

As he drew abreast of the car, a voice called out from the darkness of the back seat, 'Hey, man, you got the time?'

Before he had time to recognize something familiar in the voice, Pym had taken a step toward the car and had tilted his watch to catch the glow from the street light and had said, 'It's –'

He didn't see the back door fly open, or the crouched figure dart out of the car at him. He felt something grab his belt, saw a blur of car and street and lamplight, heard his skull strike steel and felt a terrible pain in his head as he was flung to the carpeted floor of the car.

Then something was happening to his trousers, and the pain in his head was gone, replaced by a piercing agony in his testicles.

He tried to thrash away, but whatever had his testicles gripped them even tighter, and a foot stepped on his forehead. Bile rose in his throat.

The voice spoke again, and this time he recognized it instantly.

'Vice grips,' said Teal. 'Got 'em from Brookstone. Nice, eh? Got this little wheel here, I can tighten 'em right down. See?'

Pym would have thought it impossible, but the pain got worse. He tried to scream, but the foot on his forehead pressed harder, driving his face into the footrest.

'Or, if you're a good boy, I can loosen 'em, too. See?'

The pain eased some. The car pulled away from the curb. It stopped – a red light, probably – then started again.

Pym felt sick. He thought he might faint. Then Teal must have backed the screw wheel down some more, for the pain eased again. The foot slid off his forehead onto the floor of the car.

Slowly, Pym turned his head and looked up at the owner of the foot. He could see nothing but a short, lumpy, dark figure sitting back in the seat, wearing a dark hat that covered his face in shadow.

Then he turned his head farther and saw Teal kneeling over him, holding the vice grips, grinning.

Pym thought before he spoke, desperate not to say anything that would cause his balls to be broken. His impulse was to say, 'What do you want?' Instead, he said, 'What have I done?'

'It's what you didn't do. You didn't do what I told you.'

'It's only been –'

'They know.'

'What? Who?'

'The Americans know about B-12.'

'How do you know?'

'We know. Look. Believe it: we can tap their typewriters in their embassy, we know what they know. And they know what we know. These days, the world has got a bug up its ass. Everybody knows everything.'

'*Do* they know what you know? Do they know you know that the information he was passing along is bad?'

'We don't know if they know we know. But we know they know about him.'

Pym flicked his eyes at the dark figure. 'Who is he?'

'Don't ask.' Teal rotated the vice grips, and Pym gasped. 'Okay?'

Pym's fingernails scraped at the floor of the car. He grunted and nodded and wished he would faint.

'Okay,' Teal said, relaxing his grip. 'They haven't caught him yet. You gotta blow it wide open before they catch him, 'cause if they catch him first, he'll disappear. And if that happens –' Teal glanced at the dark figure '– you disappear. The only person who'll know where you are is you, and take my word, you'll wish you didn't.'

'All right. First thing tomo –' The word dissolved into a strangled scream, for Teal had torqued the vice grips hard. Pym had a second's hope that his testicles would tear away.

'Tonight, chummy, tonight.'

The car stopped.

The pressure on Pym's balls vanished as Teal removed the vice grips. What remained was a gnawing, nauseating ache.

Teal grabbed Pym's lapels and pulled him upright, reached behind him and opened the door, stepped backward out of the car and dragged Pym after him.

'You have till "Good Morning, America",' Teal said. He turned Pym around and pushed him toward the sidewalk, then stepped back into the car and slammed the door.

Pym found himself gazing up at a glass office building over the entrance to which, enclosed in a smart white circle, were the letters ABC.

He didn't have to look, he knew that the car hadn't departed. Teal and the dark lump were waiting to make sure he went into the building, where a security guard was visible behind a desk reading a comic book.

He tucked his shirt in, made sure his fly was zipped, and carelessly jangled his abused balls, which retaliated with a spasm of pain that made him stagger.

What was he going to say? Peter Jennings!

He must look like a wino out for a night's prowl. At best, they'd pitch him back out onto the street; at worst, they'd call the police.

An accent. Maybe he could put on a Russian accent. Americans were suckers for accents. Something about the inferiority feelings inherent in a young culture. A wino with no accent was just a wino, but a wino with an accent might be a prince or a count or a duke: you have to listen to him, at least hear him out.

He didn't know if he could do it. He had spent so long eradicating all traces of his Slavic heritage that he wasn't sure what Russian sounded like.

But the odds were, he knew more than the security guard.

He pulled open the glass door and walked across the marble floor.

The guard, a young white man with a Zapata moustache

345

and a bad complexion, looked up from his 'GI Joe' comic and said, 'Yeah?'

'I am a Russian person, Pinsky by name. I would like please to see Mister Peter Jennings.'

'Right,' the guard said, and his little eyes scanned Pym's torso, searching for the telltale bulge of a concealed weapon. 'Write him a letter.' He returned to the adventures of GI Joe.

'But you see, I am having a story that will be interesting him very much.'

'Sure.'

'It is involving espionage spies.'

'Yeah?' The guard eyed Pym again. 'Whyn't you tell it to me?'

'No. What I am having to say is for Mister Peter Jennings' ears only.'

'Tough, then. Write him a letter.'

'I am pleased your union has gained for you such fine job security. You can perhaps direct me to the offices of CBS?'

The guard closed his comic book. He licked his lips and looked at Pym, who smiled affably down at him. The guard picked up his phone and dialled four digits and said something into the mouthpiece that Pym could not hear because he cupped his hand over the mouthpiece and whispered.

Pym looked behind him, out through the glass doors. The car still sat at the curb.

An elevator door opened behind the guard, and a young woman approached the desk. The guard tipped his head at Pym.

The young woman was pretty but hard as nails. Pym decided she was a case officer assigned to handle kooks.

'I'm Paula Strong,' she said. 'May I help you?'

Pym repeated what he had told the guard.

'First of all,' said Miss Strong, 'Peter Jennings works in New York.'

'Of course,' Pym said uneasily, for he had forgotten that all three network news shows originated in New York. 'I was not demanding a personal confrontation.'

346

'Second, I'm afraid you'll have to be a lot more specific before we can put you in touch with any of our senior people.'

'Pretty lady – Pym flashed what he hoped was an ingratiating smile '– you have heard perhaps of Colonel Penkovsky?'

'Yes.'

'Then you should be being grateful I am not demanding to see the senior person he insisted on seeing.'

'Refresh my memory. Who was that?'

'John F. Kennedy.'

'Well, Mister . . . Pinsky, is it? . . . I think it's safe to say that Penkovsky had a lot to offer.'

'So, dear lady, I assure you, do I.'

Pym smiled again – a sincere, ingenuous smile – and allowed Miss Strong a long moment to appraise him.

'Follow me,' she said, and she turned toward the elevator.

The last image Pym saw before the elevator doors slid closed was of the car idling at the curb.

'There is a back way out of this building?' he asked.

'Sure. Why?'

'People who tell you things like I am telling you must always know if there is a back way out.'

'There's nothing the Russians like more than seeing us chase after the little brushfires they start all over the world. Spend money, send supplies, finance counter-revolutionaries, maybe even send troops – Christ! flush the resources of this nation down the john, spend ourselves into bankruptcy, trying to do the impossible.'

Burnham was on a roll. Ideas that he had never known he had, notions that had never coalesced into ideas, snippets that had never been articulated into notions – were racing around in his head and leaping out of his mouth, like passengers abandoning a sinking ship.

The President let him run. He sat back on the couch and sipped his bourbon and listened.

'What we don't realize is, it doesn't work! Ever! We're like Pavlov's goddam dogs: we hear the buzzwords like "Marx" and "socialism" and "people's republic of any dippy thing", and right away the bells ring and we holler "Russia!" and threaten to send in the Marines. What happens? The peasants say to themselves, "Who needs this?" and they turn to the guy who *isn't* hollering at them, and who's that? Bingo. Russia.

'Suppose we let them alone, even help them, maybe we retain some influence over them, maybe we can tug the leash once in a while to keep them from doing something stupid to their neighbours. But once we've driven them into the arms of the big bear, we can't say squat about what they do, so all that's left is to try to overthrow them.'

Burnham's mouth was dry. Without thinking to ask, he walked to the cabinet bar and reached into the refrigerator for a can of coke. He seemed not to realize where he was, until he saw the Presidential seal on the glass into which he poured the Coke. 'Oh!' he said, embarrassed. 'Sorry. I'm –'

'Go on, go on,' said the President. 'I think you're about to have an opinion. You're saying we should let Honduras go and be damned?'

'No, sir, I'm not. I'm saying we should stop pouring money into trying to overthrow everybody. I think we should sit down and talk to the Hondurans and the Nicaraguans. And the Russians. I think we should say, "Do what you want, but here are the limits." And just like in Cuba, the limits are things that could threaten us or their neighbours, like long-range aircraft and missiles. Then I think you, sir, just like Jack Kennedy, should go on television and tell the world what those limits are, nice and reasonable. We'll give them aid, we'll help them feed their people, we won't interfere with the way they run their lives. If they want to go socialist, they can go socialist – they can become the people's republic of ding-dong, that's great – and if the Russians want to pump a lot more of their own GNP into the effort, so much the better, BUT – if they start invading

348

people, or if they start importing missiles – and with satellite technology what it is today we can tell if one of those two-bit colonels has a boil on his nose – then the world has to know we'll go in there and crush them like a bug. That, Mr President, is my opinion.' Burnham smiled. 'I think.'

The President chuckled. He heaved himself off the couch and went to the bar and poured himself some more bourbon. He came back and sat down and rolled the ice cubes around the glass with his finger. 'I agree,' he said at last.

A wave of pride surged through Burnham. It felt wonderful.

'We're gonna get our butt kicked.' The President sipped his drink. 'Some people gonna say we're running scared. You know: abdicating the American leadership role, allowing the citadel of democracy to crumble. All that crap.'

'Let them. Right is right, and we're right.' The righteousness of his words tasted bad in Burnham's mouth, so he added, 'Which is easy for me to say since my ass isn't on the line.'

'It will be,' the President said with a smile. 'If you're wrong, I'll have you crucify yourself in my memoirs. You think history'll bear us out?'

'Who knows? As they say, history is a fickle strumpet. You play to her, and she gives you a chancre on your posterity. Look at Truman: one generation thinks he's a disaster, the next crowns him a folk hero. Coolidge: a nobody until Ronald Reagan fell in love with him. Every President should have Polonius' advice engraved on his desk.' Burnham stopped, again appalled at himself. 'Good God, listen to who's lecturing! I'm sorry, sir.'

'Don't apologize for speaking your mind.'

'No, sir. It's just . . . I have trouble believing I have anything worth saying, let alone defending.'

'Let me be the judge. I'll tell you when it's time to apologize. Can you put together some notes for tomorrow morning? I'll get the leadership in here around ten.'

'Of course.'

'I'm not gonna let them off the hook. They're coming on the line, with me or against me.' The President yawned and looked at his watch. 'Sack time,' he said, and he stood up. He put a hand on Burnham's shoulder and walked him toward the door. 'Tim, for a person who thinks he's worthless as a cup of warm spit, you did good. Can you be proud of yourself?'

'I think so. I intend to try.'

'Do, 'cause if you can't be proud of yourself for this, for helping your President and your country and –' he waved at the window '– I believe this, all those unborn, well then, you might's well drop back and punt.'

'Thank you, sir.' Burnham reached to open the door.

'Who's Polonius?' the President asked.

'In *Hamlet*. You know: "To thine own self be true, and it must follow, as night the day, thou canst not then be false to any man."'

'That's good. Save it. We're gonna need all the ammunition we can get. You mentioned Truman. You remember what he said: "If you can't stand the heat, get out of the kitchen"?'

'Sure.'

'Think you can stand the heat?'

'So far.'

'So far!' the President laughed. 'It hasn't even started to get warm yet. But I hope you can, Tim, 'cause I've got more'n a year to go, and you're gonna be my chief cook.'

Before Burnham could reply, the President had opened the door, ushered him into the hallway and closed the door again.

Burnham stared at the door for a second and then felt someone watching him. He looked up into the eyes of a gargantuan Secret Service man who appeared to have had all his motors for facial expression surgically removed.

Burnham didn't want the Secret Service man to think he had been expelled from the Oval Office like an Avon Lady

350

or a Jehovah's Witness, so he said with authority, 'He's going to turn in now. Back to the Mansion.'

The agent nodded and reached under his jacket for a walkie-talkie.

Burnham walked down the hall, past Epstein's offices, where the night shift of secretaries laboured on the banks of humming copiers, word processors and typewriters. He waved at the secretaries as he passed, and one of them did a double-take when she saw him – surprised, Burnham assumed, to see that anyone else was working round-the-clock in the service of the nation.

He turned at the end of the hall and walked toward the West Lobby. The building no longer felt forbidding to him. It was warm and welcoming, a safe haven, a second home. He belonged here.

Maybe Sarah was right about commitment, he thought. He had found something to believe in, he had done well, had had his worth affirmed by none other than the President of the United States, and had been rewarded by a promise of even greater commitment.

He felt alive, involved, important – altogether better than he had ever felt in his life.

Outside, he started along the path toward the West Gate.

He heard behind him a car accelerating up West Executive Avenue, then the squeal of tires as the car braked and turned toward the West Basement.

Idly curious, he left the path and walked to the edge of the grass to see who was so frantic to get to work at ten-thirty at night. It was a black sedan, with a red light flashing from within each side of its grillwork.

Mario Epstein.

No peace for the wicked, Burnham thought, and he passed through the West Gate and hailed a taxi cruising Pennsylvania Avenue.

The intersection of Wisconsin Avenue and M Street was packed with taxis, buses, double-parked private cars, motor-cycles, bicycles, skateboarders, pedestrians, drunks, dancers, panhandlers and junkies, so Burnham

351

paid the driver and left the taxi and walked the four blocks to the apartment.

Wisconsin Avenue was a continuous party, and Burnham wanted to join in, to share his own elation, to have people clap him on the back and congratulate him and buy him drinks. Solitary triumphs were no fun at all. But Eva was waiting for him, and she would celebrate with him and would love him and – as important right now as love – appreciate him.

The thought of her made him quicken his pace.

A blue sedan was parked fifteen or twenty yards this side of the entrance to Burnham's building. Burnham would never have noticed it if it hadn't been cozied up so brazenly to a fire hydrant. The Georgetown police were notoriously gleeful towers, and Burnham enjoyed a fleeting fantasy of the car's owner, well oiled, returning from an evening of revelry to discover that his GM mid-size had been removed to some remote burial ground where only a fool would go at night.

Suddenly there was movement inside the sedan, and before Burnham could obey his instinct and look away (never stare at anything surprising, was the rule, for many surprising things will take offence and put a bullet in you) he saw a cascade of wonderfully red hair belonging to a woman who had locked her face onto that of an unseen man and was trying either to suck his brains out or administer a novel form of CPR.

Burnham smiled benignly and walked on to the gate that led down to the entrance to his garden apartment.

'Where can we reach you?' asked Paula Strong as she pushed the button for the service elevator.

'Nowhere,' said Pym. 'I am nowhere.'

'We'll have to. You only gave us half a loaf. I mean, it's a dynamite half a loaf, don't get me wrong, but it's still half a loaf. Like, we'll need some names before we can go with anything.'

'I will reach you. As soon as I am getting names, you are

'getting names.' The elevator arrived; it was padded with movers' quilts, and two big trash barrels stood against the far wall. Pym stepped inside.

'Push B,' said Paul Strong. 'When you get to the basement, turn right, then right again, and the exit door's straight ahead at the end of the corridor.'

'You have never seen me.'

'Seen who? I don't know what you're talking about.'

Pym was bewildered until he saw her smile. He said, 'Clever lady,' and pushed B, and the door slid closed.

He had given them an *hors d'oeuvre* tantalizing enough to whet any journalist's appetite. He had told them about Q Clearance, which had earned him instant credibility because the deputy bureau chief had thought that only he and a few other Washington insiders had ever heard of Q Clearance. He had described himself as a low-level courier drawn unwillingly into the conspiracy by Soviet blackmailers who threatened to send his ailing mother to the gulag, impelled by loyalty to his adopted country to expose this perfidy yet fearful of going to the authorities lest he be deported or jailed or sent back to Russia. And he had detailed roughly some of the documents that had passed through his hands.

Then, once his credibility was firmly established, he had purposely shaken it by insisting that he could not identify either the American mole or his Soviet contacts. He wasn't a hundred percent positive, he said. Yet.

He had given ABC nowhere near enough to run a responsible story, but had teased them quite enough to make them eager for more.

He had decided in the elevator going up that he would not give ABC Burnham's name or his code name, B-12. Let them press for it and endure the government's evasions, equivocations and prevarications, all of which would take time, precious time for Pym and Eva to disappear – separately, with neither of them knowing where the other was, so that if either was caught the other might stay safe.

It was the least he could do for Eva, and, as he saw it, Eva was the only person to whom he owed anything. He appraised his gratitude as professional, not personal or parental, but then he found himself feeling happy in the hope that she might escape, that some part of him might endure – might even someday prevail, in some tiny outpost of achievement – and he realized that he had under-estimated the power of genes. Tenacious little devils.

He had no idea how Burnham would react when Eva told him what was happening, but he prayed that Eva would have the sense – the selfishness, the base instinct for self-preservation – to do the one thing that could save her life: run.

He pushed open the exit door and looked out into an alley filled with trash cans. He let the door close quietly behind him and walked tip-toe to the end of the alley. The sidewalk was deserted. He waited a moment, listening for footsteps, then stepped out onto the sidewalk.

'Going somewhere?'

The words kicked Pym backward a step. He stopped, frozen.

Teal sauntered out of a dark doorway. 'I *thought* you might pull something like this,' he said. He reached for Pym's arm. 'Come on.'

Pym was like a dying man: ghastly images of torture and loneliness and death raced across his brain.

But there was a difference: he had decided not to die.

He ducked away from Teal's hand.

Teal took a step, stretching to grab Pym, and his legs were spread like a hurdler's.

Pym planted his back foot and sprang forward and slammed his right hand into Teal's crotch and heaved upward, lifting Teal a foot off the ground. His fingertips groped for substance through the flimsy fabric of Teal's cotton trousers, and when he felt it, he made a fist and squeezed as if he would mash it into paste.

Teal shrieked. He flailed, scratching Pym's head, trying to find his eyes, but Pym drove his left elbow up into Teal's throat and forced him back against the alley wall. He ducked his head and rammed his shoulder into Teal's gut, pinning him against the wall and holding him off the ground, and then he could use two hands to crush Teal's nuts. He told himself he was squeezing juice from an unripe lime, or wringing the last drop of water from a washcloth.

Teal was still screaming – a high pitched wail like a cat on fire.

Then Teal fainted. Pym felt Teal's musculature sag, and he backed away and let Teal slide to the pavement.

Pym touched his face and looked at his fingers. He felt raw bands across his cheeks, but there was no blood.

He looked out into the empty street, and listened, and when he was certain he was alone, he left the alley and walked quickly down the block, staying in the shadows of the buildings.

With worldly goods amounting to sixty-two dollars and eighty-eight cents, an American Express green card, a Revlon nail clipper and a handkerchief, Foster Pym turned the corner and abandoned four and a half decades of life.

Thirteen

Burnham sat on the end of the bed. Eva sat at his feet, hugging her knees, tears streaming down her face and falling into the maroon pattern of the oriental carpet.

He felt numb, as if all feeling had been sucked from him and all that remained was a shell of bones and nerves that somehow maintained a form of life. He wasn't angry, he wasn't sad, he wasn't afraid. He wasn't anything.

An epigram repeated itself in his head: no good deed ever goes unpunished. It was like a pop song with a catchy tune; it wouldn't leave him alone. It demanded all his attention, drove all other thoughts from his head. No good deed ever goes unpunished.

It was pissing him off. He began to get angry, and because he sensed that it was healthy for him to get angry he goaded himself. Stupid shit! Your life has just gone down in flames, and you're thinking in jingles.

He jumped up and shouted, 'Jesus Christ!' and kicked a chest of drawers and howled, 'Fuck!'

Eva sobbed, for she knew he was cursing her.

Burnham looked at the chest of drawers, at the new dent in the old wood. *It* wasn't sorry. *It* didn't regret a thing. *It* didn't care what Burnham thought of it.

Then he laughed, and laughing made him feel better, so he sat down again. When he saw Eva raise her head and gaze at him with her glistening eyes. He put out his hand and ran his fingers through her hair.

'Are we through?' he said.

'Through what?'

'Through feeling sorry for ourselves.'

Eva cocked her head like a curious dog. 'Don't you want to kill me? she said. 'I'll understand if you do.'

'Good.' Burnham laughed again. 'That's a comfort. You'll be lying there dead, but I'll know you understand.' He leaned forward and kissed her. 'Why would I want to kill you? I love you.'

'But look what I –'

'What's done is done. Life is a long salvage operation. You save what you can.' He smiled at himself. 'Very profound. I wonder where I heard that.' He took one of her hands. 'What shall we do?'

'What *can* we do?'

'That's the point. Let's figure it out. As a friend of mine says, "The need of doing is pressing, since the time of doing is short." I imagine,' he said, toying with her fingers, 'that the smartest thing is for me to turn myself in. Cut our losses.'

'No! You can't.'

'What d'you mean, I can't?'

'It's too late. The damage would be horrible.'

'What can they do? Put me in jail.'

'I mean the damage to the country. Yesterday, day before, you could've turned yourself in and it would've been very quiet. Nobody would've had to know a thing. They might've even let you go, or tucked you away somewhere. By tomorrow the TV people will know, and once you turn yourself in they'll have to go public with it. How'll that look? You told me the *British* looked stupid in the fifties. How about the President? His right-hand man is a Russian spy? He'll be finished! The country'll be a bad joke. No. The only way to keep it quiet is to stay hidden. Then the White House can deny everything.'

'So we may have some time.'

'I wouldn't count on it.' Eva looked at the floor. 'The only thing that makes sense to me is for *me* to turn myself in.'

357

'What? Why?'

'Tell them the truth. *You* didn't pass the documents. *You* didn't know anything about it. They'll have to let you off the hook. They can't prove anything different.'

Burnham shook his head. 'No good.'

'Why not?'

'You're a spy, I'm a fool. You go to jail, I get fired. I'm unemployable, I have no money, and with you in jail I have no life. No I think we'll fire a few big guns and try to get out of this mess.' He stood up, walked to the head of the bed and sat down by the telephone.

'Who are you calling?'

'The President of the United States.'

'At midnight? What're you going to tell him?'

'That's he's gonna hear a lot of garbage about me, that I didn't *do* anything, that I'll explain it all to him when I see him and that he shouldn't go off half-cocked and do something he'll regret.'

'He'll listen to that?'

'Beats me.' Burnham shrugged. 'But I owe us a try. I think he might. We get along pretty well.'

Burnham dialled 456–1414, and when an operator answered he said, 'This is Timothy Burnham. It's important that I speak to the President.'

'He's in the Mansion, Mr Burnham.'

'I know.'

'Asleep.'

'Wake him up.' There was a pause, and Burnham said, 'I wouldn't ask this if it wasn't important.'

'Yes, sir.' Again the operator paused, and Burnham could hear another voice in the background. 'Hold a sec.'

There were two clicks as the call was transferred.

'Tim? How are you, my friend?'

It wasn't the President.

It was Mario Epstein.

All Burnham could think to say was, 'I was trying to reach the President.'

'He asked me to take his calls,' Epstein said. 'You must've tired him out. Where're you calling from?'

'It can wait, I guess.'

'Can I help?'

'No. I'll see him in the morning.'

'Hold on a –'

Burnham hung up. He didn't dare keep talking to Epstein. Better to be rude than to say too much, especially since he didn't know how much Epstein knew, and to say anything might be to say too much.

'So much for –'

There was a knock on the door – three sharp raps.

He said to Eva, 'Expecting someone?'

She shook her head.

He looked at the door. 'Who is it?'

'PEPCo,' said a man's voice. 'We got a report of a gas leak.'

'Just a second. Gotta find my pants.' Burnham leaned down to Eva and whispered, 'Put some shoes on. Get some money and anything else you need.'

'Why? Who –'

'Just in case.' Burnham felt for his wallet and his White House pass, and he tip-toed to the door. A brass lozenge covered the peephole in the door, and he slid it aside and put his eye to the hole.

He saw a forest of flame-red hair, and behind it, the shoulder of a man.

Well, at least now he knew.

Holding his breath, he backed away from the door.

'Let's go, mister!' said the man. 'This isn't something to fool around with.'

'Right. Right with you.' Burnham beckoned to Eva as he backed toward the French doors that led out into the garden.

She pointed at him, wanting to speak, but he held his finger to his lips – and backed into the end table beside the bed, knocking over a lamp and the telephone, which struck the floor so hard that its bell rang.

Burnham heard the crash of a heavy foot against the wooden door.

He opened the French doors and led Eva into the garden.

Behind him, he heard something about 'under arrest' and another slam of foot against the door and a woman's voice saying, 'Get him!'

The garden was jungle dark, a confusion of vines and plants and stubby trees. There were three six-foot walls, two leading to adjacent gardens, the third into the back alley.

They stepped into a flower bed by the far wall. Burnham bent his knees and cupped his hands and boosted Eva. She teetered for a moment at the top of the wooden wall, then swung gracefully over it and landed on her feet in the alley.

A silenced pistol was fired – a nasty 'thwup' sound – and the bullet must have struck the stone floor of the apartment for it ricocheted with an angry whine and then destroyed something made of glass.

Burnham tried to hoist himself over the wall, but as he crouched to spring, his feet sank into the soft fertilized loam of the flower bed. His jump dissolved into a squoosh.

He tried to haul himself up the wall, but the angle deprived him of the strong muscles in his shoulders and back.

'Can I help you? asked Eva from the alley.

'I don't know how. If they get me, you run.'

'They won't get you! Climb!'

'With my fingernails?'

'And your toes. But mostly with your head. Tell yourself you can do it. Convince yourself.'

'That's –'

Another shot was fired, and this time it was followed by the sound of the door swinging open and slamming against the apartment wall, and by running feet and enraged voices.

'Now!' Eva said.

And, triggered by Eva's voice, Burnham told his muscles to explode. Like a child fleeing a neighbour's dog, he scrambled and clawed his way up the wooden wall, balanced for a split second and then fell head-first into the alley in a heap of soiled seersucker.

'Stop, Mr Burnham!' the red-haired woman called out. 'You're only making things worse.'

'Worse?' Burnham called back. 'What's worse than a bullet in the brain?' He and Eva crept along the alley toward the street.

'We're just s'posed to bring you in.'

'Sure,' Burnham shouted. 'That's why you're shooting at me.'

They reached the street and they ran, first down to N Street, then over two blocks, then down a couple more, until after three or four minutes Burnham was convinced they had lost themselves in the maze of Georgetown. They ducked into an alley to catch their breath.

'Where can we go?' asked Eva. 'We can't go to my apartment. The Russians'll be watching that. For sure, we can't go to your house. And we can't just waltz into the Y. It's –'

'Wait a minute.'

'What?'

Burnham looked out the end of the alley. At the corner he saw a lighted phone booth. 'Be right back,' he said, and before Eva could protest, he was gone.

A bell tower in the distance was ringing the twelve chimes of midnight when Burnham led Eva into another dark alley. A rat scuttled between the garbage cans, and a roused cat knocked over a bottle in pursuit. At the end of the alley was a steel door, and Burnham knocked twice.

'Where are we?' Eva whispered.

Burnham smiled. 'Waltzing into the Y.'

The door swung open on rusty hinges, and Hal said, 'Come in, children. Be quick.'

He shone a flashlight on the floor for them and led the way down a dingy hall. 'They've had a man outside for the past couple of hours, pretending to be a wino.' Hal snickered. 'The only wino in Washington who wears Corfam shoes and a Rolex watch.'

Halfway down the hall, Hal stopped at another steel door. Faded stencilled lettering said 'MAINTENANCE – keep out'. Hal inserted a key into the imposing brass lock, turned it and pushed open the door.

Lights went on automatically, illuminating a cozy den decorated in impeccable conservative Yankee taste: leather club chairs worn shiny and comfortable, an antique four-poster bed covered with a Rhode Island quilt, Winslow Homer prints, brass lamps on cherry red tables.

'Wow!' Eva said.

Hal smiled. 'My lifetime to sanity.'

'How did you –'

'Garages sales, flea markets, hearing about this and that from here and there.'

'Do they know?' Burnham asked. 'Upstairs?'

'They don't know and they don't care,' said Hal. 'Their attitude about everything is, If it ain't broke, don't fix it. I make sure it ain't broke. I have the only key. You'd be safe here forever. But I don't imagine you want to stay forever?'

'A day or two,' Burnham said. 'Till we can sort things out and decide where we can go. If anywhere.'

'You want to tell me what's wrong? I'm the soul of discretion.'

Burnham shook his head. 'The less you know, the better for you. I've mixed you up too far in it already.'

'It's serious, though, isn't it?'

'Yes, Hal. Very.'

'You sure I can't help? I have a devious mind.'

Burnham hesitated, then said, 'All right. See if you can work this out: how do you get two people out of the country, with no passports and very little money, and with the entire Federal Government looking for them?'

'My!' Hal said.

Eva kicked off her shoes and said to Burnham, 'If we're going to run again, I've got to close my eyes. I'm ex-

362

hausted.' She spread her arms and let herself fall backward onto the bed.

The press of her weight on the mattress must have tripped a hidden switch, for instantly the room was filled with the pulsing, throbbing beat of Ravel's *Bolero*.

Eva sat up and said, 'Christ!'

'Apologies, my dear,' Hal said, a blush suffusing his pasty face. He touched a spot on the wall, and the music stopped.

The grin that had started to split Burnham's face now froze. 'My God!' he said.

'Oh don't be such –'

'No no,' Burnham said to Hal. 'It's not that.' The motor of his mind, which had been resting at idle, slipped into gear and began to race. 'I think I . . . never mind. What time is it?' He looked at his watch. 'Do you have a mirror?'

'There's a bathroom over there.' Hal pointed. 'What *are* you –'

'You don't want to know,' Burnham said as he opened the bathroom door and stood in front of the mirror and dusted off his suit and retied his tie. 'Your tape just gave me an idea, that's all.' He spoke to Eva. 'If they get me, you leave first thing in the morning. You should be able to make it alone. I'd try Canada first. I'd –'

'Where are you *going*?'

'Just thought I'd stop in at the office for a few minutes.' He kissed her.

'*What?*'

Burnham said to Hal, 'D'you have a briefcase?'

'A briefcase? Me?'

'How about a squash bag?'

'Not down here.' Hal found a Gucci shoulder bag. 'How about this?'

'Good.' Burnham took the bag. 'I'll be at the alley door in exactly an hour. If I miss, try a half hour later, then a half hour after that. If I'm not there then, say a prayer for me.' He reached for the doorknob and said to Hal, 'Thanks. Whatever happens.'

363

This was like Russian roulette but with worse odds. Burnham thought as he crossed 17th Street and stared along the last block to the White House. All or nothing. And there was no way to find out which it would be without committing himself. He would give his name and show his pass, and if Epstein had put an APB out on him with the White House police, he was finished. He was betting that Epstein hadn't thought to do it yet, that it hadn't occurred to Epstein that Burnham would be so stupid as to walk back into the White House. Unless Epstein thought he was crazy, in which case every White House policeman would be sitting at his post with his finger on the button.

Burnham's footsteps rang out in the still night. He wished he could creep up on the White House and peek over the shoulder of the guard at the West Gate to see if his name was flashing on an electronic hit list. But the concrete bulwarks and security fencing, the bright lights and electric gates and bulletproof-glass observation windows, made sneaky arrivals impossible. These nights, one approached the White House like a submissive dog – all smiles and waggy tails and floppy ears, and keep your hands out of your pockets.

So he continued noisily down the block, clutching the Gucci bag in one hand and his White House pass in the other. He tried to imbue his step with a confident bounce. He didn't feel like slinking into Federal prison.

He turned in at the West Gate. Through the window he saw the guard leave his seat and turn to the door at the gatehouse and, his right hand resting on the butt of his pistol, take a half step outside.

Burnham held his breath and forced a smile and raised his White House pass for the guard to see.

The guard took the pass and compared its picture with the reality of Burnham.

What would the words be? Burnham wondered. 'Wait right here'? 'Hands up'? 'Gotcha!'?

The guard squinted at Burnham and said, 'You're either awful late for yesterday, or awful early for today.' He returned Burnham's pass and motioned him through the gate.

'Working hard to build a better tomorrow,' Burnham said, and he stepped quickly out of the circle of light.

There was another guard, at the desk inside the West Lobby, and he looked up when he heard the door open, and when he recognized Burnham his languid face snapped to attention.

'Mr Burnham!' he said.

Oh-oh, Burnham thought. Goodbye. Visions of Danbury and Allenwood danced in his head. He said, 'That's me.'

'Just the man I wanted to see.'

'Oh?' Burnham said weakly, thinking: this is some laid-back arrest.

'I hope you don't mind, but –'

'Don't worry about it.'

'You know a four-letter word for "mine entrance"?'

Burnham's mouth dropped open. He stared at the guard. 'I . . . beg . . . your . . . pardon?'

'Mine entrance. Four letters.' The guard tapped his pencil on the crossword-puzzle book open on the desk.

Burnham felt little rivulets of sweat running down the insides of his thighs. 'Adit,' he said, and he spelled the word.

'Adit. Great. Hey, thanks a lot.'

Burnham's fingertips felt numb as he reached for the door that led to the interior corridors of the West Wing. His underarms were beginning to itch, he tasted a salty hint of blood in his saliva, and the outer limits of his peripheral vision were slowly closing in.

He wasn't afraid – the symptoms of stress overload were old acquaintances – and, thinking about them now, he was surprised that they hadn't arrived sooner. Discovering that he was a spy, being chased by Federal agents through the alleys of Georgetown, facing the prospect of a life of penal servitude – these were triggers that a months ago would have reduced him to a drooling, suppurating, dysfunctional

365

corpse. It was testament to the effect of his relationship with Eva that he had gotten this far.

Maybe we are what we eat, he thought, but we're also what we love.

As soon as he got to his office, he reached into the bottom drawer of his desk and found a box of Snickers bars. He ate one in three bites, and his system, deprived of sugar for eight or ten hours, now cried for more, so he ate another one. Then he lay on his couch and waited for the glucose mellowness to wash over him.

Gradually, like water running out of a sink, the itching and the bleeding and the numbness drained from him, and when he opened his eyes his vision had returned to normal.

He grabbed the Gucci bag and walked down the hall to Epstein's suite of offices. They were dark. Even Epstein had to sleep sometime. He entered the outer office, turned on a desk lamp, shut the door and looked around the room.

A bin, Dyanna had said. Where would you keep a bin? The desks were clean of all but personal paraphernalia, the file cabinets closed and locked. He tugged on one of the drawers in one of the desks. Locked. The bin could be in a deep bottom drawer. How do you pick the lock in a desk? With a paper clip?

There were two doors in the back of the room. One led to Epstein's inner office. The other was a locked closet.

Screwed, Burnham thought. The best laid plans . . .

He was about to turn and go, to abandon himself to life as a fugitive, to sleepless nights and spastic colitis and cosmetic surgery, when he noticed that the hinges on the closet door faced out, not in. The door couldn't be opened, but it could be removed.

He slipped off his belt and, with its brass buckle, forced the hinge pins up to where he could grip them with his fingers and pull them out. When the door was secured only by its own weight, Burnham tugged on one of the hinges, and the wood slab fell off its mount and thumped onto the carpet on its edge. Burnham supported the door and held his breath, praying that the guard in the lobby would be too

366

intent on finding a five-letter word for an Indian potentate to pay heed to any single distant noise.

He pushed the door against the wall and looked into the closet. It was full of office supplies: paper and paper clips, pencils, rubber bands, tape, glue, stationery, stencils, typewriter ribbons and a couple of folding umbrellas.

On the floor of the closet was a plastic bin about the size of a liquor carton, half-full of used audio cassettes and micro-cassettes. He kent down and opened the Gucci bag and culled the bin for all the micro-cassettes. There were three or four dozen. Then, because room remained in the Gucci bag, he filled it with regular cassettes.

Before he replaced the door – propping it on the toe of his shoe so he could fit the sections of hinge together – he removed a roll of Scotch tape from the closet.

He opened the door to Epstein's inner office. He thought he remembered that Epstein's private bathroom was behind and to the right of the massive mahogany desk.

When he was finished in the bathroom, he backed slowly out through the suite of offices, looking left and right, trying to focus on everything, wanting to have disturbed nothing.

He leaned down to turn off the lamp on the last of the secretaries' desks, and he noticed that the ashtray wasn't clean. It was empty, but not clean, which meant that this secretary had worked later than the cleaning staff and when she had finished for the night, she had dumped her cigarette butts but hadn't bothered to wipe the ashtray.

On a whim, Burnham stepped behind the desk and examined the secretary's IBM Displaywriter. He saw that she had left discs in the toaster-like device beside the main machine. He turned the word processor on, and when the letters IBM flashed on the screen to show that it was ready for action, he removed the diskette, read its label, replaced it, armed the toaster, pushed 'request,' typed in the name of the diskette, commanded the machine to display its contents, and stood back as an army of green letters advanced on the screen.

It was at the top of the list: 'Burnham memo.'

Burnham told the machine he wanted to see the Burnham memo, and, obediently, the machine, showed it to him.

It was dated today, eight a.m. It would be printed and distributed in – Burnham looked at his watch – three and a half hours.

It was addressed to the White House police, and it instructed all gate officers to, on sight of Timothy Y. Burnham, apprehend him, confiscate his pass, escort him to the West Basement and notify Mario Epstein's office immediately.

Burnham told the IBM machine to erase the memo. He typed a new one, substituting Epstein's name for his own, instructing the police to notify the President as soon as Epstein was apprehended. Then he ordered ten copies of the memo and, as each came off the printer, signed it with a dramatic 'W.' He slid the copies into an inter-office envelope, slugged it 'Rush' and, on his way back to his office, dropped it in a routing cart. The memo would greet every gate officer at the change of shift.

Mischief, Burnham admitted to himself, puerile mischief. But it would provide a suitable beginning for Mario Epstein's memorable day.

He sat at his desk and typed out the Honduras notes for the President. He knew it was a reckless, probably dangerous gesture – he had already missed the hour mark with Hal, and he would likely miss the hour-and-a-half mark, too – but he felt an obligation to the President, to himself and (he was interested to discover that he actually believed this) to the country. He might crash and burn, but he would leave a little legacy.

The notes were six pages long. He clipped them together, walked them into Evelyn Witt's office and placed them in the centre of her desk.

Back in his office, he removed from their frames his signed photos of the President and, along with a folder of memos in the President's handwriting, slipped them into

368

the Gucci bag. Someday, perhaps, they would mitigate his infamy in the eyes of his children.

He left a note for Dyanna, wishing her well and offering to provide exculpatory testimony, should anyone attempt to tar her with his brush, and apologizing for purloining her micro-cassette recorder, which he took from her desk and put in his jacket pocket.

As he passed out through the West Gate, he stopped and listed with the guard a name – the name of a visitor to be cleared through to see Mario Epstein at ten o'clock that morning.

A tapeworm. That had to be it, Ivy decided. No other way to explain an eighteen-year-old boy who never gets any more exercise than going tippety-tappety, tippety-tappety on a computer keyboard all day long eating a breakfast every day of almost a dozen fat, doughy pancakes and half a pound of bacon and a pint of whole milk, and he stays as skinny as a lizard.

Ivy stood at the stove and flipped four more pancakes. Jerome sat on a stool at the kitchen counter, eating as fast as his mother cooked and watched a 'CBS Morning News' interview with one of those people whose daughter had just had a kidney transplant from a baboon. The morning shows must keep a whole warehouse of those people available to be trotted out on slow news days.

Jerome didn't care about kidney transplants or baboons. If there was no news about supercomputers or computer piracy or computer software, he wanted to watch about baseball: he didn't care about the game, but he loved the statistics. They were graspable, quantifiable, recordable. They represented order to Jerome. He kept a disk with the statistics of every member of every team in the American League East, and he updated it every day.

So he switched channels on his brand-new Sony twelve-inch colour TV. Maybe 'Good Morning America' would have something about baseball. After all, David Hartman used to play ball.

The words were out of David Hartman's mouth and vanishing in the ether before they imprinted on Ivy's mind. Something about spies, he said. Something about the White House.

She went rigid. She stopped breathing and aimed her hearing at the TV set. But whatever it was had gone.

'What'd he just say?'

'Nothing,' said Jerome.

'Don't tell me "nothing". I heard him. About the White House.'

'Rumours. He said there's rumours about someone leaking documents from the White House, and maybe there's spies involved. They're working on the story. That's all.'

Ivy flipped the pancakes. How serious could this be? She flipped them again. What was she supposed to do? She flipped them a third time. What *could* she do? Flipping pancakes wasn't helping at all. She piled them on the spatula and dropped them on Jerome's plate. They weren't done, they'd taste like mucilage, but Jerome wouldn't care. Bulk, that's what he cared about, bulk and maple syrup.

She went into her bedroom and shut the door. She tried to dial Mr Pym's phone number, but her dialling finger shook so badly that she punched the wrong buttons and got that annoying, mocking intercept buzz from the phone. She grabbed her left index finger with her right fist and – as carefully as a policeman fingerprinting a suspect – pressed the seven numbers.

The phone rang five times before a man's voice answered with a cheery, 'Hel-lo'. It was a happy, singsong voice. It sounded like honey would sound, if honey had a sound.

'Mr Pym?'

'Why, no. He's not here right now. May I ask who's calling?'

'Mrs –' Don't be stupid, Ivy told herself '– just a friend.'

'I see.' The voice lost some of its treacle. 'I'm looking for him myself. I'm a big customer of his, and I have a big order for him. When did you see him last?'

'What're you doing in his house?'

'Looking after it for him. I expected him back by now.'

'Maybe he's gone on holiday.'

'Maybe he has. If you'd just give me your –'

Ivy hung up. Were the TV people on to Mr Pym already? Was that fellow trying to keep her on the line till he could trace the call? If David Hartman had Mr Pym, how long could it be before he'd come knocking at her door?

No thank you. She'd had her fill of TV people. After she spoke her mind about that Mengele fellow, she'd had calls from a bunch of kooks. Morning, noon and night, even a couple after midnight. Some had called her a Communist. Some had called her a barbarian. One guy had wanted to know exactly how you go about skinning somebody.

She called her supervisor and said she was sick and asked how much sick leave she had accumulated.

More than a month, her supervisor said, but why did she want to know? Was she that sick?

'I'm afraid so,' she said. 'This could be the end.'

She returned to the kitchen and asked Jerome how much money he could get for her as soon as the bank opened.

'Why?' Jerome asked.

'Your Uncle Buggywhip's sick. I have to go to him.'

'In Bermuda?'

Ivy nodded. 'But if anybody asks, you don't know. I told 'em at work it was me that's sick. Say I'm at one of those fancy sanatoriums where they don't give out information about the patients.'

'How long you'll be?'

'A while, I expect.' Ivy touched Jerome's head. 'Don't you worry. You're a big boy. It's time you struck out on your own.'

'I told Hal,' Eva said. 'I had to, if we're going to ask him to help us.'

'Sure. Fine.' Burnham shook himself awake and accepted a cup of coffee from Eva, who sat on the edge of the bed. 'What time is it?'

'Nine-thirty.'

'Will he do it?'

'Ask him yourself.' Smiling, Eva pointed across the room.

Burnham rolled over and propped himself on one elbow.

There was Hal, proud as a schoolboy on graduation day, standing like a model in the middle of the room. He was wearing new white espadrilles, pressed white ducks, a lavender Ralph Lauren Polo shirt, a foulard ascot and a blue blazer so well worn that its elbows shone. His skin was the colour of meringue, against which his teeth stood out like drops of amber.

'Reporting for duty,' Hal said, and saluted. 'How do I look?'

'Perfect. Don't change a thing. You sure you want to do this?'

'Timothy, my life is a monotone of dirty towels, forsaken sweat socks and shower drains clogged with unmentionables. I've forgotten what a thrill feels like.'

'If something goes wrong, you could –'

'So I'll move on, to another town and another Y, or maybe I'll get lucky and find a tennis club. At least let me have the memory of excitement.'

'It's yours. Got the tape?'

Hal grinned and patted the side pocket of his jacket.

'Let me brush my teeth, and I'll rehearse you.' Burnham climbed out of bed and walked to the john. 'By the way, you're cleared through as Mr Prince.'

'Hal Prince.' Hal savoured the words. 'Prince Hal. Dashing. I like it. Suppose he won't see me.'

'He'll see you,' Burnham said. 'I guarantee it.'

Hal departed at a quarter to ten. At ten of, Burnham sat on the edge of the bed, with Eva beside him, and dialled the White House number and asked for Epstein's office.

Burnham heard the secretary draw a short, sharp breath when he identified himself.

He said immediately, 'Don't put a trace on this call. I'm in a phone booth in Bethesda. I know all the tricks, and I'll hang up before you can get to square one.'

'But –'

'Just put me through. Now.'

'Yes, sir.'

Epstein came on the line, as amiable as a puff adder. 'Well?' was all he said.

'In about eight minutes, you're gonna have a visitor, Mario. See him.'

'Fuck you!' Epstein shouted. 'Who do you think you are, giving me orders? Listen, you two-bit phony, you're as good as crucified. If you think I'm gonna –'

Burnham let Epstein fulminate, venting his rage and frustration. He wished only that he could have seen Epstein's face as he arrived at work this morning and found himself locked in the basement, surrounded by armed guards.

'Mario,' Burnham said pleasantly when Epstein had run out of steam, 'you're in over your head. Unless you want to spend the rest of your life as the special assistant to the assistant vice president of the Allstate Insurance Company, you'll do what I tell you. Now get up and go into the bathroom.'

There was a pause while Epstein challenged his ears and composed a new outburst. 'I'll see you burn in hell, you . . . you Communist.'

'You'll be sorry, Mario. Look how I've already spoiled your day, and it's not even ten o'clock. Don't you want to know what else I did at three o'clock in the morning? Sure you do. You don't want another nasty surprise. Fore-warned is forearmed.'

When Epstein said nothing, Burnham repeated, 'Now get up and go into the bathroom. Pick up the phone in there.'

Burnham heard the telephone receiver clunk against the wooden desk top, and the wheels of Epstein's chair roll across the plastic carpet shield, and the bathroom door open, and then the phone click off its hook on the bathroom wall.

'Good,' he said, trying to picture Epstein standing

by the toilet, his face lived. 'Now pick up the toilet seat.'

'God d –'

'Pick it up, Mario! And tell me what you see.'

Burnham closed his eyes, willing himself into the bathroom with Epstein. He saw Epstein lift the toilet-seat cover and find nothing and want to slam it down but instead lift the toilet seat itself, and there, between the two little rubber bumper buttons, see Scotch-taped to the underside of the toilet seat –

'A tape.'

'A micro-cassette, to be precise. Take it into your office and listen to a little bit of it. I'm sure you'll recognize it, and when you do, I know you'll be eager to see the chap who'll be visiting you in about . . . five minutes.'

'Why sh –'

'Because I have all the rest of them, Mario, all the ones that were in your closet there, the ones that go back God-knows-how-many weeks, starring you and all kinds of fascinating folks saying things – I haven't had time to listen to all of them – that would probably set the capital ablaze and for sure would cause the President to stick a Roman candle up your ass and blow you all the way to Uranus, let alone the interesting dilemma they'd pose for the Justice Department, since taping other people's conversations without telling them is an awkwardness especially for someone in your exalted position.

'The fellow who'll be coming to visit you will have another tape for you, Mario, to prove his *bona fides*. It's a particularly juicy one – you refer to Benjamin Winslow as being like Stevie Wonder, you have to lead him from pillar to post – and the fellow will give it to you as a gesture of good faith. Listen to what he has to say, Mario, 'cause if I hear that you didn't . . . well, you better buy yourself a couple extra television sets 'cause your mother'll be calling you tonight to tell you that you're all over the evening news!'

374

Burnham spat out the last few words and slammed down the phone.

'Wow!' said Eva.

'Mondo macho.' Burnham smiled. 'I feel like Charles Bronson.'

'You think he'll see Hal?'

'I know he will, unless he's gone kamikaze overnight. He doesn't dare not. But whether he'll do what Hal will tell him to do . . . that's something else. I have faith in Dr Johnson.'

'What's he got to do with this?'

'He said patriotism is the last refuge of a scoundrel. I don't think Mario's so close to the end of his rope that he'll suddenly turn patriotic. None of this *"I regret that I have but one life to give to my country"* crap for Mario. He's enough of an egomaniac to see that when defeat is inevitable, there's wisdom in compromise.

'I hope.'

Fourteen

They sat on the bed, eating Vietnamese food that Hal had ordered according to Eva's meticulous guidance.

'What time is it?' asked Eva.

'Three minutes later than when you asked last,' Burnham replied. 'Seven forty-eight.' He said to Hal, 'What's it like out?'

'Raining. It's been raining all day.'

Burnham and Eva had not been out of this room in more than thirty-six hours. Hal had brought them razors and toothbrushes and shampoo and deodorant, had used Burnham's bank card to collect several hundred dollars in cash, had taken all their clothing to a one-day cleaner. They had read and watched television and made love and watched more television and made love.

'Shall I pour gasoline over you and set you afire?' Burnham had asked as they reclined on the rumpled sheets.

'If that turns you on,' Eva said. 'But why?'

'It's appropriate, don't you think? Here we are in a bunker, waiting to see if we'll live or die, and your name is Eva, and –'

She bit him on the shoulder. 'No Hitler jokes. I'm a very sensitive person.'

'You're the only kid on the block who can object to Hitler jokes because they make your mom look bad.'

At seven fifty-seven, Hal plugged in the portable TV and brought it over to the bed. 'You care what network?'

'ABC,' Burnham said. 'They've got the ammunition, so they'll fire first.'

The Presidential news conference began exactly at eight o'clock. Epstein had attempted to schedule the news conference for last night, as Hal had requested, but two of the three networks had complained bitterly about the short notice: one had scheduled a live prime-time special featuring every pop singer in the world (most via satellite) in a simultaneous rendition of the song 'Food, Glorious Food' as a tribute to the starving multitudes in Africa; the other was locked into a baseball Game of the Week that promised to garner great numbers because of the participation of the Mets' rookie pitcher Corns McGinty (already 10–0 on the season), who pitched in one baseball shoe and one ballet slipper due to an agonizing podiatric affliction which he refused to have corrected for fear it would disrupt the perfection of his balance on the mound, a refusal supported by his opponents as well as his teammates, for Corns threw a baseball faster than Kevin Curran could serve a tennis ball (somewhere around 130 miles an hour), and if his balance were to be disrupted to the point where a pitch got away from him, the batter would likely spend the rest of the season in a dark clinic.

Burnham supposed that he could have forced the news conference for last night, but the risk was that only one network would broadcast it, which would have meant that seven-eighths of America wouldn't have watched it.

The President looked tired and, it seemed to Burnham (though he was aware that he might be projecting his own feelings onto the President), a little sad.

He opened with a short statement about Honduras. He reiterated his pledge never to send American boys to fight in a foreign jungle unless and until he discerned a direct threat to the security of the United States. He refused to impose the American democratic ideal on people who showed no inclination to embrace it. He described the aid packages he had proposed for Honduras and Nicaragua. He said he had directed the Secretary of State to schedule 'full and frank discussions' with Honduras, Nicaragua and the Soviet Union, and that he hoped to meet soon with the Soviet premier. Finally, he said he recognized that there were some in the Congress and in the country at large who advocated a stronger, more confrontational stand against socialism in general and the Russians in particular, and he wanted to reassure them that he was not giving the forces of revolution a free hand to poison this hemisphere. He recalled the Cuban missile crisis of 1962 and pledged to respond to any similar challenge with similar force. For emphasis, he closed with a couple of the more stirring lines from John F. Kennedy's inaugural address.

Exactly as Burnham had urged him to do.

A frisson of pride made the hair stand up on Burnham's arms, and he took Eva's hand.

Then the President invited questions.

As always, the first question was from the senior wire service correspondent, a blowsy woman who liked to ask outrageous questions ('Is it true, sir, that you've been seeing a psychic?') that attracted attention from the fringe media (Paul Harvey, 'Entertainment Tonight', *The National Enquirer*) and made her a celebrity worthy of inclusion in *People's* list of Washington eccentrics.

Tonight, though, she knew that the eyes and ears of the nation would be on the burgeoning spy scandal, and so, with a malevolent leer at ABC's gadfly Sam Donaldson, she stole his precious air and said, 'Mr President, ABC's been telling the world they're about to prove you've got spies working under your nose right here in the White House. What d'you have to say to that?'

'Sally,' the President said, favouring her with the recognition of her name and then turning to the television cameras and – more in sorrow than in anger, it seemed – addressing the American people, 'there are times when every President wishes that the First Amendment could be put on "hold" for a little while.'

A nervous titter rippled through the audience, for these were the high priests of the cult of the First Amendment, and any suggestion of an assault on their sanctum was a sacrilege.

'But as soon as he thinks that, he chastises himself, for he knows that a free press is the bulwark of a free society.'

Having thus made suitable obeisances at the altar of investigative reporting, the President felt at liberty to proceed.

'I wish ABC had come to me before they reported that story – that rumour, 'cause that's what it was and it didn't become a story till a lot of people chose to believe it without checking on it – 'cause I would've told them what really was going on and appealed to them to let it run its course. But they didn't and that's their right.'

A few reporters coughed in polite disbelief.

'That's good,' Burnham said. 'I wonder who thought of that.'

'I did,' said Hal, beaming. 'I reminded Mr Epstein that there was no way to confirm what never happened, so the President might as well take the offensive.'

Burnham smiled. 'You must've had a good time.'

'A fiesta.'

'. . . sick of having rumours fly around,' the President was saying, '' 'cause a rumour uncontradicted grows up into a kind of fact, and before you know it it's an accepted truth.

'So here's what happened – the unvarnished facts: we'd been hearing for some time that there were leaks coming out of the White House. Nobody said they were intentional, nobody said they were serious, but if there's one piece of real estate that America can't afford to have leaking, it's the White House.'

'Is that true?' asked Eva.

'Yup,' Burnham said. 'It's what he'd been told, and it makes sense, so it must be true.'

'And so, unbeknownst to any other member of the White House staff, I brought in an agent to work directly for me – he was a staff assistant, sort of a jack-of-all trades – and I arranged for him to have access to the topmost of all top secret documents . . .'

'Unbeknownst to him, too,' Eva said.

'No,' said Burnham. 'He's convinced he was following his instincts. He knew I was working on some secret mission all along, and now he's being proved right.'

'. . . spurious, of course,' continued the President, 'excellent replicas of the real thing that would have – and did – convinced anybody, including the Soviets. This assistant was encouraged to handle the documents in a routine, even careless fashion, for we were eager to see when and if their contents surfaced.'

'He can't *believe* that!' said Eva.

'Oh yes he can.' Burnham smiled. 'Remember, Lyndon Johnson said his grandfather died at the Alamo, which was utter horseshit, but he believed it because it was imporant to him.'

'. . . *did* begin to surface,' the President said, 'in another piece of Washington real estate, this one owned by our friends from the Soviet Union. How did we know? Well, with today's technological wonders, it's almost impossible to keep a secret unless you keep it right here –' the President touched his temple '– and never tell another soul. Some of you may remember the typewriters in our embassy in Moscow. The Soviets put sensors in those typewriters that read what was being typed and broadcast it to them as it came out of the typewriter. You'll be glad to know we have gremlins of our own. Every electronic signal the Russians send out of their embassy is intercepted by us and decoded and examined before we send it on its way. This is oversimplified, but I'm sure you understand. They prob'ly have some we don't know about, and we won't know about 'em till we find 'em, but we *will* find 'em.'

'Mario briefed the hell out of him,' Eva said.

'Everything Mario holds dear was on the line – his job, his access, his power. Besides, Hal briefed the hell out of him.' Burnham assumed a Presidential tone and said to Hal, 'You did good, son.'

'. . . month or so,' said the President, 'we found that the leaks were in our standard routing procedures for documents. Too many things are classified these days, so the currency of classification has been devalued. When requisitions for toilet paper are classified "secret", it's hard to take secrecy seriously. Some documents were misplaced. Some were thrown in the trash instead of being shredded. They all became bait for the scavengers the Soviets have planted around every capital city in the Western world.

'I called the Russian ambassador and told him what we'd found – a courtesy call, you might say, since I have reason to believe that when they found out we were feeding 'em bogus intelligence, they were the ones called ABC and sicced 'em on our trail – and of course he denied everything.'

Sam Donaldson couldn't contain himself. Beet red, he jumped to his feet and pre-empted Sally's follow-up question. 'Are you saying ABC was used by the Russians? Sir.'

The President turned slowly toward Donaldson, a placid smile on his face. 'Why hello, Sam.' he said. 'Used? Gosh, I'd hate to think that sophisticated journalists could be used. Deceived, maybe.'

'And could you tell us . . . sir . . . what's happened to your . . . secret agent?'

'That, I am pleased to say, is none of your business.' The President turned to face the cameras. 'He is an American of untarnished patriotism, happy to work without public recognition in the service of his country. I wish we had more like him. Suffice it to say –'

The cameras closed on the President's face. His eyes were moist.

Burnham held his breath.

'– that this man I will not name has been awarded a medal I will not name, a medal he will never see. Next.'

The President pointed at a reporter in the back of the room, who rose to ask a question about the deficit.

Eva squeezed Burnham's hand. 'He's either a hell of an actor,' she said, 'or he really loved you.'

'Let's go,' was all Burnham could say.

Fifteen

Evelyn Witt didn't see the letter until she uncovered her typewriter. The unmarked white envelope had been slipped between the paper bale and the platen. Her name was written on the envelope in ink, in a handwriting she didn't recognize.

She slit open the envelope. Inside was a sheet of yellow legal paper wrapped around another, smaller envelope on which was written 'The President.'

She unfolded the yellow paper and read:

Dear Evelyn:

If you'll be so kind as to give the enclosed to the President, I'll be forever in your debt.

I'm already in your debt more than you will ever know, but that's another story.

If ever you think of me, I hope it will be with a scintilla of the affection with which I think of you.

Timothy Burnham

Dear Timothy, she thought. She had warned him that the life of a Presidential favourite was spectacular but short, like the life of a moth. She wondered where he was, what he was doing. She wondered what had happened to him. It was all very mysterious.

But her years in the White House had accustomed her to mysteries without resolutions.

She picked up the smaller envelope and took it into the Oval Office.

The President was leaning back in his chair, with his feet on the desk, reading the editorial page of the *Post*.

'Morning, Mr President,' Evelyn said.

'Morning, Evie. Seen the *Post*?'

'Not yet. Good news?'

'Better'n a spot on the lung.' The President swung his feet to the floor. 'Honduras pitched out all their Soviet advisors. Even Boy George concedes it's just as well we didn't start World War Three over a bunch of bananas.' Boy George was the President's nickname for George Will.

'This was on my typewriter,' Evelyn said, and she passed the envelope to the President. 'I don't know how it got there.'

'What is it?'

'It's from Timothy Burnham.'

'Oh yeah?' The President smiled as he tore the end off the envelope. 'Where's he at?'

'I don't know. Like some coffee?'

'Yes. Yes, thanks.' The President kicked his feet up again and leaned back.

He had thought of Burnham at least once a day in the two weeks since he had disappeared. Normally, the President's mind was disciplined enough to keep him from dwelling on what had been or what might have been: enough new problems surfaced every minute to keep him fully occupied. But it was those new problems that brought Burnham to mind – minor things, mostly, things on which a fresh, unbiased, honest and unafraid opinion could cast a helpful perspective. Cut through the bullshit.

The new fellow Epstein had given him, nominally as his Appointments Secretary, was as useful as a third nostril. An ass-kisser, scared of everybody.

The President never stopped long enough to realize it, let alone articulate it, but he missed old Tim.

He had been right about Tim all along, and he accepted Tim's sudden departure as part of the price he (and all

Americans) had to pay for maintaining the nation's security. It had been worth it just for the pleasure of watching Mario eat crow, sit there looking all splotchy and nervous and having to admit that Tim was better wired than he was.

The President smoothed the sheet of yellow paper on his thigh.

Nice handwriting, for a man, he thought idly. Most men's handwriting looked like scrambled eggs.

Dear Mr President:

It's better that you don't know where I am or what I'm doing, but I wanted to let you know that you were right – about a great many things.

You suspected that I had an 'in' with the Russians, and you were right, though it's a different kind of 'in' than I, for one, realized.

You felt that we should not go off half-cocked and invade Honduras – I didn't tell you, you knew it, all I did was show you that you knew it – and you were right. By now I imagine the rest of the world is catching up with you. But you were first.

You helped me, in ways you'll never know, to discover what's right about myself, and for that I thank you.

As time goes by, you may hear things about me that make you question the faith you had in me. For what it's worth, I flatter myself that you were right to have that faith.

If the fur does fly about me, I hope you'll remember what my friend Samuel Johnson said: 'As I know more of mankind I expect less of them, and am ready now to call a man a good man, upon easier terms than I was formerly.'

With respect and gratitude,

TYB

The President read the letter again. Then he leaned forward and pushed the intercom button on his desk.

'Evie,' he said, 'this Samuel Johnson Tim refers to. Who does he work for?'

384